By Dust & Duty

The Forgotten Heirs, Volume 1

K.C. Phillips

Published by KC Phillips, 2024.

SEE BACK FOR PRONOUNCIATION GUIDE AND GLOSSARY OF TERMS.

.

.

.

.

.

.

.

.

.

First Print Edition | March 3rd, 2024
Published via Smashwords by K.C. Phillips

.

.

.

Cover design & illustration by Andriy D.
Copy editing by Ramona Mihai
Developmental Editing by Regina Sage & Fiza Abbas

Table of Contents

.
.
.

For the self-loathers, the mirror-avoiders, the pain-hiders, the over-thinkers:
may your journey toward loving yourself be as beautiful as you are.

.
.
.

Our Moons and Suns

Excerpt from 'A Childhouse History of Veirbos' (Version Four, N.S. 923)

A millennium ago, the Old Sun shone its light upon Veirbos, and all was lush and live.

But the children of the Old Sun did not attend their Duty as we do. Instead of earning their boons, the people spent their days taking from the gifts of land and Sun and moons–giving nothing in return.

Eventually, the Old Sun grew tired of their greed. It abandoned Veirbos and its people, taking with it all but the bare rock upon which they lived and the three moons that they worshiped.

The children of Veirbos' Old Sun began to suffer and die.

From afar, another sun looked upon Veirbos and took pity. It shone its orange light upon them, vowing to watch over Veirbos forever more, if only its people vowed in turn to not take its gifts for granted.

And so, the New Sun gave them light.

But still, they had no Water.

Saddened by the suffering of a people they loved dearly, the three moons of Veirbos–Siga, Tella, and Pri–sent bits of themselves through the wide cracks that fissured down to the planet's core. Those sacrificial offerings became fertile springs of Water's raw elements.

"From these that we give," Siga–the largest moon–told them, *"make a spark and forge Water."*

1

So they did: the gases came to flame on a spark, and Combustion left well-earned Water behind.

With the New Sun's light and that precious Water, our ancestors grew seeds from the time of the Old Sun, and our people had nutrition and clothing.

Ever since the New Sun, we have toiled in this cold, unforgiving desert and performed our Duties. From the Fabricators who shape metal, to the Masons who carve rock and the Molters who melt it into glass, to the Hortisans who grow plants, to the Runners who carry trade, to the very Combustors that still spark our moons' gifts: all grueling Duty is in service to the Water that we need to survive and in honor of the New Sun that took pity on our people.

And while the rock of Veirbos has been long since ground to dust, and the fissures have spread so wide and so deep that traversing our planet comes at great peril, still we have taken nothing for granted: hoping that our grueling Duty will one day prove to all of our suns and moons that we are worthy.

Prologue | Another Realm

"Please," I beg. "Please don't go. Don't make me go. I'm not ready." But already, the presence is fading away. I struggle as I am torn apart from it, feeling its sudden absence as an overwhelming emptiness in my being.

This place is home, and I don't want to leave. I have only just found it.

The desperate need to stay here–to return to the presence's side and wrap myself around it–consumes me.

"I'll find you," I call into the growing blackness that steadily devours my newfound home. "I promise I will find you!"

I am fading fast now, almost gone; but just as the last of that beautiful light winks out, I hear four words echoing back to me across the expanse:

"We will find each other."

Chapter 1

22 Turns Later

I*'m probably dying,* Ereta thought with grim acceptance and just a smidge of dread.

She turned in a circle in front of the cleanroom mirror and noted (again) that instead of moving with her, the nagging tug behind her eyes remained fixed toward the left wall as she rotated. And surely, *that* wasn't normal. She stared at her reflection, her dull gray eyes wide with fear, her chest rising and falling in rapid pants. Her heart pounded. *I'm definitely dying.*

...But surely, it wasn't *that* serious? It was likely just a quirk of aging. *People always complain about random aches and pains appearing as they age, right?* Yes, it was probably that. She was only 26 turns, which all things considered, she didn't think was old enough to be experiencing the breakdown of her mind and/or body, but the evidence seemed to suggest the contrary. So, she probably, almost *certainly,* wasn't dying; at least not immediately.

But then again, what if I am?

Jace knocked on the door. Again. "I'm not getting any younger," her flat voice carried through the door.

"Neither am I," Ereta replied solemnly, the truth of those words another nail in her likely imminent coffin. Because aging *was* dying, wasn't it? *Isn't everyone dying, all the time, from the moment they're bor-*

"I need time to pamper. What in the Crown Lord's spit are you up to in there, a head-to-toe powdering? You're just going to get grimy all over again on your Shift."

The word Shift snapped her out of her panicked reverie. *"Cold fucking burn me,"* she muttered aloud to herself. How much time had she wasted staring at her own reflection and spinning in moons-cursed circles? She had, in fact, meant to powder off–but the powder jar and scrubbing rag still sat untouched on the bathroom shelf, as did the scant layer of dirt and sweat that covered her skin. So now, grimy and with no time to spare, overcome entirely by a different sort of panic than that of a moment earlier, she whipped the door open and rushed into the hall...

...Only to immediately collide with Jace. The impact sent Ereta ricocheting backward onto the hard stone floor, her left hip bearing the brunt of a bruising collision. She gritted her teeth against the grating swell of pain.

"What the *fuck,* Ereta?" Despite having just been hurled into the opposite, equally hard stone wall by their clash, Jace still managed to sound thoroughly bored.

Ereta rearranged the disheveled curtain of black hair that had fallen in front of her eyes before letting her gaze drift upward. "Sorry," she muttered. In response, Jace's pale, delicate features briefly regarded her with the kind of regal indifference Ereta imagined the Queens of the Old Sun might have envied. She stumbled to her feet as her housemate returned to adjusting her form-fitting linen shirt, paying special attention to fluffing her ample breasts as though the tumble had significantly displaced them. Seemingly satisfied, she tossed her long, auburn hair over her shoulder and started toward the cleanroom door.

"The powder drain's full," Ereta murmured in warning. Jace brushed past her with another dismissive flick of her hair, saying nothing. And *shit,* if Ereta was honest, she really didn't care either.

They'd probably wait until the dirty powder pile was cresting the soles of their feet through the Lords-damn floor grate before they bothered to empty it. But they liked to maintain the illusion that the chores mattered to them, and small comments here and there about their home's cleanliness proved that they were (at the very least) *aware* of the mess.

Their similar indifference to housekeeping was one of the many reasons she and Jace got along so well. To an outsider, Jace's severity might be mistaken for dislike, or even anger; but although her friend wasn't particularly reassuring, she was unfailingly honest. If Jace had been truly upset at the encounter, she would have addressed it immediately; so when she instead closed the cleanroom door with a quiet *click*, Ereta knew with a certainty that her friend had forgiven her...disheveled breasts and all.

"The floor out there's dusty, too. We should sweep soon," Jace called a moment later through the closed door, and Ereta hummed her agreement, knowing full well that neither of them would bother revisiting the issue for at least a pentad (maybe two, if tolerating another ten days' worth of dust proved less annoying than cleaning). She felt the tug pull with more urgency behind her eyes.

She couldn't help but narrow her focus on the undeniably disconcerting sensation. She felt her heart pick up its beat as she pondered exactly *how* it would kill her. Perhaps the tug would pull her eyes until they were facing backward in their sockets, and she would be a reluctant audience to the melting of her dying brain—

Jace cracked the door open and peered through. Even though Ereta was standing, Jace looked down at her when she spoke—which, considering her friend's ever-imposing demeanor, felt fitting in more ways than one. "What is with you today? Your *Shift*."

Shit. Ereta shook her head and hurried to gather her things. She spared a glance out the window. Outside, the cold, beige expanse of desert looked as unwelcoming and dreary and unending as ever, interrupted only by the beige-and-grey stone brick of the five other houses on their small street. The New Sun had long crested the horizon: its orange midmorning light illuminating the stagnant haze of dust that perpetually saturated the air. And the moons–

Shit. Shit. Tella's soft blue glow was nearly invisible, which meant that she had fewer than ten minutes until her Shift.

She couldn't be late. In truth, she should have left several minutes ago, but her usual difficulty focusing was apparently, *distressingly* amplified by this moons-cursed tug. *Later. I'll deal with the moons-cursed tug later.*

But much like the promise of powder to be emptied and floors to be swept, all that the ambiguous self-promise did was delay the inevitable.

With two minutes to spare, she padded out of the cold, barren expanse that was Veirbos and onto the equally dreary stone expanse of the Distribution center. The Run from home had done little to settle her nerves, and the tug pulled as fervently as ever as she slowed to a walk and made for the back wall while pulling off her hat and gloves. The run had similarly done little to warm her body, but that (at least) was nothing new. The constant, frigid temperature of Veirbos' dusty desert plains was not exactly *comforting* in its familiarity, but at least it was predictable. Unlike her morning. *Unlike the tug.*

She unconsciously began to pace back and forth almost immediately: a habit from childhood that typically helped ease her too-frequent sense of impending doom. But today, it did little to allay her fears. She chanced a glance toward the Expediter's desk, where the rest of her Cohort had casually clustered: their universally long limbs outfitted in universally beige jumpsuits and overcoats.

Eight Runners out of ten. She didn't have to count them off to know who was missing.

Leelin's insistence on turning up to the distribution center with seconds to spare had long earned him annoyed sentiments from the Expediters. But he had never once been late, so there was no reason for his supervisors to admonish him formally. Ereta was constantly amused by and endeared to his small acts of malicious compliance, but she couldn't help but wish that he would hurry up today–she needed the Lords-damn *distraction* from her racing thoughts. From the *tug.*

She paced restlessly. Could it be a hallucination? Or perhaps some sort of supernatural sign of something terrible to come? She barely registered the restrained giggles that rose from the Cohort across the open space. *Can they tell that something's wrong with me–*

Leelin's chipper, booming voice echoed behind her just as the overhead bell chimed. *Perfect timing, as always.* "Good morning, my brothers and sisters in grueling Duty," he shouted a bastardization of their Duty oath through surprisingly even breaths, considering he had likely been sprinting. "I trust you all slept well and have brought unquestioning enthusiasm and bright eyes to serve our glorious Lords on this fine day?"

She sensed more than saw the eye-rolls of the rest of the Cohort. She stopped her pacing and shuffled into line behind the Expediter's desk. She half-turned to Leelin as he approached, raising her brows at him and fighting a smile of relief at his presence.

A perfect Runner in form and figure, he was tall and leanly muscled. He wore the standard beige jumpsuit and coat–nearly identical to Ereta's–but had foregone his hat and gloves. His warm-toned dark skin caught slivers of the New Sun's orange light through the windows as he glided toward her. Large sage eyes with an ever-present mischievous gleam roved up and down her form in an over-performed ogle.

"Enjoying the view, Leelin?" she asked as he sidled up beside her and knocked his shoulder against hers. The easy comfort of his presence bore resemblance to how she felt around Jace. Neither of her friends judged her or expected her to be anything other than what she was.

But whereas Jace was serious and regally superior, Leelin took everything in stride and wore his boisterous emotions on his sleeve.

"You flatter yourself, Ereta," he flashed a bright, wide smile so quickly she barely caught it before it turned to a frown with the creasing of his brows. "I was innocently pondering a professional curiosity."

Pained groans echoed from throughout the room as Kilas, a similarly tall and lithe platinum-haired man a turn younger than her and Leelin, loudly muttered something about the Lords sparing him.

"Even if *none of you*," those three words came out with added emphasis as he dramatically gestured around the room, most emphatically at Kilas, "manage to match my *impressive* paces, I find it baffling that Ereta is physically capable of avoiding Rationing each Shift due to late Routes."

Leelin bent slightly at the hip, hands clasped behind his back and eyes narrowed in concentration as if he were studying a particularly vexing mathematical equation. He stared down at her, his voice becoming low and intimate. "Tell me, little flame, how you manage a Route *at all* on legs nearly half as long as the rest of us?"

Well, not half *as long*...but he had a point. She was at least two heads shorter than the rest of the Cohort, her steps small and quick. The strides of long, graceful legs mocked her shuffle as the Runners departed each day. She could only attribute her ability to keep pace to the luck of the wind at her back (and being just *slightly* self-punishing).

Before she could reply to Leelin, Kilas' waspish voice called out to him from the front of the line, "She's probably trying to outrun your lecherous stares."

"All the more reason to keep staring lecherously, I suppose," he said to her, tipping his head as a bright grin reclaimed his face. "Lest you lose your Duty."

She smiled back at him, stretched up on her toes, and leaned in until they were nearly nose-to-nose. "Be careful, Leelin—if I come to enjoy those stares, we may *both* be delayed."

Leelin's face crumpled in a brief laugh before he suddenly lurched forward, grabbed her face with both hands, and plopped a messy, moist kiss onto her cheek. *"Hey!"* she protested with a giggle as she wiped the residue off, but Leelin had already stood stock straight, staring ahead with over-exaggerated seriousness. The line, all the while, moved relentlessly forward. She was in front of the desk by the time she turned away from her friend, the smile turning up her mouth still lingering.

"Why do you encourage him, Ereta?" the austere Expediter sighed as she gathered Ereta's deliveries for the day from a neat pile behind the desk. Mari was mid-aged and attractively featured, with a coil of hair the listless beige hue of Veirbosian dust wound neatly atop her head. Ereta had always imagined that both Mari's hair and her severity grew directly into that coil, and that if it ever unwound, so might the entire settlement.

"They find some depraved pleasure in torturing the rest of us. It's obscene, really." Kilas drawled from somewhere behind her.

"The only torture here is your fucking ceaseless *whining*, Kilas," Leelin replied through gritted teeth. Kilas was the only person Ereta knew with the ability to make Leelin lose his easy composure. It was impressive, really–but unfortunately, Kilas was also privy to his effect on her friend, and seemed to relish any chance to rile him.

Ereta turned back to Mari, suddenly remembering to answer her question. She shrugged. "Because it's *fun*, Mari."

Indeed, these moments of careless levity were often the brightest spots of her day. Whenever she struggled with fear or dread (which was often), sometimes the simple pleasure of a laugh and a smile between friends was enough to keep her going. Indeed, the world felt a tad bit lighter, her future less oppressive, even as she again noticed the tug on her eye and subconsciously turned toward it.

For just a fraction of a second, her vision was consumed by a flash of white light in the air to her left. Warmth tingled inside her. She blinked. Before she could begin to process what or where it was, the light had vanished. The sight before her was once again the plain stone of the distribution center, with the dry, cold, dusty beige-brown expanse of the Tubat-So settlement stretching far beyond its open archway.

What in all the Lords' heirs was that?

The tug remained, but even as she turned away and looked again, trying to retrigger whatever she had done, there was nothing. A quick glance at the Cohort around her– no one's expressions had changed. They all remained focused on their deliveries: shoving their burdens into overstuffed packs, reading the details of their Routes, and chatting amongst themselves. No one so much as glanced toward where the light had been.

They hadn't seen it.

There were few things in life of which she was sure. One thing she trusted completely was the acuity of her eyesight. It had been ruthlessly honed by turns of Running: darting over fissures, noting areas where the surface was thin and unstable, reacting to unnatural shifts of pebbles just before the ground cracked.

It was due to this confidence that she did not deign to attribute what she had just seen to her imagination. Besides, even though she had tended toward daydreaming as a child, that tendency had been long-suffocated by turns of dashed hopes and grueling Duty (and she had never been so imaginative as to see something that wasn't there). She concluded that whatever she saw in that brief flash had been real to her eyes; either it *was* real, or her eyes were deceiving her.

She briefly considered whether she could be losing her sanity, but without any other indicators that something was amiss, that didn't seem likely. But was the tug a sign in itself? *Not necessarily–it could be a physical ailment unrelated to my sanity.* And surely, if she were going insane, she would be hearing things as well? She had thought that the Cohort might have been giggling about her earlier, but that was grounded in reality, wasn't it? Her heart beat faster. *And surely, true visions would make more sense?* But *are* the visions of the insane bound to natural law? Likely not. *But*...was her attempt to evaluate her own sanity in and of itself an act of insanity? *Do the crazy know they're crazy? Or are you only at risk of insanity when you're positive that you're sane?*

The tug remained, and her heart raced faster, the beat so loud in her chest that she was sure everyone in the room could hear it. Panic stirred low in her belly and she felt the familiar shiver of cold dread creep along her skin. Her mind raced, and the fact that she could not seem to definitively prove (or disprove) her own mental stability became increasingly distressing.

"–in only *six hours*, my dearest. That's the fastest Western 5B Route in history. Though you can rest assured that there are some things with which I *take my time*." Leelin's loud preening about his record Route time distracted Ereta from her thoughts; even more so as she observed his bold attempt to caress Mari's flushed cheek–a move that earned him a flustered slap across the hand. He deflected by sweeping said hand carelessly through the windswept curls of his short, dark brown hair: as if that had been his intention all along. She wondered if he would manage to tempt the Expediter into his bed. At least half of the Cohort, men and women alike, had lain with him at some point. Her friend was nothing if not...charming. And handsome. *Very, very handsome–*

Stop. Friends don't ogle each other.

And that's all you are: friends.

She dumped her deliveries into her bag and glanced at the slip of paper that outlined her Route map for the day. Her heart was calming now, as if the widening separation of time between her and the flash of light somehow made it less real. Certainly, being distracted helped.

Northern Lek, Eastern Segment 2A. 36 pounds. Est. 7 hours. Two hours shorter and five pounds heavier than yesterday's extended Route, and she was glad for it.

The bell alerting them that there were only 2 minutes until departure sang through the air. Habitude turned her and everyone in the room to face North-Eastward, toward the Lek refinery. As a Cohort, they recited their Duty pledge:

Through dusted air and o'er cleaves of ground -

I vow to complete my task this day and all the days to come -

Only death or crippling injury will prevent me from fulfilling this promise:

I hereby pledge my life's Duty to Lek Tubat-So.

And by that grueling Duty, I am henceforth bound.

The words left her lips before every Route, and though she should have been used to them, they still managed to feel heavy every moons-cursed time. She idly wondered if she became *more* bound to Lek Tubat-So with each repetition of her vow. *Or perhaps each day's vow replaces the one that came before it– then again, 'all the days to come' seems to imply some level of permanence–*

All the days to come.

The vow's words echoed in her head. How many days did she truly have left? Between the tug and the white light, she felt like she was falling apart too quickly to bear. Surely, her heart couldn't indefinitely maintain the pace of its panicked beat–but until it actually stopped, regardless of when and how her life would end, the reality of her existence on Veirbos remained a constant with each minute, each vow: a too-short eternity filled with grueling Duty, fear, and endless fucking *dust*.

But sometimes, she got a smile and a laugh to keep her moving through it.

If only that could be enough.

S he took a running jump over a small fissure.

Over six hours into her Route, she was on time and stable. A steady, frigid breeze encouraged her onward toward home. She had already completed her outward deliveries for the day, all of them going to the Central Runner on the Northern Lek Route, with whom she had shared only clipped words of benign greeting and farewell in between muttering that she didn't have time to dawdle. Which, strictly speaking, wasn't *entirely* true. But she was in no mood for chit-chat today, particularly not with a random stranger.

A large, complex network of Runners connected Veirbos' messaging and parcel delivery system. Mostly, they transported communications between Lek Outposts, settlements, trading stops, and the major cities. But other parcels often required delivery, including raw materials in the form of weighted blocks. Today, she had the dubious *pleasure* of running a 15-pound block of raw iron, which she had enthusiastically traded with the Central Runner for a three-pound block of spun bamboo fiber and a small stack of letters: all destined for doorstep delivery to various Dutied in Tubat-So.

She found her way out and back to her small settlement by following the Water delivery pipes that twined their way through Veirbos. The pipes were grounded intermittently on beds of rock, their weight distribution carefully orchestrated to avoid crumbling into ubiquitous shallows and fissures that cracked their way through the dust.

As she ran beside a length of pipe that took a particularly circuitous path across the desert, it was *so tempting* to cut across the expanse to her right: bypassing a large section of the pipe and finding it again on the other side. Such a shortcut would save at least thirty minutes.

But her self-preservation instincts must have been somewhat functional because she remained on the path. It had been drilled relentlessly into their heads during Runner training: *those who forsake the Water network and venture into open desert are rarely seen again.*

The planet of Veirbos was a dusty, barren terrain littered with shallow outcroppings of rock and winding fissures–all washed in the pervasive orange light of the New Sun. Trying to way find without the Water network would be akin to walking in place: the scenery never altering, and with the persistent, nagging feeling that you aren't really going anywhere at all.

She was less than two miles outside of Tubat-So, and the Route became so familiar that she had to force herself to pay attention. Her mind tended to wander in false complacency during these stretches. Actually, her mind tended to wander all the time, but out here, indulging it could be fatal. *I know this path as well as my hand,* she thought. But then, the rote reply from Runner training echoed back to her like a foreboding poem: *The land is never static. It is ever-changing, forever in the act of becoming.*

She felt the tug on the back of her eyes pinch more acutely than it had in hours, and she let her head turn toward it without thought, halting to a rigid stop at what she beheld.

There it was again–the blinding white light–but this time, she had time to take in its form. It resembled a fissure; but a crack in the air instead of the ground, cleaving the world in front of her in two and revealing a blaze of white light. It was roughly her height, if not a bit taller. Her eyes took two or three seconds, during which she didn't dare to blink or turn her head, to adjust to the brightness.

Not just light.

A landscape of purest white, with a horizon in the far distance meeting a pale sky and an alarmingly bright yellow sun. She had never seen the sun any color other than the hazy orange that it perpetually cast across Veirbos. *Is this what the Old Sun looked like a millennium ago?*

As dazzling as the sight before her was, the twinge of feeling that accompanied it was just as enthralling, if not more so. It was a caress of pure contentment against her soul. It felt comforting, *right*, and familiar in a way she couldn't place.

Another second passed, and she noticed movement in the air–*of* the air–or was it? The white shimmered and danced in her vision, bright spots floating lazily from sky to ground, whereupon it disappeared.

It was like dust, but heavier, and moving with purpose to the ground below instead of swirling statically through the air. Her eyes began to burn in the frigid cold, but she didn't dare blink. Without thinking, she reached out her hand, and her gloved fingertips just barely brushed the air beyond the fissure. The pleasant feeling inside her intensified, just as something white began to attach itself to her glove in tiny dots. She instinctively pulled her hand back with a sharp intake of air.

But she had broken eye contact, and when she looked back up at the air fissure, it was gone.

Heart pounding a wild beat, she looked again at the white dots that remained on her glove. She removed its twin and lightly touched one of the dots. It was cold; as cold as the air, and it quickly turned to liquid beneath her finger. She repeated the experiment on each of the dots, and then they were all gone, leaving tiny patches of moisture in their wake.

Water.

A handful of times, she had seen tiny amounts of Water hardened to solidity by the cold of Veirbos, usually due to a pinhole leak in a Water delivery line. But this substance had been lighter, softer than that. And if the whole landscape had been that same bright white...

A land covered by tiny pieces of cold Water.

She thought about the stories she used to hear about Veirbos under the Old Sun. *Water in the air. Water on the ground. Changing weather.*

She balked, utterly unable to imagine that the vast expanse she had just seen had been covered in thousands–no, *millions* of tiny pieces of Water, gathering atop each other, accumulating on the ground and turning everything a solid white.

Without thinking, she began to run. She ran harder, more desperately, than she had all day. Maybe harder than she had in all her life. Her eyes were wild, darting around the air in front of her, searching for more cracks in the air: both hoping and dreading that she would find one again.

She didn't know why she felt so frantic. *What am I running from? What am I running to?* She only knew that she couldn't stay still. Her instincts screamed at her, louder than the wind pounding past her ears: *something is wrong. All is not as it should be. You are not safe.* As if remaining in a place where she had seen the thing that she didn't understand would lead her to madness, if it hadn't found her already.

But the picture of what she had seen chased after her, easily keeping pace with her racing thoughts. There was no escaping it. All that she knew to be true fought desperately to hold on as it was rattled by memories of an experience that defied it: *there is a place where cold Water coats the ground for mile after mile.* Where Water, the thing that dominated every waking moment of her life with its creation and desperate consumption, *fell from the sky*. And that feeling–of warmth and contentment–its absence now felt almost painful. It reminded her of emerging from her dreams and left her with the sensation that everything–that her entire Lords-damn *life*–was just...*wrong* somehow.

You are not saf–

The ground beneath her was air and wind, and blackness enveloped her.

Chapter 2

She barely had the time to comprehend what was happening before the ground slammed into her feet. The shock vibrated through her bones, her knees buckled under the shock of her landing, and she crumpled to the ground. How long had she been falling?

Her heart raced. Every part of her ached. But the worst part, by far, was the brutal reality of what had just happened.

Dust bury me and cold fucking burn me.

I fell into a moons-cursed fucking fissure.

She allowed herself a moment to marvel at the fact that she wasn't yet dead. Of all of the Runners who had been swallowed by fissures in Veirbos' history, she knew of none who had been successfully recovered. As far as she had known, all fissures opened directly to the core of the planet. She briefly wondered if that was where she had landed.

But no, she hadn't fallen *that* far. She'd only been weightless for a few seconds. And indeed, when she dared to look up, she was relieved to find that she could still see a slice of familiar orange sunlight in the distance above her.

She reached her hands out into the pitch black. She imagined that, if there were light to see, the place she had landed might look like a tall, wide hallway. She was able to discern walls in front of and behind her, and the gap between them seemed to be about five feet wide. She could not find walls to her left and right, and didn't dare shift her feet too far in either direction for fear that the ground would give way and her fall would resume–and she didn't dare push the luck that had seen her first fall halting well above the planet's core.

She felt up and down the two expanses of the wall, her nails digging into rock and soft dirt, scrambling for a purchase that would support her weight. But everywhere she touched, the dirt crumbled, and the small pieces of rock gave way.

Not safe, indeed.

Her breathing accelerated, and she felt the cold chill of panic winding its way into her bones. She would *die* down here, and it would not be quick or painless. She still had Water in her canteen, but if she drank it, it would only prolong her life–which she wasn't entirely sure was a good thing given that there was absolutely *no way* out of this fissure. The gap was too wide for her to wedge herself between the walls and climb, and besides, there was no solid place for her hands or feet to grip. *No way out. This is how it all ends.*

But falling deeper–all the way to the burning core of Veirbos–*would* be the better end. The faster end. Although being confronted by death scared her, she would rather embrace it quickly than live to suffer at its side for days until it got close enough to claim her. *Just a few steps further, it could all be over now.*

Before it gets any worse.

Maybe she had been naively holding onto the hope that *something* would change in her life. That it wouldn't always be endless days of dust and grueling Duty. She thought that all hope had long ago been locked away inside her, too painful to bear. But now, she knew it had lingered. She *felt* the last of it disintegrate. There would be no better future.

There would be no future at all.

Her mind swirled. She had lived most of her life amidst crawling, suffocating tendrils of panic and dread, but she hadn't known the true meaning of those feelings until this very moment. She thought about Jace: about their easy honesty and the home they had made together. She thought about her smooth stone bed and light sheets. About the dusty sunlight illuminating her room through the window panes each morning. She thought about her Cohort. About Leelin, her best friend: his smile and Kilas' answering sarcastic eye-rolls. Mari's charming irritation. Laughter and moments of levity.

That was *the good part, and you didn't even know it.*

The panic and despair spiraled. It fed off of itself, growing larger and stronger with each second that she indulged its presence until it consumed her entirely. Her entire body started shaking, and she felt both too hot and too cold all at once. Tears sliced through the dirt on her cheeks. She couldn't see. Couldn't hear. Couldn't fucking *think*.

There was a loud roaring rising in her ears. Her heart thumped a frantic tempo. She shivered and shook more violently, and her breaths were coming too far too shallowly and quickly.

On a good day, her thoughts were scattered. Worried. Disjointed. But now? She was so far gone into the panic that she couldn't even fucking think in full sentences–just words and fractions of sentiment.

Dead -
going to die–
am already dying–
hurts–
scared–

After what could have been minutes, or hours (or seconds?? *Who the fuck knows*), she became distantly aware of another sound: a lower tone. Not a pulsing beat, but a broken, inconsistent spattering of noises.

At first, she ignored it, but the longer it lingered, the more present it became.

"Ereta–"

Her name?

"Ereta."

Yes. She really *had* heard her name. She focused on the sound, sharpening her mind as best she could through the blur of racing, all-consuming terror.

"Ereta, can you hear me?"

Yes. I can hear you.

She opened her mouth to respond, but the sound would not come out. It was as if the link between her speech and her thoughts had been severed by the sharpness of her terror. She opened her mouth again, but all she could force out were a series of rapid, too-shallow breaths.

She screamed in her head: *Yes, I'm here, I'm alive.*

But the words wouldn't, *couldn't*, take form on her lips.

Probably for the best. It's probably just a hallucination anyway. One last comfort of hope as your mind turns into goo.

"Ereta! Can you hear me?"

"She's gone," a shaking voice said. And...she *knew* that voice. *Leelin.* Her heart lurched. Maybe this wasn't a hallucination? *Leelin is here.*

The other voice was sharp and unfamiliar as it clipped back, "No, she's not."

The words were spoken with a surety that settled into her bones. In a moment of steadying clarity, she knew that the voice was right. She could not die here, and she *would not* die here. Others had seen her fall, somehow. She hadn't been that far out from the settlement before she fell, maybe a quarter mile or less, considering her frantic dash away from the air fissure. They must have spotted her fall from a distance and come to help. And now, instead of (logically) assuming she was dead, they were trying to save her.

But her survival depended on her telling Leelin and the other voice that she was here. Alive. If not, they would leave and she would stay... left alone to suffer an inevitable demise. *Unless this really is a hallucination*—she stifled the unwelcome thought before it could overwhelm her.

Ereta closed her eyes. Breathed as deeply as she could. Before she found her way out of this fissure, she needed to repair the severed tie between her thoughts and her voice. She needed to fucking *calm down*.

She breathed, focusing on the sensation of air moving through her. *In. Out. In. Out.* The breaths started out shallow and quick, but with each intentional deepening of her air intake, she felt her body settle a little. She breathed slower with each inhale. Deeper. And, more quickly than she could have hoped, she felt the panic begin to recede, just slightly. Her swirling thoughts slowed as well, and though the fear still clouded her, she was no longer entirely at its mercy. Another few breaths, and she was in at least *partial* control of herself again.

She opened her mouth and yelled with every ounce of strength she had. It was as much a plea as a war cry. A celebration of her own strength and the triumph over her fear:

"I'm here! I'm alive!"

"**E**reta!" Leelin's strangled sob of relief caressed her ears. They had heard her. And although she was still down here, still stuck, there was hope now. She wasn't alone.

"We're going to get you out, Ereta," the strange voice yelled down at her. It was a man, she thought. His voice was icy. Determined. Strangely calm.

Yes, I will get out of here. I will live.

"Ereta is down there? What happened? I saw you two running over—" She knew that voice, too. Bellat, another member of her Cohort. She could see her in her mind's eye: pale face lightly kissed by lines of age and wisdom, with soft blond and silver hairs framing her tender countenance in short, wispy strands. She didn't know the woman well, but Bellat had been kind in their limited interactions.

Once caught up to speed, Bellat fell into the role of caretaker, gently reassuring her, "Ereta, everything is going to be ok, sweetheart. How are you feeling? Do you need Water? Or maybe an allot—"

"Can you see the light at the top of the fissure?" the stranger interrupted, assessing. She breathed in deeply again, relieved that he (whoever he was) was here. Leelin seemed panicked, almost frantic, and Bellat was so worried about caring for her that she might have inadvertently kept Ereta down here for Lords-damn hours... focus trained on trying to make Ereta's circumstances at *the bottom of a pit* more comfortable.

But the stranger? He seemed...pragmatic. Unclouded by emotion. The kind of person who would face putting out a fire and cleaning the house with the same steady, determined efficiency. *Relax, the opposite of you is here.*

"I can see a sliver of the light from the surface, but I can't make out anything specific."

They parried questions back and forth. How long had she fallen for? Did the landing break her legs, or could she stand? Were the fissure walls solid and jagged enough for her to climb?

"You're no more than 30 feet down. The impact of a fall longer than that would have shattered your bones." She couldn't fathom *how* the stranger seemed to casually know that statistic, but no one questioned him.

"Unfortunately, there are no ladders that tall on the settlement," he continued. *How in the Lords does he know all of this random information?* "We need to lower a rope down."

"I'll go look for one," Bellat offered.

"So will I," the stranger said.

And Ereta's heart kept pounding. "Please don't leave me alone here," she begged to one, or both, or all. Because if she were left alone again? She was concerned that her currently manageable fear might swell to consume her completely.

"Never, little flame." Leelin's voice was a balm to her nerves. "We'll simply entertain ourselves while they do all the work. What'll it be: a recounting of one of my recent sexual misadventures, or a rote recitation of the Runner's training handbook?"

She sobbed out a laugh. How did he always manage to do this—bring light to even the darkest places?

She replied in a shaky voice, "Are those my only two options?"

Leelin's indignant scoff echoed down the fissure. "Of *course* they are. Lords, Ereta, we've been friends for Turns—do you know me at *all*?"

Chapter 3

"...Much of the planet's surface is highly unstable and cannot bear significant weight. The most stable outcroppings of rock are already in use as anchors for the Water pipe network. And so you, the Runners, must carry in your Duty the burden of transporting all other supplies and materials across our planet." Leelin's bored drone finished as Bellat and the stranger began to lower the rope they'd found. "By *far* the worst of the two options I gave you, little flame."

"My heart rate is high enough already without being aroused on top of it," she called upward in reply.

It had been nearly half an hour since the stranger and Bellat had left, the entirety of which she spent pacing in small circles while listening to Leelin's tedious recitation of the Running handbook. She was slightly calmer than she'd been earlier, but her grasp on level-headedness seemed tenuous at best.

She sucked in a sharp, relieved breath when the rough fiber of the rope finally brushed against her hands. She grasped the tether in her fists and tugged firmly. It held.

"Alright, we've got you, Ereta. Can you climb?" Leelin called down the fissure.

"I can try." She gripped the rope and tentatively lifted her feet. She scrambled them against the hanging rope and pinched it between her ankles. She began to bend her knees while her arms pulled her weight upward. She barely gained a few inches after a strong effort, and lost what she gained immediately as her grip failed and she landed, hard, on her rear. Both of her Water canteens were ejected from the pockets of her pack by the impact, and she fumbled to find them again in the dark.

"Climbing is harder than I thought, give me a moment."

She set her feet back on the ground and then jumped back onto the rope again, meeting the same end result.

"If you tie the rope around yourself, maybe we can pull you up!" Bellat called down. She wasn't confident enough in her knot-tying abilities to be sure that such a sling would hold, even if she *did* manage to make one that could support her weight for however long it would take to haul her out of the fissure. She didn't want to risk another fall. Maybe the second one *would* shatter her bones.

"She can climb out." The stranger was convincing, even if she was entirely certain he was wrong.

"How? I keep trying to pull myself up, but my legs and hands slip off–"

"Tie a loop in the bottom of the rope," the stranger instructed, "large enough to slip one foot into."

"I don't know if I can tie a knot strong enough to hold–"

"It just has to hold your weight for a moment."

She did as he asked, despite her self-doubt. "Ok."

"Put your foot through the loop, grasp the rope, and then lean back and lift your other foot off the ground."

She did as he prescribed. Her dubious knot held. "Ok, I'm...dangling."

"Now put your free foot on the wall in front of you and take your weight off of your looped foot. Then remove it from the loop and place it on the wall as well."

"But when I tried to climb the wall earlier, it crumbled–" she started.

"Yes, because your fingertips have less surface area and couldn't find a purchase. At this angle, your feet will distribute your weight evenly enough that the dirt will provide a solid surface."

So, again, she did as he asked and found that, aside from a few clumps of dirt skittering to the floor, her grip on the wall felt solid. "Ok, I'm on the wall."

"Good. Now start moving upward: one step up while one hand moves up, and then the other foot and other hand."

It felt a bit awkward at first, and her hands and arms and shoulders were burning within moments. But she kept moving, one leg and one hand at a time.

You can do this. Probably.

Maybe.

She started to feel panic bubble again, clouding her thoughts. But the stranger knew what to do. She could trust him. He knew the exact height at which falls broke bones, suggesting that he had at least a passing familiarity with handling crises. Plus, he was calm, and rational, and thoughtful: *the opposite of her.* So, logically, if she felt an utter lack of faith in herself, she knew she could trust him completely. And *he* thought she could do it.

Step by careful step, she made her way upward. Her hands moved up the rope. Her feet scrambled against the wall. Even though bits of dirt and rock fell from under her treads, the surface held, just as the stranger had said it would.

She took occasional pauses as she climbed, during which she shifted all of her weight to her legs and gave her screaming arm muscles a respite. The darkness stretched beneath her, the light rising closer. She made steady progress and felt tenuous hope begin to replace the dread of certain death.

Before that dread had even eased completely, she felt hands grasping onto her wrists, and her weight was lifted upward. Light bathed her skin. Grasping hands dragged her out of the fissure and laid her down on solid ground. She stared upward, unblinking, at the sky.

And she smiled.

Had it been only this morning (...and also a few minutes ago) that she had pondered death in lieu of life? That sentiment felt distant as she felt the promise of a future stretch before her. She was swept up in the thrill of it: where there had been doom, there were now endless possibilities and countless fates. Compounding actions, decisions, experiences weaving together in a web: innumerable combinations of a possible path through life. *This is what hope feels like.*

Two faces craned over to interrupt her view of a sunset-flushed expanse of sky; her eyes pulled to focus on a stranger.

Her breath caught–she was immediately pinned by eyes that were sharp and assessing: pits of rich, dark brown glowing with sparks of crimson, like blazing firewood. They studied her with determined efficiency and brazen, unbroken contact, seeing more than she wanted to show. They *searched* her.

What will they find?

A slight movement had her gaze sliding to the other face, and her heart stumbled. Leelin's handsome features were crumpled into a mix of emotions too complex for Ereta to discern. The dust on his face was set into stark relief by tracks of clean skin that stretched from both eyes–*tears?*

She felt the web of her future shift as a decision settled into her bones: she would not let life simply happen to her anymore, action stifled by anxiety and self-doubt. Her future was hers to weave as she saw fit. She stared with wonder at the man who had felt so saddened at the idea of her death that he had shed his own body's Water in grief.

Her dearest friend. Her flirty, handsome–

–*very* handsome–

She didn't think. She just pushed up onto her hands and crushed her lips to his.

At first, he was still. Barely a heartbeat passed, enough time to wonder if she had misjudged. *Why did you assume this would be ok? You should have asked him. You are* insane *to think he would want you. Oh Lords, this is going to be so incredibly awkward. Can he ever forgive–*

Suddenly, his shock receded, heralded by a desperate, crushing answer of his lips against hers. Leelin's hands gripped the sides of her face and pulled her closer, deeper.

She vaguely registered Bellat's surprised chuckle.

This kiss wasn't soft or tender. This was a kiss of *life*; a celebration of defiance against impossible odds.

The moment was broken by a loud, impatient, and pointedly unsubtle *"Ahem"* from behind them. She broke the kiss with a press of her hand against Leelin's chest, returning the grin that eased onto his face.

They both turned to face the stranger.

His unnervingly keen gaze instantly found hers, searching her (again) through narrowed eyes framed by dark, furrowed brows. As he stared, she observed the face that housed those unnerving eyes. It was almost intimidating in its precision: all sharp angles and defined features. She took peripheral notice of tanned skin and dusty, sweat-tangled brown hair that barely brushed his brows.

"In a rush, Milo?" Leelin snapped with his usual booming confidence. All traces of worry or despair had vanished. He leaned toward Milo, flashed bedroom eyes, and added in a lover's whisper, "Or just impatient for your turn on my lips?"

Bellat, sitting behind him, rolled her eyes at his back. Ereta smiled at her, and she returned it with seemingly genuine warmth.

Milo (to his credit) did not lean away. His eyes narrowed at Leelin for a fraction, before landing back on her. "Perhaps you *should* be in a rush," he replied. "Midmorning Runner Shifts are ending in 6 minutes." He got to his feet in a brisk, efficient motion.

"I already checked out for the day. And since when do you keep track of the Runner Shift schedules?"

Milo leveled a severe look at Leelin. Bellat's expression morphed into one of dread. "But... Ereta has *not* checked out."

Oh. Oh, no.

She had been so happy just to be *alive* that the reality of her shift ending had not crossed her mind.

Although her Route had been given a seven-hour time *estimate,* each shift had a hardline time *limit* of eight hours. A few times a quarter, they were given extended Shifts lasting longer than eight hours. Unfortunately, today was not one of those days, and she had yet to complete the last part of her Route: local deliveries.

There was no way she could finish in six minutes. Which meant that she would be Rationed.

Well, hope had felt nice. While it lasted.

***Despite being only a quarter mile outside of Tubat-So, she didn't make it back to the distribution center until 15 minutes after the end of her shift. The local deliveries had taken her around the outer edges of the settlement; the penalty for not completing them was instant reassignment to combustion at the Lek. She was already going to be Rationed, but there was no reason to shirk her deliveries and prematurely resign herself to the most dangerous job on Veirbos.

When she arrived at the center, Bellat's look of defeat, completely obvious despite her attempt at a smile, told Ereta that there was nothing to be done. She checked out formally and received a Ration slip from Mari. She rushed to explain the circumstances (leaving out the part about the air fissure, since she *still* wasn't entirely convinced that she hadn't hallucinated that). But Leelin, Bellat, and Milo had already told their side of the story while she finished her Route.

It changed nothing.

"Ultimately," Mari spoke to her with the solemn severity of a teacher giving a bad grade to a student they liked, "runners are responsible for detecting and avoiding fissures. You *chose* to accept that responsibility when you first took your oath."

And so Ereta accepted the Ration with a grimace. "Thanks. I'll frame it."

"Watch your tongue, Ereta. I'm still your supervisor, and this isn't my fault. It's yours."

Ereta hoped that her shame was evident in the slump of her shoulders, the burn of her cheeks, and the breaking of her voice as she replied, "I'm aware. I apologize."

At least she didn't have Duty tomorrow. She needed the break; the Ration would take effect in two days' time.

Walking outside, the four of them ambled mindlessly toward the social hall on the southern edge of Tubat-So. But surprisingly, she found that she wasn't ready to part with this unfamiliar feeling of hope. *Not yet, anyway.* So, despite the bleakness of her Rationing, she decided to revel a little while longer in the bliss of surviving what should have been a death sentence.

Bellat came up to her side, wrapping her in a half-hug as they walked. "I'm sorry, sweet Ereta. It isn't fair." Bellat's steady gentleness was a salve for her nerves, and Ereta regretted that she hadn't gotten to know this kind-hearted woman sooner.

Leelin threw his arm around her. "Nothing would have changed Mari's mind about your punishment. She didn't even seem to *entertain* my offer to take her to bed in exchange for leniency."

Ereta ignored him, brushing his shoulder off and fighting back a smile at his persistent levity, which he *refused* to censure no matter how bleak the circumstances.

"It is what it is. I missed the fissure. It's my fault. I appreciate you all advocating on my behalf," she said in a surprisingly steady voice. "Especially you, Milo, considering we barely know each other."

"It was nothing." Milo kept pace slightly behind the rest of the group. His brow remained furrowed as he stared ahead. She idly wondered if his face was stuck that way: a permanent look of fierce discernment.

"How did you know that would work? The rope and the wall, I mean?" She had never heard of anyone using a rope in that particular way, to climb against a wall, and she couldn't imagine why they'd need to.

"Math," he replied with a shrug.

A beat of silence passed. She supposed that answer was all she was going to get. She tried again, curiosity overcoming her usual resistance to engage strangers in conversation.

"How do you and Leelin know each other?"

"We're neighbors."

And...at that, it was abundantly clear that Milo wasn't interested in chit-chat. *Fair enough.*

She turned to Leelin. "How did you even find me?"

"We saw you fall in. Milo and I were walking home together from our Duties. One second, you were there, running *impressively* fast," he leaned over and knocked his shoulder against hers. "The next second, you just... disappeared. I might have thought I imagined the whole thing if Milo hadn't been with me. I've had *nightmares* less distressing." He paused. They were at the social hall doors. Milo and Bellat proceeded through, the latter pulling Ereta into a quick embrace and plopping a kiss on her cheek before disappearing inside.

Leelin's eyes dropped to the ground. "I thought you were dead," he said, barely above a whisper.

She could see the pain in his expression. Seeing what he had thought to be her death had clearly been traumatic for him, and that feeling must have lingered despite her survival.

"But I am not dead. Because of you." She grasped his chin with her thumb and forefinger and lifted his head until those sage eyes locked onto hers. "And tonight, I plan to *live*."

He smiled and grasped her face, leaning in to brush his lips against hers.

She felt the whisper of his warm breath as he spoke, *"Yes, little flame, we will live."*

Chapter 4

In the social hall, stone benches crowded around rough-cast metal tables in clumps. It seemed as though half the settlement was out tonight, stuffed shoulder-to-shoulder around the tables, engaged in riotous games of *Intali*. The much-beloved game was the ubiquitous non-Duty pastime of Veirbos citizens, and Ereta and her friends were no exception.

She was four hours into a game with Bellat, Leelin, two Tubat-So Dutied she didn't know, and Kilas. When Leelin had first seen that Kilas' table was the only game with open seats, he had loudly declared, *"Over my frostbitten corpse,"* grabbed her by the arm, and begun to drag her toward the exit. Bellat and Ereta had grabbed him by his shoulders and steered him back toward the game against his will.

"The best way to get the better of him is to ignore him, Leelin," Bellat had encouraged as they dragged him toward the table. *"He knows he gets under your skin, so he pushes."*

When Milo hadn't sat down next to them, Ereta had glanced around the room, surprised to find that he had disappeared completely from the social hall. *Why even come inside if not to join in a game?*

Now, she sipped from her nearly-empty canteen. Her cards were good, but she had lost too many hands already by riding the sense of invincibility gained from today's near-death experience. Her losses were a prudent reminder of the danger that hope held, no matter how tempting it might be.

"*THE CROWN LORD'S SWEATY BALLSACK!*" Leelin swore loudly and slammed down his cards. Kilas smiled wickedly and reached for Leelin's canteen. He carefully poured a measure of Leelin's Issue into a small betting glass and swallowed it down, punctuating the action with a loud sigh of refreshment and a sodden smack of his thin lips. "I thought you would be better at Intali, Leelin, after all of these turns whoring yourself around the card table." Kilas' venomous drawl of the word *whoring* made Ereta bristle.

Leelin's face was burning red, but he managed to restrain his anger enough to volley some of his usual wit in a lilting tone: "*Of course* you assume all copulation to be transactional, Kilas. Is paying for it the only way you've found a willing partner? I suspect no one has climbed into your bed free of charge."

"I suspect *you* would. If I asked nicely."

The leash on Leelin's anger snapped. In a flash, he slammed his hands down on the table, bracing himself as he leaned across it and brought his face just inches from Kilas' own. Leelin's voice dropped to a tight, barely-constrained whisper as he spoke: "*There's not enough Water in all of Veirbos that could compel me to touch your rotten pric–*"

Bellat interrupted their hateful back-and-forth by announcing the roll of the next turn of dice. Kilas continued to shoot Leelin taunting smiles as they played, and she had to lightly pinch Leelin several times to keep him from launching himself across the table. She decided to play her hand despite her better judgment, and lost. *Again.* The woman to her left, against whom she had been betting, poured out a measure of Ereta's Issue and transferred it into her own canteen.

As was customary for each round, a new hand began with small tablets of *Olchate* being passed around and greedily consumed by all players. Along with Intali, the substance was one of the only things in Veirbos that existed purely for enjoyment. It softened the world for those who took it, casting a warm, fuzzy glow around the edges of a sharp and unforgiving existence. Ereta swallowed her tablet–savoring its numbing slide down her dry throat–and dealt out another hand of cards.

She didn't often spend her nights at the social hall for several reasons, not least her disinclination to be social. Her free time was mostly consumed by sleep as she chased the peace and comfort that her dreams always brought.

But tonight, she was part of Tubat-So, and the pure joy of effortless camaraderie (not to mention the entertainment of watching Kilas and Leelin rip each other to pieces) carried her through hours of gambling and revelry.

Leelin pushed open the door to his home. It was dark and smelled distinctly masculine, like sweat and stone. Despite their closeness, she had never found occasion to visit him here. His house was where he took lovers and slept, and not much else. Most of their time together was spent during or just after shared Shifts, and the very occasional evenings at the social hall when Leelin managed to convince her to join him, usually by flashing a thoroughly indecent smile that weakened Ereta's knees.

She stepped inside, the entryway opening to a small, open living space with a single door that she guessed led to a cleanroom. There was an entry table littered with odds and ends. As was customary on Veirbos, the raised platform for the bed had been carved directly from the stone of the house's floor: its center dipping into a shallow bowl littered with thin cushions and airy linen sheets. The room also contained a dresser, and a Water Issue holding the last few drops of Leelin's daily allotment. *Everything needed for trysts and sleeping, and nothing more.*

She stumbled further into the room, a bit unsteady on her feet. Leelin and she had both emptied their Issues at Intali and taken six (or was it seven?) rounds of Olchate by the time the first player in their group, a Dutied she didn't know, had passed out on the table, signaling the formal end of the game.

"Ask the lad, the on- the one with the beard?" Leelin pondered, nearly shouting, "–I *know he* saw it–saw *Kilas*," he spit his name like it was poison on his lips, "–he was *cheating*. I've never been so sure of anything. You saw it, didn't you, lil' flame?? Or did you *sense* it? The *lies*, I could practically taste them–in the *air*." His hands gestured in a wide sweep, as if showing her the air he spoke of.

Never mind that cheating at Intali was incredibly difficult to pull off, she knew Leelin's conviction came only from his unwillingness to admit defeat in anything, *especially* against Kilas.

"Could be, could be..." she indulged him, pulling off her coat and letting it land on the floor. "We'll have to challenge him, to a–" she hiccupped loudly, "to a *rematch*."

"*Yes.* A rematch. Honor *demands* it!" Leelin declared as he shucked off his coat in similar fashion and plopped down onto his massive bed. His hand in hers, he tugged on her arm until she tumbled gracelessly onto his lap. She winced slightly when the bruises on her rear (souvenirs of her fall into the pit and subsequent falls from the rope), collided with Leelin's muscled thigh. As far as injuries went, she could have had much, much worse.

She met his sage eyes, her voice dropping low and her gaze morphing into something between a challenge and an invitation. "What do *you* know of honor, Leelin?"

His voice sobered a fraction. "The most honorable thing a man can do is serve others," he began with a smirk, "you know," he brushed a kiss against her lips. "The standard selfless acts." A kiss along her jaw. "Giving Water to the Dutiless," his lips teased her neck. "Sharing my allotments with the hungry."

He nipped at her ear and lightly nuzzled the skin just behind it with his nose. Her skin tingled at the contact, and her entire body warmed.

A whisper: "And when beautiful women look at me with want in their eyes, I am happy to offer them services of a *different* sort."

"Those services are not entirely selfless, are they?"

"Oh, they are most certainly not."

His mouth returned to hers. They caressed each other's lips, tongues dancing and breath coming in increasingly rapid pants. His hands gripped her hips before sliding to her back and pulling down her zipper. She returned the favor. He stood, pulling her to her feet with him. Their jumpsuits peeled off in a blur, carelessly tossed in a heap on the floor.

They paused, standing nearly bare before each other, covered only by their undergarments.

And she shamelessly drank in the sight of him.

Dust bury me, he is utterly magnificent.

With both of them standing, his chest was at her eye level, a cool shade of brown dusted lightly with swirls of dark hair. Her eyes began to travel downward in a long caress. She took note of the hard, lean muscle that corded his arms, of a taught and chiseled abdomen. Dark undergarments obscured his arousal, but she glanced a long, sleek outline pressing against the fabric. Her gaze halted at his thighs: Lords, his legs were so *long*. His physical proclivity for Running was visible even when he was fully clothed, but standing there nearly naked, he looked like he had been *made* for traversing the world. Brutally efficient lines of thick muscle stretched over his long, sleek legs. His body looked as if it was poised to erupt into action at any moment: coiled like a spring, ready to push into the air.

Despite the power that he radiated, Leelin's steps toward her were feather light and silent. His was a carefully honed sort of strength, executed in graceful lines and deliberate movements even under the influence of several rounds of Olchate.

She tilted her head back to meet his gaze as he stalked close, savoring the exquisite tension that saturated the air between them. It caressed her and beckoned: *live, Ereta.*

And so she did.

I t is strange for a friend to become a lover. For all of their familiarity, it felt disarmingly intimate to caress the body of a mind she knew well.

Most of Ereta's previous lovers were visiting Dutied from other Leks and settlements, or those she met while on overnight Routes to faraway cities. A few were acquaintances she met at the social hall in Tubat-So, although she tried to avoid trysts with those who lived so close. She had learned that lesson when she lived in the Lords' City.

All of her previous lovers (save one) had come to pass with efficient trading of flirty banter and, as soon as she was relatively sure they would agree, a hasty invitation to return to her home. She rarely, if ever, saw them again—and the lack of attachment was a boon. No pain. Just a few moments of blissful pleasure to break up the dreariness of her days.

But to see her friend—a man with whom she had shared laughter, teasing, and carefree banter—in this private, passionate way? In some ways, it felt like she was violating something precious. Crossing a line that could not be uncrossed. Then again, Leelin had bedded so many Tubat-So residents that she wasn't sure his bedroom manner had ever been *truly* private. Lords, the stories she'd overheard from the Cohort *alone*–

Those thoughts faded to the background as Leelin, between kisses on her neck, untied the band across her chest. Both hands caressed and kneaded her breasts, then one slid down, his fingers dipping underneath her lower undergarment. An entirely involuntary, sharp inhale passed between her lips as he lightly caressed the most sensitive part of her. She felt his lips turn up against hers, forming what she knew to be a cocky grin silently preening at her responsiveness. Electricity tingled in his touch, and spread out in shivers of pleasure as he began to slowly circle his fingers around her clit.

The rational part of her brain knew that Leelin would later brag to her, preening about how his *expert* fingers had reduced her to a shivering, gasping mess, entirely at his mercy.

Two can play that game.

Her hands began to caress his chest with languid touches, drifting across his abdominals, and down, until she felt the edge of the cloth that separated their skin. She removed her hand, and then gently danced her fingers on the ridge of his arousal. A feather light touch; barely a touch at all. She ensured there was no rhythm to it, no predictability, as she alternated between dragging her fingers across his length and lightly pressing her palm against him.

She felt Leelin's tension growing with every brush of her hand. He bucked his hips into her touch, desperate for more friction, and she pulled back. He pulled back from her, in turn, letting his fingers drift into the ghost of a touch against her skin.

"Must we torture ourselves, little flame?" he whispered in her ear.

She was about to agree that no, they shouldn't, when he added, "We both know who will emerge from this victorious." He leaned down. "It seems you simply can't resist me. You kissed me *twice* today, and now, you're seducing me into your bed–"

"This is *your* house."

"All the same."

Her eyes rose to his face. She smiled, and her fingers dipped below his waistband, making searing eye contact as she grasped him firmly in both hands.

"F-uccck," he groaned in full voice and dropped his hands to his sides. Involuntary actions, like those he had elicited from her moments before.

She did her best impression of his cocky grin as her hands began to gently stroke him, rotating slightly as they passed up and down.

He tugged off his undershorts so smoothly that she wasn't sure it had been a conscious effort and not a reflexive one. He looked dazed, utterly transfixed by her touch. And despite herself, she was nearly lost in the pleasure of touching him. The rigid, smooth skin of his cock was a promise of what was to come, and she felt her untouched skin jolt in a current of heady need.

She saw a moment of clarity pass over his eyes, and he began to crouch downward. Her strokes continued as he dipped lower; then, so quickly she barely registered movement, his hands darted out and grasped around her backside. He tugged her upward, hands sliding to cradle her thighs as her legs bent. He rose to his full height again, and shot a mirror of her grin back at her. She realized only then that her hands had slipped loose of him.

With lithe grace, he began to stride through the room with her in his arms, until she felt her back brush the wall behind them. He pushed her against the cold stone, anchoring her with his arms. She felt the brush of his hardness against her center. He angled his hips to coat the tip of himself in her wetness and then set to making idle strokes across her. A sound somewhere between a gasp and a moan left her lips. His smile stayed plastered on his face; ever the cocky, triumphant winner; but his eyes turned predatory with lust.

After several strokes against her, all eliciting *shameless* shivers and gasps and moans, he angled himself away just slightly. She mourned the loss of contact—until he pushed inside in a long, smooth motion.

Both of them were making sounds now. *The game of winners and losers has come to a close.*

"Call it a tie," she murmured.

He laughed, deep and gravelly, and sank in deeper and deeper, until he touched a place so far inside her that she felt a twinge of ache. He began to rock in and out, slowly at first. As his pace quickened, she looked up at his face, beholding a man lost to all motivations beyond those of carnal need. For a person so effortlessly cocky and smug, this level of rawness was strangely...vulnerable?

She leaned in and kissed him with fervor, fingers interlacing behind his neck. His pace quickened, and their panting became more desperate. She moaned loudly, feeling every sensation where his body met hers so vividly that the world faded away. She was distantly aware of his arms adjusting. He lowered her to the ground and pulled himself out, flashing a grin at her. He grasped her shoulders and turned her around, seemingly beyond words, which was rare for him. Then, she saw his hands come around her, palms pressing against the wall, his front fully enveloping her back. He kissed her neck and shoulders, and reached his right hand between them. He guided his length back into her from behind, and his right arm snaked around her front, where it began fervently stroking her most sensitive spot. His pace accelerated, left hand firmly clutching her hip, until she could hear the slaps of his thighs on her rear. So quickly, the tension that had warmed her center all this time passed a threshold and became an urgent, distracting ache of pleasure. Her moans were more like yells as he drove into her harder, cock pistoning and fingers circling with exquisite roughness.

Her responding movements were frantic reflexes that sang her body's need. She felt raw and real in that moment with him, their bodies communicating in a language more ancient than words.

She was distantly aware of her own scream of pleasure as release crested and rippled through her body in bursts. He almost instantly tensed and growled with his own, and she relished every stroke he gave her as they rode through their pleasure together.

Moments passed, their ragged breathing slowing. They pulled apart.

Their circumstances settled around her like a cold wind: two friends, naked, covered in each other, raw and vulnerable after sharing their bodies. She turned to look at him over her shoulder. He looked trepidatious, just as she felt.

But maybe knowing more of Leelin didn't mean she had to pick between the friendship she knew and the pleasure they were only just exploring. After all, she had quietly lusted after him for *turns*, never letting it get in the way of their friendship. Perhaps friendship and pleasure could live together, side-by-side, for as long as they both wanted?

She turned and leaned against the wall. "I'm glad that the bedroom is one circumstance in which you are not faster than me," she slid into their usual dynamic with surprising ease.

It seemed to take a second for her words to register. Then, Leelin's usual grin appeared, growing so genuine, so large, so filled with happiness and laughter and affection that she swore it could have lit up the night sky. "If I had known it was a race, be assured I would have done things differently."

And she grinned back just as widely at her wonderful, silly, cocky, beautiful friend.

Interlude | Another Realm

The world is different here, but it feels right. It feels like home. I am sure that I have never before known the meaning, not until this place. That belonging calls to me, a song of my heart and soul that settles deep into my bones. It shakes loose the tension, the fear, the dread, the consuming, ever-present cold. I can't remember where those feelings had even come from, or why they had consumed me, and I do not care. Now, warmth and love radiates from within me, and I want to live in this moment forever.

There are colors and lights swimming in my vision, unformed and liquid. The air is strange...both heavy and light, layered in an aroma of sweet, bright scents.

I look down at myself, greeted by an indistinguishable tangle of shapes and colors. I have no body. I am part of the air, part of the tangle. Everything is loose; unbound, as if the universe is bleeding its very essence around and through me. I absorb the sights and sounds and smells and tastes.

My memories begin to form into solidity, as if waking from sleep and reminding oneself of what is real and what is not.

After a moment, the space in front of me shimmers. The presence is there, and it is calling to me. The sensations of home and rightness radiate from within it.

I focus until the bond between me and the presence clarifies—and words are coming forth. The presence is speaking directly into my head, and it is...beyond voice. Purer. It communicates with feelings and

51

intention through our bond, and I understand its language as if I had been born to it.

"...saw you there. The space behind you was just endless brown. You reached out, but then you pulled back and the gap closed. I couldn't really see you, but the gap... it felt like you. Like this."

I feel a hand grasp mine, and I look down. Yes, it has the shape of a hand, but that same mix of colors and light makes up its essence. It is of the air and apart from it. But the duality doesn't bother me. Not when the sensation of holding that hand...

I will never get used to it. If this place had felt like home before, it is nothing compared to how that hand feels in mine. It is the answer to every question I've ever asked, and even those I don't know to ask. It is a song in my soul, bright and gleaming. A connection to a presence that I know as well as myself. Better.

The presence is so beautiful that I want to fall to my knees and sob. Belonging, and deep, perfect love replaces a vast emptiness in my heart.

This. This is everything.

I lean into the presence and grasp it against myself. I hold it there, its essence bleeding into mine. It grasps me in return.

I wish, as I always do, that we might never part. That we could stay here for eternity.

"It's not fair–" I begin, using that same wordless bond, "I-I can hardly stand it, to know this feeling, and then lose it–I don't care who I am in the other realm. Nothing matters but this. It-it isn't fair–" frustration and sadness fill me, and while I am not sure if I can cry in this place, but I know that tears would be falling if they could.

"I know, Ariame." Love radiates from the presence as it grasps my face in its hands–at least that's what it feels like. I still can't see any details beyond light and color.

"But if this is the only place we can be together for now, we will savor it, and we will keep fighting to find each other in the physical realm."

There have been thousands of these meetings, here in this place, with this presence. I remember them all.

"I know," I say softly. *Knowing doesn't lessen the pain.*

This place is real, of that I am absolutely certain, but I also know that this realm is not the same as the physical one I live in. I don't know who I am in that world. What I do with my time, what I look like, or what I call myself. That existence and this one, while intertwined, are kept apart.

"What were you saying before? Something brown?" *I feel a sense of urgency surge. Our time here, as always, is limited. Soon, we will be dragged apart again. We always try to make the most of these moments, attempting to find any possible solution to our struggle... some way to integrate our existences and find each other in the physical world.*

"I saw you. I know that I did. In the physical world. It was different this time, Ariame. At first, I was here in our realm, but you were not. Then, there was a flash of your presence. It went away so quickly that I barely registered it. But it happened again, and it stayed for longer. I saw you. I know it was you. I could feel you, just like I feel you here. Perhaps you were in your physical form, but I couldn't make anything out. You were...hazy. There was brown everywhere behind you. I reached toward you, and then you pulled back, and you were gone."

"I remember, Embrase," *I whisper, using the name I had long ago given the presence in this place.* "I don't remember my waking life, but I recall a moment when there was a..." *I search for the word until it clicks into place,* "...a fissure in the air. Maybe a shadow of this place leaked into that world. Whoever that is, whoever I am... I felt you, too."

"This changes everything," *Embrase whispers. Still, we embrace each other, our edges melting together and intertwining. Separate, but not.* "We've never been able to remember anything from the physical world before."

"How do we make it happen again?" I ask, even as I begin filtering through my memories seeking the answer for myself.

"The string!" Embrase's excitement washes over me, bright and tangy. "We have to do it again."

"Do you think that's what made the fissure possible?"

"It has to be. It's the only thing we did differently last time."

I pull out a thread of my essence, clear and bright.

"We should make it longer this time, to see if the length correlates to how long the tether lasts," Embrase mutters as they pull out a thread of their own. We lay them across each other and begin winding.

When we are done, the shining tether of our entwined essences is nearly twice the length it had been last time. Embrase had come up with the theory that if we connected themselves in this way, there wouldn't be time for the tether to be pulled apart before we returned to the physical world, allowing us to keep some form of connection in our waking lives.

I still couldn't believe that it had worked, even briefly.

Each time we come here, we try something slightly different. It had started with our vow, spoken at the moment we pass the edge between this realm and the physical one. We have tested innumerable ideas in the hopes that one might bridge the gap. And something finally has.

We pass the remaining stretch of time wrapped in each other, communicating through our bond, basking in the love and wholeness of our love. Too quickly, I begin to feel the drag of the physical world coming to tear us apart, as it always does. Despair and panic wash over me. "I'm not ready, Embrase," I choke out the words with a sob, tugging the presence close to me in a gesture that feels like bringing our foreheads together.

"It never gets any easier." Embrase's sharp pain caresses my own. "I promise that one day, we won't have to part. Wherever I go when I leave this place, know I am thinking of that future. Of you. Of our eternity together."

The tingle of our essences pulling apart becomes more pronounced. It hurts. It feels like emptiness. It feels cold.

I fiddle with the string, twisting it tighter, double-checking that it is secure. Warmth radiates from Embrase, and I look up. We gaze at each other, not needing eyes to behold. It is recognition that runs deeper, purer than sight.

"Ariame. Someday, we won't have to part."

"Embrase. I am yours in every realm."

Our vows to each other ring warm and true between us, softening the agony as our essences are brutally ripped apart. The colors and shapes of our mutual realm pull away.

But the string remains; strong and gleaming.

As we both begin to fade into the darkness, my thoughts drift to the names we gave to each other in this place, long ago. The identities that declare what, and who, we were to each other despite the time and space that separate us.

'Ariame. Air of my life,' they had named me.

'Embrase. Fire of my soul,' I had named them in return.

As always, I chant a promise–one to myself as much as Embrase–again and again as the world fades to black. "In all realms, we will find each other."

Chapter 5

"We will find each other."

The words echoed in her mind, just as they did every morning. She fought to retain the lingering sense of peace and wholeness, but it drifted away as wakefulness sunk its unforgiving claws into her. No matter what happened in her life, the fact that her dreams would always be a refuge of soul-deep contentment grounded her—even if the specifics of those dreams were never within her ability to recall.

Most nights, she took a sleeping tablet in the early evening in order to both avoid the fits of panic that tended to strike her when the world was too quiet, and to sleep for as long as possible. She wanted to stay in those dreams that always left her feeling *whole*. But last night—

She stiffened as memories rushed through her. *The fissure. The social hall.*

Tentatively, she shifted her arm back and felt the brush of a warm body against her skin. *Leelin.*

I'm still at Leelin's house. I must have fallen asleep here, after...

Suddenly flushed, she turned her head to look at him, but as soon as her eyes moved, she felt it: stronger than yesterday, more insistent.

The tug.

Her heart began to pound as she recalled that blazing white place, the brush of warmth against her when she reached out to touch the air fissure. She had been so caught up with escaping the ground fissure, and then playing Intali, and then Leelin–she hadn't had the wherewithal to truly ponder the air fissure. Her tendency toward distraction was a problem at the best of times, but even more so when compounded with a tangle of heightened emotions and confusing experiences.

But for some reason, sleep had keenly reminded her of the feeling she had when reaching her hand toward that other place, and it rekindled the desperate curiosity and fear that had consumed her yesterday. That had caused her to run straight into a moons-cursed fissure.

Suddenly, lying still felt impossible. She needed answers, even though she hadn't the faintest idea what her questions should be. Whatever they were, she didn't have much time to find out–her Ration Route was tomorrow. This was her last day of assured life and limb, and she felt compelled to spend at least *part* of it finding out what that place had been. And, despite herself, she couldn't help the swell of hope she felt: maybe she could escape there, into that place of cold Water, and wouldn't have to complete the Ration Route at all...?

She rose out of Leelin's bed, situated like a shrine of worship in the middle of the room, and began to pull on her clothes. He snored lightly, remaining in a deep sleep despite the noise she made as she clumsily dressed. She glanced around for the direction that the tug insisted on. *Outside.* And she wanted to follow, despite everything from yesterday. Something deep within her called to it. She needed to know more.

As she grasped the door handle to leave, guilt halted her. What in the fucking dust was she doing? Abandoning her best friend's bed like he was an anonymous one-time lover? She should say goodbye. That's what friends did, right? Did *they* normally say goodbye? She couldn't think straight–no, they didn't normally go out of their way to exchange formal goodbyes–*well–we* normally *don't spend the night in bed together.*

Indeed, things between them were different now, even though she didn't know exactly *how.* Leaving without a word might give him the impression that she thought of their encounter as a mistake that she didn't want to acknowledge in the light of day.

But was it a mistake? It had been...really good. Both the pleasure and the easy comfort of each other's company in the hours after, when they had held each other and talked and joked until sleep came. Now, looking down at Leelin's peaceful, sleeping form, she wasn't sure–was it more than just that: pleasure and friendship? She supposed they would find out, and she wanted to travel that road *with* him. No good would come from not communicating. They were in this, whatever it was, together, and she wasn't willing to risk losing the friendship that meant so much to her.

She grimaced at the fact that her impulsivity and curiosity had consumed her to the exception of behavioral norms and the barest consideration of other people's feelings. *I need to fix that.*

She walked back over to the bed, crouched down at his side, and gently kissed his cheek. Leelin's eyes fluttered open. He grinned at her. She grinned back.

"I decided not to sneak out while you slept–to save your ego from the implication that I didn't enjoy myself."

He yawned. "I *know* that you enjoyed yourself. If you think you hold such sway over my self-esteem after just one night, little flame, perhaps it is *your* ego we should be concerned about." His cocky grin was shining as he yawned again, deeper, and lazily stretched, limbs (somehow) becoming even longer. "And now you've chosen to disrupt my beauty rest. How will I have the energy to *entertain* you today?" His husky tone and a brush of his thumb against her lips made it clear exactly what kind of *entertainment* he had in mind.

She pulled back. "Such a sense of self-importance in the morning. What makes you think I need entertaining? Perhaps I have plans."

"You can tell the people you made plans with to join us. I wouldn't mind."

No, of course he wouldn't.

"I'm afraid that without your beauty rest, you're just not pretty enough for that to be tempting." *A lie.* "Perhaps after you get a full eight hours." She patted his arm, making an effort to ooze condescension.

He yanked her down to the bed and wrapped his arm around her. A kiss on her neck, and a voice in her ear, "You wound me, little flame. Lower your standards just this once, and I'll make it worth your while."

"Is that what you say to all of the people you want to sleep with?"

"Since *you* seduced *me*, I suppose you'll never know."

He undid a few of her jacket buttons, creating a gap through which he slipped a hand to squeeze her breast. She shivered at the touch, part of her still stuck in that place of self-conscious yearning for a man she wasn't beautiful enough to bed. *He could never be interested in you, not in a sexual way*, she thought—even while he enthusiastically fondled her breast.

"I really *do* have plans, Leelin..."

"Cancel them." His kisses trailed up and down her neck as he kneaded her chest; the rest of her body still covered in thick layers of clothes.

Yes, cancel them. But the tug lingered in her mind, and she again reminded herself that since she would be Rationed tomorrow, this day off was her only opportunity to figure the mystery out. *After all, tomorrow's Rationing will likely kill or maim you.*

"I won't say I'm not tempted, but I really have to go. Perhaps later, we can meet up to assault Kilas as revenge for last night's game?"

His brow twitched downward at the sound of Kilas' name. Lords help the man next time Leelin saw him. She was joking about assaulting Kilas, but she realized too late that Leelin might find such a suggestion totally reasonable. "Alright then, cruel woman, it's a date." He pecked her cheek and pushed her off of the bed. "Now run along, you're disturbing my rest. I want to be especially beautiful when I pummel that cheating prick into the dust." Leelin, apparently, hadn't seen it as a joke.

She made her way toward the exit and opened the door. Frigid air assaulted her. She turned back, drinking in one last look at the stunning man sprawled on the bed. "Sweet dreams," she called out to him, and shut the door behind her.

Once outside, she felt grateful for the cold air, if only due to its lust-abating effects. She closed her eyes and tried to focus on the tug. As she did, her chest began to feel a bit hollow: as if it were a Water Issue emptying drip by drip. It was a strange sensation, an emptiness of feeling that, despite her usual moodiness, felt completely foreign. *Maybe this is what focusing feels like? You don't have much experience with paying attention.*

When she opened her eyes, temporarily blinded by the flash of early morning light, she caught fleeting movement out of the right corner of her eye. *The fissure?* The tug was pulling her that way, so it must have been the cause. She turned toward it and began walking through the alley that separated Leelin's small stone house from its neighbor.

Passing around a bend, she saw Milo at the end of the alley, taking slow, tentative steps toward something out of her line of sight.

She wasn't sure why, but before she could think better of it, she was calling after him. "Milo!" she shouted, and his head whipped toward her.

Chapter 6

Without so much as a word of greeting, Milo's gaze instantly whipped away from her, back toward where it had been fixed.

She strode up to his side and followed his gaze, which seemed to be aimed at nothing but the barren, sprawling desert of Veirbos beyond his and Leelin's small neighborhood.

Suddenly, she was starkly aware that she had no reason for calling out to him. She had nothing to say, and despite him saving her life yesterday, she barely knew him.

She decided to pretend that they had known each other for turns, if only to soothe her own awkward affect. The tug pulled her onward, beckoning–but she had started this conversation, and she had to say *something*.

"What are you up to? Do you have a Shift today?" she prodded gently in greeting.

"I–no. Not today." He was distracted, his eyes frantically searching the desert in front of him, lips parting. His hands were balled into tight fists at his sides, knuckles draining to white.

Something seemed off. She reached out her hand as if to grasp his shoulder, but thought better of it. Hadn't she told herself after brashly kissing Leelin that she would no longer presume to invade others' personal space without permission? *Some people don't like to be touched.* "Is everything ok?"

Slowly, Milo turned his head toward her—his gaze calculating, fierce, piercing.

After a moment, his brows softened a fraction, and his ember-glow eyes dimmed. His head dropped, eyes staring blankly at the dust. He shook his head. "I-I don't know."

She barely knew Milo, but looking confused, or lost, didn't suit him at all. It felt unnatural for him to not know what was going on. The tug pulled, but her concern and curiosity at Milo's seemingly uncharacteristic behavior compelled her to dig just a bit deeper. *I still have all day to follow the tug. This will only take a moment. Maybe I can help him.*

She saw a faint tremor flit across his shoulders.

Is he...shaking?

Dust bury her, she hardly knew this man, but her impulsivity took control of her arm before she could stop to consider if what she planned to do was wise, or even remind herself of the thought she had only moments earlier about asking permission before touching. She reached down and grasped his wrist with her hand, tugging lightly back toward the alley.

"Come on. Let's go inside, it's too cold to be standing around."

He stayed rooted to the spot, eyes drifting back up to inspect the desert.

"Milo?"

A long moment dragged between them as she waited for him to respond. He finally turned toward her, and his eyes fell back down to the ground. He tugged against her hold on his wrist, and she let his arm drop. He softly spoke under his breath: "I'm fine."

"You don't seem fine."

"You don't know me well enough to analyze my moods." His voice, which had remained sharp and precise throughout their previous interactions, now sounded distant.

She shrugged. "True," she hesitated, "but some things are self-evident. I don't feel every fire that burns, but I'm sure that none burn cold. I don't think it's in your nature to be uneasy."

His eyes lifted to hers, and her breath rushed out.

She was instantly both transfixed and intimidated by the bright flecks of crimson that glowed in consideration. His eyebrows furrowed a bit more, and his head cocked slightly to one side. *He sees too much, he sees too much—*

"W-what is your Duty?" she stumbled the question out without much thought, desperate for something to break the intensity of his gaze.

"Combustion," he replied, the sharpness back in his voice.

Wait–what??!

She balked at him, mouth hanging open. "Are you serious?"

"Usually."

She felt her conviction to cut this interaction short in favor of following the tug slip away, because this news was, truly, *shocking*. Combustion was the most dangerous, most demanding job in all of Veirbos. It was typically reserved as a punishment Duty, or one of last resort when a person was too injured to perform their usual tasks. A combustion career ended in death more often than not.

For a healthy, seemingly strong man of about her age, being assigned to Combustion was rare. He had to have committed some kind of serious offense against the Lords to be Dutied there.

"What did you do?"

One of his brows quirked up. "I didn't *do* anything."

Not a punishment. So that meant he had to be incapacitated to the exclusion of every other Duty. She carefully, attentively looked him up and down again, searching for evidence of a severe injury.

He was taller than her (not that that was saying much), but shorter than Leelin. An average height, maybe an inch under six feet. It was still hard to tell under his heavy coat, but he was definitely more...solid than she had first realized. It wasn't excessive, but the kind of natural muscle that a person builds over a lifetime of consistent, daily physical efforts. It was well-distributed, functional strength; muscle with purpose and utility.

She wasn't sure when her gaze changed from searching for injury to something else. Ogling was too strong a word. She was just...surprised. His eyes were so intense that she hadn't bothered before this moment to look at the rest of him. And what she found–

"I wasn't maimed in Duty, either. I chose Combustion."

Right. You had been staring. Looking for injuries.

She dragged her stare back to his. And then, his words sank in–

She blinked, her eyes widening until she was sure they bulged out of her skull. "You *chose* combustion?" He nodded. "Why in the Holy Crown Lord's spit would you choose a job that will kill you?"

His gaze didn't falter from hers as he shrugged and replied, "I like the heat."

"Yo-you *like the heat.*"

"Yes."

She stared at him. She was sure she looked ridiculous, mouth agape and eyes protuberant, but she couldn't for all the Water on Veirbos come up with a response to that.

He stared right back at her, the corner of his lip twitching upward in...*amusement?*

She hadn't seen Milo throw a countenance even approaching a smile. But this–her disbelief at his casual disregard for his own life–was *funny?*

"Ereta?" His eyes searched hers, and she hoped her utter disbelief was sufficiently conveyed that he didn't expect her to respond.

After another moment wherein she failed to muster words, Milo decided to try and explain himself. *As if volunteering for combustion warrants any explanation beyond declaring: 'I'm insane.'*

"It really isn't as dangerous as it's made out to be. Combustion is a straightforward formula. Combine the right amount of energy–heat, in this case, with atmospheric gasses in a closed environment, and the gasses will fuse together to form Water. Most Lek explosions happen when Dutied Combustors don't understand the reaction, use the wrong types or amount of materials, or don't maintain the integrity of the reaction chamber. The process is highly exothermic, so any leak or breach can cause an explosion instantly."

Her mouth drew closed as she watched and listened to him explain his Duty. As he spoke, his former tension and quietude eased. He became animated, hands gesturing in precise movements to illustrate his words, many of which she didn't understand. For the first time since she met him, his brows un-furrowed completely.

"–and it's really quite interesting, at one of the old Lek grounds–I was able to roughly calculate the amount of gas that was being processed when the explosion happened. And where it happened, as well. I have some firm guesses as to how."

He lowered to his knees in the dust. *What is he doing?*

He didn't stop talking as he began to draw shapes with his finger.

"All I had to do was measure radius–so that's the distance from the center point to one edge point of a circle, like this–of the burn marks left in the rock, and then take into account the *shape* of the explosion–its radius was largest on the side where the break happened and then diminishes around the outer edge–to determine the failure point, and then estimate from those numbers the amount of energy the explosion created. From there, it's just simple math to find the inputs that created those outputs. We can use this formula–"

He began writing letters and symbols messily in the dirt.

What in the Crown Lord's spit is he talking about?

He finished writing, and she focused her attention back in to hear him finish: "–if we were able to apply these same formulas in reverse, we could dial in the reaction so that it was predictable. It's all so straightforward when you just take a moment to study it. But apparently *no one* ever thought to do this before, which is just *lazy, don't you think?"*

His eyes darted up and connected with hers. This time, the contact felt different. The same intensity, but instead of searching for answers, or information, he was searching for something else. *Understanding? Validation?* He looked excited as he got to his feet. Almost *hopeful* about her response. She was suddenly aware that she was holding something precious in her hands: Milo's raw enthusiasm.

Although she wasn't entirely sure how to nurture it, she refused to be the one to crush it. The idea of stripping flickers of happiness from anyone on Veirbos was abhorrent to her. *But what to say?*

"This is... you figured this out on your own?" she stumbled the words out.

He nodded, and a smile, broad and genuine, formed on his face; it took every ounce of her self-restraint not to gawk at the transformation. She had been tacitly aware of his handsomeness when wearing his usual expression: a furrowed brow and narrowed, blazing eyes. But sporting a wide grin, eyes shining in excitement? He was *striking*, everything about his sharp, angular features eye-catching against warm tan skin. His tousled brown hair framed his face and gave his otherwise precise features an air of ruggedness. And still, those deep brown eyes sparkled with flecks of smoldering crimson.

He began speaking again, enthusiasm still peaked. *You're staring again. Snap out of it.*

"–few people helped. But that was why I volunteered. I grew up within walking distance of the old North West Lek Refinery grounds. I would go there nearly every day from the ages of seven to 17. That's where I developed a hatred for the cold," he added, as if this aversion to the weather on Veirbos was unique, and every person on the planet did not share his sentiment.

"Anyway, a few elders in my village were survivors of the destroyed Lek, and they let me ask them questions about Combustion in exchange for doing household chores. By the time I was ready for Duty assignment, I had figured out the math and the formulas for Combustion and I knew I could do it. *Safely.*"

He said the last word with a small puff of his chest. Even Ereta, with her admittedly minimal ability to read social cues, could see the pride that radiated from him.

"Milo, this is all really–Lords, it's..." she didn't have words, because she still didn't fully believe that he wasn't insane, or that it was possible to make combustion *safe*. Also, much of what he explained was so complex that she struggled to recognize the words, let alone understand them.

But he seemed to have completely forgotten whatever had been bothering him earlier, and she didn't want to ruin this...whatever this was.

Best to keep him talking. Ask more questions. "How confident are you that it's safe? Are you really not worried at all? I mean, just being *near* all that fire has to be a little bit dangerous."

"But it's warm."

She pinned him with an incredulous look. Milo's lip quirked up again as he continued. "The risk is not significant enough to cause concern. Knowing the Dutied here, this Lek would have been lost to explosion already if I hadn't stepped in when I did. This is the third Lek I've served in, but I made sure the others were fully trained on the process before going to the next one. I'll probably leave this one in a quarter or two. It's already been two turns, and there are Dutied here who are nearly ready to take over. Once I finish teaching my method at all of the Leks, I'm hoping I can go to the Lords' City and get permission to do some experiments. You know, find other ways to make the Water process more efficient. Or assist at one of the Greenhouses. I've been developing a new strain of bamboo that uses less than half the Water of what we currently grow."

From the same man whose responses to her questions before this had been one-word answers, she could hardly believe that multiple full sentences were pouring from him with the barest encouragement.

"Developing it? As in growing it? Here?"

"Yes, I have a few different plants, although the clones are still in progress—"

Don't you dare. You have things to do. The tug—

But reasoning with herself was futile; curiosity had already won out. "Can I see?"

He stilled, his brows raising a fraction before resuming their usual furrow. He studied her, eyes darting slightly back and forth as he searched her face.

"You want to see my bamboo plants?" His voice was quiet, but retained its edge.

"Very much, if that's alright."

A beat passed. She was excited—she had never seen a living plant before. As a child, not yet disillusioned, she had dreamt of what Veirbos might have looked like under the old Sun. Whether it could, someday, look like that again: green, lush, and thrumming with life—

"I can't. Not now."

Something crashed downward in Ereta's chest, her eyes lowering to the dust. The hollowness that was as natural to her as breath felt more prominent in the wake of dashed hope. "Ah. Alright then."

She could feel him staring at her again, but she kept her focus downcast. *This is embarrassing. Why am I so...disappointed? I have to follow the tug, anyway. This is a good thing. The right thing.*

But now, she didn't know what to do—she never did in the wake of rejection. *Just leave before you say anything else unwelcome.* "See you around, Milo." She turned on her heel and began to walk back the way she had come—

"Another day?" Milo's voice was sure and sharp, as usual, at her back. She stopped short. Her heart quickened, and despite knowing better, she felt hope flutter in her chest. She made an effort to stifle it before it could get out of hand. *He's just being polite, the offer isn't sincere. If it were, he would be specific as to when.*

She answered him over her shoulder: "Sure. Another day," and walked away. Despite her surety that she remained an awkward, unwelcome, presumptuous person, she couldn't help but wonder as she walked out of the shadowed alley and into the orange light of the sun if maybe...maybe Milo's offer *had* been genuine?

Hope would be the death of her.

"**A**re you ready for tomorrow?" Jace asked, her voice far too flat to convey the enormity of the question she asked. Ereta was back at their house, taking small sips from her Water Issue. Last night's activities had not left her as dehydrated as she had feared, and her Lords-provided Issue—which, as a Runner, was several servings larger than the standard—had refilled overnight.

"Of course not." Tomorrow, she would be Rationed for her Shift.

The nutrition allotments being withheld for a day would be uncomfortable, and the loss of the stimulant laced into all Runners' nutritional gels would make her Run more challenging, but it wouldn't kill her.

The Water Rationing might, though. Turns ago, Rationing had been consistent across all Duties, and it meant the loss of all nutrition and all Water for a full Shift. However, after it became clear that Runners could not survive a full Water Ration, the rules had been amended to allow Runners half of their Issue. For other, less physically demanding duties, Rationing remained a total withholding.

Despite the amendment to the rules, Runners still died from Rationing, and those who survived were typically injured severely and permanently by dehydration.

"Have you seen the Ration Officer yet?"

"No."

"When are you heading over?"

Ereta considered. She needed to report to the Ration quarters before midnight, but her Shift was at 5 in the morning, and she wanted to get a full night of sleep. Any physical advantage could make the difference between life and death tomorrow.

"I think I'll sleep here from 6 to 10–if you're willing to wake me up, please and thank you–and then drink the rest of my Issue slowly and finish it as I arrive at the quarters. Hopefully, just before midnight. Then I'll try to get some more sleep before the Shift."

It was the best plan she could come up with, allowing plenty of sleep and letting her hydrate up until the last possible moment. She knew that a similar strategy had been used by other Rationed Runners.

Not that it had saved them in the end.

She sipped her Water glass.

"So..." Jace's flat voice turned unnaturally casual. "Who did you fuck last night?"

Ereta nearly spit out her mouthful of liquid. She just barely managed to clamp her lips together in time to block what might have proved a lethal waste of Water. Her wide eyes snapped up to Jace, who was leaning against the counter, arms crossed and head slightly tilted: the picture of informality. *It doesn't suit her at all.* Ereta swallowed. "Pardon?"

"You didn't return home, which means it was someone who lives here." She considered for a moment. "Unless you bedded a traveler in the barracks, but you're too insecure for such a public display."

True. "Go swallow dust, Jace," Ereta replied, still taken aback. Why was she surprised that Jace had figured out something that was, she had to admit, fairly evident? Jace was sharp, and her knowledge of the goings-on around Tubat-So was as much due to her love for gossip as it was a strategic effort to remain at the top of the social ladder. Ereta had told Jace for turns that her talents were wasted as a Route coordinator. She would make a wonderful Attendant at the Lords' Court, where whispers were prized over all else. Perhaps even over Water.

Jace studied Ereta's face. She felt the flush of heat on her cheeks intensify under the scrutiny. Silence stretched, during which she swore she could hear Jace's brain churning as she deciphered the sparse clues before her.

Please don't guess please don't guess please don't-

"*For Lords' sake...*" Jace's normally flat voice was accented by chagrin. "*Really,* Ereta? *Leelin?*"

Dust bury me.

Ereta turned and walked toward her room. She made a conscious effort to keep her chin up, which proved a foolish combination with her frantic scramble to leave the room. She walked directly into a chair, tripping and landing face down on the cold floor. Her hands caught her weight, and a quick inventory told her she was, mercifully, uninjured. She turned onto her back, and her eyes met Jace, who moved to stand over her.

She didn't even seem to notice that Ereta was on the floor as she continued, "I know you're attracted to him, but Lords, Ereta, he's so...flippant. Cocky. It's irritating to *talk* to him, let alone *fuck* him—"

"You're one to talk!" Ereta's pulse began to pound, and the heat on her face remained even as her sentiments shifted from embarrassment to ire. She stood and resumed her retreat from the room.

Jace scoffed at her back. "Oh, come on. That was *ages* ago, *before* he had bedded most of the settlement. We weren't even Dutied yet."

Ereta knew that Jace and Leelin had been together several times in their youth, and she tried to convince herself that this fact didn't make her jealous. *Tried, and failed.*

Both of them being exceptionally attractive, it wasn't surprising that they had explored each other as adolescents. They had grown up together in Tubat-So's childhouse, as had most of the residents of the settlement.

Ereta was a rare exception, having moved to Tubat-So from the Lords' City at 18. She shoved down thoughts of the childhouse where she had been born and raised, but not before *his* face flashed across her memory. *My first and only love.* She shook her head, skirting the thoughts as best she could manage before they dragged her down into an all-too familiar sadness.

Jace had followed Ereta into her room, catching the door mid-slam and walking in as if she were wholly unaware that she wasn't welcome. "So, what, are you two *together* now? Is that why you're being so Lords-damn sensitive?"

"No—well, cold burn me, I don't know! We're not 'together', as in *together*–It was just..." she threw her hands up. "I don't know! A bit of fun!"

"You don't have fun." Jace stated the words with the flat confidence she might have used to comment on the weather. *Of course it's cold. Of course Ereta doesn't have fun.*

Ereta made every effort to put coldness into her voice. To make it clear that this discussion was unwelcome and entirely *over.* "Well, I almost died yesterday, and it's likely I will die tomorrow, so I suppose those were reasons enough to make an exception."

She had already filled Jace in on the fissure incident, although she needn't have bothered. Jace probably knew that Ereta had fallen in before she even hit the ground.

"How was it?"

That was unexpected. Ereta had thought that her reasoning, and perhaps her sanity, would be questioned further given Jace's incredulity.

"It was..." she struggled to form her feelings into words, "...a reminder that life can be good."

Jace stared at her for a long moment, then broke into a rare smile and shook her head as she walked out of the room. "Lords help you, you're in *deep*."

Ereta said nothing. Her thoughts were painfully loud in the silence: *Yes, yes you are.*

Chapter 7

The tug's pull didn't lead to a single point. It led her around without pattern, often pulling sharply in one direction just to yank the opposite way a few minutes later.

At each firm tug, her head turned to meet the pull. But she saw no flash of white, no crack in the air.

She had been walking around for hours, and had gleaned nothing of value about the tug.

The sun was beginning to set, and the usual orange glow of Veirbos was darkening to red. Sunset on Veirbos always gave her the unsettling sensation of walking through a planet of blood. *That's not untrue. The dust is drenched in the blood of Rationed Runners. Soon, yours will drench it further.*

She shook her head, trying to avoid that particular line of thought. She had found that indulging her pessimism tended to make it worse, and if sufficiently emboldened, it would spiral so far downward that she would be reduced to a blubbering mess, rocking back and forth with her knees clenched to her chest, knowing for a certainty that she was dying.

She didn't have time for that today. Or the Water to spare on tears.

The journey had taken her slightly outside of the settlement. She began to wander back toward Tubat-So, taking periodic sips from her canteen as she walked, thinking about uplifting things. Trying to construct a thorough recreation of Leelin's muscles in her mind was a successful distraction.

She arrived home with a little time to spare. She took a non-stimulant allotment: her last nutrition until after her Ration Shift day. That fact didn't make the sweet, salty gel taste any better.

She chased the nutrition down with a long gulp of Water and a sleeping tablet, then indulged in a thorough, full-body powdering off before changing into nightclothes and stumbling into her bed.

Ereta closed her eyes and felt her body melt into the cool, enveloping stone of her bed. She barely had time to worry about her imminent doom, or think about the muscles of beautiful men, before she was pulled into sleep.

There was no familiar echo of words as her consciousness returned. She didn't feel the familiar warmth and comfort, either. The dreams didn't *always* come, and she had found through trial and error that they were less likely to occur outside of her usual sleeping hours. That didn't make it any less disappointing.

Jace's hand was lightly shaking her shoulder. "It's 10. Time to get up, *your Grace.*"

She smiled weakly at the chiding nickname that Jace had given her: a reminder that anything she did for Ereta's sole benefit was not servitude, but a *favor* that carried the expectation of repayment.

"You're the queen, not me. I'm surprised you didn't pull a muscle when you leaned on the counter earlier and tried to feign informality."

Jace rose and began to leave Ereta's room. She paused at the doorway.

"Try not to die, Ereta."

"I'll do my best."

Jace left the room, leaving the door cracked slightly open. Her loud voice cut through the quiet a moment later, coming from further down the hall: "I don't want to have to find another housemate."

Ereta smiled and got up. They had been housemates for turns now. They had first met when Ereta, as a fresh Dutied Runner in Tubat-So, had stumbled into the wrong building while looking for the distribution center. She had found Jace there, fastidiously tracing out Routes on a large map pinned to the wall. Jace had told her in no uncertain terms that her presence was unexpected and unwelcome, and Ereta had fumbled out an apology. Jace had responded to that apology with another insistence that she "get out", and Ereta had spoken without thinking (as usual) and called her a frigid bitch.

She could still remember the smile that crept onto Jace's face at that, and her asking if Ereta was in need of lodging, which she was. And that had been that.

Ereta's clothes were only slightly moistened with sweat, but the loss of Water made her cringe. She used the cleanroom, walked to her Water Issue, and filled a glass: taking small sips of it as she strolled back to her room to stretch. The looser her muscles were at the start of the shift, the better. Her bruises from her fall still ached as she went through the movements.

With an hour and a half still left before she needed to depart for the Ration quarters, she planned to spend the time continuing to drink small sips and stretching lightly. If she timed it right, she would finish off her Issue just before her midnight arrival at the Distribution Center.

She took a deep breath and worked to calm her already pulsing nervousness. Despite her crippling fear, she had to use this time to think through her strategy for the Run. But the urge to get up and pace the room reared with a consuming ferocity–

There was a knock on her window.

She started, and loosed a tiny yelp (nerves already on a thin edge). But as she pulled back the curtain, and saw Leelin smiling back at her, she felt the fear abate. Still, her heart continued pounding. *From dread, definitely from dread.*

She motioned at him to walk around to the front door, and met him there a moment later. She quietly let him in. "What are you doing here?" She realized only after speaking that her words could be taken as rude. "Not that I'm not happy to see you," she hastily added.

"Did you forget our date? Perhaps slapping Kilas' smug face isn't as important to you as it is to me."

She grinned, and was still not entirely sure if he was serious. "Why the window?"

He leaned in and grabbed her face as he kissed her. They stumbled backward until her rear end hit the counter. He lifted her up onto it, seemingly without effort, and then craned his head around to kiss her neck and whisper in her ear, "*Stealth,* little flame."

Oh.

Yes, this made sense, even though it stung. *He wants this to be a secret. He's ashamed. Of course he is, you can't blame him, especially with his stunningly gorgeous former lover in the next room. You're a step down. Or five steps. A whole staircase–*

He hadn't stopped kissing her neck. "I couldn't have *her Haughtiness* interrupting our precious little time together tonight, which she surely would have done had I alerted her to my presence by knocking. I can hear her now: *Leelin, shut up, why are you here? Get out.*" He mocked Jace with surprising accuracy of tone, timbre, and (likely) content. She smiled as the truth of his words cracked the resignation of her former, bleaker, assumption.

Jace's voice sliced through the intimate silence. "Leelin. Why are you here?"

The resemblance was uncanny.

"You should read fortunes," Ereta told him as he straightened and turned his head toward Jace.

"Isn't it obvious?" he asked her, voice returning to its normal lilting bounce. "I'm here to perform last rites for the condemned."

Suddenly, Ereta was swept off the counter in a smooth motion and swung into Leelin's arms. He cradled her knees and her head, her side pressing flush to his chest. She loosed an entirely involuntary giggle.

"Ereta has to prepare for tomorrow. Get out."

"That's two for two!" Ereta noticed, her lighthearted glee a stark departure from the mood she had stewed in before his arrival.

"It's true, I *can* read fortunes." He said, smiling at her before his head turned to look at Jace. "Ereta's fortune is that you will leave us alone all evening."

"This isn't a game, Leelin. You're willing to sacrifice Ereta's last hours of preparation for the sake of wetting your cock? *Anything* can turn the tides of survival on a Ration Route. She needs to rest, and drink."

"Remind me, Jace, which one of us is a world-class Runner? Which one of us might know best *exactly* what Ereta needs for tomorrow?"

"I will not allow you to fuck her Waterless just because you've decided that you suddenly like her cu–"

"Enough." Leelin's voice was loud, and harsher than she had ever heard it (save for interactions with Kilas). He gave Ereta a small smile. "This is why I didn't knock on the door."

"I trust him, Jace," Ereta said, and it was true. First and foremost, Leelin was her friend, and she didn't believe he would be so careless as to...'*fuck her Waterless.*'

"Ereta..." Jace's voice was a plea. "I know you like him, Lords know why, but a crush isn't worth sacrificing your *life*–"

"Luckily, neither of us need your permission. I just need hers." He looked at her again. "What'll it be, little flame? Feel free to kick me out if I'm unwanted. My ego will survive."

She looked at Jace. "I'll be fine, Jace, I promise."

"You can't know that."

"I think I can, if I take a fortune teller to my bed."

Leelin barked a laugh, turned with her still in his arms, and strode off toward her room. Ereta had time to yell a high-pitched, "Goodnight!" to Jace before the door slammed behind them.

"**D**eeper."

"I can't go any deeper."

Well, this was unexpected. Even after a heated few minutes of kissing and touching (and Leelin's muttered complaints about her being "all sticky" with sweat), it appeared he really *was* going to use his Running experience to help her prepare.

He had spent the last 30 minutes leading her through a series of stretches. She was currently positioned with her hands on the floor, elbows straight, one leg outstretched behind her and the other folded perpendicularly beneath her chest.

"Just a *little* deeper," he encouraged, and she obliged, sinking down a fraction and grunting slightly at the pull. She held the pose until she started to shake.

"Good. Now Water."

She sipped at her glass, which contained the rest of the day's Issue. The glass orb that held her daily Water allotment had emptied all too quickly, and would not refill via the pipes of the Water network until after midnight. Her last glass was a little over half full. *Or maybe half empty.*

"Are you sure you want to push the opening?" he asked her, as he took her foot into his lap and began massaging it lightly.

"Not at all, but it seems like a sensible choice. Take advantage of my lingering hydration early into the day, try to etch out some speed, and then slow down as I dehydrate. I'll save my Water for the second half of the Route, unless it's over 8 hours, in which case I'm fucked no matter what I do." An extended Route on a Ration shift was not something she had heard of happening, but she didn't want to assume it wasn't possible.

"I really think you might be better off starting slow. The lower your heart rate, the less Water you'll lose to sweat."

"But the colder I am, the faster my heart will beat to maintain my body temperature. Won't I be better off starting warm by picking up my pace a bit?"

"But if you push too hard at the beginning and sweat, you'll get chilled as you slow down and the sweat cools you further. And then your body will have to toil extra hard to maintain your temperature anyway."

They continued breaking down the pros and cons of various pacing strategies, and all the while, Leelin massaged her. He moved from her feet to her calves, and then up to her thighs, and then she was sprawled on her stomach as he massaged her rear. At the first touch, she had fought a sharp intake of air as the pain of her lingering bruises flared. Leelin eased back the pressure, but didn't stop his machinations. He lingered there long enough that it became clear the action was no longer purely functional. Not that she was complaining.

"What time is it?" Leelin asked her in his usual lighthearted inflection.

"How should I know? I'm face down on the floor."

"I'm finding it difficult to divert my attention long enough to check."

Ereta rolled over and sat up, peering out the window to check the position of the moons. Siga was waxing in earnest.

"It's quarter past."

"Wonderful." He pecked her cheek. "Back on the floor now, little flame."

"I think you've massaged me thoroughly enough."

"I disagree. And as the superior Runner, my opinion holds far more weight than yours."

She settled back onto her stomach, and his hands cupped her ass once again. He trailed his fingers over her flesh, squeezing, teasing, exploring. Her bruises didn't even hurt anymore.

"At what point does a massage become a fondling?" she pondered aloud.

"Oh, my sweet innocent flame. It's been a fondling since the start."

She huffed a laugh.

"Leelin, as much as I want to, I don't think it's a good idea–"

"I know that being Rationed is frightening," his voice had turned somber. Soft. "But you can do this. I believe that you can. When I first saw you join the Cohort, I was sure that you would be Rationed on your first Route. Everything I know about Running tells me that these *tiny* legs, lovely as they are," he squeezed her thigh, "should not be able to keep pace on a Dutied Route."

"Leelin, I–"

"You surprise me every day, little flame. You surpass all expectations. You are strong, and determined, and fast. If I could bet my Water on any Runner in the Cohort making it through a Ration unscathed, I would pick you."

She knew that crying would be irresponsible, but his beautiful words and his raw, intimate voice made her want to fold into his arms and sob away her Issue.

"Thank you," she whispered, her throat tight as she fought back tears.

"I know you get nervous. I know you're *always* nervous–I believe that your biggest weakness is getting in your own head. You need to relax. Trust yourself. You can do this." She didn't trust herself, but his confidence in her was uplifting.

His hands had begun teasing her inner thighs, and her breath quickened. The combination of his sensual, slow touch and his sensual, slow words was distracting her from the sense of foreboding, and she realized that might have been his intention all along.

Ereta rolled over and leaned up, resting her head on his chest. He stroked her back lightly.

"Take a sip of Water, little flame."

She did, and after she put down the glass, he leaned forward and kissed her softly. He lightly pushed her shoulders back until she was prone on the floor.

"Now, I am going to help you relax, and you are going to burn this memory into your brain. Call it...something to motivate you to return home safely."

His head lowered, and he lightly kissed her stomach just below the hem of her nightshirt. Her breath became shallow and her pulse quickened.

"Deep breaths. Relax. I want to keep your sweating to a minimum."

His hands brushed her hips, grabbing lightly onto the band of her night shorts and pulling them off. Bare from the waist down, she savored the feel of the cool ground contrasted against the heat of his body, his hands, his breath. He kissed her lower, trailing down her stomach, hands gently caressing her outer thighs. One hand broke away, sliding down to her ankle. He lifted it until it rested on his shoulder, and then lifted the other one. His kisses continued, and when he lightly brushed his lips against her clit, her gasp of pleasure was entirely guttural.

She felt his smile against her sensitive skin, and his tongue flicked out to begin teasing her. He pulled away slightly, but before she could protest, she felt his tongue's hot, wet warmth drag across her center.

Dust bury me–

His tongue plugged inside of her, and his fingers found her clit to begin making slow circles.

He worked quickly. Efficiently. With practiced expertise. He wouldn't drag this out, she knew: the longer her heart rate stayed elevated, the more sweat she would lose. More quickly than it ever had, her pleasure crossed a threshold into pulsing, inevitable tension.

When his tongue and fingers swapped, she yelled out. He sucked and nipped her, tongue dancing, fingers pumping in a steady, quickening rhythm.

"Come," he muttered under his breath. Then, he sucked hard.

Cold burn her, she obeyed. Her climax shuddered through her body, her muscles clenching around his fingers as sweet, exquisite warmth overtook her.

He worked her through each shuddering swell, until she was melting into the floor, muscles utterly languid and feeling more at ease than she had in turns. Possibly ever.

He dropped several kisses onto her sex and her thighs, before lifting his head. Their eyes met over the flush of her skin.

He was silent for a long moment as their quickened breaths began to slow.

"*Lords,* Ereta, you are so fucking beautiful."

Wait–what? Beautiful? She felt her eyes widen in disbelief. No one had ever called her beautiful. And his words were his truth, it was undeniable from the earnest look in his eyes. She couldn't help the single tear that quickly welled and dripped from her eye. He leaned forward and wiped it away, cupping her face to kiss her.

They parted. She leaned her head against his chest, and he resumed stroking her back.

She barely got the words out through the tightness in her throat: "So are you."

The sensation of her last sip of Water sliding down her throat was not as terrifying as she had expected.

Ereta had done everything she could to prepare, and after Leelin's *services*, she was feeling... good. Strong, but not tense.

Ereta and Leelin walked together from her house to the Distribution Center. She had dressed in her full Running outerwear, but for the walk, she had stuffed her hood and gloves into her pack. They took their time, holding hands, chatting and teasing.

As they approached the center, they banked left instead of heading straight through the main doors. Around the side, there was a small outbuilding. *The Ration quarters.*

She glanced up at the moons. Siga was nearly at full rise, meaning it was close to midnight. She had just a few minutes before she would be sequestered.

When she lowered her gaze from the sky, it was pulled to a shadowy figure, leaning stiffly with one shoulder against the small building.

"Milo, I'm glad you're here. I showed impressive restraint by not bedding Ereta tonight, but my seams are still stretched. Your attentions would be most welcome."

Milo pushed off of the building and walked up to them, ignoring Leelin just as Ereta did.

"Are you feeling prepared?" he asked her, furrowed brows assessing her body, scanning for weakness.

"As prepared as I can be."

"Rationing is a ridiculous practice," he muttered. He looked tense, a bit keyed up, his words even more tightly clipped than normal.

"Watch your tongue–If the Ration officer overhears, you'll be punished for blasphemy," she warned him in a low tone.

"It is a truly weak authority that feels a need to punish its citizens for voicing valid criticism."

Ereta shifted with discomfort at the words. It was rare that anyone openly criticized the Lords, or the intricacies of the system that they presided over. To do so was to be at their mercy, which was notoriously fickle when it came to matters of critique.

"Quite an attitude tonight, Milo. Are you simply here to brood and wax poetic about the injustices of life, or is there a further purpose to your lurking in the shadows?" Leelin teased Milo with the ease of a long-time friend. She wondered how close they truly were. It was hard to picture the two of them: one serious and unyielding, one lighthearted and teasing, spending any amount of mutually enjoyable time together.

But maybe opposites made good pairings, because Milo's lip quirked up slightly at Leelin's words.

"I brought you something."

He walked into the deeper shadows of the building, and Leelin and Ereta trailed after him. "This is foreboding," Leelin casually noted. Milo swung his pack off of his shoulder and rummaged around in it for a moment. He pulled out a small piece of bundled cloth and shoved it into her hands. She took it, feeling that it was wrapped around a small object. She unwrapped the cloth to reveal a filled sachet...

"What–what is this?"

"It's a nutritional gel. I have experimented with making my own. It's perfectly safe. Eat it."

"Milo, I can't–"

"Yes, you can. I made it. It's technically not an allotment."

It was illegal to trade allotments of any kind outside of Intali games. Even giving allotments in acts of charity was illegal, though it didn't stop people from staging games so that they could quietly pass Water and nutritional gel to those in need.

The rule was enforced particularly harshly before and during Rations–that was partly why the punished were sequestered in Ration quarters and escorted through their Route by a Ration officer. They were watched at all times during their 24-hour Ration period to ensure non-interference.

Having only a few scant minutes left, she took the gel into her mouth...and *moaned*.

It was the finest thing she had ever tasted. Sweet and salty danced on her tongue, but not in the aggressive, antiseptic way that the Lords-provided allotments did. This dance was a thing of lithe beauty–a delicate combination of flavors that she was sure would ruin regular allotments for her forever.

"Oh my *Lords*, Milo, this is *so* good–how did you–"

"Quickly. We're low on time," Milo instructed, and he pulled out a canteen from his pack.

She swallowed the last of the gel and stared at the canteen, which he was now holding outstretched...to her. She was silent for a moment as his offer sank in.

"*Absolutely not.*"

"We're not arguing this. This is *collected* Water, not an allot–"

"*Collected?* What does that even–it doesn't matter. It's *illegal.* You'll be punished–"

"You're forgetting that I'm already Dutied at combustion. I'm currently suffering the worst punishment on offer." He shoved the canteen into her hands. It felt like holding something poisonous. Or explosive.

She held it back out to him and shook her head. "You don't know that. You don't know what they'll do."

"Ereta." He moved swiftly, and before she registered what was happening, he had grabbed her by the shoulders. She looked up at him, finding that he had pinned her with that fierce, determined gaze. "You are drinking this Water."

"So *bossy*, Milo. Tell me, do you have much practice with dominat–"

"Shut the fuck up, Leelin." Milo's voice was cold and cutting. His gaze did not leave hers. "Drink."

Her hands shook slightly. He eased his grip on her shoulders, and she undid the clasp of the canteen, attempting to deepen her too-shallow breathing. The canteen felt full. It may have held a quarter Issue. She had never done anything this forbidden–

"It's ok. I promise. Drink. Quickly, we're nearly out of time." Milo's voice was slightly softer, but no less steady and sure.

She remembered being at the bottom of the pit, hearing Milo's voice and trusting its surety more than her own. He was clearly smart, and confident. Despite herself, she believed him that this was ok. She took a deep breath.

You're a fool.

She tipped the canteen back and drank deeply, chugging down each gulp with a desperation that was more fundamental than thirst. She was...*hiding evidence.*

She finished the canteen, and Milo hastily shoved it back into his pack.

He placed one hand back on her shoulder, met her eyes with his, their crimson streaks seeming to cast a glow into the night air between them. "You will be fine."

And with that, he left, walking with steady purpose back into the waiting silence of Tubat-So.

She could hardly breathe. They stood there in silence for a long moment as Milo's form disappeared into the night. *If anyone finds out, what will they do to him? What will they do to me, and to Leelin? We participated, we are complicit–*

"You know he filters his piss."

Leelin's words sliced through the blur of her fear.

"Excuse me?"

He held his hands up in the air in a gesture that implored her not to blame him for telling the truth. "It's *probably* not what he gave you. But it could be. He *does* make Water that way. I've seen it."

She stared at Leelin with incredulity.

"I mean–I didn't *see it,* not the act of him, *you know,* piss–"

"I get it," Ereta said, laughter coloring her voice a fraction.

"He probably gave you some other Water. He has a whole bunch of experiments for Water. But I'm just saying, it's a *possibility* that you drank his piss."

Ereta laughed out loud, heart feeling lighter. She was grateful for Leelin's ability to cut through the starkness of any mood with remarks that were so...*utterly wrong* that they ended up being just right.

"Thank you for that, Leelin," she said flatly, but she meant it.

"No need to thank me," he said with bravado, hands again held up in the air as they walked back around to the Ration quarter entrance. "It's my job to tell you the hard truths, no matter how disgusting and piss-flavored they may be."

"Let's hope the nutritional gel didn't have a similar origin."

He smacked a hand to his forehead. "Oh *Lords,* I didn't even *think* about the gel. What combination of Milo's excretions do you imagine were mixed to form *that*?"

"I don't even care, it was *delicious*–I wish I excreted anything that tasted so good," she replied.

"Ohhhh, Ereta...but you do." She laughed again and smiled. He smiled back, winked, and opened the door to the quarters for her.

She walked, smiling, head high and heart steady, into her punishment.

Chapter 8

"Oh, good. Ereta. I was worried you would be tardy." Mari ushered Ereta inside and attempted to shut the door, but was halted by the slap of Leelin's arm against the iron. He lazily slid against the door and leaned there with exaggerated sensuality.

"My, my, my, what do we have here? You're looking *ravishing* tonight, Mari."

Ereta watched the exchange, sure that it would be entertaining enough to distract her from the fact that her Rationing was imminent.

"Leelin, you need to leave. I don't have time for you tonight." Mari backed up a step. As if extra distance would do anything to stop him from flirting.

"So...you *will* have time for me another night?"

"Get. *Out.*" She pushed against the door with the words, and Leelin stumbled a few paces back, giving her a little bit of compliance before halting the door's swing again.

"You're not the first person to say that to me tonight, Mari, and it wasn't successful for her, either."

He winked and his eyes flashed to Ereta. "You can do this, little flame. You ok?"

It was a genuine question. "I'm ok." *Truth? Lie? Who knows anymore?*

"I expect you to return to me, preferably unscathed."

"I'll do my best. I owe you a date."

Mari spared a look at her, eyebrows raising a fraction–and then scoffed while shoving her entire body weight into the door. Just a sliver of Leelin's face was visible now, sage eyes bright and comforting as they stayed locked on her.

"I can't wait." He made a strained noise as the door was shoved harder. "Mari, enough with the games, darling. *Surely,* you and I can find a way to make this whole messy Ration business disappear; perhaps you can let Ereta off with a warning, and in return, I'll–"

"OUT!"

The door slammed shut.

Mari leaned against it, panting slightly. She straightened her beige linen shirt as if in an attempt to regain her poise.

Ereta turned to survey the Ration quarters. There was a hallway stretching from where she stood to an open-doored cleanroom on the other end. On each side of the hall, doors stood closed, housing what she presumed to be the chambers in which she would sleep for the rest of the night (and tomorrow evening).

"Your Ration officer is already sleeping. She came from the Lords' City this morning."

"Ok."

"Your Rationed Issue is in your bedroom. The door on your right."

"Thank you."

"You're welcome."

Mari made to leave, but paused at the door. Ereta wondered if Mari would delay her exit in an effort to avoid running into Leelin. But she cracked open the door, and spoke without turning back to Ereta, "I hope you make it."

Before she could reply, Mari had whisked out of the door and shut it behind her.

I hope so, too.

And that, at least, was true.

E reta didn't dream at all.

She had half-expected her dreams to be elusive during her earlier nap, but to not have them at all during the night? That was unprecedented and disconcerting. *An omen? A harbinger of my death today–*

A loud knock startled her, but didn't wake her: she had already been awake, unfortunately, for nearly an hour (as best she could guess). There were no windows in the cramped bedroom of the Ration quarters. Just an uncomfortably small stone bed, her pack, and her Rationed Water.

The Issue they had used for her Water allotment was half-empty–or, she supposed, half-full, depending on your perspective. She just wished they had just filled a smaller one completely. It would have been less bleak-looking.

She rose and stretched–realizing that she was, mercifully, dry–perhaps the only positive thing about not dreaming last night had been that she also hadn't sweat. She opened the door for the person she assumed would be her Ration officer–

Her breath caught at the figure she beheld.

Standing effortlessly straight, with a look of pure indifference on her face, was the woman who had made her who she was today.

By ruining her life.

"Good morning, Ereta. I have the pleasure of serving as your Ration officer today." Voice like an airy song, Hista was as beautiful now as she had been eight turns ago. Tall, graceful, almost impossibly slim, with warm blond hair that fell to her waist in silky straight strands. Her eyes were blue, but not like Kilas'. Hista's eyes were a deep, rich blue: a color Ereta hadn't known existed until she had seen those eyes for the first time in the Lords' City. The only changes in Hista's appearance were the slight lines of age that now pulled at the corners of her eyes, but they somehow only served to enhance her beauty–make it more sophisticated.

You are staring.

She knew it, but she couldn't stop. She could feel the stale air drying her wide eyes as she gazed, unblinking, at Hista's perfect face. *This can't be real. Maybe you're having a nightmare. You've never had one, so you wouldn't know–*

"You will be in receipt of a secondary Ration if you do not begin your Route before the sun hits five."

Yes, of course she would. And that would be a death sentence that no amount of possibly-pee-derived illegal allotments could prevent. But still, she couldn't force herself to stop staring in disbelief at the personification of her unbelievably terrible luck.

Hista cocked her head. "The Caretakers used to read me stories of creatures that lived under the Old Sun. There was one creature–tiny, with skin of midnight, and large blades on its back that it used to glide through the air.

"It was said that their bulging eyes were larger than their heads, or maybe even larger than their bodies. Though entirely harmless, they were repulsive. A tiny nuisance with huge eyes, flitting around, refusing to recognize that it was unwanted. I had trouble picturing them until I met you."

And there it is.

The fact that Ereta had anticipated the storytelling taking some kind of brutal turn did not do much to soften the blow. Hista was an artist whose medium was cruelty. She found tiny cracks of self-doubt in others and carved into them until they were gaping holes of insecurity. Pouring acid on the open wounds was just her way of ensuring her hard efforts never healed over.

Hista watched her words strike true. It reminded Ereta of Intali: how one might draw a winning hand and bait others into placing large bets, only to smugly set the cards down and ruin everyone's day.

Sentiments around the table of, *"I should have known better,"* and, *"I didn't think you had it,"* or even, *"I can't believe I fell for that again,"* were useless; the game was already lost.

The shame she felt allowed her to finally break her stare, if only to let her gaze drop to her feet.

"Ten minutes," Hista's voice was steady–melodic and sickly sweet, the beauty of it somehow potentiating the venom of her words.

It made Ereta sick.

Hista turned her back on the woman that she had eviscerated, not for the first time or, Ereta thought, the last. Her beautiful blond hair disappeared from view as she entered her own room and closed the door behind her.

Ereta had been born in the Lords' City, as best she knew. The Childhouse there was the largest of any on Veirbos. Rows of cribs became rows of tiny beds as she aged alongside the hundred and twenty-four other children born in the City during the same turn as she.

She didn't have a lot of memories of her early childhood. There was nothing particularly notable about it; most everyone on Veirbos had been raised similarly. Except Heirs, of course.

Most citizens were dosed with a contraceptive that prevented pregnancy, intentional or otherwise. Only high aristocrats in the Lords' court had the honor of breeding. Aristocrats typically had many children in pursuit of an Heir, with those babes who didn't meet their needs being sent to the Childhouse. The specific quality or manner that defined Heirship was a closely guarded secret, and the rarity of a true Heir was sufficient to cast them in reverence.

The Dutied Caretakers who served the Childhouse raised the spare children from babes. They nursed them, nurtured them, played with them, and taught them in a manner that would ensure their actualization as obedient Dutied adults. Staggered Shifts and shifting Duties ensured that the children never formed strong attachments to any specific caretaker. Though the spare children were not treated cruelly, neither were they loved.

Ereta's first memory was at the age of three: waking from a dream, filled with feelings she would someday understand to be contentment and love.

Her second memory was at age four: sliding down the side of her stone bed onto the floor, climbing back up to repeat the process again and again, with a boy her age by her side.

His face adorned many of her memories of childhood. They spent countless hours together–playing, talking, or just enjoying quiet moments in each other's presence.

At age six, Ereta remembered feeling anxious for the first time. That night, she had trouble sleeping. Her desperation to rest and find the comfort of her dreams only served to make sleep more elusive; and as she stared into the darkness, her heart started pounding. She felt a sudden and overwhelming urge to get up and start pacing the room. She walked up and down the rows of beds, counting her steps as she went, for what might have been hours. She wasn't sure why she did it, just that she *knew* something terrible would happen if she didn't.

At some point during her laps, some of the other children woke. They started whispering and pointing at her. Whenever Ereta passed their beds, she could hear them giggling and whispering, *"Look at her, look at her, look at her."* That mantra would follow her for the rest of her childhood, spreading in whispers whenever the other children found her behavior to be strange or entertaining.

But that first night, when her friend woke to whispers and giggles at Ereta's expense, the boy came to her side and walked with her. They talked for several minutes about nothing in particular. Ereta's face was flushed in embarrassment, but she felt like she couldn't stop. After a while, he stepped in front of her and took her hands. *"Let's go back to bed, 'Reta."* His eyes were steadying, and she found that she finally felt strong enough to let go of the compulsion and return to bed.

Ereta continued to struggle with overwhelming urges to engage in strange, repetitive behaviors that served as the only balm to a nagging sensation of impending doom. She would tap her foot, or try to count grains of dust in the air, or aggressively powder her hands repeatedly until they cracked and bled. Even as the *look at hers* continued, she found that the only way she could reliably stop was when her friend came up to her and steadied her with his presence.

As they got older, he would tell her about his ambitions: of being strong enough to be assigned a prestigious, high-ranking Duty. Ereta had no such ambitions—in turn, she would tell him about her daydreams of worlds where plants grew lush and green, where Water was in the air and sky, where you could feel the warmth of the sun on your skin. He would sit and listen, smiling at her, but always his response was the same: *"Why do you bother imaging things that cannot be? Why can't you just be happy with the way things are?"* And always, she answered: *"Because everything could be so much more beautiful!"*

Gradually, Ereta started to notice that she felt feelings other than friendship for the boy: strange, new feelings that compelled her to be near him. To touch him. To hold his hand, to run her fingers through his hair.

And he returned those gentle touches.

Their first kiss was at age 13. They were outside in the cold of night, sitting on the steps of the Childhouse, looking up at the moons. He told her he wanted to kiss her, and she replied, *"That sounds good."* The turns passed, and the innocent, gentle kisses of youth turned to the passionate tangling of tongues and lips and teeth. It turned to touching and caressing and, eventually, making love. The first time he had her, it happened on the floor of a supply closet in the Childhouse. It was awkward and uncomfortable, but it still felt *so right*. Lying in each other's arms in the aftermath, she whispered into the darkness that she loved him. He leaned down, kissed the top of her head, and whispered against her ebony hair, "I love you, too, Reta."

The boy grew in spurts, seemingly becoming taller with each passing day, even as Ereta remained the same height. At 16, he was so much taller than her that he had to pick her up by the waist in order to comfortably kiss her. The boy's form was ideal for Running, the Duty scout told him. The scout had the boy do some test trials, at which he excelled, and which led to the Lords' Court offering him an incentive to choose Running as his Duty: the promise of a large, luxurious apartment in the Court.

By contrast, Ereta didn't particularly care what her Duty was. The most important part of her life was her all-consuming love for the boy. Wanting to stay with him, she decided to choose Running as well, hoping that a shared Duty would ensure that they never had to part; not for a single day.

They entered Runner training together at age 17. Ereta was, by a wide margin, the shortest person in the training Cohort. The first day, a woman called Hista walked in: beautiful and tall and graceful. She looked at Ereta, and a flash of some indiscernible emotion crossed her face before she smiled. Wholly ignorant of the cruelty lurking behind Hista's smile, Ereta smiled back.

Hista had been a trainer, only two turns older than their Cohort and in her prime as a Runner. She taught the training with efficiency and had no patience for mistakes. It was either keep up or be left out. Despite Ereta's size, despite everything about her that made her different and unlikely to succeed in a Duty where lithe forms and long, muscled legs excelled, she kept up.

And Hista *hated* it. She began singling out Ereta for special drills early on. She would have Ereta woken before dawn to perform sprints across the Childhouse grounds, wearing nothing but her bedclothes in the frigid air, until she became sick. During training classes, she would taunt Ereta constantly, *"Do that again so everyone can see a demonstration of poor form,"* or, *"Perhaps the growth of your brain was stunted, just as the rest of you was."* The other children laughed (except for the boy, who looked at her with genuine pity), and the *look at hers* continued.

But the boy held her hand as they fell asleep each night in their adjacent beds. And she knew it was worth it. *Anything* was worth it if they could be together.

Driven by the all-consuming desire to stay close to the boy she loved, Ereta endured it all, even as the punishments became crueler. In the last quarter of training, she was separated from the rest of the group because, as Hista put it, she was "tarnishing the quality of the Cohort."

Her solitary training was, in actuality, Running full Routes alongside the fully grown and fully trained Dutied Runners of the City. She was given extended Routes with heavy deliveries four days out of every pentad, and still, Hista woke her before sunrise each morning to perform sprints until she vomited.

She could still remember Hista leaning down beside her on the dust, Ereta's stomach contents on the ground beside them, as Hista whispered, *"It's not good enough. Why have I bothered putting so much effort into helping you? You should have never disgraced this Duty with your presence. You're an ungrateful, lazy little bitch, and that's all you'll ever be."*

As training reached its final pentads, Ereta's self-hatred had grown to become an all-consuming entity. Her compulsions worsened, and fits of panic seized her as she drifted off to sleep each night, bringing her back to consciousness hugging her knees, crying, and shaking violently until the boy's soft words and gentle caresses eased her to sleep.

The boy, now a man, turned 18 before Ereta did, and passed his trials with record-breaking paces. He moved into his promised apartment, assuring her that she could come with him as soon as she turned 18 and passed her trials. They saw each other only a few times a pentad at most; he was fully Dutied now, after all, and she was still living in the shared quarters of the Childhouse.

On her 18th birthday, Ereta took her final trials. She was shocked when she passed them all with time to spare and was sworn into Running with her first oath. She wanted to surprise the man with news of her success, and after leaving the trials, she walked to his apartment to finally begin their life together.

She traveled to the tall central building of the Court and walked up flights of carved stone stairs to arrive at the apartment. She had never been there, not yet, and had to get directions from passersby. When she finally found it, she opened the door with a smile.

The room was large and open. In the center, there was a lounge, with its delicate cushions tossed onto the floor, and on the lounge–

Hista's beautiful, naked body was perched on top of the man, his hands caressing her hips. The man didn't hear Ereta come in, and so as she stood there, eyes wide and too disbelieving to shed tears, Hista looked at her, smiled, lifted her hips, and impaled herself on the man's length. She maintained constant eye contact with Ereta as she continued to move up and down on him. The man moaned: a sound of pleasure that Ereta knew so well, that she had coaxed from him so many countless times. Hista leaned down and kissed him, and he kissed her back. She pulled away, looking at Ereta still, and spoke to him. "How much do you love me?"

"*Oh my Lords,* Hista, you're the love of my life. Of *course,* you are. You're perfect. You're fucking gorgeous. I love you so Lords-damn much."

Hista's body looked like it had been carved out of stone. Her silhouette was slender and graceful, her skin delicately pale over ridges of smooth muscle, her long blond hair hanging silky around her shoulders and brushing the delicate pink peaks of her round breasts. "Mmmm and tell me we'll be together forever."

"Of course we will, baby. You're gonna stay here forever, with me, and I'm gonna fuck you in this apartment every day for the rest of our fucking lives."

Hista kept moving up and down on him.

"What about Ereta?"

The man paused before answering. She could hear his quickened breaths in the silence. "What about her?"

"She thinks she's going to live here with you when she passes her trials." Hista's movement didn't stop. She slid up and down, his cock disappearing inside her again and again as she spoke.

The man reached up to palm Hista's breasts, and she moaned, eyes still glued to Ereta, who wasn't sure she was breathing. Who might never breathe again.

"She definitely won't pass the trials. There's no way. She's too... small. You've said it yourself: those legs are too short to make the minimum trial times. Even if it were possible, she's too fucking worked up all the time to make it through. She'll probably end up running in circles or sobbing in the dust, knowing her. Poor thing. And then she'll be assigned to Lek Combustion somewhere, anyway, and she'll leave the city. It's just you and me now, baby."

"I just get jealous sometimes, and I worry that you will pick her over me?" Hista smiled cruelly at Ereta out of the corner of her eye as she spoke.

The man laughed. "You don't have to worry about her, baby. She's... she's a lot. She's *too much*. I've been with her my whole life, and I've stuck by because I felt bad, you know? And because I didn't have anyone else. But then I met you, and I realized how good it could be. I feel bad that she's gonna fail and go to combustion, but honestly? I can't fix her. I've tried. She's not my problem, not anymore–not when I have *you*..."

He gripped her hips and flipped Hista onto her back, kissed her, and lifted himself up to begin pumping into her again. But as his head raised and his eyes caught sight of Ereta, he faltered.

"OH my *Lords*, Reta, what are you doing here?!"

The man got up in a rush, pulling on the bedclothes that had been tossed on the floor amidst the cushions. Hista simply stood, her slim curves utterly breathtaking, wearing only her cruel smile of satisfaction.

Ereta said nothing. He approached her quickly and grabbed her by the shoulders.

"You're not supposed to be here, Reta, how *the fuck* did you even–"

"I passed the trials." Ereta's voice filled the air, but she couldn't recall thinking the words, let alone forming them.

"You...what? Really? The Running trials? What are you–?"

"I'm sorry," she whispered, voice breaking, but tears still refusing to fall.

"Sorry? For what? Reta, *I'm sor*–you were never supposed to see–"

"I didn't know I was too much. I didn't think you minded helping me. I never wanted to be a burden to you. I just love you."

"Oh, Lords, Reta, I–I love you too, you're *not* too much; you're just not..." the man's words trailed off. He brushed a hand through his hair, and then moved that hand to cup her cheek. He lifted her head, and their eyes met.

"Tell her." Hista's voice was melodious, and she was still stark naked, leaning casually on the lounge.

"I–Hista and I, we're–*fuck*, I didn't think you'd *pass*, Reta. If I thought you'd pass, I never would have let you get your hopes up about living together. I would have told you about me and Hista quarters ago. I–"

"Quarters ago?"

He was quiet for a long moment, hand still cupping her cheek. "I'm sorry, Reta. I'm so sorry you had to find out this way. I just wanted to protect you, *honestly*–I thought you'd have to move away, and I didn't want you to think I had chosen someone else, didn't want you to have to endure that, you know?"

"Protect me," she repeated his words back to him, eyes still locked on his.

"I've done that our whole lives, protected you." His hands fell and he grabbed hers, squeezing them. "I thought if I could make you more... normal, keep you calm, stop you from doing those things that you do–if I could make you more normal, those other kids, they wouldn't make fun of you."

"Normal?" she whispered the word.

"Yeah, Reta, you know, the way you are, you know how much I love you but... you're different. You're not like the rest of us. I can handle it, you know I can, and I wanted to help you and try to make you better. But I realized a while ago that I'm just one person, you know? I can't change someone, not if they don't want to change, not if they're broken–"

"Broken," she repeated.

"Well, not broken, but–Lords, I don't know how to say any of this! Reta, *why did you come here?*"

She took a long moment to gather threads of her scattered thoughts, attempting to make something like an answer. All that came out in the end were four words. Four words that had meant so much to her, that she had been working toward for turns. That she had endured so much for: the promise of them keeping her grounded in purpose.

"Starting our life together."

He was quiet and squeezed her hands again before pulling her into a hug.

"You've always had so much hope that things could be...*perfect*. But that's not how the world is. Things don't just magically pan out. You have to accept things the way they are. It wouldn't hurt so much if you were just more...realistic. *Lords,* I've been trying to tell you that for turns."

He paused, waiting for a response, of which she had absolutely none besides the gentle tremor that hummed in her muscles.

"You know we'll always be friends, right, Reta? And I do love you, just–just not like *that*. Me and Hista, we're together now, and you and I, we can be friends, alright? Just like we always were. I'm sorry you had to find out this way, but isn't it better that you know now? Maybe you can find someone else, someone who's better at handling all of your...well, you know. Someone who can put up with–"

He stopped himself, pulled out of the hug, and shook his head. "It doesn't matter. Just know that I love you, Reta, you're my best friend. I'm so sorry, I never wanted to hurt you. Can you forgive me? Can we just go back to how things used to be? Just be friends?"

Her eyes moved back to meet Hista's. Hista, who put on an exaggerated pout and then grinned.

She shook her head. "It's not your fault. It's me that's too much. I'm sorry I've been a burden to you."

I'll always be too much.

A quarter later, after trying to live and Duty at the Lords' City as a Runner alongside Hista and the man, Ereta wanted to die. She wanted to disappear into a fissure and never emerge.

Despite the man's promises, they didn't spend any time together at all, and even at their Duty shifts, they didn't talk. Sometimes, she would catch him glancing at her. He would smile, and the sight would make her want to live again for a too-brief moment before reality crushed back into her awareness. *You're too much.* She stopped allowing herself to daydream, to hope. The man had been right. It hurt too much.

One day, an Expediter visited from Lek Tubat-So, saying they needed a Runner to transfer to the settlement permanently. They planned to have a competition, from which the worst-performing Runner would be selected for the Duty. But they didn't need to hold that competition in the end.

Because Ereta volunteered.

And so, she left the Lords' City and the love of her life behind.

Chapter 9

E reta's nausea might be attributed to any number of the things currently happening.

It could be due to the exhaustion she felt. She was six hours into her Rationed Shift, with three hours remaining–because *of course* Hista had given her an extended Route, which was (apparently) allowed on Rationed shifts, if unprecedented in Tubat-So. Her legs felt like jelly, and her head pounded. The pack on her back held the standard Ration pack weight of fifteen pounds; she wasn't actually delivering anything, the weight was just part of the punishment. The expediters wouldn't risk a delivery not arriving due to the (possible, if not likely) death or maiming of the Rationed Runner.

The nausea could also be due to her fear. She was pretty positive she would die today. Any doubt she'd had about that fate had been thoroughly abolished once she learned that she had to complete an extended Route.

But it was likely just muscle memory of some kind. Most of her Runs with Hista had culminated in her vomiting on the dust, and at this point, her body associated the woman's cruel voice with the sensation of throwing up.

"You'll never make it at this pace, Ereta," Hista told her for the tenth or eleventh time.

"I'm aware," Ereta called back over the roar of the wind. It would be impossible for her to finish on time, even if she picked up her pace significantly for the rest of the Route, which she did not have the physical ability to do in her current state. If she finished at all, she was already destined for Combustion.

"It was luck alone that got you through your trials. Maybe that, and your *silly little crush* on my husband. But you don't have anyone to motivate you this time, do you, Ereta? No one waiting for you at home?"

Husband husband husband husband

The word hit Ereta like a slap across the face. She stumbled slightly. She didn't know they had gotten married, but she supposed she needn't have been surprised.

Hista scoffed at the clumsiness. "Unbelievable. You're a disgrace to this Duty."

Ereta said nothing, letting the words wash over her. She was becoming numb now. They barely stung. Hista waited for Ereta's response, and at her silence, decided to keep twisting the proverbial knife.

"So that's a no, right? No one special at Tubat-So?"

"No." Ereta answered under her breath. *A lie.*

"Not even friends?"

"No." *Another lie.*

"I would say that my husband was the only one who pitied you enough to tolerate your presence, but I happen to know for a fact that you are lying to me."

Ereta's heart, already pounding hard at the effort she was exerting, picked up its pace. Her vision turned black around the edges as she felt her panic rising.

"Yes, what's his name again? The expediter told me. A *very* handsome man, your friend. Breathtaking even, if she's to be believed."

Ereta still said nothing. Hista knew his name; she wouldn't have let Mari walk away without telling her.

"Oh *that's* right. *Leelin.* Leelin, Ereta's handsome friend." She could hear the smile in Hista's voice. "That's all he is, right? A friend?"

Say nothing. Do nothing. Just keep Running.

A long moment of silence was broken when Hista clapped her hands together. *"Oh,* how wonderful–more than a friend? Another fruitless crush? Or were you able to wrangle him into your bed somehow? Perhaps you gave him allotments in exchange. I can't *imagine* he would do it without payment, not if he's as handsome as Mari says."

Ereta stared ahead, not daring to blink behind her hood. *"Shut up,"* she whispered without thought.

"Excuse me?"

Ereta stopped cold. She did not turn to face Hista. She spoke again, louder this time: "Shut the fuck up, Hista." Hista laughed, and she felt her pack shift against her back. Hista walked around to Ereta's front. She was holding...

Ereta's canteen. The canteen that held the remainder of her Water, a little over half full. She had been pacing herself carefully, hoping it would raise her chance of survival despite the odds.

Hista opened the canteen, turned it over, and held Ereta's gaze as she let the Water fall into the dust. She tossed the canteen to the ground beside them, the low thud of its impact ringing like a death bell.

It's over. Ereta fell to her knees in the dust. Without Water, she would be dead in an hour or less if she kept running at her previous pace, let alone the pace required to make up time.

"Leave me. *Please.*" She didn't want to die with Hista here. She needed...well, she needed her friends. But that wasn't possible. The next best thing would be dying alone.

"Oh, I intend to. But before I go, just know this."

Hista grabbed Ereta's chin and tipped it up so that their eyes met. Those eyes, which had held hers as Hista fucked the love of her life.

Hista's voice was low, but no less like a beautiful song, as she spoke. "I hated you from the moment I saw you. How *dare you*, your whole body barely the size of one of my legs, think you can be one of us? Running is a *sacred* duty, it keeps our planet turning. And you disgrace it with your presence. I already hated you for that disrespect. But I had lusted after the beautiful man in the training Cohort from the first day, and when I found out that *somehow*, you had manipulated him into sharing your bed, I hated you even more. So I got rid of you.

"But remember this, Ereta. With him, and with this Leelin? It's *pity* that compels them to indulge you. It's always been *pity*. My husband still pities you, you know. He used to talk about it sometimes, in the couple of turns after you left. About how he wished he could have let *'poor Reta'* down easy, because your face when you found us was so *moons-cursed pathetic*. Do you know how much of a waste of space you are?"

Tears welled in her eyes. The waste of Water didn't matter, she was dead anyway.

"*Say it*," Hista pushed.

"Yes."

"Good."

Hista turned to walk away, to leave Ereta to her death in the desert.

"Oh, by the way, I'm going to fuck him, too. Your handsome friend at the settlement? *Leelin?*"

Ereta choked out a sob then. She couldn't help it. Tears began sliding down her cheeks.

"He will choose me, just as my husband chose me, and I'm going to ride him exactly the same. I bet you can picture it, can't you?"

Ereta said nothing, just sobbed aloud, voice sounding raw as skin against shards of glass. "Your pathetic suffering will be over soon. You will be dead, and Leelin will forget all about you, just like we did. Just like everyone will." She registered Hista's retreating footfalls.

"*Fuck you.*" She let those words come out as loud as she could manage, packed with all of the venom and shame she felt. She had nothing left to lose. Nothing left to fear.

Hista's footsteps stopped. She heard the woman walk back toward where she knelt in the dust.

And a hard kick to her back sent her sprawling, face-first, into the ground, her nose cracking into pieces. As Ereta fell out of consciousness, she heard Hista's voice like a song on the wind: *"Look at her, now."*

Her eyes fluttered open sometime later. She didn't know how long she had been out. The thirst was painful. The world spun in front of her, a blur with blackened edges. Her muscles ached. Her head pounded. Her heart felt weak and stuttering in her chest. *Not long now.*

The tug pulled relentlessly at her eyes, as it had for the past three days. The effort to keep her eyes open was too great, and she let her lids drift closed again, idly wondering if it would be the last time. She let her thoughts drift to the fissure she had seen in the air. The white dots that were cold Water, coating the land for miles in every direction. She remembered that landscape, and that warm, wonderful feeling she had gotten when the fissure had opened. She tried to imagine it again, painting the picture in her mind.

Light flashed in front of her eyelids, and she was proud of the efficacy of her imagination, even while dying. But then, the warmth returned, and there was no way she could *imagine* that feeling–

She opened her eyes.

The fissure sat before her, wide and open to reveal the sprawling expanse of white.

She crawled toward it, desperate. She thought of Leelin, and Milo, and Jace. Their faces filled her mind, replacing the cruel grin of Hista, as she crawled toward hope.

Muscles screaming, she pulled herself across the ground until her face breached the fissure. A gloved hand crossed the barrier, and she put it down into the white dots, feeling them condense beneath her weight. She moved further, and soon, her whole body was inside, creating a small crater in the thick layer of white. She grabbed a handful of the powdery, soft substance, and as she did, she felt it begin to melt. Water fell in small drips from her fist. She raised the melting ball to her mouth and dropped it in.

Water.

It was glorious, cold Water that melted from the powder to slice down her parched throat.

Ereta had taken dozens of handfuls of the powder into her mouth before she took a break. She knew that, given how severe her dehydration had been, she needed to give herself time to recover. She didn't want to drink too much at once and make herself sick.

The contented feeling this world gave her warmed her heart (if not her body), and was enough to keep her grounded. Panicking would *not* be helpful, not when she had so little energy left to lose. She needed to stay calm and let herself rehydrate if she had any hope of returning to Tubat-So. The hope that she might live to return to her friends flickered within her like a tiny flame struck into life. She let it grow and spread, no longer concerned about the pain that disappointment might bring. She *needed* hope, she realized. Without it, there was no point in trying.

She continued drinking (eating? it was mostly solid, after all) the cold Water as hours passed. Exactly *how many* hours passed, she couldn't be sure—the yellow sun was not the one she knew. *Another world.* She was in another world. Being nearly dead had dulled her awe at the realization: the fissure had been a doorway, and here she was, in a place where Water was everywhere. Abundant and cold and beautiful.

The fissure had closed behind her after she crossed the barrier, and as she slowly regained her faculties, she had the troubling realization that she wasn't entirely sure how to return to her world.

The cold powder beneath her had melted into Water with her body heat, and she now had a different problem: she was wet and utterly freezing. For the time being, there was no fierce wind to worsen her cold; but still, she shivered, expending far too much energy than was wise considering the hours-long Run she had to conquer to get back to Tubat-So.

But before that Run was a remote possibility, she had to deal with several more pressing issues: the foremost being that she needed to figure out how in the Lords' spit she was supposed to return to her world.

She thought and thought, but although her dehydration had eased significantly, her exhaustion and hunger were making it hard to concentrate on anything.

How did you open the fissure to get here?

She thought back on her last moments in Veirbos, when she had pictured this landscape of cold, white Water. She had tried to remember the warm feeling that enveloped her heart in its presence. And that imagination had somehow manifested the fissure before her.

It wasn't hard to imagine Veirbos. She closed her eyes and saw it clearly in her mind. The fissure, however, did not appear.

The tug pulled at her eyes gently, steadily, as it always did. She wondered if it was pulling back toward Veirbos? Or somewhere beyond even this world in which she currently sat? This world that she had longed to see, to feel, even as she felt herself begin to die. And her hope had been realized–

Her thoughts guttered at the realization. *Longing. Hope.* Before the fissure had appeared, those feelings had been as strong and clear as her mental pictures of the white Water landscape. Maybe that was the key to opening the fissure back to her world.

But try as she might, it was nigh impossible for her to long for Veirbos. She hated Veirbos. She didn't truly want to return, she just wanted to get back to...

To...her friends. They were what made her planet a place worth fighting for. She closed her eyes again, picturing Veirbos, but instead of empty, dusty expanses, she pictured Leelin smiling as the orange glow of the sun tinted his skin. She pictured the stone of her home, where Jace would make haughty comments and spend far too long staring at herself in the cleanroom mirror. She pictured the alley outside of the Ration quarters, where Milo, with his fierce gaze, had made her eat the most delicious allotment she had ever tasted. She pictured climbing out of the fissure two days ago and lying on her back, staring at the sky, with new, intoxicating hope filling her mind with possibilities of what might be.

Orange light colored her eyelids; orange light so different from the yellow of the sun in this place, and she knew it had worked. She opened her eyes and looked through the fissure that led to her friends. To home.

Chapter 10

The last sip of her canteen fell past her lips just before she crossed into Tubat-So. She had walked instead of Run for most of the way, muscles aching from the intense shivering that had refused to ebb during the entire return journey. The soaking wet of her clothing had not dried until she was over halfway back, and the freezing wind that blew at her back had only chilled her further.

It was past midnight now, and she guessed that it had been five, or maybe six hours since she had climbed through the fissure back to Veirbos' dust. She hadn't thought to check the time until she had been well on her way. Maybe she had been in shock. Maybe she still was.

The fissure had stayed open long enough for her to retrieve the canteen that Hista had emptied and fill both of her containers with the powdery, cold Water from the other world. She had purposefully finished both canteens before entering the settlement grounds; if she were found with Water outside of her Ration allotment, she–

Wait, what *would* happen to her? She was already going to be assigned to Combustion for not finishing her Ration Route in the allotted Shift time. She knew that, and while she didn't necessarily accept it, it seemed like the least of her problems at the moment.

She wasn't sure she could save herself from severe punishment, but an inquiry into how she had acquired extra Water might end up implicating her friends, especially Milo, and she wouldn't let that happen.

She stumbled her way through Tubat-So, careful to avoid fissures; how ironic would it be if she fell into a fissure now, when she had already defied so many odds to survive? Her fingers and toes were numb and her muscles felt as if they were being sliced apart with tiny knives.

As the Distribution Center loomed in the distance, she picked up her pace. A figure began moving toward her from its watch by the entrance, moving quickly, its form solid and sure. A flash of red as she felt a body collide with her own—

She was warm. The pleasant aroma of wood smoke tickled her nostrils. It was *so Lords-damn warm* here, and she felt safe, here in the arms of...*wait, who in the Lords is this?*

"I never doubted you. Not for a single moment, Ereta." A familiar, steady voice that she *knew,* but was simply too far gone to identify, whispered as her knees shook and her vision began to swirl. She was exhausted, and in pain. She just wanted to *sleep.* "You did it. It's over now. You're safe."

She believed the voice. *Yes. You're safe. You can stop fighting.*

She felt her knees buckle as the blissful blackness of unconsciousness cradled her once again.

"**L**ook at her."

The woman's even words were low whispers, but they still struck Ereta's ears as clear as a punch to the gut. Those *moons-cursed words*—they were the absolute last thing in the world she wanted to hear. *Am I dead? Is this some kind of eternal punishment?*

"I *am* looking at her. She's beautiful."

Ok, maybe not punishment, then.

"She's a fucking mess. We have to take care of it, who knows how long she'll be out?" That was Jace's voice.

"Do. Not. Touch. Her." Leelin spoke slowly, emphasizing each word as if Jace were an infant not yet wholly versed in language.

"You are not my Lord."

"No, but I *am* much bigger and stronger than you. Also better-looking, not that that's strictly relevant, but it bears repeating."

Jace scoffed. "You want her to wake, days from now, covered in filth and stinking like a cleanroom pipe?"

"I *want* her to get the rest that she needs to recover. It's only been two days since her last cleaning, she's fine! If you insist on fussing over her like she's an heir fresh out of the womb, you'll wake her, or at the least, disturb her—"

"If she were capable of waking, this wouldn't even be a problem!"

"She should wake on *her own* terms, in *her own* time, not because she's being pawed at—"

"*Pawed at?* If one of us should be ensuring that the other isn't pawing at her, it's me."

"Oh, please. I have more honor than that."

"What do you know of honor, Leelin?"

Ereta smiled to herself, remembering asking Leelin that exact question just before they ended up in bed together. Leelin laughed out loud, obviously remembering, too—the sound was as clear and bright and beautiful as ever. "If only you knew the depths of my honor, especially when it comes to Ereta. Now stop trying to make her your vanity project and let her rest for the Lord's—"

"It's *vanity* to brush out the mats of her hair? To powder off the sweat and dirt? Imagine if she wakes up to this! She'll be horrified—"

"She is perfect just as she is."

It felt blissfully normal to hear Jace and Leelin argue, and she was at least 80% sure that she had, in fact, lived. She wiggled her fingers and toes, most of which felt oddly distant and a little numb. Slowly, she began to shift around, her body's sensations returning one by one.

The first thing she noticed was the ache. It was a dull, constant pressure that clamped down on every single muscle. Even her Lords-damn eyelids pulsed with a throbbing tenderness.

The second thing she noticed was that she was incredibly warm, which felt like an indulgence that she had never wholly experienced (let alone truly appreciated) until that moment.

The third thing she noticed was that she was dry–both of the moisture that had clung to her from the powdered Water and of any sweat. *No dreams, again.*

Her eyes fluttered open.

The ceiling was unfamiliar–a high, curved arch of stone bathed in soft orange light.

She felt the tug pull behind her eyes, a steady presence that made the corner of her lip twitch up. She knew what it was now, and she knew how to return to that wonderful place where Water was endless and warmth suffused her heart, if not her skin.

She turned her head to the left, and the fuzzy image before her slowly took shape. Jace and Leelin were standing by the wall of an unfamiliar room, facing each other with crossed arms and frustrated expressions. They had not stopped arguing while she had been lost in thought. She focused on their conversation again.

"–you should probably leave anyway. The room is at least ten degrees colder with you in it."

"As her *best friend*–"

"*No,* I am her best friend."

Jace scoffed, again. "You're cocky because she chose to take you to bed the other night instead of heeding my advice, but don't misunderstand what part of your body she was choosing. It wasn't your brain."

"We'll just ask her who she prefers when she wakes up."

"Let me see what I look like before I choose sides," Ereta's voice sounded like stones scraping together, and felt like it, too. Her nose throbbed with the slight movement of her lips. She barely pushed the words out, but her smile was genuine, even if her sentiment was not. Lords, she loved both of them so much her heart felt like it might burst.

"Ereta! You're awake! Thank the Lords, I–"

Jace shoved in front of Leelin. "Oh, Ereta, I'm so sorry, you must be *mortified–*"

Leelin checked her hip with his, sending her stumbling slightly to the side. "*Do not* put words in her mouth." He spat the words at Jace before turning to Ereta and softly smiling. "You look beautiful, little flame."

She looked up into Leelin's sage eyes and let the happiness of the moment consume her, until she remembered–

"Hista."

"What?" Jace had recovered and stood calmly (for now) next to Leelin at her bedside.

"Hista. Tall, blond?" Her heart raced. If Hista knew Ereta was awake, there was no telling what she might do. Her reappearance in Tubat-So was proof that Hista had not stayed with Ereta until she confirmed her death, as was protocol for Ration Routes. Her survival meant that Hista had failed to do her Duty. And then there was Leelin–oh, *Lords,* had she been too late? Had Hista already–

"Oh, the Ration officer? She left the day of your Shift, before you even returned. *Really* irritating woman. So bossy–even bossier than *Her Majesty* over here." Leelin indicated to Jace with his head. "I do not envy you sharing that Shift with her."

Ereta felt a surge of relief that Hista was gone, and likely ignorant that Ereta had lived at all. She was only slightly relieved that Leelin seemed irritated by Hista, but that wasn't necessarily mutually exclusive with him allowing her into his bed. But she couldn't ask, didn't *want* to ask, not here. Not now. And it didn't matter anyway, did it? *Don't go there.*

As she replayed her time with Hista in her mind, an utterly unimportant memory skidded to the forefront. Her dry, chapped lips nearly split with the wide grin that took over her face.

"What is it, little flame?" Leelin asked, returning her smile and leaning close to brush a stray hair out of her face.

"Apparently, Mari thinks you're *breathtaking.*"

She had been unconscious for four days in an infirmary bed. And while she didn't *quite* 'stink like a cleanroom pipe' (as Jace had so tactlessly put it), she was certainly grateful for the opportunity to clean herself up. She was unsteady on her socked feet–likely due to a combination of recovery from dehydration and the fact that she hadn't eaten in over five days–so a Dutied Nurse had assisted her to the cleanroom, helping her undress.

When she looked down at her bare toes, she couldn't manage to stifle a sound somewhere between a yelp of surprise and a scream of horror. Of her ten toes, only four remained. Both of her big and little toes were reduced to nubs, as were the second and third toes on her left and right foot, respectively. Gruesome-looking stitches pulled the skin tight at the apex of each nub. The Duty nurse stroked her back in soothing motions as she explained that Ereta had suffered frostbite: the deadened digits were amputated the first night she returned. Not that she had thought Running would be a possibility after she failed her Ration Route–but the loss of her toes was stark proof that she was unfit to return to her former Duty. It also partially explained her unsteadiness on her feet.

A glance in the mirror told her that Jace was right–she did look awful. Her nose was blackened with bruises and swollen to the apples of her cheeks. Strategically-placed strips of sticky bamboo tape held the shattered bones in place for healing. She was immensely grateful to have been unconscious when they set her nose, not to mention the amputations. Her hair was a tangled mess of knots, sticking up at odd angles and littered with bits of dust and debris. Her forehead and cheeks were covered in scabs and scrapes. *"You look beautiful, little flame,"* Leelin had lied, even as his eyes had sparkled with earnestness. She smiled to herself.

After powdering off her body and letting the Nurse tend to her matted, dirty hair, Ereta redressed in a set of the ill-fitting bedclothes provided by the Infirmary and returned to her bed. It was night now, and Leelin and Jace had been forced to leave hours ago. She ate two nutrition allotments, drank Water, was given some sort of absolutely *fabulous* medicine that made her entire body feel weightless, and fell quickly into a thick, heavy sleep.

Two more days passed in hazy bursts. Her dreams returned as she slept each night. The warmth and comfort of them was so pleasingly similar to the feeling she had gotten in the other world.

She slept during the day as well, the naps intermittent and dreamless, whenever she wasn't being visited by Leelin or Jace (or, most entertaining of all, Leelin *and* Jace). Bellat visited a few times as well, which was a welcome surprise to Ereta. On Bellat's first visit, she came bearing a tiny iron Runner figurine that she had been found many turns ago, just outside the Lords' City. *"I asked a Connection from the Court about it. Apparently, it's a token that Runners in the City get from the Lords for their retirement, to thank them for their turns of Duty. I think it's fitting that you keep it."* Ereta had tucked the tiny figure into her pack.

With Leelin and Jace, Ereta mostly kept it light: playing rounds of Intali on her bed, joking with each other about nothing in particular. But just as Ereta's very brief, very sparse description of what had happened on her Ration Route hinted that she didn't want to recount the memories, so too did Jace and Leelin's tense overview of the hours after Hista had returned and announced Ereta's death beg that there be no prying into specifics.

Even though her toe-nubs were not healing particularly quickly, she practiced walking on her "new" feet as much as she could. Her muscles hurt less with each day, but the loss of her toes had completely thrown off her balance, and entirely different muscles began to ache as her body compensated for the change in ambulation. She took loops around the Infirmary with the Nurses, and her habit of counting her steps as she went was painfully reminiscent of her childhood. Luckily, there was no one to *look at her*, because the building was otherwise empty.

On the third day after waking, Jace and Leelin were on Shifts during visiting hours.

The morning passed in a blur of intermittent naps, sips of Water, turns around the room, and brief respites spent lying in her small stone infirmary bed staring blankly at the ceiling. It was during a particularly long indulgence of that last activity that Ereta heard soft footsteps echoing through the room. Her eyes pulled to her left, and glowing ember eyes met her own. *Milo.*

"Hi," she said, a bit timidly. Although she had effortlessly categorized Milo as her "friend" while dying, the uncomfortable reality of how little they knew each other still insisted upon itself: *you should feel more awkward, you barely know him.*

"Hi," he replied, and his brow was scrunched, hands clasped behind his back as he stopped a few feet away to look her up and down (or side to side, as it were). She felt like an object being studied for clues; but she had done the same to him just a few days prior, so she supposed it was fair. "How are you feeling?"

"A few ounces lighter," she joked, lifting one foot from beneath the sheet and wiggling its remaining toes.

He cocked his head to one side and approached the bed with interest. He reached his hands toward her foot–but he stopped before he made contact. "May I?"

"I...suppose?" There was hesitancy in the way she drew out the words, but Milo didn't seem to notice, and jumped at the permission. He lifted her leg up by cupping her heel, perched on the edge of her bed, and lowered her foot back down so it rested on his lap. With intricate gentleness, his warm fingers prodded and pinched the skin around her wounds. "Not great," he summarized his inspection under his breath without further explanation. "Can you flex and bend your toes again?" She did, and the pain was less disconcerting than the phantom feel of her missing digits.

He nodded. "And the other." It wasn't a question, but Ereta allowed the inspection to proceed anyway. She didn't know why, but she trusted his assessment as much, if not even a bit more, than that of the nurses. He rose, replaced her foot gently on the bed, and walked around to the other side to repeat the entire process (even down to the "not great").

Done with both feet, he walked right up beside her head and leaned so close that her next inhale was suffused with his scent. The smell of wood smoke filled her nostrils–*wood smoke*. The realization hit her like a slap to the face.

"It was you," she whispered to him. His fingers had already begun prodding at her nose, but she barely noticed. "When I came back after the Ration, it was you there, waiting. You–grabbed me."

"Yes." So they were back to one word answers?

Over the past few days, she hadn't thought about the man who had greeted her when she returned from her Shift. The memory was so foggy that she hadn't even been sure it was real, but now, his smell was so distinct that it dragged the entire encounter to the forefront of her mind.

"How did you know? To wait for me, I mean?" His prodding at her nose paused, and those eyes pinned her again. She wanted to shrink back from them, but there was nowhere to go.

"You're a survivor. You'll always be ok. Especially when the odds are against you."

Her eyes widened at his conclusion, not sure what to make of it. "But you couldn't have known that I would make it. *I* didn't know."

He resumed prodding her nose one more time, and then stood straight. "It was obvious. Don't look so surprised."

"You don't know me well enough to analyze my moods." She crossed her arms and spit his previous words back at him with equal parts venom and lilt. Was she joking? She wasn't sure. This was all so strange. *A survivor*—she had never thought of herself as a survivor. She always felt more like some world-weary, broken heap of a creature desperately crawling from near miss to near miss and hating the journey along the way. But maybe...that's all survivors were? *You don't have to come out of a trauma whole in order to live through it*, she realized with sudden clarity. *You just move on as best you can with whichever toes you have left.*

Milo had known that she would make it back, and she had. He had waited for her outside the Distribution Center through the night. Through the long hours after Hista had pronounced her dead. While Leelin and Jace had grieved for her, he had patiently waited for her to return. "*I never doubted you. Not for one second.*"

He seemed to read her thoughts somehow, as if those too-sharp eyes could see straight through her skull and into her mind. He grinned slightly, brows remaining in their steadfast furrow. "Nowhere does fire burn cold, Ereta."

Chapter 11

"**F**UUUUUCK OFF, MILO, YOU UTTER WASTE OF WATER!" While that wasn't the nicest thing Ereta had screamed at Milo in the preceding hour, it wasn't the meanest, either. He fought the quirking up of his lips with every insult she hurled in his direction. He seemed to find her anger (if not her pain) amusing.

Leelin, on the other hand, didn't fight his smile at all. He seemed to revel in her temper.

"Did you ever wonder *why* I call you little flame?"

"You can fuck off as well, Leelin." Ereta breathed in heavy pants, sweat drenching the bed beneath her, hands clutching her sheets. Leelin and Jace were each holding down one arm and one leg; they fought to keep her still while Milo worked his needle through the nubs where toes had once been. It was the day after he had first come to see her, and all three happened to share a non-Shift day. It was a convenient time for Jace and Leelin to be used as living restraints against Ereta's flails of pain.

"I always assumed it was some kind of childish euphemism." Jace seemed entirely unaffected by Ereta's pain, or anger, or any of the other moods swirling about the room.

Leelin scoffed. "Not everything I say is about sex, you know."

All three of them spared him an incredulous glance, but then, *dust bury her and cold burn her,* Milo was positioning that Lords-damn *needle–*"Milo, I swear by the Crown Lord I will cut off the rest of my toes and make you swallow them if you dare–FUUUUCK!"

Milo chuckled at that, but his attention was firmly on her toes. In between bursts of anger from the pain he was inflicting, Ereta had to admit that he looked rather amusing. He had (somehow) warped small pieces of glass into half-spheres that he wore over his eyes, held together and looped over his ears with small bits of wire. When she looked down at him from this angle, his eyes through the deformed glass looked four times their normal size, making them even more intimidating than normal when they focused on hers. He had explained that the glass made small objects appear larger, allowing him to complete small, intricate, torturous, movements (such as stitches) with confidence.

"*Why* couldn't you have done this while I was unconscious?" She whined at him. Lords, she sounded pathetic, but she didn't have the energy to care.

"Yesterday was my first non-Shift day since your Ration." He had already told her that several times, but it still seemed an inadequate excuse for the torture he was inflicting. Her eyes were wild and bulging as he pulled the long thread tight against her skin, tied it, and used a sharp blade to cut it short. "There, that wasn't so bad, was it?"

She sneered at him with bared teeth.

"*You're welcome* for fixing the nurse's inadequate stitches that would otherwise have gotten badly infected and plagued you with turns of recurring pain. Your heartfelt gratitude means the world." She huffed at his words. After everything he'd done, he had the nerve to *tease* her?

...Not that he was wrong.

"I don't see how she can thank you when you refused to even *consider* sewing on donated toes." Leelin had offered Ereta his toes many times that day, each instance met with Milo's perfectly reasonable explanations as to why such a procedure wasn't plausible.

How Milo knew all of this– how to stitch wounds and assess broken bones? No one thought to question. After all, fire burned hot, and Milo understood things.

"Even if that were possible, which I'm not confident it is, your toes would not have fit her-"

"The intimidating size of my appendages has never stopped Ereta before."

"*Not everything I say is about sex,*" Jace mocked in a poor impression of Leelin's voice. Milo cracked another grin. Ereta's patience had gone out the door and into the dust with her screams of pain, but she couldn't quite deny herself a giggle.

After all, at this moment, life was...pretty good. Relatively speaking.

"And now, the nose," Milo declared as casually as if he were announcing something uninteresting and inevitable, like the sun rising.

She chuckled, low and deep and threatening. "Ohhh Milo. Over my fucking *frostbitten corpse* will you be going anywhere *near* my nose."

Hours later, alone in her bed with her nose reset into a straight line by the torture devices that Milo had the nerve to call hands, Ereta reached into her pack and pulled out the tiny iron Runner figurine: a reminder that she was, indeed, a survivor. She clutched it against her chest and began to drift off to sleep.

And despite everything? Her life was, indeed, pretty good.

Twelve days had passed since Ereta's Ration Route, and she finally was allowed to leave the infirmary. The nurses had been awed by the fastidiousness of Milo's ministrations. They even offered to apply with the Lek to take some of his Duty into their service, which he declined, but not before he offered to stop by whenever they would like him to consult on injuries. When Leelin had balked at the idea of anyone volunteering to do extra Duty for free, Milo had said that the infirmary was "interesting" and that the opportunity to help would be "enlightening." He was always saying things like that—to Milo, every tiny facet of the world was brimming with the potential to be fascinating, if only one cared to look.

Ereta and Leelin left the Infirmary in the midmorning, her wounds bandaged and her body bundled in layers of outerwear. The cold still hit her like a slap in the face, and she decided at that moment that she would do pretty much anything to avoid being cold again in her lifetime. Milo's earlier words to justify his Duty felt less frivolous to her now: *"I like the heat."* Maybe Combustion wouldn't be so bad, despite the likelihood of a painful death. At least she would die warm.

She still hadn't dared to think about the fact that she would be assigned to Duty at Combustion soon. None of her friends had broached the subject. The nurses had given her two more days of injury leave before she had to report to the Tubat-So Court, where she would be forced to resign her Runner's oath, sit through a reprisal of her Ration, and finally be assigned to her new Duty. The notice about her post-Ration Court appearance had, ironically, arrived at the infirmary via Runner.

The other thing she hadn't dared to think about was, of course, the incident with the fissure. It was now clear that picturing the fissure was a crucial part of opening it, so it seemed prudent to avoid thoughts of it entirely until she was back home, alone. She didn't want to accidentally trigger it in anyone's presence, partly because she didn't yet understand the implications, and partly because of the lingering fear that the whole experience had been in her head.

Ereta yelped in surprise at the feel of steady hands wrapping around her back and knees. "This is entirely unnecessary!" she decreed in protest as Leelin swept her into his arms. "I need to practice walking anyway."

"Life would be incredibly *dull* if we predicated our actions based on their necessity." he replied with a waggle of his brows. "Besides, since I couldn't give you my toes, this is the least I can do."

They ambled through the dust, and only when Leelin's house became visible in the distance did Ereta realize where they were headed. "Why are we going to your house?"

"Why wouldn't we go to my house?"

"Because all of my clothes and belongings are at mine."

"Yes, but your house also serves as Court for a certain nosy, self-important, fire-headed queen, whose presence over the next several hours would be detrimental to my plans."

"Plans?"

"Oh, little flame, did you really think that losing a few toes would make me desire you less?"

"I'm not sure." She paused to consider. With a still mottled, bruised visage and scabby stitches covering her feet, she didn't feel particularly desirable. Not that she usually did. But, she supposed, she didn't look much different except for her missing toes. "Some people have a strong inclination for feet, or so I hear. It could have been my toes alone that drove you to my bed, and if that were the case, a change of heart regarding our trysts would be understandable."

"An *inclination for feet?*" Leelin's brows knitted together, and a grin crept up his face.

Ereta shrugged. "Jace told me about it. Something she's heard about at Court."

"And?"

She thought for another moment. "And... if that were the case, I would hold no ill will or judgment for your proclivities, and would look forward to an enjoyable platonic friendship."

Leelin looked at Ereta with something like surprise, his eyebrows raised and the earlier grin now absent from his face.

"You're serious."

"Of course I'm serious. I would never judge you–"

"Not about the feet. About the friendship."

"Oh I–" she was suddenly at a loss for words. *Is this it? We're having this conversation now?*

Leelin placed her down on the dust just outside his house and looked at her with earnestness.

"We haven't had this conversation yet, and I think it's well past time." *That answers that.*

Her heart began to pound with the realization that this talk might be the end of one or both parts of their relationship was not out of the realm of possibility. And losing him? She couldn't bear–

Leelin sighed loudly. "There is nothing..." his words trailed off, as did his vision, which focused on the open desert behind her. "There...is nothing more important to me than keeping this," he wiggled his pointer finger back and forth between them. "I've always found you attractive. I find a lot of people attractive, but you are beautiful in a way that's so much *more*..." he trailed off, and she took the silence as an opportunity to share her truth with him.

"I've always found you attractive, too."

A self-satisfied grin eased onto his face at her admission. "Good to know."

He paused again, deep in thought, before he next spoke: "Ereta, you're beautiful like..." his eyes were far away, and he lifted his hand, fingers dancing gently in the wind. "You're beautiful like the air." She stayed silent, unsure if this was a compliment.

"Sometimes unseen, but ever-present. You don't *want* to hide, or stay invisible, not really–so when I throw you something," he reached down and grasped a handful of dust, "you catch it, and together we make it soar." He opened his palm, and they both watched as the wind took the dust swirling away, dancing against the orange glow of the sun, going nowhere in particular, but on a journey just the same.

He turned to look at her, his face was uncharacteristically serious. "I don't need to fuck you, Ereta, to appreciate your beauty, and to love you. Don't get me wrong, I *really enjoy* fucking you, but I should have..."

She stayed quiet. She didn't know where this was going and was too terrified to speculate.

"I should have told you from the outset that no matter what happens between us, no matter if we fall in *that* kind of love, or find other people who are a better fit, or even recruit a sizable harem of willing lovers," they both smiled at that, and he grasped her hands in his. "*No matter what*, I need you in my life, because you're as fundamental as air–my best friend in this world."

She smiled up at him, and in that moment everything was perfect, because he was her best friend, too, and always would be.

"So I should have asked you before we added this additional perk to our dynamic, if staying friends with me despite it would be doable for you, because *nothing* is worth risking our friendship, and I'm sorry if I did, and I will fix it if you let me–"

"There's nothing to fix, Leelin." And it was true. If she never enjoyed his body again, she would be ok with that, because he was right. Their friendship eclipsed it all. "I was the one who took that step, and I'm sorry I didn't say anything first. I just got...impulsive. When I got out of that fissure and saw you looking at me, and you had shed your tears, it was..." she swallowed a knot in her throat at the memory. "I saw you and I just *knew* you were mine, and that you were beautiful, and that you loved me. I wanted to feel that love in every way I could, because you were proof that there was someone in this world who would be sad if I were gone, and that made me grateful to be alive."

His face was as raw and open as it ever was, and after a moment of basking in the bond that was as strong as steel in their hearts, he spoke, "Maybe we weren't being careless by not talking about this. Maybe we never *did* risk our friendship. I think deep down, we both knew that nothing ever could."

W ell, yeah, the friendship was all well and good, but the sex was pretty great, too.

Ereta was delighted to find that the absence of six toes did not have much of an impact on her ability to enjoy Leelin's body. She tested her theory three times before she was satisfied with its veracity.

Her still-healing nose did get in the way a little when their kissing got too frantic, but it was a minor inconvenience at best.

As the sun finally dipped below the horizon, Ereta and Leelin rolled apart, panting and drenched in sweat.

She lay there for a long moment, catching her breath, feeling the cool air against her drenched skin, before abruptly bursting into laughter.

"FUCK!" She must have startled Leelin, because he jumped what looked like a foot off of the bed.

This only made her laugh harder, until tears fell down her cheeks. She hadn't even known that tears came from anything other than sadness. Her laughter continued.

"I know that I must have missed something, and I would appreciate it if you enlightened me. Having a lover devolve into a fit of laughter after bedding me is not great for my self-esteem."

Ereta's laughter began to calm enough that she could clip out a few words as she wiped her eyes, "I–I'm s-sorry–it's just so–" she was glad that Leelin had already been thoroughly seduced, because the snort that burst out of her was probably the least attractive sound she had ever made. Leelin began to chuckle along with her.

When she finally caught her breath, Ereta was grinning ear to ear. "It doesn't matter anymore, Leelin. None of it matters, and it's just so *ridiculous*–" she started laughing again.

"Ok..." he drew out the word with the cadence of a sober person trying to have patience with a friend who had indulged in one too many rounds of Olchate. "What doesn't matter?"

"Sweat! Tears! None of it! Don't you see?" She turned to him and grasped his shoulder, giving him a gentle shake. "I am drenched in sweat and tears and other bodily fluids, and it doesn't *matter*, because I don't have to Run anymore–" her giggles returned with a vengeance.

He smiled at her with gentleness, likely concerned that she had lost her mind, but she felt saner than she had in days. Quarters. *Turns.*

"I don't have to worry about it anymore. *None of it.* Dehydration, Routes, pacing, rest, injury–it doesn't *matter*. I can do whatever the fuck I want, because the consequences that I've always been so terrified of have already happened–but instead of being miserable, I just feel...*free!*"

Leelin began to chuckle, and loosed a snort that rivaled hers for least attractive sound ever made. "I guess Jace was right after all." He paused and gave her a smirk so smarmy it should have been illegal. "I did fuck you Waterless, didn't I?"

They fell against each other and laughed until Ereta's sides were aching and her face was wet with tears.

Chapter 12

When they had finished laughing (or at least temporarily tired of it), Leelin had insisted that Ereta get dressed so that he could walk her home. She didn't particularly want to go home, mostly because she was warm and didn't relish the prospect of going back outdoors.

But Leelin *refused* to let up, insisting that she needed to be home in her bed to eat and sleep, not to mention drink more Water, since she had only gotten half of her daily Issue from the Nurse that morning. It was just after seven when they approached her front door.

"Are you coming in?"

"Oh, most certainly, little flame."

"What was the point in us coming back here if you're just going to stay here with me anyway?"

The cocky grin on his face was accented by a carefree shrug. "I probably have an ulterior motive."

She huffed at him, irritated that she had been forced to endure the cold walk over for no reason. She swung the front door open–

A loud chorus of, *"WELCOME HOME, ERETA!"* was barely audible to her ears over her own startled swear.

There were people in her Waterroom. Many people. Tens of people. More people than had ever been there before. Her gaze swept the room and was halted by Milo's ember-flecked eyes. One of his eyebrows cocked and the corners of his lips turned up.

The sensation of a body slamming into hers released another pump of adrenaline, and someone was hugging her tightly–

"Welcome home, sweet Ereta!" Bellat's voice hummed warm in her ear.

"What is this?" she asked no one in particular as Bellat pulled out of their embrace and draped her long, slender arm over Ereta's shoulder. She gestured to the room. "*This* is a party. For you."

"I–" she didn't know what to say. She'd never been to a party before. She had been invited to a few, but she always assumed her presence at such events was not genuinely wanted, and that invitations were mostly shows of politeness. Her eyes darted around the room. Dust bury her, her *entire Cohort* (or former Cohort, she supposed) was there. And some people she didn't know at all. And Jace–

"Hey, Ereta, welcome home," she absorbed the utterly unnatural smile plastered on Jace's visage. *Fire does not burn cold, indeed.*

The room was quiet. For the Lords' sake, were they expecting her to say something? She cleared her throat and attempted to quiet her nerves, or at the very least, ignore them. "Thank you– thank you all for..." Her heart was pounding in her ears. Their eyes were glued to her in expectation. *Look at her, look at her, look at her.* She had the sudden urge to vomit, but that would only serve to draw their attention further. She tried to speak through the oscillating peaks of nausea and panic, "Th-thank–"

"Cold burn me, Ereta, we're not so evil that we'd force you to make a speech. Come on, debauchery awaits us." The spotlight suddenly off of her as Jace pulled her to the common area, Ereta got a sudden and unfamiliar urge to hug her, which she imagined would be a lot like hugging a particularly beautiful pillar of stone. Her heart calmed, but she was sure that the lingering pallor of sweat and nausea was plain to everyone who glanced her way.

Cushions had been assembled into three large circles on the floor, each surrounding Intali supplies: cards, dice, betting glasses of varied sizes, and small bottles of Olchate tablets. She took a seat in one of the circles and was surrounded by her friends: Bellat at her left, then Milo, then Jace, and Leelin at her right. Jace grabbed the cards to begin dealing their first hand as Bellat passed around the Olchate. The other party goers dispersed to fill the other circles and begin games of their own.

"Is this seat taken?" Kilas had already begun to sit on the empty cushion beside Leelin before receiving an answer. *Oh, this will be a fun evening, indeed.*

Leelin snatched the cushion off of the floor just in time, and Kilas inadvertently plopped directly onto the cold stone floor. "*Yes,* this seat and every other seat in every single room in which I will ever sit is taken where you're concerned." Kilas' movement to snatch the cushion back was a blur, but it was not stealthy enough to trick Leelin, who tightened his grip on the fabric. They held the cushion between them, faces getting close as their respective efforts to pull it out of the other's grasp grew more fervent. "Let. *Go.*"

Kilas smiled with a wickedness that, Ereta had to admit even as a somewhat neutral bystander, was a bit infuriating.

Bellat was fidgeting, eyes shifting between the two men. "There's no reason for this to devolve into a fight, can't we all just enjoy a nice, quiet, respectful game?"

"I doubt it," replied Kilas. A vein bulged on his forehead.

Ereta spoke up, "Leelin, do you remember that night after Intali?"

"*Not now,*" Leelin ground out between clenched teeth. His muscles flexed beneath his shirt. A shine of sweat began materializing on his forehead. He was clearly putting all of his strength into muscling the cushion out of his opponent's grip, and vice versa. They appeared evenly matched.

She spoke a bit more urgently, "That night, we had a *discussion*? About the nature of *honor...*?" She hoped she wouldn't have to spell it out for him in front of Kilas: that Leelin had strongly suspected the man of cheating and had planned to challenge him to a rematch. There was no need to mention aloud that the plan somehow evolved into one of punching Kilas in the face only a few hours later.

Impossibly, Leelin tensed further. He did not relinquish his grip on the cushion as he slowly turned his head to face Ereta. A smile crept up his face, so cruel that Ereta actually shivered. "*Yes,* little flame, thank you for reminding me." All at once, he let go of the pillow, and Kilas tumbled backward onto the floor under the weight of his own strain. Leelin was over him in an instant, caging him in with his body, nose nearly brushing Kilas', a finger digging into his chest. "Listen to me, you treacherous little fuck. I *know* you cheated the last time we played. And while it makes me sick to inhabit the same room as you for fear that air you have breathed will poison my lungs, I am going to *allow* you to sit at this table tonight and play a *fair rematch* in defense of mine and everyone at that table's honor, which you, as a cheating piece of shit, have insulted. But if you dare to even *think* about trying to squirm your way into a win through dishonorable means, rest assured I will beat your stupid, ugly face with a cleanroom pipe until your outside is covered in as much shit as your insides."

Kilas listened as Leelin thoroughly dressed him down, that wicked smile taking up residence on his face again as he cocked his head. "Does convincing yourself that you were cheated make you feel like a man, Leelin? Certainly, *mounting me* in public must serve the same purpose."

Leelin grabbed Kilas' shirt in both fists as if preparing to slam his back into the floor repeatedly. Kilas leaned up to speak into Leelin's ear. Ereta caught sight of Milo and Bellat rushing up to Leelin just as she heard Kilas' barely audible whisper: "Tell me again, while your cock is poised above me, how you loathe us to share breath."

But in an instant, Milo and Bellat were there, prying Leelin away from Kilas by the shoulders. If one could see and hear death, Ereta was sure it would have been plain to Kilas in the expression on Leelin's face and the growl rumbling from deep in his chest. She and Jace joined in, hauling Leelin away to Milo's former seat on the far end of the table, and she wasn't sure that he wouldn't have murdered Kilas right there had they not intervened.

Several tense minutes later, with assurances from Leelin that he was sufficiently in control of himself to proceed with the game, everyone returned to their seats, with Milo taking Leelin's former place beside Ereta.

"Is this what I missed by not playing with you last time?"

"More or less. This was a tad more violent."

"The use of past tense seems optimistic."

"Well, you know me...nothing if not an optimist." She hoped that her sarcasm had been evident and that he didn't actually think her some dreamy-eyed child. Milo's lip quirked up as if to silently assure her that it had been.

Something nagged at her memory, and without stopping to wonder if she was being too forward, Ereta let her words flow out freely. "Where *did* you go that night, at the social hall? We thought you were going to join us for a game, but you just...disappeared."

He was silent for a moment. "I got distracted."

Better than a one-word answer, but not by much.

The game went on. Ereta lost each of the three rounds that passed by in a blur of chatting and good-natured teasing. Well, mostly good-natured. Kilas was attempting to bait Leelin into another fight with wicked, taunting smiles. Her friend's entire being was eerily still with tension as he seemingly fought a desire to launch himself across the table.

A dice roll heralded the fourth round's beginning, and Ereta swallowed down her Olchate with a sip of Water as she considered her cards. She wanted to play badly, but her chances were arguably worse than with her previous three hands, all of which she had lost. But there was still a chance that the round would play out in her favor. She'd seen worse odds pay off at the Intali table. And, she realized with a smile to herself, she could spare the Water now. She wasn't a Runner anymore.

She pushed two betting stones forward to lock in her bet.

The round continued on, and with every passing turn of betting, the possibility of winning the hand diminished slightly, until finally she poured out a triple bet measure of her Water into the glass and passed it to Kilas.

Milo leaned over slightly and spoke under his breath. "You were telling the truth earlier."

"About what?"

The corners of his mouth tipped up and his brows climbed high on his forehead, disappearing behind a curtain of shaggy brown bangs.

"You *are* an optimist."

Apparently, her sarcasm hadn't been clear enough. *Dust bury me, this is why I shouldn't attempt humor.* "What? No–"

"You've played *every single round*, despite having really, truly terrible cards."

She scoffed. "They weren't that bad."

"Oh, yes they were." He smiled broadly, a sight that still unsteadied her a fraction for some reason she didn't care to parse out. "Take this latest hand, for example." He leaned over and plucked her cards off of the table, fanning them out in his hands. "Do you know that if you played those exact cards in 1,000 rounds, you would lose 999 times?"

"I did not. I'm not sure how you do, either."

"Well, it's simple math. There are four possible outcomes that exist where your cards make a winning hand. There are, roughly, 4,000 possible combinations of card distributions available for the other players. Those are one in one thousand odds, and still, you decided to try. What does that make you if not an optimist?"

She shrugged. A smile tugged at her lips as she replied, "I just wanted to play; I didn't think about the odds. And it helps that I have nothing to lose." That wasn't true, of course. She had already lost a significant amount of her Water and still had half a canteen left to recklessly barter. Perhaps what she meant was that she didn't *care* if she lost. The loss wouldn't kill her, not anymore, and the freedom of gambling away so much Water without fear was liberating. It was *exhilarating*. Choosing to play with bad cards was like pouring her Water into the dust. There was no real reason to do it, but it made her feel powerful to know that she could, and that was a victory in and of itself.

The hours flew by and the game wore on. The other games that had taken up around their house slowly ended, and some guests took to sitting and standing around Ereta's table, watching their game play out with interest. Intali was not particularly engaging to watch under normal circumstances, but the addition of Leelin and Kilas' rivalry added sufficient entertainment for a group of onlookers to form.

"Hey, Boss. This the girl?" A man with a deep, roughly accented voice spoke from behind the table. An accent from far west of the Lords' City, if she was hearing it correctly.

Milo's head whipped around at the address. His brow was drawn down, and interpreting the tension behind Milo's mouth and the slight color in his cheeks, she thought he might have been startled. Ereta turned to look at the man who had spoken. He was small in stature, perhaps only a few inches taller than her. His bright orange hair reminded her of the sky at noon; it hung in tight curls around his pale, weathered face—though he didn't look much older than her for it. Layers of brute muscle were generously heaped onto his compact frame.

"Oh, Chegg–yes, this is Ereta, the person I told you about who will likely be joining us at the Lek."

"Hey, 'Reta." Chegg's thick, gravelly voice didn't obscure his dropping of the "E" at the beginning of her name. Hearing the all-too familiar nickname made her wince. "Heard a lot about ya. Sounds like you'll keep Milo's hands real full at Duty." He clapped Milo's and Ereta's shoulders at the same time, and she was nearly pushed down to the table by the impact. Lords, this man was strong. And...forward.

She pushed back against Chegg's arm, straightening herself. His hand did not leave her shoulder.

"Well, Milo, please elaborate on the ways in which you expect me to be a handful." Her voice sounded loud in the sudden silence of the room. *Hadn't everyone been deep in conversation just a moment ago?* Leelin barked a laugh from his place at the table. Everyone's eyes were on her. Or maybe on Milo. Maybe both?

Milo started, voice even, "I never said–"

"Yes, ya did. Don't be shy, now; ain't no sense lyin' about it. Ya said she's a real character, all excitable and impulsive and brave, and that she's gonna wanna get her hands dirty on day one." Chegg's hand rose from her shoulder a fraction before clapping back down in two small, firm pats. Ereta's eyes widened, and she turned from Chegg to face Milo. Their gazes met, and she stared at him as Chegg continued, "Don't you remember? You told me, 'Chegg, I ain't met anyone like her.' That's what ya said. Ya said she's gonna be a natural at Combustion, and that I best not underestimate her just because she's small and pretty. Ya said small and pretty things are the most dangerous of all. More deadly than the big, ugly things, because ya can't see 'em comin' 'til they're real close, and that's when they're most...well, fuckin' shit, I can't quite remember the word," he was silent for a moment, and his fingers drummed on Ereta's shoulder, "...captivatin', maybe?"

Ereta's mouth was parted slightly. She couldn't look away from the ember glow of Milo's eyes. They stared at each other in silence for another moment. His brows were still furrowed, and a grin emerged on his face. "Yes. Captivating. Thank you, Chegg. No one has called poor memory one of your faults, have they?"

"No, can't say they have."

"Nor brevity, I suspect," Jace added without looking up from her cards.

"Can't recall ever hearin' as much."

Her heart was racing from the sudden attention on her. Or maybe it was from prolonged eye contact with Milo, which had at once made her feel both small and powerful.

"It certainly sounds like Milo. There's nothing he loves quite as much as pontificating endlessly about the nature of life," Leelin drawled with a grin, hand gesturing elegantly in the air as he pushed stones forward in a bet.

Milo's face turned indignant as his eyes snapped to Leelin. "I don't pontificate."

Ereta chuckled. "Oh, yes, you do."

"You seem all quiet and reserved when people first meet you, but once that communication door opens? You go on and on *and on*, spouting off grand truths like you're a scholar of old," Leelin said.

"Name one time—"

"Easy. Do you remember what you said to me when I forgot to bring back my rubbish bin last pentad? *'When Siga fades under the light of day, does that mean that it ceases to exist? Or is it simply out of our sight for a time?'*" Leelin's impression of Milo was remarkably accurate- his voice deepened slightly, the cadence becoming steady and sharp even under the heavy influence of Olchate.

"That's not what I sound like," Milo grumbled, sounding uncannily similar to Leelin's impression.

There were some rumbles of laughter throughout the room, Ereta's included. Leelin seemed energized by the audience.

"Or how about this one–*Most of the failures of this world are due to a person giving up their efforts without realizing how close they were to succeeding.*' That's what you said when Ereta fell into the fissure, and I told you she was gone, but you didn't think so. And actually, you said that again the other night when you refused to leave your post at the Center because you were *so sure* she would be back any...moment..." The room was deathly silent as Leelin's words trailed off. He looked at Ereta, who gave him a small, sad smile.

Jace broke the quiet with a groan, "*Nice,* Leelin. Care to rehash anyone else's traumatic near-death experiences while you're at it? For the Lords' sake, it's *her party.*"

He attempted to clear his throat, but only managed to loose a small hiccup. "I'm sorry, Ereta, I didn't mean–it's just that I'm very, *very* intoxicated."

"As am I." she paused. "'*Fear of a mere moment spent in great pain might tempt us to endure a lesser pain forever. But to agonize needlessly for all our lives, no matter how tolerable each moment might be, isn't that the greater suffering in the end?*'"

The laughs came louder at Ereta's admittedly poor impression of Milo. She felt a tinge of guilt. Those words had been just what she needed at the time. When the nurses had initially set her nose, the bone had impeded her breathing slightly, and she felt an uncomfortable pinch whenever she smiled. She was willing to accept that discomfort permanently, but Milo encouraged her to endure the pain of resetting it, and she was glad she had. She hadn't intended to use his sentiment as a spectacle, but the tension and sadness were broken, and that had been her intent. Still, the last thing she wanted was to embarrass Milo back into one-word answers.

She was relieved when he simply huffed and seemed to fight a smile. "I stand by all of those sentiments."

"As you should," Ereta said. "You wouldn't be nearly as infuriating if you were wrong."

"That's true," Leelin chimed in. "If you were wrong, or stupid, it would be easier to ignore you. Have you ever even had a casual conversation that didn't end in the other person having an existential crisis?"

Milo chuckled. "Lords, I certainly hope not." Her responding laugh blew out as a snort. He grinned at her, one side of his lips tipped up and a dimple forming on his cheek.

"Well, I think we can all agree that whether you're brief or verbose, your words are never wasted, Milo." Bellat smiled at him in that warm, welcoming way of hers. Ereta quietly appreciated, if not envied, the way that Bellat could say something reassuring without coming across as condescending. The woman's manner was so Lords-damn *tactful*.

"Thank you, Bellat," Milo replied with a nod.

"I hate to be the bearer of bad news, but this is, in fact, an Intali game and not a social roundtable," Kilas said.

"Yes, let's *please* get on with the game," Jace agreed. "Ereta, your bet?"

Down to the last third of her Water, and despite her mediocre cards and better judgment, Ereta pushed a betting stone forward to secure her place in the round.

Milo ditched his cards, as did Jace. Leelin increased the bet, and Kilas matched it. Ereta matched it as well. Heart pounding in anticipation, she watched as the last of the dice rolled out onto the table. They did nothing to help her situation, but she couldn't very well back down, not after she had already gambled so much on the hand. What a waste it would be to give it away now...

She decided that she would be uncharacteristically bold and try to frighten Leelin and Kilas out of the round. She rarely played aggressively. Perhaps they would believe that she truly had a winning hand? She doubled her last bet, steeling a confidence into her manner that she didn't at all feel.

"What do you *have* in that tiny hand of yours, little flame?" Leelin smiled at her while drumming his fingers on the table. He maintained eye contact with her for a long moment, smile widening. *No no no no–*

"I'll match," he lilted with the cheery tone of someone responding to a particularly flattering compliment. He pushed his stones forward on the table. Her heart raced. This would be a particularly grand loss. A few seconds passed–

"Double," Kilas spouted in a transparent mimicry of Leelin's tone.

Ereta looked down at her stones, which represented all of the Water she had left for the day. She didn't have enough to match Kilas' bet. She could do nothing. Resigned, she pushed her cards forward in a reluctant late-round ditch. "Fuck you both," she muttered.

But Leelin wasn't paying attention to her. He was staring at Kilas, eyes narrowed, and she could have sworn she heard his heart pounding from a few seats away.

"All," he said, the word low and almost gravelly. The onlookers gasped in surprise, as did Ereta. Leelin pushed all of his stones forward.

"That's breathtakingly stupid, even for you," Jace noted. He ignored her.

Kilas had not broken Leelin's glare, and with likely deliberate slowness, his face transformed into a wide, wicked grin. He cocked his head to one side. "Match."

Another gasp echoed across the room. Alls were rare in Intali, and practically unheard of for Runners, for which such a bet could prove deadly if it preceded a Shift. Leelin had bet two-thirds of a canteen, which was just...reckless.

"Do you have a Shift tomorrow, Leelin?" Ereta whispered at him, though she was sure everyone could hear.

"Yes."

Fuck.

"But... so does he." Leelin matched Kilas' grin and flipped his cards.

Kilas didn't even spare a glance at Leelin's cards before flipping his own in turn. Everyone leaned over to assess the table, and the onlookers crowded around, desperately craning for a peak.

"Dust bury me," Milo whispered.

Leelin looked down, and after a few moments, his face paled, features becoming stony. "No. *Absolutely not.* You fucking *treacherous, cheating little ballsack of a man—*" Leelin's voice started quiet, but his rage grew in the timbre and volume of his voice as he spoke.

Kilas flexed his fingers and used his pinky to slowly push the betting glass before him toward Leelin. "Be a good little whore and pay up."

"A whore wouldn't pay—" Ereta started, but Milo gave her a tense shake of his head, and she thought better of getting involved. He subtly stood and started inching over to Leelin, likely intending to restrain the man if things turned physical, which she knew they would.

"You fucking *cheated.* I told you what I would do to you, *I told you*, and still you *dared* to insult everyone at this table—"

"Enlighten me, please, as to how I could have possibly cheated." Kilas examined his nails, affect completely undisturbed.

Leelin slammed his hands on the table. "How in the Lords should I know? I'm a man of honor. I couldn't possibly think in the slimy manner with which you—"

"Oh, please, *spare me.*"

"An extra set of cards, or someone–" Leelin turned to look at the onlookers gathered behind him. "One of you was looking at my cards and signaling to him?"

Ereta got up and hurried over to Leelin. She palmed his cheek and turned his face away from the innocent bystanders. He was still as stone. "Leelin, my heart, I think he just... got lucky. I'm sorry."

Milo broke the silence he had maintained throughout the exchange, not releasing his stare from the table as he spoke, "It's the only hand he could have beaten you with. But I do not think he cheated, brother." He leaned down and grasped Leelin's shoulder. His voice lowered, and became soft in a way Ereta had not heard from him before, "You had him beaten until that last roll. Any other outcome, and he would have lost. I was watching, he didn't even touch his cards after the first round. The odds were not in his favor, but his win was genuine."

Leelin did not break his eye contact with Kilas as he took a deep breath and leaned over the table. He pulled the betting glass to him, filled it, and took another empty one from its place in front of Jace and filled that as well. He grasped a glass in each hand, made a low sound in his throat, and...*oh no.* He dropped a large glob of spit and mucus into one glass, and then the other. They floated there, slightly yellow and entirely too large. Leelin smiled, genuinely, and pushed the glasses back to Kilas.

Kilas didn't even flinch. He grabbed the first glass and chugged it down. Ereta thought she might be sick. He took the second glass and downed it as well.

It was an unthinkable insult to drink the won Water of such a large bet in one go. It was customary in Intali to transfer large bets back to the winner's canteens, with only small sip-sized bets being drunk directly from the glass. To drink so much all at once, it was so wasteful that it almost hurt to watch. The body can only use so much Water at a time; Kilas was, in truth, *pissing away* Leelin's Water.

Leelin didn't even look angry anymore. Although she was not normally skilled at interpreting emotions, she knew what depression looked like, and it was written all over Leelin's face. She had seen that same expression every Lords-damn time she looked in the mirror.

"Good game," Kilas said, standing in one fluid movement. He threw his cushion at Leelin, who caught it in reflex. "I'll see you at Duty tomorrow, Leelin." With a last, cruel smile that reminded Ereta of how Hista had kicked her into the dirt before leaving her for dead, Kilas strode out of the room and out of the house, the majority of the other partygoers leaving in his wake. She was about to run after him, but when she glanced around the table, she realized that Jace had drifted off to sleep at her seat, and the game was indeed over.

"**W**hat *happened* between them?" Bellat asked Ereta as they walked back to Leelin's house. They had left shortly after the last few straggling guests had departed and Leelin had helped Ereta carry Jace to her room.

Leelin and Milo were walking slightly ahead, their arms draped around each other's shoulders. *Brother*, Milo had called him. Ereta hadn't even heard Leelin mention Milo until the incident with the fissure. But there was clearly love between them, and a familiarity that ran deeper than she had initially assumed.

"I don't know. I guess they became close, living next to each other. They're just so...*different*. They don't seem like they should get along as well as they do."

"Wh-wait, who are you talking about?"

She stilled for a moment, trying to think through the haze. "Who are *you* talking about?"

"Leelin and Kilas."

"Oh." Ereta paused to collect herself. She felt a little embarrassed that her private thoughts had caused her to misinterpret Bellat, but the Olchate helped her let it go before she spiraled into self-consciousness, as she surely would have if sober.

"I'm not entirely sure. They were in the Childhouse together; Kilas is younger by a turn, I think. I heard that there was an incident of some kind between them, but have never gotten any details. Leelin doesn't like to talk about Kilas. Whenever I've asked, he's changed the subject."

"Based on their interactions tonight, I fear that they will come to blows sooner than later."

She frowned. "I hope someone intervenes when they do." She didn't know who would win in such a fight, but the implications for Leelin were unfavorable no matter the victor: would he be beaten, broken, or killed—or would he be Rationed in punishment for his beating, breaking, or killing of Kilas?

They walked on in companionable silence for a few minutes. "You know, they *are* an unlikely pair." It took Ereta a moment to realize that Bellat was looking at Milo and Leelin, her head tilted slightly to one side. "But perhaps all the best friendships are made from unlikely pairs."

Ereta smiled at that and looped her arm around Bellat's. "Perhaps." Bellat smiled back, and understanding passed between them: that Ereta was claiming the sweet, gentle woman as her friend.

Leelin fumbled with his front door and stumbled in, Ereta and Bellat following behind. Milo broke off in the direction of his house without saying a word.

Once inside, Leelin collapsed onto his bed with a groan.

"I'm concerned about your Shift," Ereta said. "You could be on the cusp of Ration if you get an extended Route."

"I know," Leelin groaned, drawing out the words against his pillow. "But what was I to do?"

"Not engage him?" she suggested.

He scoffed. The noise was muffled. "That would only goad him on."

"How could ignoring him possibly—"

He sat up abruptly. "*Everything* goads him on. He always anticipates my responses and takes some sick pleasure in seeing his predictions come to fruition. If I ignored him, he would insist that it's because he's getting to me—"

"He *is* getting to you!"

"You don't *understand.*" He flopped back against his pillow, hands covering his face.

"Help us understand, Leelin," Bellat chimed in, voice gentle but insistent. "What is it about him that makes it so hard for you to walk away?"

"I just don't want..." he sighed, let his hands drop to the bed, and was silent for a drawn-out moment as he stared at the ceiling. When he spoke again, his voice was quiet. "When he wins, it makes me feel like...like I'm a Lords-damn child again. It's this feeling of being helpless, and it *terrifies* me, and the fact that it terrifies me—that *he* has the power to terrify me—that makes me so angry I could just—*ugh!*" He covered his face with the pillow.

"That makes sense," Bellat replied. "But the only reason he still has that power is because you allow him to. I know it's hard, but you can choose how he makes you feel. You can choose to let it stick and build up until you collapse under the weight, or you can let it slide off of you like cleaning powder. But never forget that it is *your* choice."

He was silent at that. Ereta gave Bellat a nod of encouragement, even as her words sank in. *Never forget that it is your choice.* Her thoughts went to Hista. She had never thought that she had a choice but to feel small and pathetic when Hista spoke to her. Cold burn her, just thinking of the woman sent Ereta looking uncomfortably inward: forcing acknowledgement of the deep, painful truth that she would never, ever be good enough. Not good enough for her chosen Duty. Not good enough for the people around her, for her friends, her Cohort, her peers, her betters.

But perhaps most devastatingly, not good enough for herself.

Could she really choose not to feel that way? Could she choose to accept herself as she was instead of wishing she could be someone else? But knowing her own worth, even if it was knowing that she had very little of it, was at least an honest way to operate in the world. Wouldn't anything else just be lying to herself, and wasn't that even worse? She loathed to imagine living happily if she must also be ignorant of the fact that people pointed and laughed all the while. *Look at her look at her look at her.*

The front door opened. Milo walked in, pack around his shoulders. "We thought you went home," Bellat told him.

"I did go home. To get supplies." He shucked off his pack and walked it over to Leelin.

"Supplies?" Ereta inquired, her memories flitting back to the canteen of Water that Milo had given her before her Ration Route.

Indeed, Milo pulled two massive canteens out of his pack. "Luckily, unlike your Ration, Leelin won't have his Water monitored. We can just replace what he lost. Canteen?" he asked Leelin. Ereta stared wide-eyed at what Milo had brought. It was nearly an entire standard Issue's worth of Water.

"You can't," Leelin protested. His voice shook slightly.

"I can do whatever I want, and you'd do well to remember that. Canteen?"

Ereta grabbed Leelin's pack and fished out both of his canteens. "Here."

"Thank you, Ereta," Milo took them from her and sat to begin transferring the contents to Leelin's bottles.

"I don't need all of that. I only lost–"

"Yes, yes, I know. But no one ever died from being over-hydrated. And I have extra. We can't have anyone else Rationed and transferred to combustion as trainees; I don't think I would have the patience to handle you both at the same time." Leelin grinned at that. Ereta wondered if Milo had purposefully infused his wording with innuendo to lighten his friend's spirits.

"I don't think *patience* is what you would need," she replied, smirking at the two men. Leelin chuckled, looking more like his usual self.

"And *I* don't think you'd find anything else lacking," he replied smoothly. Their eyes met, both grinning. But Ereta's smile fell as she took in Milo's gaze. There was something...*different* in the way he looked at her this time. Almost like the crimson coals of his eyes burned slightly hotter.

"What do you mean by *extra?*" Bellat's voice cut through the silent tension with uncharacteristic sharpness.

Milo blinked and looked toward her. "Ah, yes, I uh–" he cleared his throat. Leelin's brows raised. "I have these experiments that I perform to generate or collect Water in different ways. All of this," he gestured to the canteens he had just filled, "came from those experiments, so giving it to Leelin does not detract from my Issue."

"That's..." she trailed off. "I didn't know that was possible."

"It's impossible to know everything that's possible. But you can certainly try, and you'll figure out a lot along the way. What is life but a series of questions waiting to be asked and answered?"

Everyone was quiet.

"Like a scholar of old," Leelin broke the silence, voice chiding.

"You ought to be kissing the ground this man walks on," Ereta told him. "He saved you from your own stupidity. You should be grateful–*respectful*–even if you *are* drinking his piss."

Leelin grinned.

"Wait, what?" Bellat chimed in. "*Dust bury me,* that's your–"

Milo's hand had come up to rub at his temples in tiny circles. "Leelin, I swear to all the Lords..."

"But is she wrong, brother?" Leelin radiated pure glee at the opportunity to poke fun at his friend.

Milo opened his mouth to speak.

"Wait! Don't tell him," Ereta jumped in. "It's better if he has to wonder." Milo furrowed his brows at her. "You know, just like I had to."

Leelin laughed, deep and booming. Bellat chuckled.

"Tell me again that I don't need patience," Milo replied, shaking his head, but she could see his lips fighting to tip up, and that new, hotter burn in the embers of his eyes held steady.

Later, after Leelin had fallen into a deep, drug-heavy sleep and Bellat had left for home, Milo and Ereta stood alone. "I should head home, too," he said, and began collecting his now-empty canteens from the floor. He packed his bag and slung it over one shoulder, turning and heading toward the door. "Goodnight, Ereta."

She didn't think before she spoke, which was becoming an irritatingly common habit when she was around Milo, "What were the odds?"

He stopped, turning his head slightly to glance back over his shoulder. He was smiling. She didn't need to clarify that she spoke about the bet between Leelin and Kilas.

"One in 42,305."

She was silent for a moment, considering. "Kilas' optimism puts mine to shame."

He walked to the door and opened it to the frigid night. "When the day comes that I witness you scoff at greater odds, I will remind you of this moment. Perhaps then you will finally accept that you're the most Lords-damn hopeful person on this entire planet."

The door clicked shut behind him, and Ereta was left alone in the dark. She wasn't sure which made her shiver: the ghost of the frigid outside air caressing her skin, or the echo of Milo's prophecy in the silence.

Interlude 2 | Another Realm

T his time, I come to awareness all at once. In this place, I am not
aware of much outside of my current consciousness... but I can feel
that time has passed since I was last here, stretching over the blackness
that obscures the place between.

Embrase takes a little longer to fade into our realm than I do, but
I am patient. Sometimes, when the fog of that other realm lingers too
thick, shedding it to emerge into our true selves is difficult. Heavy. Slow.

I can sense that fog now, obscuring Embrase's essence. I can still feel
the beautiful warmth that emanates from them; I always can. But they
are leaden, suffocated by the lingering embrace of physicality. That is
alright. I am here. I will remain here until they come to me, and we will
spend whatever time we have holding each other until the world comes
(as it always does) to tear us apart.

I focus on the tether—now frayed but still present, which held true
in binding us across the expanse of another realm. Our plan is working.
I try again to focus on the blank space: on that time that passed between.
It is not truly blank, but so far away that its contents are polished into a
distant obscurity.

But today, as I glance across it, something stands out.

I train myself on the errant protrusion that is stark against the
smoothness of unknowing. It is slight, but it is there, reaching toward
me.

It is a memory.

A world of white. A meager stretch of faint beats that held a tepid awareness—a closeness. A hint of Embrase filling only a fraction of the empty places within my physical self. Then, a flash of brown, and nothing.

I recall that white space—a short stretch of time during which I stirred just slightly within that other form, feeling my own emotions and senses briefly merge with that of my corporeal reflection.

It has only happened once before: just after the tether was first tied. And this time, it held longer, its affect more potent.

The sensation of this memory is unsettling. My other self felt Embrase's slight presence as something entirely unfamiliar to them. Is that the reality my they are bound to? One where there is nothing but bleak emptiness in all the places where Embrase's love and light and beauty should be? I shudder at the thought. To know a reality without them is unthinkable.

My heart aches for my reflection: forced to suffer a life without Embrase, and cursed to not know the depth of that loss.

But maybe that can change. Maybe we can change it. I think—I hope *we've already begun to.*

"Ariame," Embrase calls to me as the final dregs of shadow slough from their spirit.

I go to them in earnest, and we wrap ourselves in each other, taking a moment to bask in the sensation of being reunited.

"Do you remember?" I ask through our bond as I curl impossibly closer.

"Yes," they reply. They squeeze me back. "Brown and white."

I echo that memory back to them, and we find that our recollections mirror each other.

All too aware that our time together is limited, Embrase grabs at the tether, and we both begin to inspect it. It held beautifully through everything, and the fray within its tendrils takes only a moment's effort to smooth back into place. Embrase insists that we reinforce it even further, until they are satisfied that it will once again hold through the strain of our separation.

"I think your body was in pain," Embrase tells me. I can feel their sadness, comingling with the joy they feel that we've made progress toward uniting. "I couldn't do anything to help. I tried, Ariame. I reached out for you, but even though you were closer, you were still far away. I pulled on the tether. I called for you. I tried to go to you. I did everything I could think of. I'm sorry it wasn't enough."

I recall experiencing some sort of unfamiliar discomfort, but it paled in comparison to the vast, torturous emptiness of Embrase's absence. "To know that some form of me exists without you? That is the true pain. But it is a pain I treasure—I can only know it because I have felt its equal in love. I'd rather suffer the emptiness of having lost you than live without knowing you at all."

I feel the first stirrings of the darkness then, as though it heard my words and seeks to test the truth of them. It begins to claw at us, dragging us apart bit by painful bit.

Embrase reaches for me a final time, holding me close as they whisper down our bond: "If love is pain, then you—air of my life, my soul's mate—are the most exquisite torture."

"I love you," I say, feeling the truth of their words as the agony of our separation once again consumes me. Exquisite torture.

"I love you," they reply with a final reverent caress.

As always, I chant into the darkness as it consumes me:

"We will find each other."

Chapter 13

"We will find each other."

Ereta woke in Leelin's bed, feeling the strands of her dream slip away. There was a rustle of fabric to her right, and a whisper, *"Fucking sweaty ballsacks–"*

She glanced toward the sound and found her friend hopping on one leg as he attempted to pull on his tread without losing balance. It took several attempts before he was successful. With his back to her, he stood straight and shoved his arms through a thick, beige outer jacket.

"Enjoying the view?" he asked without looking her way.

She stretched, and replied with a yawn. "You flatter yourself." He looked at her over his shoulder and flashed a grin. "You heading out to Duty?"

"I suppose, although I could probably be convinced to delay my departure for a minute or two. Maybe even three, if you're feeling particularly salacious this morning." He eyed her nearly-naked form sprawled over his bed, and waggled his eyebrows in silent question.

She snorted. "I need at least four, I'm afraid. I'll leave with you." She began looking around for her clothes, which she had tossed somewhere on the floor before climbing into Leelin's bed the night before.

"In just your underthings? What a treat for the neighbors."

Neighbors. Her face flashed hot. She only knew one of Leelin's neighbors, and the idea of crimson, glowing eyes fixed on her scantily clad figure made her feel...odd. Unsettled?

"You don't have to leave, you know. You can stay as long as you like. Stay until I get back, and I might even be able to spare you *five* minutes," Leelin drolled.

She pulled on her clothes as quickly as she was able and made for the door behind Leelin. "As much as I would love to lounge naked in your house all day while pining for your return, I should get home. I don't think Jace will be thrilled to wake up and find that I left her to clean up the mess from the party on her own. And I have a big day tomorrow." She didn't mention that the reason she wanted–*needed* to go home was to experiment with the fissure in solitude. She still hadn't told Leelin, or anyone else for that matter, about her experience. About the cold Water that had saved her from certain death.

They walked together to the Distribution Center. Ereta's balance still wavered slightly, but the walk felt good. She couldn't remember the last time she had gone so long without physically exerting herself. She felt tense with inactivity, as if her body yearned to expend the energy it had accumulated during nearly three pentads of rest.

"Don't you usually run to Duty?"

"Yes, but I'm quite early today." He waggled his brows.

"Aaaaand why is that?" Leelin never turned up to Duty early. "Dust bury me, Leelin, not Kilas, *please* don't do anything stupid–"

"*No.* Not him. Not today. Different Shift." They approached the distribution center, and she reached out and squeezed his hand.

"I'm sorry. I didn't mean to..."

"You never have to apologize to me, little flame," he smiled at her, "but rest assured, I do have a bit of a show planned for you this morning, if you care to watch."

She paused on the threshold. "Am I even allowed inside anymore?" Her heart picked up its beat. This was such a familiar feeling, to walk into the distribution center in the soft orange glow of the morning sun. But she would not have a Running Shift today. *Not ever again.* The realization felt strange, as though she hadn't truly processed it before that moment.

He grabbed her arm and pulled her through the door and out of her thoughts. "Probably not. But better to ask for forgiveness than request permission, in my view."

They walked inside the center and crossed the room. As they passed, the Cohort turned to wave and smile in her direction with something that looked uncomfortably like pity on their faces. She *hated* that; she didn't want their pity.

Leelin ambled up to the Expediter's desk, and Ereta suddenly knew exactly what Leelin had planned–

Mari looked up at their approach. "Ereta? You can't be here."

"Don't worry, Mari, she's with me."

"That means nothing to me, Leelin," Mari replied dryly, pinning Ereta with a familiar sternness. "You have to leave. It's against protocol–"

"Methinks that someone, my dear, dear Mari, is avoiding the matter at hand." Leelin leaned forward, hands braced on the desk. "I heard a *fascinating* tale recently."

"If you don't vacate the premises, Ereta, I'll have to call security."

She felt a twinge of annoyance that her presence suddenly, *somehow*, was considered a hazard. She'd come here nearly every day for eight turns. Would a few more minutes really do any harm? But as she turned to leave, Leelin grabbed her wrist to stop her.

"Mari, we need to have a discussion, you and I. There will be no calling of security. Besides, I don't know how you might call for *anyone*, when you're so clearly *out of breath.*"

"I am perfectly well, actually." Her voice was clipped. Red crept up her neck and cheeks.

Leelin leaned in, his face coming close to Mari's. "Are you, *really?*"

"Y-yes." Mari took an audible swallow.

"That's not what *I* heard." He was smiling with the wicked indulgence of someone who just discovered a piece of salacious Courtly gossip.

"I really do not have time for whatever childish game–"

"Well, what else could you have meant by calling me breathtaking? *Surely* you were describing your actual state–" Leelin broke off mid-sentence and feigned a sudden epiphany, performatively slapping his hand to his forehead with a loud *thwack*. "Or *wait*, it *couldn't be* that you're attracted to me, could it?"

Mari's features stilled, and her face managed to both pale and redden even further at the undeniable realization that she had been caught. "No," she gritted out between her teeth. Whether it was a plea or a statement or a denial, Ereta couldn't tell.

"Oh, *yes*, Mari." He strode to the other side of the desk and walked around her in a wide circle, eyes pinning her to the spot. He stopped at her back and leaned toward her ear. Ereta could see Mari's shoulders rising and falling with quick, frantic breaths. "I think that's *exactly* what you meant, since you appear to be breathing just fine."

"I–I don't know what–" she stammered, but it wasn't very convincing.

He resumed his strides and faced Mari again, the desk no longer between them. "You know I love the games we play, Mari." He raised Mari's hand to his mouth and gently kissed it. Mari looked as if she'd just been caught in the midst of setting the settlement aflame. "Pretend all you like that my presence does not affect you. I know the truth, as I always have, that you desire me as I desire you. And perhaps I will oblige you yet; you need only ask."

Mari's mouth was partially open as she met Leelin's gaze. He smirked at her. She remained speechless. Leelin broke their eye contact and looked around the woman. "I'm guessing that these are my deliveries? This pile with my name on it?" He didn't wait for her response as he leaned down and gathered the packages under one arm. "I'm glad we had this chat, my dear. I look forward to the day, or preferably night, when you call upon me." He leaned forward and kissed her hand one last time, softly murmuring against her skin, "I know that the delay can be *exquisite,* but please have mercy on me and do not dawdle too long."

Leelin walked away from Mari, who was still as stone for a painfully long moment. She cleared her throat, "I-Ereta, you are not allowed–"

"Yes, yes, she's on her way out." Leelin swung his full pack onto his back and pulled Ereta by the arm toward the door.

"That was unnecessary," she chided him, although she knew that Mari had been intrigued despite herself. It had always been clear that the woman found Leelin desirable. Despite her denial, she stared at him often, and blushed with his attentions. Besides, had Mari truly been aloof, Leelin never would have continued flirting. Despite his lasciviousness (or perhaps because of it), he was remarkably adept at reading people, and never pursued anyone who truly wasn't interested.

"She started this. My first turn on Duty, she told me I was too young for her. 'You're just a boy. I only entertain men.'" *Another uncanny impression.* He scoffed. "I was a man when I turned 18, I'm a man now, and she'll have no doubts that I'm a man when I bed her." They had just crossed the threshold to the outdoors when he turned toward her, frowning.

"What? What's wrong?"

"I didn't even realize..." He shook his head and grabbed her hands in his. "Ereta, I know that for all we have discussed the nature of our relationship, we haven't quite established any...rules. And I have never been one for monogamy, surely you must know this, but my flirting with Mari wasn't meant as a slight to you, nor was I implying that I wished to stop our trysts."

She raised her eyebrows at him and smiled as he continued to struggle with the words. She hadn't even really thought to be jealous, not of any of the people with whom Leelin flirted. That was just who he was.

"Leelin, I–"

"You know this has nothing to do with you, I have just never considered the idea of being with one person–"

"Leelin!" She grasped his shoulder and shook it lightly, a wide grin on her face. She couldn't help it, he was just so Lords-damn adorable. "Fire does not burn cold."

He paused. "What?"

She had forgotten that the phrase, which seemed to come in handy quite often, was only understood between her and Milo. She shook his shoulder again. "Do you think I don't know you at all? What kind of friend would I be if I expected you to forego your very nature on my behalf?"

He blinked at her, a small grin forming on his face that still held a trace of wary disbelief. "So...were I to take another, it wouldn't bother you?"

"I used to believe that there was one person for everyone. But I don't think that's true. And you just wouldn't be *you* if you stopped trying to tempt everyone on the Lords-damn planet into your bed. Your heart is too large to be given to only one person."

He smiled and elbowed her lightly. "What else do I have that's too large for only one person?"

"Oh, shut up." She gave him a playful shove in return. "Were I to take another, would it bother you?"

He snorted. "Of course not."

"I don't think I am made for monogamous love, either. I tried it once, and that is a pain to which I will never be vulnerable again. Non-monogamy doesn't bother me, as long as it's my *choice*," she paused. "And I think you mentioned something about building a sizable harem of lovers. I would be loath to stand in the way of such ambition."

Leelin smiled at her with a hint of sadness in his eyes. She looked away, not wanting pity, and not wanting to dwell on her past. She had told him only sparse details about the man she had loved before coming to Tubat-So. "I know you have been hurt, little flame, but don't give up on love just yet." The two-minute warning bell rang, and he pulled her into a brief, crushing embrace, lifted her feet off the ground, and kissed the top of her head before striding back inside. He shouted back to her over his shoulder: "What was it you said? Fire doesn't burn cold?"

After hastily picking up the remnants of last night's games, Ereta had retreated to comfortable solitude. Jace was still asleep, and would likely remain so for hours more.

Sitting in her room, Ereta took a long sip of Water from her canteen and a deep breath. Her heart was pounding. She wasn't sure why she was so nervous, having been to the cold Water planet before. But, to be fair, she had been nearly dead at the time, and doing so again while fully conscious was a much more frightening concept. She had life to lose, now.

She had been avoiding thoughts about the air fissure since waking in the infirmary. Whenever she let herself think about how close she had been to death, she felt a little bit sick. The whole experience had been traumatic in a way she didn't yet know how to process. Not to mention that she had feared thinking about the fissure might rip it open in plain sight of others.

She took another deep breath, shook her head, and closed her eyes. She still felt the gentle pull of the tug behind her eyes. It was so constant that she barely noticed it anymore. The sharper pulls which had come in the first few days of the tug had not happened since.

She focused, picturing the bright, white expanse of cold Water that stretched for miles in every direction. She pictured the strange yellow sun of the other planet. She tried to remember that feeling of warmth that suffused her soul when she touched the barrier between worlds.

Her heart continued pounding as she tried and tried to hold the images and feelings still in her mind. It was harder than she remembered. Forcing her mind to not wander in idle thoughts or spirals of worry proved more challenging than she had anticipated.

Nearly twenty minutes had passed when she opened her eyes again. Her room was coated in the orange glow of Veirbos' midday sun. There was no hint of a yellow glow, no expanse of white.

She sighed, tucked her legs beneath her, and closed her eyes again. How had she done this so easily last time? What was different now? Or, most worryingly, had she imagined it all from the start?

She felt the stirrings of unease deep in her belly. All her life, a persistent sense of impending doom with no discernable origin had plagued her. It tended to take root most fervently during the times when she allowed her mind to idle.

She took deep breaths, trying to think of anything else and failing miserably. She wanted to feel how she felt when she woke from dreams: grounded in a soul-deep contentment. She tried to focus on the memory of that feeling, as if she could manifest that state of ease if only she wanted it badly enough. And *Lords,* did she ever–

A flash of bright light from behind her eyelids. She whipped her eyes open, and stared at the air fissure in front of her. The white, cold plain lay beyond it, beckoning her forward, calling her somewhere that felt more like home than anywhere on Veirbos ever had.

She rose onto her knees and reached out with one hand to brush the opening that cut through her world and into another. Her whole body rippled with a pleasant, warm tingle at that barest touch. Though her heart was racing, she was no longer afraid. This felt *right*, and she knew in her bones that there was nothing to fear. She stumbled to her feet, careful to keep her eyes unblinking, and took a step over the threshold.

In the cold Water planet, the light was almost painfully bright. It set the landscape into blinding lucidity. Everything felt so real, almost *too* real. It was as if a thin veil of dust and orange light had been laying on top of her vision in Veirbos, and here, it was pulled off to reveal something more...vivid. More clear.

She took a deep breath in and was rewarded with air that felt strangely smooth. It was grainless, textureless, beautiful, clean air. *No dust.* The tiny brown specks that had polluted every single inch of her life since birth were gone in this place.

She turned around and looked to where the fissure had been. She wasn't surprised to find that it was gone, and had anticipated that the portal might close as it had during her Ration. But she had reopened it then, and she didn't see any reason why she wouldn't be able to do so again.

She knelt in the cold Water. It crunched beneath her and compressed itself several inches downward. She lifted her hand and plunged it into the white substance, pulling it back with her fist filled. She brought it to her lips and took a small bite. It changed texture in her mouth, flowing down her throat as pure, clean, cold Water. She had so many questions that she couldn't begin to parse them out. Why did the white Water compress under her weight?

When she had first seen this place, and again during her Ration, the white dots had been falling from the sky. But now, the air was clear of them, and still it sat on the ground below. Where had it come from, and why?

She moved her hand through the substance with a hand that she was only now realizing should have been gloved. In fact, she had on none of her outerwear, and was already beginning to shiver. *Dust bury me, I won't last long in here without it.* Why hadn't she thought of that before even attempting to open the fissure again? Perhaps she had been in denial that it was even possible. Perhaps she had been afraid to get her hopes up too high that this place was real.

She moved her hand back and forth, pushing the cold Water aside, digging lower and lower. Her hands became frantic, scratching at the increasingly dense layers of cold Water. What was beneath it? She was leaning forward now, her body tipping downward into the small hole she had dug. The substance was so hard now, so dense, that clawing at it did little. But she could still feel its wetness, the way it turned to liquid beneath her fingers. If she could just get some sort of tool, maybe something sharp and made of iron, like a knife–

"Hey! You!"

She stilled and held her breath in some attempt to maintain control of her racing heart, and slowly pulled backward out of her small hole. The light was so Lords-damn bright. She squinted against it, willing her eyes to adjust in the direction from which the voice had sounded.

Before anything further than the edges of her vision had solidified into clarity, she heard a strange sliding, crunching sound. Closer and closer, louder and louder, it approached.

A figure came into clarity. Two figures? She wasn't sure.

"By the forge, you're a scrawny little thing." The figure stepped above her. This was one person–the tallest, *largest* person that Ereta had ever seen. Light brown eyes were set into dark golden skin. Her features were full, shapely, and a bit pointed at the ends. She had the beginnings of age lines around her eyes and lips–lips that were tipped downward slightly.

Most striking of all was the woman's clothing. Ereta had only ever seen clothing the color of linen or bamboo, both a dusty beige-ish brown. This woman had clothing in shades of deep red. A large jacket with a deep hood. Thick, cushioned gloves that covered her hands completely without any demarcations for individual fingers. Deep red pants that lay over the *strangest* treads Ereta had ever encountered; the tops were clearly rubber, though it, too, was red. But the *bottoms*–they were long strips of what looked to be iron, bent slightly at each end. They sat flush to the cold white powder, stretching out two feet in each direction. The woman held a long, slim iron bar in each hand.

She snapped her fingers in Ereta's face. "Oy! I'm trying to ask you a question." The woman spoke with a strange, melodious accent. She struggled to her feet. Her whole body was shaking violently. She hugged her arms to herself, seeking both comfort and warmth.

"I'm not one to pry into anyone's personal affairs, but exactly how is it that you came to be way out here without skis, or a pack, or a jacket?"

Skis? She cleared her throat and attempted to project a confidence that she didn't feel. "Well, I...I forgot my jacket," which wasn't a lie, nor was it a convincing explanation. But she had no good reason for not having a jacket, not to mention a pack or whatever in the dust *skis* were.

"How in the blazing forge could you forget a thing like your jacket?"

"I wasn't thinking," she replied honestly.

"Obviously not! Well, where'd you come from, then? And what're you doing digging a hole in the snow? Trying to build an igloo? Or give some Skier a nasty fall, eh?" The list of words she'd never heard grew frustratingly larger, and the woman walked over to Ereta's hole to look in. "There's nothing in here."

"Well, no, I was trying to find the bottom."

"Heh! The bottom of what? You won't be finding anything except ice down there."

She would have asked what in the Lords "ice" was, but thought better of it. She couldn't think of *anything* to say that would be clear of suspicion, so she was silent for a moment too long, staring wide-eyed at the woman.

"You're not from around here, are you?"

That was an easy question to answer, and truthfully. "No, I am not."

"Your accent, never heard nothing like it. And wherever you're from–they must not be feeding you very much at all! Look at the state of you! I've got more fat on one arm than your whole body!" The woman slapped her arm for emphasis. "Did you walk all the way from Brafta, Tiny? You should be heading back, before you freeze to death."

"Ah–well, yes, I should head back there. Thank you. I'll just be a few more minutes here. It was nice to meet you..."

"Ima! Name's Ima. Good to meet you too, Tiny. Maybe I'll be seeing you at the settlement. We can grab an ale, and you can tell me what exactly you've been up to out here."

"My name's Ereta," she corrected, since *Tiny* wasn't a name she was particularly fond of. "And thank you. That sounds...good." She didn't understand the offer to "grab an ale," but it was clearly meant to be some offer of hospitality, even though she had no intention of telling Ima what exactly she had been up to.

"You sure you're gonna be alright out here? Here, you can take my jacket–" Ima began to undo the buttons on her large red overcoat.

"No, that's very nice of you, but really, I'm fine! I run hot, actually." Her body betrayed her lie with a visible shiver. "But before you go, you mentioned...the snow?" She guessed that the word referred to the white powdery Water.

"What about it?"

"Well, what exactly...is it?" *Is that too strange to ask? Cold burn me, is she going to know I'm–*

Ima gave a booming laugh and clapped Ereta on the back. "So you have a sense of humor, eh? They'll be all over you in Brafta, Tiny. Buncha horny, drunk bastards can't resist a lass with cheek, even though your cheeks themselves are a bit wanting." Ima winked.

"Pardon?" What in the Lords was this woman talking about?

"Your *ass cheeks*, tiny. They're wanting. But don't fret–I'll get some meat on you yet, starting by filling you up with a big bowl of stew when you come for that ale."

"That sounds...good. Thank you, Ima. I will see you later, then?" She hoped Ima would take her not-so-subtle clue to leave, since Ereta did not plan to open a fissure in front of the woman and she was very nearly frostbitten.

"That you will, tiny! Stay warm out here, and don't be falling into any holes."

Lords, if only Ima knew how prudent *that* advice was. Ereta watched as the woman pushed against her poles, and the strange iron strips glided into motion across the white Water, which she supposed was *snow*. She gasped as Ima continued to push her poles downward, propelling herself across the plain effortlessly, gaining speed with each stroke, though her feet never moved up or down. Within seconds, she was moving so quickly that Ereta could barely keep track, and all too soon, the tiny speck of red was completely out of sight.

"Dust bury me and cold burn me," she swore aloud loud to no one as the tiny dots of white began to fall from the sky once again.

Chapter 14

"Ereta LC965-R, Dutied Runner of Tubat-So, born of the Lords' City in the 965th turn of Veirbos around the new Sun, you are here today to answer for your failure to complete your Ration Route in the allotted Shift time. Please step forward."

The Tubat-So Court's hearing room was intimidatingly large, with a domed stone ceiling that echoed the Duty Councilor's voice to a booming clarity. Most places in Veirbos were plain and unadorned, but the Court was an exception: its stone walls adorned with thousands of intricate carvings. The three Duty Councilors sat before her on a raised platform. They loomed behind a massive stone table that had been carved from the room itself, and standing beneath it, Ereta felt even smaller than she normally did. She stepped forward at the command while attempting to steady her breathing. She knew what was coming, but that didn't make the reality of it any easier to experience.

"Do you deny your failure?" the same councilor asked. He was an older man, prominently featured and thin-lipped with flecks of gray dusting his dark hair and a scruff of wiry beard to match.

"I do not," she replied. The echo of her own voice in her ears was startling. She listened to her words as they bathed the room before fading. *I do not. I do not. I do not.*

"Very well. We have already heard testimony from the Expediter who issued your Ration. Mari TS945-E, and unanimously find that the initial Ration was just. Your failure to complete your subsequent

Ration Route in the allotted time means that your Duty as a Runner will be terminated henceforth, and you may choose to accept your new Duty assigned per the laws of the Crown Lord of Veirbos, or you may reject all Duty and live by your own means. What is your choice?" It really wasn't a choice. Living by her own means would mean that she would no longer receive any nutrition or Water Rations, or her housing stipend, or clothes, or anything at all. She would be forced to live on the streets at the mercy of passersby.

"I will accept the Council's Duty assignment."

"Very well. From this day forward, per the Crown Lord's Laws, the council transfers you to serve at the Tubat-So Lek in the Duty of Combustion. You will henceforth be known as Ereta LC965-RC." The counselor banged a large stone onto the table in front of him. "Please step forward and retrieve your oath."

She did so, stepping up to the platform and accepting a small slip of paper from the councilor. She stepped back.

"The words you will now speak constitute a binding contract with the Crown Lord of Veirbos, and may only be broken by death, the Crown Lord's pardon, or this Council's unanimous decree. Please recite your Duty oath."

"With fire and air I will forge all life's Water.
I vow to complete my task this day and all the days to come -
Only death will prevent me from fulfilling this promise:
I hereby pledge my life's Duty to Lek Tubat-So.
And by that grueling Duty, I am henceforth bound."

The vow was nearly identical to the one she had taken as a Runner, excepting the first line and the removing of "or crippling injury" from the exceptions to which her promise would be upheld. Indeed, crippling injury would not be a factor that expelled her from Combustion. This would be her Duty until death. She thought back to her Runner's oath; how she had wondered if the vow became more binding with each recitation. Now she was sure that it didn't. Simply by reciting a new vow, she had forsaken eight long turns of Runner's oaths. It was an almost laughably simple process to renounce her former life for a new one. So she spoke the new words, but didn't really feel their weight.

"Let it be so. Before we adjourn, there is another matter to which we must attend. Prior to your arrival at the Distribution Center on the night of your Ration, your Ration officer had signed all official paperwork certifying your death on-Route."

She said nothing, but her heart started pounding. She had avoided thinking about this: about the fact that Hista had failed in her duty by leaving Ereta while she still lived. She hadn't wanted to consider what it meant–

"The council will send word to the Lords' City for Ration officer Hista LC962-R to appear before this Court in seven days' time. That hearing will be an opportunity for Hista to explain the circumstances under which she failed her duty. Prior to that, we must enter your official testimony into the record. Please describe to the Council the circumstances of your Ration Route."

Ereta took a deep breath. Hista would return to Tubat-So in a little over a pentad. In a brief moment of panic, she had wondered if the woman had already been summoned and if she might be forced to testify with Hista in the room. She was relieved that wasn't the case. She started detailing the Ration Route, shying away from the booming echo of her own voice, but continuing on as best she could. She left out the parts of the story that included anything about Hista's feelings toward her, or her cruel words, or her crueler actions. That testimony would be her word against Hista's, and Ereta didn't like her odds.

"...and then I collapsed forward into the dust. I think that I must have passed out. When I woke, she was gone," she finished. It wasn't a lie. She *had* collapsed forward (...after being kicked squarely in the back). *Look at her, now.*

"And how much Water did you have remaining at the time?"

"I..." *cold burn me, I have no idea how to answer that.* The truth was that she had no Water when Hista left, since the woman had poured out the rest of her canteen. But the Council wasn't stupid. They knew that making the journey back to Tubat-So with no Water was impossible, so she had to lie and say that she had at least *some,* or else they would investigate her further. She certainly wasn't going to tell them about the air fissure or the snow planet. She nearly chuckled aloud to imagine their reaction to her tale, a display which would have been wholly inappropriate. She bit the inside of her cheek and tried to focus.

"I cannot recall how much Water I had remaining. Only that when I woke, I had recovered some of my strength and was able to finish the Route."

"Do you have any memory at all of your Water levels during the last part of your journey?"

"No, I'm sorry. I don't," she lied.

"Very well. We may require you back for further testimony, depending on the outcome of Hista LC962-R's own. Should such testimony be required of you, you will be excused from your Duty in order to give it. Until then, you will report to the Scheduling office to receive your Shifts and any other materials needed for your new Duty. Your Water Issue will be replaced with one of standard size, and your nutrition allotments will no longer contain any stimulant. Please return any other Running supplies, including your treads, canteens, and pack to the Scheduling office by sundown today. All of your other boons, as granted to the Dutied, remain unchanged. Do you have any questions?"

"No, thank you."

"Ereta LC965-RC is dismissed and her Ration case is hereby closed."

The councilor once again banged his stone onto the table. The echo of it in her ears remained long after she left the Court and walked home. It was the sound of her fate sealed.

But then again, it wasn't, was it? She thought of Ima, and of the air fissure. There was another world—a world she could now visit at her will—where Combustion likely didn't even exist. Where people glided across the ground with speed at least three times that of the fastest Runners on Veirbos. Perhaps she could escape there, and find a way to build a new life for herself. But then her thoughts turned to her friends. She didn't want to abandon them here. But could she bring them with her? If they could, would they come, leaving everything they knew behind?

Before she dared to ask them, she decided that she needed to learn more about the snow planet. She had to find out about their Duty. Did it exist, and if so, how was it assigned? Was there a way for her and her friends to make a life for themselves without being exposed as outsiders from another world? She resolved to find answers to that question, and any others she could think of, as soon as she could. Maybe if she planned well enough, she could have a plan set up for all of them before she even brought it up. If she planned for every imaginable complication, she could bring them to the snow planet without issue. They could live a life where they never again worried about Water, if she could just convince them to leave Veirbos behind to toil in its own dust.

That night, she returned home from the Scheduling office where she had dropped off her Running supplies and received her new ones, excepting her new Water Issue, which had to be installed by a Dutied Water Technician and would arrive later in the pentad.

Her new treads were missing the spiked rubber grips of her old ones. They were simple, and a lot less comfortable, too: woven of thick layers of linen cloth instead of rubber. She kicked them off and deposited her new, smaller pack and canteens on the floor. She started to walk to her room, and paused.

"Jace?" She listened for a response and none came. She went up to her friend's bedroom door and knocked lightly. "Are you home?" The door remained closed. It was quiet and dark. Resolved, she pulled her new treads back on, retrieved her pack, and retreated to her own chamber.

She lit the room's candles, casting the space into a dance of soft light and deep shadows.

She settled onto the floor and began to picture the snow planet. She hadn't been back since the day before, having just barely managed to reopen the fissure back to Veirbos before the cold became an urgent safety hazard. It had taken her hours to warm up sufficiently for sleep to come.

But she had time now. Her first Combustion Duty Shift would take place the next morning at 8. But she had the whole evening alone to explore the snow planet, and with her outerwear and pack in tow, she was hoping to stay a bit longer than last time–

Last time. She got up and made her way to the Waterroom. Hanging on a hook by the basin was a large iron utility knife. She grabbed it, glad to have something that she might be able to dig with when the snow became too dense for her hands, and returned to her previous place in her room.

She was just beginning to focus on the memory of the snow planet when a knock sounded on her window. Her eyes shot open. *Cold burn me, I don't have time for this right now.* She rushed over, unlatched it, and swung it open: revealing Bellat and Leelin's smiling faces. Leelin's smile turned to a look of feigned horror as both of his arms shot straight up into the air, eyes on her left hand. "Whatever I did, it wasn't me. I swear it!"

She glanced down at the knife that she was still clutching. The knife that she had no good explanation for, other than the truth. Yes, the truth–why *not* tell them now? She was struck with a sudden impulse of wanting, *needing* to share her secret. She was so Lords-damn tired of carrying this alone. She wanted her friends to know that she was working on a plan to save them from this dust-forsaken place. Maybe they could even help her if they were willing.

"Do you have time to come in and talk?" she asked.

"Can we talk on the way? We're going to Intali," Bellat told her with a gentle smile.

She paused and shook her head, feeling a surge of disappointment. She didn't know what to do. The fact that she was so desperate to tell them everything couldn't reconcile the twinge of hesitation she felt at making them vulnerable. What if she couldn't arrange their escape before Hista returned, and her friends were questioned by the Lords? She didn't want them to share the burden of this secret unnecessarily, nor be implicated in her illegal actions on the Ration Route. She also didn't want to give them hope if her idea of escaping proved futile. *Perhaps it's better if you figure things out first, without them.*

Still entirely unsure if she was doing the right thing, she swallowed and answered them, "No, I can't play tonight. I have a shift in the morning."

Leelin scoffed. "So what? You're not a Runner anymore. Why would you need to be well-rested just to stand in a room all day, making big fuck-off fires?"

Bellat shot Leelin a disapproving look. "You don't think she should be well-rested for a Duty so dangerous that a single mistake could kill her and everyone on the settlement?"

Leelin scoffed again and waved a hand in dismissal. "She'll be fine. Milo will be there. He's so controlling about his *precious* Duty, I doubt she'll lift a finger all day. Though listening to him prattle on about adjusted Combustion formulas might be a grueling Duty all its own."

"I really can't tonight, I'm sorry. There are some things I have to take care of. You go ahead." She didn't want to ruin their evening. And if tonight went well on the snow planet, perhaps she would have the beginnings of a plan in place to fill them in on.

"*Things to take care of* with a massive knife in your hand?"

"Yes. And as long as I'm holding this massive knife, I don't think your mere words can compel me to explain myself."

He scoffed for a third time. "*Fine.* But I reserve the right to barge in here at two in the morning to upstage your massive knife with my massive Water winnings. Among other massive things." He winked at her.

"You'll do no such thing," Bellat admonished him. "She needs to rest. And *you* shouldn't be placing anything close to a massive bet tonight. Not after last time, and especially without Milo around to bail you out."

"You're both being so fucking responsible. It's really Lords-damn *annoying.*"

"Will *you-know-who* be there tonight?" Ereta asked Bellat in a conspiratorial whisper.

"I don't think so," Bellat replied with a shake of her head. "He has an extended Route tomorrow."

"It would be a fatal mistake to underestimate Kilas' stupidity," Leelin murmured.

"Get out of here," she told them with a smile and a nod of her head toward the Social Hall. "My big knife and I have things to do. Have fun."

"*Fine,*" Leelin relented with an exaggerated sigh, hooking his arm around Bellat. "We'll debauch ourselves without you tonight, little flame. But you owe me."

"In what way do I *owe* you?"

"*Clearly,* for the disappointment I will suffer at the lack of your company."

"Since when is your disappointment my responsibility?" She raised her brows at him.

"We don't Duty together anymore. We have to spend time together when the moons are out. That's *my* time." He slapped his hand on his own chest possessively.

"So now you own my nights? I don't recall agreeing to that," she fought a smile, and her heartbeat quickened despite herself.

He began striding away, still arm-in-arm with Bellat, before yelling back over his shoulder, "The moons rise and set each day, little flame. I've yet to find any evidence that they don't revolve around me."

The crunch of the snow beneath her feet and the warm sensation in her chest welcomed Ereta to the other planet. She looked up at the sky. For all of the planets' differences, the moons were the same here as they were on Veirbos: three of varying sizes, and their position seemed similar to that of her own moons at the time of her departure. She made a mental note to take more precise records of the times on future visits.

She welcomed a deep breath of smooth, chill night air. *Maybe I could be happy here,* she thought. But that dream still depended on a lot of factors. She needed answers to a few very fundamental questions before she could begin daydreaming (or nightdreaming, as it were) of her future on the snow planet.

She knelt. Her hole from the day before was still there, but had been lightly dusted with a covering of new, fluffy snow that she could see smoothing over her previous marks. She wondered at it for a moment, brushing it with a finger. Those small snows that had fallen from the sky as she departed the day before–those were the tiny little pieces that made up this massive, unending landscape. She struggled to comprehend the time it must have taken for the millions of tiny snows to amass into the thick layer on which she sat.

She took a firm grip on the knife and lowered herself into the hole. Steadily, she began chipping, wondering what she would find beneath the snow.

Nearly ten minutes later and after minimal progress, she abandoned her effort. Sure, she had wondered if there were fissures or even Water pipes like on Veirbos, but those questions were not in any way urgent. They were futile attempts to ground herself in some sort of familiarity despite the bizarre foreignness of this planet. Cold burn her, her tendency toward being swept up in small tasks and consumed by sparks of curiosity could prove problematic to her plans at best. She needed to *focus*.

She resolved to spend her time walking to the settlement Ima had mentioned, where she assumed she might be able to inquire about Duty assignments, or at least 'grab an ale' with the snow planet woman.

The walk was difficult. Every step had her feet sinking into the snow up to her knees. Before ten minutes had passed, she was panting from effort. *Lords, am I this out of shape? Or is walking in snow really that much harder than normal walking?*

A short while later, a familiar gliding sound came from behind her. *Ima.* She turned to see a figure riding through the snow on the same long iron strips that Ima had used, but as they approached, she knew that this was not Ima. This person was taller, his features distinctly masculine, sporting a puffy brown beard over most of his face. She waved at him to pull his attention.

He angled his iron strips and skidded to a stop a short distance away. "What in the blazes are you doing out here?" he called to her.

"Hello," she replied to the stranger, ignoring his question. His accent reminded her of Ima's, spoken with that same musicality. "I was wondering if you could tell me how far the nearest settlement is."

"Well, sure–that would be Brafta. It's three, maybe four miles that way," he pointed toward what she thought, based on the moons, was North. "But you're gonna have a heck of a time getting there without skis."

"*Skis...?*" Her tone implied a question, one she hoped he wouldn't balk at. Or laugh at, as Ima had.

He gestured to the iron strips on his feet, as if in explanation. "Yeah, your skis. How did you get all the way out here without them, anyway? *By the forge,* do you even have snowshoes?"

"Well, no, I don't think so," and that certainly wasn't a lie. At least she now knew what to call the strange metal strips. *Skis.*

"Then what in blazes happened?"

"I was...it's a long story. Thank you for your help, but I won't keep you any longer," she hinted.

"You sure? I could send somebody–"

"No, really, that's fine. I..." her mind raced for words that made a hint of sense. Then, confidently, "Ima is bringing me my *skis.* And then I will use them to travel across the *snow* to *Brafta,* where we are going to *grab an ale* and–" she searched for the phrase, "–and then, Ima is going to fill me with *stew.*"

He looked at her for a long moment, shrugged and then spoke, "Well, alright then. Good luck out here, I guess." He gave her one last look that seemed to question her sanity. She couldn't help but smile in return, proud of her seemingly successful attempt at communicating with the snow people.

He pushed his poles into the snow and began to slide off. As he did, she heard him call back to her: *"And don't forget your snowshoes next time, for the Lords' sake!"*

She didn't know what that meant, either, but one word stood out: *Lords.* So there were Lords here, too. Perhaps this planet would have Duty as well, then? She tucked that information away for later and continued her trudging walk.

A long while later, with the moons of the snow planet high above, she decided she should probably head back home. She did have a shift tomorrow, after all...but she had walked a decent distance from the point at which she'd entered the air fissure. Did that mean that if she opened one at her current location, it would be translated to somewhere else on Veirbos? Somewhere other than her room?

She needed to test that, but there was no way to covertly do so from where she was, since she wasn't sure how far she had walked. She could accidentally open a fissure into the social hall, for the Lords' sake. With a sigh, she began a frustratingly slow trudge back toward her hole.

Back at her point of entry, she resolved that she would perform an experiment. Obviously, walking through the snow all the way to Brafta was not an option. Dust bury her, four miles at that pace would take *hours*. Too many hours. And she didn't yet have any skis, or the knowledge of how to use them. What if, instead, she could walk or run the four miles north back in Veirbos, and open a fissure directly into the snow town? It *might* work, if the distance on both planets was measured similarly, and if they lined up.

The problem with that plan was that she knew nothing of Brafta, and risked opening a fissure directly into a public space. Surely *that* would draw an unacceptable amount of attention. A problem for later, though–for tonight, she needed to do a small test of her theory.

Standing at the place where the fissure had opened, she imagined her bedroom. She resolved to open the fissure on the far side of the room, which wasn't much of a test, but would be a good starting point. She paced to her best estimation of the spot in her head, sat down, closed her eyes, and thought of home.

Minutes later, she felt a shift in the air in front of her before she opened her eyes. The air fissure opened to the far-left corner of her room.

Exactly where she had hoped it would.

Chapter 15

Ereta stepped into the shadow cast by the two tall structures looming over the Lek refinery. She tried not to indulge any superstitious sense of foreboding that naturally accompanied stepping out of light and into darkness. *Poetic.*

"I'm here for my new Duty," she told one of the two Lek security guards flanking the doors.

"Name?"

"Ereta LC965-RC," she replied with a wince. Her new last name carried with it an implied shame; the former Running designation (R) and new Combustion designation (C) bearing a testament to her Duty failure.

One of the guards nodded sharply, as if he had been expecting her. "This way," he motioned with his hand for her to follow. The front door opened to a narrow, dim hallway that stretched the length of the building. She was greeted by abrasively loud banging and crashing noises that echoed at irregular intervals, seemingly originating from just beyond the hall.

The guard brought her to a large closet filled with specialized Duty clothing. She was outfitted with three identical jumpsuits (all wispy thin, beige, and long-sleeved), a pair of matching thin gloves, slightly scratched and grimy-looking safety glasses, a pair of large rubber over-treads with hammered iron toe plates, and a handful of one-inch square keychains, each branded with her full name.

"Your Combustion clothing is not allowed off the premises. Laundry is done once a pentad; be sure to mark your suits so they are returned to you," he told her in a bored drawl. She trailed him into a room at the end of the hall: a locker room, with several haphazardly-placed stone benches, three partially ajar cleanroom doors, and rows of narrow metal lockers spanning two sides. He gestured to an empty unit on the left side of the room. "You can use that locker for your things. Go ahead and change, and then meet your Shift supervisor in the front hall. I'll tell him to expect you." He left, and she took a moment to fasten a branded keyring onto the rivet of each of her new supplies, marking them as hers. Hoping that she could finish changing before anyone barged in, she quickly stripped herself of her outerwear and regular clothes. She felt strangely vulnerable standing there in just her underthings. Ereta wasn't necessarily shy, but there was a particular discomfort in being nearly naked in an unfamiliar place filled with people she didn't know.

She redressed in the light Combustion jumpsuit. It was airy and soft to the touch: barely cloth at all, really. Despite being the smallest size on offer, the material swallowed her and hung several inches past her wrists and ankles. She rolled the overlong cuffs, donned her gloves and safety glasses, pulled her treads back on, and slipped the thick rubber over-treads on top. Finally, she stashed the extra jumpsuits and discarded clothing in her locker and exited the room.

Back in the hallway, she spotted a man who looked to be about 40 turns, or possibly a bit more, leaning against the wall with his hands in his pockets, projecting a casual confidence that led her to believe he must hold some position of authority. "Hello, are you the shift supervisor?" she asked him.

"What?" he called back over the grating noise of the Lek. "You gotta speak up in here, it gets real loud!"

"Sorry!" she replied at a yell. "Are you the shift supervisor?"

"Yeah. Garil. And you are..." before she could answer, he reached down and snatched at the small, square metal keychain that hung off of the jumpsuit's zipper. "Ereta," he read. "Nice to meet you, Ereta. Welcome to the Lek."

She nodded. Wordlessly, he pushed off of the wall and began walking: one hand still stuffed into his pocket, the other lazily beckoning for her to follow.

Garil led her to a door on the far right of the hall. He braced himself against it and turned the handle. It swung open, slowly, and with what looked like great effort. "It's heavy," he yelled in explanation over his shoulder. "You might need to get someone to help you open and close it."

As the door opened, the noise became deafening. He held up a hand and leaned backward out of the doorway, reaching over to a rack on the wall that was lined with rubber and metal objects. He took one, fitting the round cups at each end over his ears and sliding the bar on top of his head to tighten them. "Mufflers," he said by way of answering her unasked question, and she copied him by fitting a pair onto her own head.

As soon as they were on, the uncomfortably loud roar of the Lek dulled to a moderately loud hum. It was an instant relief to her senses. Garil pushed the door open the rest of the way, and stepped to the side–

Heat enveloped her body, but the sensation was not unpleasant, and she was immediately grateful for her light clothing. She stepped forward into the doorway, and could only gawk at what she beheld.

A massive room stretched out in all directions. Pipes of various sizes and shapes were sprawled over the ceilings, floors, and walls. Narrow walkways ringed each of the massive metal capsules that stood in straight rows throughout the space. Eyes wide and heart beating rapidly for a reason she didn't fully understand, she walked toward one of the five capsules that made up the first row. It was even bigger up close. Perhaps six feet tall and twice as wide, with several pipes reaching up from the floor or down from the ceiling to join with its dull iron surface. A slender tube wrapped around the capsule in tight rings spanning end to end. *Lords, it's fucking massive.* She was struck with a sense of awe at the size of the operation before her, and she didn't bother to dampen her sudden urge to touch the massive metal capsule–

She yelped in surprise when strong hands grasped her shoulders from behind and yanked her backward, taking her outstretched hand with her. "*Stay behind the line!*" A familiar voice yelled near her ear. *Milo.* He turned her around and looked down into her face with a stern visage, brow furrowed in a way that made her feel like she was a child about to be scolded. He pointed at the floor, where a white line ran in a wide rectangle around the capsule. "You *never* cross that line unless the Combustor is locked out!"

She nodded and took a lumpy swallow. "How do I know if it's locked out?" she yelled back.

"Dust bury me, did Garil not give you the safety brief?" Milo's crimson-flecked eyes scanned the room before narrowing on Garil, who had resumed his leaning posture against the wall of the chamber, looking thoroughly bored. Milo grabbed her wrist and gently tugged her along with him as he strode up to the supervisor.

"Garil!" he bellowed as they approached. "I have told you this so many Lords-damn times: you *absolutely cannot* let anyone into the Combustion chamber until they complete the safety briefing–"

Garil waved a hand in lazy dismissal. "Give it a rest, Milo. That safety briefing isn't Duty-bound. We didn't even have one before you arrived."

"*Exactly!*" Milo yelled back, face reddening with barely-restrained fury. "You *didn't* have one, and do you know what happens in Leks without safety measures? *People die.* Or the *entire fucking settlement* gets blown to the damned moons. Often, both!"

He threw up his hands in a gesture of frustration, and after a moment, Garil returned an unbothered shrug.

"It's never blown up before," the older man mused.

"*For the Lords' fucking sake!*" Milo yelled. "Just because something has never happened before doesn't mean that it can't happen in the future. Accidents are unpredictable by nature, and being complacent about procedure is a sure way to increase their frequency and severity–"

"Good Lords, I told you to *give it a rest,* Milo!" Garil looked at Ereta and rolled his eyes in an attempt at commiseration–clearly thinking that she shared his annoyance at Milo's fastidiousness–and strode away.

Milo watched his supervisor amble deeper into the Lek with a look of burning fury. When the man was out of sight, Milo grasped Ereta's wrist again and gently tugged her toward the door. He pushed it open in one smooth motion, and they stood in the hallway alone. He pulled off his mufflers and she followed suit. "Sorry about that," he mumbled at her, still staring at the closed door as if his gaze could pierce through the stone and track Garil's movements. He ran a hand through his messy brown hair, which subsequently fell right back into his face. It was only then that she noticed the sheen of sweat covering him. His face and brow were glistening, and tiny beads of moisture ran down his neck before disappearing behind his jumpsuit. The thin, damp fabric clung to his chest and arms, outlining thickly sculpted cords of muscle–

Stop staring, it's just muscle. You've seen lots of muscles, she chided herself with a shake of her head. "That's your boss?" she inquired, and his head snapped back to her.

"Unfortunately, yes." They were both silent for a moment, staring wordlessly at each other.

"So...you said something about a safety briefing?" She prodded in an attempt to pull him out of what she assumed was a still-simmering internal rage.

"Yes," he paused. "You *should* have been given the briefing before you *ever* stepped foot in the Lek. I could give it to you, I suppose but..." he pondered something, head slightly tilted, and then tipped one corner of his lip up. "Wait one moment. I have an idea."

"And don't you be touchin' no metal, or be sure you'll be findin' your hand burnt clean off faster than ya can blink," Chegg told her, wiping his hands across each other as if in demonstration. "And ya gotta watch out for the compressors, and them fans. Them blades are terrible sharp, and fast as a Runner needin' the cleanroom, and if ya get caught between 'em, you'll be reduced to..." Chegg narrowed his eyes in concentration. "Sorry, boss, what's the word?"

Milo stood at the back of the locker room, arms folded, as he watched Chegg give the safety brief to Ereta. Apparently, Milo had been training several Dutied to do so, and this was Chegg's first time, which she had to admit was obvious.

"Reduced to viscera," Milo supplied.

Ereta grimaced. "Lords, is being so graphic about it really necessary?"

"Absolutely," Milo replied. "Being clear about the reality of these dangers is the only way that people will take them seriously."

"Of any way to go, I reckon the compressor would be the worst of 'em. That machine'll take a man and grind him into a human homogate in two seconds flat," Chegg snapped his fingers.

"*Homogenate.* A human *homogenate,*" Milo corrected, but his tone was patient.

"Right. And what that means is, you'll be crushed real quick-like, and crushed so small that all your bones and skin and bits go to liquid, and all mix together into one fuckin' big puddle of person."

Ereta's grimace intensified. "*Cold burn me; that is fucking disgusting.*"

Milo stepped out from behind her and nodded. "It's gruesome, yes, but it's the truth. And now you'll have that visual in your head every time you near the compressor, and it'll make you careful. Fear is the best incentive for safety."

"I reckon so," Chegg agreed. "Any questions, 'Reta?"

She paused a moment before answering, "Actually, yes. What is the purpose of the safety gloves if your hands will burn off despite them?"

He flipped through the safety binder, the papers making a thick shucking noise with each hasty turn, his eyes darting back and forth across the pages in search of an answer. Finally, he slammed his pointer finger down on a page. "Ah! Here it is. *'The safety gloves keep your hands from gettin' dry and chapped in the heat.'*"

"Wait, really? Dry hands?" Ereta snorted. "That doesn't seem very important at all in the wake of being warned that I might become a puddle."

Chegg looked at Ereta, then starting rushedly flipping through the safety binder again as if it would contain a response to her idle observation–

"*'Some of the safety procedures may seem trivial, but every accident is preventable and it is all of our responsibility to reduce risk in any way we can,'*" he read with a tone of pride.

Huh. Dust bury me, that thing is thorough. Chegg flipped back to his former place in the safety binder and resumed reading. "'Another benefit of the safety gloves is prevention of small cuts on the fingers as a result of paper edges slidin' along the sk–"

"Seriously? These are for *paper cuts?*" she interjected as she waved her hands in front of her, indicating the gloves. "Why wouldn't you make them massive and thick, and maybe rubber so that they can't, I don't know, *burn through and melt your hands off?*"

Just as Chegg motioned to start flipping through the binder for an answer, Milo responded, "Heat-proof gloves would imply that there is any circumstance under which it is acceptable to touch the metal. Which there is not," he stated in a flat tone.

Chegg's booming laugh suddenly filled the locker room. "But that ain't the full reason, is it, boss?"

Milo eyed Chegg with obvious irritation. "No, it's not," he forced out through gritted teeth. Clearly, there was something he didn't want Ereta to know, which only served to make her urgently curious about what it might be.

"What's the full reason?"

Milo sighed and looked up at the ceiling as if searching the stone for patience. "When I got here, there were no gloves at all. So I submitted a proposal–"

"A *long* proposal. He spent nearly a whole *quarter* on it. About as thick as this thing," Chegg patted the safety binder.

"Yes, *thank you,* Chegg." Milo spat. "I submitted a very long proposal for safety gloves, and these," he waggled his gloved fingers, "are what the court sent me. They said I had been 'sufficiently convincing,' but they didn't have the resources to provide anything more substan–"

"And all the lads call them 'Milo-gloves' and say he requested 'em cause his hands are soft as a babe's, and cause he ain't want callouses to roughen his grip." Chegg made a suggestive gesture to accompany his explanation.

Milo was standing with his face in both hands, eyes downcast and head shaking as if in denial. Ereta was beaming, and barely containing her laughter. "So why do you wear them at all, then?"

Milo sighed and crossed his arms. "Because if we don't, and the Court ever visits and sees we aren't using them, they'll never consider one of my safety petitions again." he paused, then added, "And because *nobody* wants a paper cut, Ereta."

The safety brief had taken over an hour, but Ereta felt a sense of confidence when she recited her new Duty oath and followed Milo and Chegg back into the Combustion chamber. The lessons she had learned played themselves over and over again in her head as they mazed their way through the massive space. *'Don't step past the white lines. Don't touch the metal. Check the vessels for lock-out before approaching. Look out for tripping hazards. No pranks. No running. No stapling of anything other than paper.'*

Some of the rules were so random that she supposed they were only in the binder because common sense hadn't proved sufficient to prevent them. *I wonder who got stapled, and where.*

They walked to the back left corner of the Combustion chamber. There was a solid iron door, with a large stamped metal sign across it:

CAUTION: DO NOT ENTER

And just below that, another sign, engraved crudely but meticulously as if by hand, that read:

THIS MACHINE WILL KILL YOU,
AND IT WILL HURT THE WHOLE TIME YOU ARE DYING

Milo tapped at the door with his knuckles. "This is the compression chamber. There is never any reason why you ever need to go inside. Stay away from it. It's not locked right now, but I have a petition submitted to get a lock installed, or to remove the door completely and install another means of access for maintenance purposes. But until then," he rapped on the metal again, "steer clear, and if you ever see anyone near it, pawing at the handle or some other stupid shit, please come find me immediately."

She nodded and performatively shuffled a few steps backward away from the door with her hands up in supplication. The muscles in Milo's cheek twitched, and she wondered if he was suppressing a grin.

As they continued their tour of the space, Ereta found that the hand-engraved signs were a common sight. They were mounted to various doorways and pipes and pieces of machinery with overly specific, dire warnings about how the machine would maim or kill its user. Just as in the safety briefing, the descriptions were...graphic, and she preferred to live in blissful ignorance of the meaning of words like *evisceration* and *cephalotomy* and *degloving* (which she didn't think had anything at all to do with the removal of one's Milo-gloves).

Other signs decorated the walls of the chamber with bits of more general advice:

CARELESSNESS IN THIS VICINITY WILL LIKELY BE FATAL

and

THESE MACHINES DO NOT HAVE BRAINS, SO YOU MUST USE YOUR OWN

and her personal favorite,

PLEASE AVOID DOING ANYTHING THAT BEGINS WITH: "HEY, WATCH THIS."

She knew the words of wisdom and warning were all Milo's doing, and she grinned to herself. *Like a scholar of old.*

They finished their walk of the room's perimeter and saw Garil leaning against the wall again. Milo's brow furrowed and his lips formed a sneer. He approached the man. "Ereta has received the safety briefing, so she is now permitted into the chamber," he yelled, perhaps a smidge louder than was strictly necessary.

Garil yawned in Milo's face and stretched his arms over his head. "Sounds good."

"So you'll do that from now on, right? Give the briefing before bringing new people in here?"

Garil shrugged. "I don't see why I should. You always end up doing it for me."

Milo's fury banked on his face, and quickly morphed into something else entirely. Something like... disgust. "She could have *died*. We *all* could have *died! Does that not bother you *at all?*"

Garil shrugged again. "Why should it? You always do all the bothering for me, too."

Milo was quiet for a long, tense moment, before he spoke, "The price of apathy is usually greater than the reward, Garil. The day will come when you pay that price," he shook his head, and his tone turned somber. "I can only hope that you don't kill us all along with you."

An hour later, Milo finished giving his tour of the Lek. She was shown the Oxygen collection tower, which was the larger of the two structures that had cast their shadows over her arrival that morning. The other structure, it turned out, was the Water tower: where all of the Water was collected, stored, and eventually sent along the pipes across Veirbos.

There were fifteen Dutied in the Combustion chamber of various ages, genders, and physical ability. She had long been taught that those Dutied at Combustion had earned either pity, fear, or hatred; but that perception was challenged with each person she met. Many had visible injuries, but they got along fine: toiling just like everyone else, some of them using wheeled chairs or canes, some operating machines by touch instead of sight. To feel pity for them felt like an insult to their mettle, especially when many of them saw to grueling tasks that were beyond her own physical abilities.

She assumed that those without injury, visible or not, must have been punished like she was. She had always imagined the punished as either tough, gritty people who thrived on the edges of lawfulness and morality, or Rationed Dutied with broken spirits. She was therefore surprised to find all of the Dutied at the Lek (with the notable exception of Garil) exceptionally welcoming and warm. In fact, many were friendlier than the Runners of her former Cohort, and she noticed that the perpetual sense of "other"-ness that she had always felt around new groups of people was not present in their company.

"Alright, we're coming up on the hour," Milo told her in a raised voice, pointing to the dust-filled hourglass that sat on the back table, one of its time lines nearly met. "Are you ready to see how the Water gets made?" She nodded, and he beckoned for her to follow. They approached one of the capsule-shaped metal Combustors that stood in the middle of the room as a loud bell clanged. "That's the hour marker," Milo explained. "We'll be working on a few different units this hour. They're marked by column and row. This is unit C7. We're going to start a new cycle." He crossed the white line that surrounded C7, and Ereta almost called out in warning before taking note of the large metal bar that was attached to the side of the unit. *It's only safe to cross the white line when the combustors are locked out,* she reminded herself with a silent nod. Milo beckoned her forward. He knelt on the ground and grabbed a length of rubber tubing. "This is your Hydrogen fill line," he told her. "It's attached to this pipe, which runs to all of the units in the Lek," he pointed to a metal pipe that was sticking out of the floor beneath the machine, "and that pipe runs from the natural hydrogen spring in the fissure beneath us. All Leks are located on top of these springs. We can't perform combustion without them." He brought the tube to meet a metal fitting on the Combustor, twisting it until it was securely connected. "We fill the unit with hydrogen for exactly 27 seconds, which we can measure using this timer." He motioned to a small hourglass (or, she supposed, a 27-second-glass) with an 'H' carved into the top and bottom. She had her own set of hourglasses that he had given her during their tour, and she pulled them out. He nodded in approval and put his hand on the gas lever at the base of the hydrogen pipe. "Ready?" he asked, and she put one hand on the lever next to his in agreement. The corner of his lip tipped up. "Three, two, one–" they pulled the lever, and Ereta flipped over her 'H' hourglass. When it ran out, they pulled the lever back into place and Milo had her disconnect the fill line. They repeated a similar process for the oxygen fill line, which was on the right side of the Combustor and used an 'O' timer to track 18 seconds of fill.

Milo removed the lockout bar from the unit. They stepped behind the white line. He leaned over and down to speak closer to her ear, "That unit is now full of a highly explosive mixture of gasses," he explained, "and we are going to give it a spark." They walked over to the left side. A metal rod protruded three feet out of its side at a slight angle. "When we push this rod forward, it will strike a flint inside the unit. It's going to be very loud, and hot. Are you ready?" She put her hand beside his on the flint rod and nodded. "Three, two, one–" She felt Milo give the bar a hard, fast push.

Suddenly, everything was dark and bright and quiet and loud all at once. The explosion filled her senses, roaring in her ears, the heat quickly becoming overwhelming. Strangely, it was so loud that she couldn't see, which didn't really make any sense. For a terrifying moment, she wondered if the fire had broken free of the chamber and the explosion was consuming her–but then, as quickly as it had come, the noise dissipated, and her vision returned. Milo was next to her, smiling. "Good job," he told her. "You just created Water."

She looked back at him, still a little bit shaky from the intensity of the explosion. "What happened?"

"The spark ignited the gasses, and the reaction between them caused them to create two outputs: Water and energy. The energy took form as an explosion, and the Water is left behind. The problem is, it's really hot in there, so the Water is actually in gaseous form right now, and we need it to be in liquid form. So," he walked over to a small tank to the side of C7 and turned a small metal knob, "we start a flow of cold Water from the tower outside through the coils on the unit. The Water flows through the coils and absorbs the heat before returning to the Tower. After two hours of this cycle, the unit will be fully cooled, and the Water we created can be drained. This also serves the purpose of keeping the Tower Water warm enough that it doesn't ever freeze."

For the rest of their shift, Milo and Ereta and occasionally Chegg walked around to different units together, starting more cycles and making more explosions and collecting finished Water into massive, heavy tanks. By the end of the day, she was covered in a sheen of sweat and couldn't help but smile. It wasn't as terrifying as she had anticipated. Milo had every part of the process down to an exact science, and it seemed that nothing was left to chance.

Chegg led her through the final hour of her shift, and she found that his company filled her with a sense of amiable comfort. He tousled her hair in praise and frequently gave broad, genuine smiles. As she left the Combustion chamber, she found that Chegg calling her 'Reta' no longer carried with it the sharp sting of painful memories, or any connotation with that quiet lover's whisper. How could it, when Chegg said it with a boisterous enthusiasm that made the nickname feel like being hoisted onto somebody's shoulders or clapped affectionately on the back? Their dynamic settled quickly into one of entirely platonic affection. It gave her a settled kind of comfort.

She walked into the locker room to find that the other workers on Shift were getting changed into their regular clothes, while the next Shift was changing out of them and into their Combustion clothing. Men and women alike were undressing without any air of self-consciousness, and she steeled herself to follow suit, blushing for a reason she didn't quite understand. Chegg walked around the room clad in only a very, *very* small pair of undershorts, attempting to introduce Ereta to the Dutied who were just starting shifts. Her head was so full of new names and faces that she forgot those of the newcomers almost instantly despite her best efforts to commit them to memory.

She glanced around the locker room once more, marking the faces of her fellow Dutied. "Where's Milo?" she asked Chegg.

A short boom of a laugh came from him in reply. "I ain't never heard of Boss leavin' an *hour* past his shift, let alone minutes. He gets pulled into some damn thing, or gets caught up correcting somebody's Duty, or spends a few hours making new signs to hang up. I'm surprised they ain't named the building for him, for the time he spends here." At that, there were a few chuckles and murmurs of agreement. One man—a tall, broad shouldered elder named Cresa—chimed in, "Pretty sure he would house here if they let him. He probably dreads the minutes of his commute as time wasted," to more grunts of assent.

Steeling herself against her baseless bashfulness, she quickly stripped and redressed in her normal clothes, which felt disconcertingly heavy and bulky and *crude* after so many hours in the delicate, flowing fabric of her Duty clothing. She placed her Shift-dirtied, sweaty jumpsuit into the communal hamper and stuffed her other supplies back into her locker. Just as she was heading toward the door, Milo entered. His sweat had dried completely since she last saw him, leaving little flecks of salty residue on his forehead. He looked a mess, with black stains running up and down the front of his clothing and Milo-gloves, and his hair (which was disheveled even at the best of times) sticking out at odd angles.

"Hey, boss, whatcha doin' here so soon? Ya never finish Duty on time," Chegg noted with a friendly clap on Milo's shoulder.

"Yes, well, I–"

"Dust bury me, you ain't left on time once in all the turns I've known ya. Is it because of 'Reta? You wanted to walk her home, bein' the noble bastard ya are?"

Milo's furrowed brow creased even further, his eyes narrowing at Chegg. "I'm not leaving, actually," he replied, words clipped and over-pronounced, then turned to Ereta. "I just wanted to see if you have any questions or concerns after your first day. If you're...pleased."

She thought for a moment. "I've never had so much energy after finishing a Shift. I feel like I could do it all over again and be no worse for the wear. But, you know, that's only physically. My *brain* feels tired; full, if that makes sense. I'm not used to having to *think* so much on a Shift." She rubbed her temples. Indeed, her brain felt sluggish now: it reminded her of how her mouth felt when she ate a sticky mouthful of a nutrition allotment and didn't wash it down with Water. "So please don't tell me anything critically important right now, because I assure you that it will go in one ear and out the other."

He nodded. "It's a waste that your brain was not utilized more in your former Duty. You're a quick learner. You could be a real asset here. We're lucky to have you."

"Damn straight we are!" Chegg bellowed with another tousle of Ereta's hair. "Strong little thing, you are, too! You were right about her, boss–she's small and pretty, but she sure ain't soft!"

Milo shot an unreadable look at Chegg and cleared his throat. "Well, I should be getting back. I'll see you both tomorrow," he nodded at them and turned on his heel to leave.

"See you tomorrow," she echoed back. "And Milo?" he paused and looked back, one eyebrow raised in silent question. "You were right about the heat. I like it, too." He cracked a small smile, nodded again, and left.

Chapter 16

Ereta had five straight days of Shifts. On the third day, she had walked into the Combustion Chamber to find a brand new sign unsubtly located on the wall where Garil had been leaning on her first day:

WE ARE ALL LINKS IN THE CHAIN OF SAFETY
DON'T BE THE WEAK LINK THAT DOOMS US ALL

By the end of the fifth day, she was able to confidently execute most of a Water Combustion cycle independently. Despite herself, she found that she *liked* her new Duty. The most dangerous, punishing Duty on the planet had turned out to be an engaging, fast-paced enterprise filled with open-minded, welcoming people. As she watched Chegg stealthily tie a sheet of paper that read *'give me a sincere compliment'* to the back of Milo's jumpsuit–and as she watched Milo's co-Dutied approach him for the rest of the day saying things like, "your presence is like a warm ray of sunshine, boss," and, "you're the smartest person I've ever met, boss," while everyone conspiratorially giggled–she wondered how she had ever dreaded this place.

"Our pranks used to be better," Chegg insisted. "But Milo put a stop to anything dangerous, which don't leave us with much in a place like this, where you can be sure that pretty much everything's dangerous. He's not even *really* in charge, but he acts like it, and cold burn us dry, we listen. That's why we call him boss, too. Cause that's what he is when ya think about it."

Maybe she had never fit in as a Runner, but she found with each passing day that she truly did fit in at the Lek. *A group of people who thought they belonged nowhere, finding that actually, they can belong together.*

Each evening, she returned home from her Shift and began experimenting with fissure locations for a few hours before meeting up with Leelin and whoever else was free at the Social hall. Bellat often joined, and occasionally Jace. She started inviting Chegg along, too. The man was so unapologetically himself that he fit in anywhere with a confident ease. Kilas hadn't been around since the night of the party, which Ereta knew was a bit of luck that couldn't possibly last forever.

She had the inter-planetary fissure travel down to a simple (if time-consuming) process. She would find a secluded spot on Veirbos, open a fissure to the other world, visually identify a secluded spot on the snow planet roughly a quarter mile Northward, open a fissure back to Veirbos, walk the quarter mile on her home planet, find another secluded spot, and repeat the process again. And again. And again.

Often, she had to progress in shorter distances due to visibility, which varied based on changes in terrain and/or the presence or absence of snow in the air. It was slow-going work, and she found that her head began to pound with a vengeance after opening the fissures seven or eight times in a row. On the fifth day, the massive sprawl of what she assumed was Brafta became just barely visible on the horizon.

It was perhaps a half-mile northward, but from where she stood, she could just make out the bustling figures on the settlement's edge. Beyond it, small white-capped mountains rose from the horizon. They reminded her of the mountains on Veirbos–stout yet intimidatingly sheer, sitting together in proud, broad clumps.

Brafta itself was beautiful, even (or especially) from a distance. The white snow that covered most of the land for miles around was broken by three massive, protruding shards of dark stone. They all stuck up from the ground at low angles, and each one was surrounded on all sides by stone constructions of various shapes and sizes. Thick gray smoke wended its way skyward in thin tendrils. It seemed that fires burned most everywhere in Brafta. They didn't have open fires in Veirbos, other than the small light of their braziers. There simply wasn't enough wood or oil to burn, and that fuel was better saved for more practical purposes, since combustible gasses were abundant.

She arched a wide path around the city, circling it from a far distance to identify the most sensible approach. It was hard to find a single edge of the town that wasn't teeming with activity. Luckily, nearly everyone wore the same bright red as Ima. They were easy to spot from a ways off against the stark white of snow and the dark gray of the stone buildings.

Her head pounded. Rather than suffer the trudge through the snow directly into the city, she resolved to return in the middle of the night, when (hopefully) the activity would have died down enough for her to open a fissure without attracting notice.

She returned to Veirbos on the far edge of a Water pipe, a place she had left only minutes earlier. The air in Veirbos felt so rough to her nose and lungs after breathing in the silky-smooth air of the snow planet. She sighed, and began the long walk back home, which eventually turned into a light run. It felt strange and unsteady and shockingly *wrong* to run again, but she padded forward at a steady pace until the glowing firelights of Tubat-So were visible in the distance.

She made straight for the social hall, where she found Leelin, Chegg, and Jace waiting for her. Bellat joined soon after, and they played for several hours before her and Leelin excused themselves and made the walk back to his house.

"No shift tomorrow?" he asked her with a squeeze of her hand.

"No shift tomorrow," she agreed. "You?"

"Unfortunately," he replied. "But I didn't have one today, and I had the foresight to take a nap this afternoon. I can stay up all night if need be."

She smiled, but kept her gaze fixed straight ahead. "And why might need be?"

"I missed you this pentad," Leelin replied, and sounded entirely genuine, with no hint of his usual flippant flirtatiousness.

"That's not an answer," she said.

"Yes, it most certainly is, little flame. I missed you this pentad, and the moons revolve around me, so I will stay up with you all night if that's what it takes for me to get my fill," he paused, "or give my fill, as the case may be."

They stumbled into his house in a tangle of limbs and lips and teeth and tongues, frantically yanking off each other's clothes in a clumsy rush to remove any barriers between their skin.

She grabbed his hand and dragged him over to the wall, pressing him against it by his shoulders, before sinking to her knees. He raised an eyebrow at her in silent question.

"The moons revolve around you," she told him with a knowing grin, grasping his cock firmly in her hand and stroking it. He moaned, low and rough. "And for tonight, so will I." With that, she released him and moved her lips to brush a kiss against his head. She trailed gentle whispers of kisses down and back up his length before lightly dragging her tongue across his slit. His whole body tensed and twitched in anticipation. She pulled her mouth away and realigned herself near his base. She firmly, wetly dragged her flattened tongue in a long stroke to his tip before circling it around the head. She circled and circled, indeed creating something like an orbit around his cock.

He fisted his hands into her messy black locks and tipped his head back.

"*Fucking Lords*, Ereta," he muttered into the dark silence of the room, the only other sound his ragged breaths. She smiled against his now-wet skin and, without breaking her tongue's orbit, slipped her lips around him. His hips bucked forward in what seemed an involuntary twitch that served to push him deeper into her mouth; she tutted at him and pushed him back against the wall. "Greedy," she chided, mouth still full of him to the exclusion of clarity in her words, but his responding chuckle told her that he had gotten her meaning.

She brought her hand up to grasp him from the base as her mouth continued to swirl and dance around his head. He gripped her hair tighter, and the pull against her scalp held just a twinge of pain, but she didn't mind. As she twisted her hand up and down his shaft and brought her mouth up and down to meet it, he began to shake and twitch more fervently.

"Dust bury me, I don't want you to stop, but you should if you don't want–" she pointedly tightened her hand's grip in answer before he could finish. His words cut off with a sharp hiss. "Well *fine*, then. Twist my arm about it." She playfully rotated her stroking hand in reply.

Her mouth and hand worked in tandem, her grip becoming firmer and her movements more rapid. She watched the prominent muscles on his upper thighs flex and tense, straining against his need. His hips bucked, and she planted her free hand against one side to pin him firmly against the wall as she worked his cock. She watched him; his head still tipped back, his eyes closed, his breath ragged and shallow, and saw the moment when he broke written across the planes of his face. "Fuuuuuck," he groaned, features tensing and relaxing in tandem as she felt a hot stream pour deep into her mouth. She let it trickle down her throat, and waited for him to look down at her before taking a loud, visible swallow of his release.

He dropped to his knees with her, but with his height, his chest was at her eye level. She leaned forward into him and he scooped her into his arms, kissing her deeply, tasting himself on her tongue and groaning again. As he stood and began walking to the bed, he whispered against her mouth, "The moons are still shining, and it's going to be a *very* long nigh–"

There was a loud, three-tap knock at the door. Leelin's head turned toward it, a look of confusion puckering his lips and pulling one corner tightly to the side. "Who is the bloody dust..." he placed Ereta on the bed. "Don't move," he instructed, and pulled his legs through his jumpsuit before tying the arms around his waist so that his chest remained fully bare. With his back turned, she reached for her clothes, too. Whoever it was, she was fairly certain she didn't want them to see her naked. As she began to dress, she heard the creak of the front door opening.

"Oh!" Leelin exclaimed with blatant surprise. "It's you!"

She listened intently for a response. It took a long moment to come, and was barely audible in the silence, "Don't make me say it," a familiar female voice grumbled. *Holy Lords, is that–*

"Well, well, well. Isn't *this* a shocking surprise, Mari? I wonder why you could *possibly* be here." He leaned against the doorframe, arms folded in a display of shamelessly cocky victory.

"I said, *don't make me say it,*" Mari spat out through what sounded like gritted teeth.

He leaned forward and responded in a low, tonal whisper, "Oh, I will make you absolutely *beg for it,* Mari–but in due time. It so happens that I have company at the moment."

"Oh!" Mari's surprised response was preceded by the sound of her retreating footsteps. Leelin leaned back and craned his head to look at Ereta, his wide smile and cocked eyebrow asking her an unspoken question.

"Go after her!" She gestured with a fervent sideways wave of her hands. "I'll leave! You've been waiting for thi–"

"I *will* go after her, but only to set a new...appointment. You will *not* leave. I would never kick out one lover to have another; if there are to be many in a night, I would have them at once, not back-to-back. Well, perhaps back-to-back, but what I mean is–"

"Yes, yes, I know, you're as active as a siring Lord. Now *go*!"

He grinned and nodded at her. The door shut behind him, and when the low tones of conversation drifted in from outside, she retreated to the cleanroom.

She stared at her reflection in the mirror, forcing herself to hold eye contact with a woman she had grown to both pity and hate (and maybe, *very* recently, grown to like just a tiny fraction of a bit). She thought about Leelin. She had felt the barest twinge of jealousy at hearing Mari's voice, which surprised her; she had thought herself totally accepting of Leelin's disposition toward multiple partners. And she was, and she *certainly* wasn't interested in a monogamous relationship with him. Certainly not. Definitely not.

Leelin's words flitted across her thoughts, *'I know you have been hurt, little flame, but don't give up on love just yet. Fire does not burn cold.'*

But what else could she do besides give up? She had thought she could spare herself the pain of betrayal by avoiding attachments. And she had, until recently; what she hadn't considered was that her attraction to Leelin might be something deeper. But what right did she have to feel jealous? She most certainly had no right to feel betrayed, not after their conversation about this very circumstance. What were those feelings, then, but echoes of a time when she had imagined her life as something to be shared entirely with another? A time when she had thought she would fall asleep and wake to the same face each day of her life. When she thought that alone might have been enough to make her happy.

But it wasn't enough in the end, she thought. Love *wasn't enough.*

No, she knew she couldn't love someone so hard that it made them into who she wanted them to be. She couldn't drown someone in enough love to stifle or change their very nature. That wasn't really love, anyway, was it? Maybe real love, she realized suddenly, was the willingness to accept another just as they are.

And she loved Leelin, truly, as one loves a true friend. She wasn't *in* love with him; she knew what that felt like, and with him, it was different. He was her best friend, and she did not want him to change for her; she didn't want him to change at all. He was perfectly imperfect just as he was, and she was relieved to find that imagining being with just him, and him with just her, did not bring her relief. It felt *wrong.*

With a deep breath, she let her pang of jealousy go, and allowed herself to simply be grateful for the moment in which she dwelled. *You will always have him in your life, and that's enough.*

But that didn't mean having that with anyone else would feel *right,* and despite Leelin's words and her apparent predisposition to jealousy, she was sure that the part of her that wanted–that *could* be in love with another–was damaged beyond all repair.

"W*e will find each other."*

Her dream faded as she tried (and failed) to hang onto the bliss and comfort she had felt within it.

After several minutes of staring blankly at the ceiling, she sat up in Leelin's bed and stretched. Lords, she was tired. She'd barely slept, as he had predicted, and might have been inclined to lay around all day if Leelin weren't due for a Shift soon.

The night before was a foggy haze of Olchate-laden lust. They had each other several times in various ways, and she felt a faint soreness lingering in her bones from the vigor of their activities.

She stretched again as she stood, then turned to gently shake her friend awake.

"Be gone, cruel woman," he groaned while pulling a pillow over his face.

"I didn't realize you were so eager to join me for Duty at the Lek," she replied.

He scoffed, his voice still muffled, "I will not be late, little flame, as I have mastered the art of sleeping until the *very last* possible second, and you have interrupted what could have been another..." he lifted the edge of the pillow and glanced toward the sun and moons of the early morning light, "96 seconds of sleep."

"Cruel, indeed," she muttered. "Well, anyway, now that you're up, are you coming to Intali tonight?"

"No, not tonight," he sighed and sat up. "I have obligations to attend." He winked at her and stood, stretching upward until his fingers grazed the ceiling.

"Ah," she replied with a small grin. "Mari?"

"The very same. Although I have my doubts that she'll show in the end. Her pride might prevent her from crawling back. But if that's the case, I'll simply seek her out myself, at which point her pride will fall prey to her desires, I'm sure. Either way," he summarized, "I will certainly not be at Intali tonight."

"If her pride would prevent her from coming, she wouldn't have agreed at all," she argued.

"Oh, she didn't."

She looked at him, hoping her disbelief was evident. "You said you have an obligation. An *appointment.*"

"I told her that I would be here this evening, alone, and that should she decide she'd like to visit, I would have the time and energy to oblige her. She prattled on, saying that her coming at all had been a foolish mistake, that she wasn't *really* interested, blah blah blah." He mimed a talking mouth with his hand and smirked. "I'd put the odds that she'll be on my doorstep promptly at seven tonight at 60%, give or take."

"You flatter yourself," she smirked back, "and I'd take those odds. She's stubborn."

A dreamy smile grew onto his face. "Yeah, she sure is."

Leelin had gotten ready with, frankly, impressive rapidity and was out the door for his Shift before she had pulled on her treads. She left a few minutes later, tugging on her coat as the front door clicked shut behind her and the dusty cold assaulted her senses.

She had meant to wake in the middle of the night to continue her scouting of Brafta while its residents slept, but she had been thoroughly distracted and fallen asleep promptly after her and Leelin were too spent to continue. She had been beyond forming coherent thoughts by then, anyway, let alone the coherent feelings she would have needed to produce in order to open the fissure. She resolved that she would, instead, do it tonight. After a long, long, perhaps even all-day nap.

But only a few steps into her trudge homeward, she heard a strange, loud scraping sound, and followed it through the alley to find Milo squatting in the dust, his upper body wholly engulfed by some sort of large pipe that stuck out from his house.

She cocked her head and watched him silently.

"For all the fucking Water–" he swore to himself, his words and that strange scraping both echoing and amplifying off the pipe's metal to a comedic effect. *"The dust-cursed Lords of fucking shit–"*

"Never heard that one before," she said with a giggle.

His body jerked within the pipe just as a loud *pang* of metal sounded. "FUCKING BALLS," and after a few seconds, she knelt down to peer down the pipe's entrance. He was stuffed inside with very little room to spare, but she could just make out his hands rubbing soothingly over his temple.

"Did you hit your head?" she asked.

"Yes," he replied.

"I'm sorry I scared you," she added, and it was genuine.

"You didn't sc–" he paused and slid out of the pipe in one long movement, staring up at her through messy brown bangs, his head now resting in the dust, his always-furrowed eyebrows (predictably) furrowed. He blew a stream of air at his forehead in a fruitless attempt to get his hair out of his left eye. "You didn't scare me," he finished.

"Clearly not," she agreed, and that was certainly not genuine. "I'm not one to pry into a person's personal affairs," she quoted Ima with a grin and a tilt of her head, "but can I ask what exactly you're doing?"

He groaned and sat up, still rubbing his head. "You pry into people's personal affairs all the Lords-damn time."

"I can't help my nature," she said with mock defensiveness and a chaste hand against her heart, paraphrasing what had become their oft-used idiom.

"That sounds like something that someone with an indefensible nature would say."

"That doesn't make it less true," she grinned again. "Take me as I am, or not at all."

Dust bury me, why did I say that? *And what does that even mean?*

It was his turn to tilt his head, with still-furrowed brows and crimson-flecked eyes pinning her soundly in place. Her heart began to pound in what she thought must be some form of embarrassment. The seconds dragged by.

"As you are then," he answered with a nod, and then got to his feet. Her heart calmed, and warmed slightly at this hint of tangible friendship. "It's a pipe."

"Believe it or not, I figured that much out already."

"It's a pipe that creates a negative pressure environment to encourage the flow of warm air toward cold air, effectively condensing it until Water droplets collect."

She tried, and (surprisingly) mostly succeeded, to understand his explanation. "And what part of that necessitates being *inside* the pipe?"

He knelt down and pointed into the pipe. She took the hint and knelt beside him. "Rust," he chuffed by way of explanation.

"Rust?"

"We don't really have to think about it out here because the air is so dry. But when metals are exposed to Water and air, they oxidize, and rust is what's left behind from the reaction. I should have anticipated it, but it's far easier to say that *after* the negligence has already happened than it is to plan for every single eventuality." He shook his head, and then muttered under his breath as if speaking only to himself, "Thoughtlessness renders us all agents of chaos, and good science is our helpless victim."

They stared at each other in silence for a long moment. "Was I pontificating?" he asked her, the corner of his lip quirking up.

"Like a scholar of old," she replied with a smile.

"That doesn't make what I said less true," his small grin grew a bit. "Anyway, I have to scrape off the corrosion and then find some method to prevent this from happening again."

It was her turn to furrow her brows. "Wait, how did you know it was happening at all? Do you frequent this pipe?"

His grin grew another measure. It was just shy of a full smile now. "No, not ideally. But this morning, I saw that the Water coming from down here had a strange color, and had to crawl in to investigate."

He lightly, but resolutely, slapped his own knees. "And here we are. Luckily, my bamboo plants can cope with a little rust, because *I* certainly don't want to drink it. And purifying it would be its own headache."

Before she had time to think (and, ideally, stop herself from word-vomiting this *truly* unwise suggestion, which would *certainly* only lead to her own disappointment at his refusal, not to mention that the ensuring awkwardness might degrade the burgeoning friendship she had with Milo), she blurted, "Can I see them now? The bamboo plants?"

He was silent, seemingly in thought, as he craned his head above her, his gaze directed toward the front of the house.

"Well, I *suppose* I could show you–"

"Great!" She chirped, the relief a heady rush, and she shot up to standing, turned on her heel, and started back down the alley. She felt excitement bubbling inside her, and she was powerless to resist its call. There had been a time when her life had been boring. Within the span of a few pentads, it had transformed itself into a rich tapestry of interesting and engaging things, and the unpredictability of it all was addictive.

He called after her, "–but you have to exercise caution–*extreme caution*–if you go inside. I have several delicate experiments set up that can't be disturbed. In fact, it might be better if I bring out a plant to show you, although I would prefer to not expose a sapling to the cold–maybe this is a bad idea. You should be going, anyway, I'm sure you have plans–"

"Nope. No plans." She answered with feigned ignorance of his unsubtle hint. After all, he had essentially called her nosy not a few minutes earlier, and she was too intrigued now to allow even a hint of disappointment ruin this. She had never seen a plant. "And I won't knock into anything. My eyesight is flawless and I have excellent reflexes."

His dry voice called out from behind her, "Forgive me for being wary of that claim, but I saw you run straight into a fissure only a few pentads ago."

She slowed to a stop. That was...true. Lords, she couldn't explain what had caused that uncharacteristic clumsiness, not without sounding like she was insane, or explaining the full truth of the fissures and the snow planet, which she *would* do, eventually, but right now, she wanted to see the plants. "That was not a normal occurrence. I wasn't myself."

"And *yourself* is someone I can trust in a room of delicate, dangerous objects?"

"Unequivocally," she declared with a firm nod, silently adding, "*Unless I get distracted by another air fissure tearing the world apart*", in her head.

He studied her for a long moment, nodded in return, and began to stride up to the front door. "Ok. But don't touch anything, and *please* try not to move more than you absolutely have to."

Milo pushed open the door to his house. She trailed after him. They stepped inside, and–

She stopped breathing. Maybe her heart ceased its beat. Was she dead? She wasn't sure–all she knew was that she was gazing upon the most beautiful sight she had ever beheld. "*Holy Lords...*"

Dots and streaks of colorful light shone over the room, bathing everything in reds, oranges, yellows, blues, greens, and purples. The colors danced together. They were in and of the air, the dust that hung there capturing fluid streaks of colors. Everything was veiled in the captivating light, colors swirling on every surface. She felt tears begin to well at the sight.

Milo cleared his throat, but she couldn't turn away from the colors. She took a breath, now feeling her racing heart slamming itself against her ribs. *Oh good. I'm alive.*

"What is it?" she whispered.

"What is what?"

She whipped her head around to look at Milo, incensed that he wasn't as awed as she was at the sight. *The moons-cursed colors!*

His eyes caught hers again, pinning her in place. One side of his lip quirked up as he studied her. "Oh, the prisms. I forget they're there, I'm used to them."

He pointed to the far side of the room, where small glass objects hung: a dozen or so of them tied to each of the floor-to ceiling ropes that spanned the windows like curtains.

"Prisms," he repeated the word. "They separate waves of light into their constituent colors." He walked over to the prisms and held his hand in front of one, showing her how the colorful light moved across his hand. "Sunlight comes in through the windows and *refracts*–or bends–when it strikes the prisms. Then the colors separate into individual waves, and the effect is this." He lightly stroked his hand across the ropes, causing them to sway. With the movement of the prisms, the colors spun across the room, eddying and twining in mesmerizing patterns, dancing together and apart, combining, separating, dazzling. She had never seen anything so...perfect.

As she watched the lights dance, she noticed that a large table occupied nearly the entirety of the space. A massive bamboo surface was held up by columns of neatly stacked stone. Atop the table, a variety of strange objects were spread out: glass tubes of varying sizes and shapes, intricate metal works composed of intertwining circles and rods, blocks of raw iron, a bell the size of her fist suspended within a large glass dome, a variety of large and small hand tools, scattered writing implements, tiny glass spheres, and sheets of paper covered in rows of neat, compact handwriting (dozens more of which were hanging from the ceiling on thin fibers). There were piles of dust, separated into bowls in what she assumed to be some kind of sorting system, although what made some dust different from other dust was indiscernible to her.

Scattered amidst everything were hundreds (maybe thousands?) of stones. Stones *everywhere*: large ones broken apart with shards littered in their wake, small ones that were shaped and polished to a dazzling shine, and works-in-progress that had been partially ground into fine powder. Rock hammers of all shapes and sizes lay in haphazard positions around the room, as if they had each been tossed aside after baring an exciting discovery.

She stepped forward, mesmerized. She didn't have any idea what most of these objects were for, or what Milo intended to learn from them, but the vibrant passion that radiated from the room made her heart ache.

For eight long turns, she had struggled through her days in bleak resignation, desperate for the reprieve of her dreams. The concept of engaging in the world around her would have required her actually taking an interest in waking life, which she mostly had not; not until recently, anyway. Not until the fissure and...everything after.

Milo's home laid bare the machinations of a full life, and it set the long turns of emptiness in her own life in stark relief. Tears welled for the second time today, but whether they were born of despair, or regret, or hope, or maybe all three? She couldn't tell.

Chapter 17

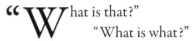

"What is that?"

"What is what?"

An hour later, she could scarcely count the number of times she and Milo had exchanged those exact words. Each time, he explained the objects she inquired about in terms that were mostly comprehensible, although when he got particularly carried away, she had to remind him that she did not know most of the words he was using. Words like *thermodynamic* and *electrochemical* and *biomassification*.

She picked up a glass orb that encased four spinning mirrored blades.

"Ah. That's a sun-powered motion device." He strode up beside her and took it from her hands, carrying it over to the windows. He held it up to the light, and the blades spun faster. "I suctioned most of the air from the orb. With the reduced resistance, the heat reflected by the blades is enough to shift the pressure around them, and they move."

She watched the blades spin faster and faster, until they became a blur. She didn't look away from the orb as she asked him, "How did you learn to do this?"

"Do what?"

She leveled a flat look at Milo and gestured in a wide arc around the room.

"Everything. All of this. How do you know how to do this?"

He furrowed his brows and tilted his head in a familiar expression of curiosity. His bangs shifted with the movement, lightly brushing against his eyelashes.

"I don't understand the question."

"You made all of this...stuff. These experiments. How did you know what to make? Or why to make it?"

"I didn't know what to make or why to make it. That's the point." Now he looked befuddled.

"Now *I* don't understand."

Milo sighed and looked around the room. He thought for a long moment, and she began to think he wouldn't answer.

"When I see something that doesn't make sense, it *maddens* me. I can't think about anything else until I figure out an explanation. The world isn't just a collection of random occurrences, Ereta, everything happens because of action and reaction. The more we are able to understand, and eventually control, those reactions...I hope that some of this will be useful–will make life better for us. Veirbos is not a hospitable place. We barely survive, and it is a struggle. But maybe...maybe we can learn enough about it that we can start to use its composition to our advantage. *Make* it hospitable. We don't just have to accept our lot at face value. There's always something we can do to make it better."

"But what could possibly be the use of something like this?" She reached out and took the orb back from him. "I don't see how spinning blades might make fissures less dangerous, or make more Water less scarce."

Milo looked taken aback. *Did I offend him?* It was an honest question, not a criticism. It was an unfortunately common occurrence for her to speak without thinking about how her words came across.

He snatched the orb back. "These are *all* very important and useful things." He gestured around the room, and she couldn't help but notice the irony that his gesture encompassed balls of crumbled paper, a two-foot-tall pyramid of empty Water glasses, a bedsheet that had been ripped into strips and tied into various complex knots, and a used cleaning powder canister filled with folded Intali cards.

But she didn't argue with him.

He seemed to read her doubt and launched into an explanation. "We can't know what is and isn't useful, because we don't fully understand the world around us. We need to test how everything works, and why it works, and maybe we can find a way to use it later on. So if I notice something, like a small piece of glass that sways in the sunlight, I investigate it until I understand why. I don't know how to 'do' any of this, I just try things. Experiment. Sometimes it works, most of the time it doesn't, but it's all in furtherance of understanding the bigger picture."

Something previously elusive clicked into place for her then. She had trouble grasping Milo's experiments because they were predicated on something she had fundamentally lacked: hope for the future of Veirbos. Perhaps, with the exception of the snow planet, hope for the future at all.

"I hope it makes a difference," she said, perhaps too quietly. Because regardless of if she got her friends off of Veirbos, she couldn't bring all 50,000 residents of the planet with them without attracting notice. And Veirbos had been the same for a long, bleak millennium, and would likely stay the same for millennia to come: long after she was gone from whatever world she lived in.

A beat passed, and she suddenly felt desperate for a distraction from her thoughts before they turned distressingly bleak. "Can I see the bamboo?" He studied her for another small eternity. Then, with a sharp nod, he turned and mazed his way through his home of useful and important things.

S he could have stayed at Milo's house all day, perhaps for multiple days, and not run out of questions to ask or objects to tinker with. The plants were so beautiful, housed inside the bedroom and scattered throughout several pots filled with dust of varying textures and colors. She had never seen any plants in person, and they filled her with something like awe; maybe reverence. It felt as though she was looking at something that was both incredibly fragile and steadfastly eternal. Plants did not naturally grow on Veirbos, not since the new Sun. As such, they were highly protected: grown in large Greenhouses on secure settlements throughout the planet. A relic of the Old Sun, the seeds used to grow bamboo, flax, and several other low-Water plants had been propagated within Greenhouses ever since the climate became inhospitable for them. The lack of other living beings on Veirbos evidenced the fact that life could not thrive here without otherwise unnatural intervention. Clothing, tools, and the nutritional allotments eaten by everyone on Veirbos all relied on the successful propagation of plant life. Under the Old Sun, when the world was warmer and wetter, she imagined that all of Veirbos had been covered in the lively greenery. Those were the daydreams that had consumed her childhood. *It must have been breathtaking.*

Milo didn't disclose how he had attained the bamboo seeds; he deflected the question by replying cryptically, *"The questions of science are above the laws of men."*

Well, if he was breaking the Lords' laws, she supposed it didn't matter, since the usual punishment for such crimes was assignment to combustion.

All of the plants, she learned, were given their own Water. Milo had multiple experiments centered on creating or capturing Water. They ranged from porous stones that absorbed moisture in the air, to the large pipe system he had shown her earlier, to that system of purifying his own urine that Leelin had mentioned. She had to feign excitement as she watched the dark yellow liquid swirl in a closed container, so as to not diminish the zeal of his explanation. She did, however, decline to *try* the purified urine-Water, despite Milo's insistence that it was *"perfectly safe to drink and measurably purer than the Water in the network."* Maybe her assumption that Milo wouldn't have given her his purified piss in a canteen had been overly sentimental. In the eyes of science, the origin of the Water didn't matter, after all.

Despite how engrossed he had been in answering her questions, Milo was all too ready to kick her out after a few hours, vaguely claiming he needed time to *"take care of a few things"*. His jitters got intense as she tried to linger, basking in the liveliness of it all. She didn't want to leave. The idea of returning to her bland, bare home was nearly nauseating.

Despite his evident anxiety, Milo gave in and told her he would show her one more experiment, which she agreed to, knowing she would just ask to see another after that. And again and again, maybe forever. If there was one thing she could do well, it was procrastinate. "It's outside. It wouldn't make sense to do this one indoors, too volatile," he muttered and opened the front door for her. She eagerly danced down the steps and into the frigid air.

"Where is it?" She asked, glancing around for hints of color or gleams of iron. The door locking behind her was enough to jolt her out of her search for the outdoor experiment.

"Apologies, Ereta, but asking nicely didn't work," he told her, voice muffled. She fumed at him, stomping up to stare at him through the glass windowpane of the door.

"So you lied?" her voice was icy. She *hated* being lied to. It was hard enough for her to relate to other people without them obfuscating their true intentions, and trust was something that had been hard for her to give freely to others after everything that had happened in the Lords' City.

"It wasn't a lie. The 'experiment' was to see how I could get you to willingly leave. And I was right, it wouldn't have worked indoors, since you *weren't leaving*." He turned to walk away, and she banged on the glass in pure indignation.

"See? Volatile." She turned away before Milo could see her involuntary grin.

She walked out into the midmorning sun and sucked in a sharp breath at the brutal cold. As she ambled back to her and Jace's house, her thoughts were occupied by Milo's experiments. By his house that was filled with life and passionate interest. By his hope, his relentless optimism that suffering of all kinds was a fundamentally solvable problem.

She had nearly forgotten the snow planet, so consumed by her own thoughts. She focused her attention back onto the sensation of the tug, feeling it pulling gently as she walked. It felt like a part of her now, like an anchor that kept her tied to the hopeful future promised by the snow planet. She noticed the tug intensifying slightly the closer she got to her house.

Milo's words flitted through her mind as she entered her warm home and removed her outer clothes.

"The world isn't just a collection of random occurrences, Ereta, everything happens because of action and reaction."

And certainly, he was right. After everything that had happened since falling into that Lords-damn fissure, she hadn't stopped to consider the *why* behind the tug, let alone her subsequent discovery of the other world. Why was she able to open a portal between Veirbos and the snow planet? Why did the other planet exist at all, and where was it? Why and how was it so similar and yet so different from her home planet? But most confusing of all, why was this happening to her? Dust bury her, she was glad that it was, but still, the question gnawed at her, *Why me why me why me*

Her thoughts consumed her as she filled her first glass of Water of the day from her Issue and chugged it down, and later as she slurped a non-stimulant nutrition allotment, and through the afternoon as she swept up the house and indulged in a long, cleansing powdering off. She did all of those things without conscious thought, her mind instead attending inward...flipping over every stone, investigating every crack, trying to figure out how everything Lords-damn fit. Trying to find that *why* which, before now, she had been content to live in blissful ignorance of.

But now, after seeing Milo's house, she was committed to getting answers.

Again, Milo's earlier words flitted back to her: *"We don't just have to accept our lot at face value. There's always something we can do to make it better."* Maybe running away to the snow planet, although it was the simplest answer, wasn't the right one. Could she find a way, perhaps, to take what she learned and discovered there and use it to improve the lives of everyone on Veirbos? Could things on this dust-cursed desert be, if not good, at least marginally *better* for everyone toiling there?

She was almost afraid to consider that, because in her heart, she knew that if she gave into that hope and it was dashed, she might not survive it. Maybe that had been the problem all along. Her natural inclination was to hope, and to dream. But she had been let down so many times that bleak resignation was an easier, and less painful, way to live.

She wasn't ready to fully succumb to hope. But she *would* explore, and experiment, and try her Lords-damn hardest to get answers.

And so she set out into the grainy cold of her world, heading toward the last location of her snow planet scouting. Her body buzzed with a keen new sense of determination: attune to the sensations of the world around her, ready to follow her instincts, ask questions, and shape her future's path even while it unfolded before her.

"**D**ouble," she called to the table around her. Her confidence wasn't a facade this time, she actually had good cards for a change. It was a shame that Bellat had to leave after just one round to get ready for a Shift tomorrow; her friend surely would have been happy to see Ereta strike a bit of rare luck. The others around the table weren't the types to fawn over winning hands, or say things like, *"I'm so proud of you!"* and, *"That's the best-played hand I've ever seen!"*

"Match," Jace responded coolly. Kilas tossed in his cards (he was measurably more tolerable when Leelin wasn't around for him to torment), and Chegg sat in not-so-silent witness after immediately ditching his hand with a scoff. He didn't have too much skill in feigning good cards; the realities of his hand were reliably etched onto his face, but at least he knew it. His penchant for brutal honesty was endearing to Ereta, even if it did make him a bit brusque.

Milo sat at the other end of the table, eyebrows furrowed at Ereta. "There's just no way. Match."

After handing over significant measures of her Water to pay for what was ultimately a lost bet, Ereta downed another tablet of Olchate and started the next round.

Their game had started fairly early, and so it finished early with Chegg's collapse on the table. It was his third or fourth game of the day by that point, and the Olchate was heavy in his features. As they left the Social Hall, Chegg was supported between Milo and Kilas, and he made valiant efforts at walking on his own without much success. He apparently lived just a quarter-mile past Leelin and Milo, which wasn't a very far distance at all. But, then again, she wasn't the one supporting half the weight of an almost unnaturally muscled man.

The group chatted as they walked, and only when they were approaching Leelin's neighborhood did Ereta have the thought that bringing Kilas this close to her friend might be ill-advised, despite the likelihood that he was likely preoccupied with Mari. They rounded a corner and passed Milo and Leelin's houses. She craned her neck to glance at the door, and make sure that Leelin wasn't anywhere in sight, which he wasn't. Their plan was to walk directly to Chegg's place, whereupon Milo and Kilas would return home and Ereta and Jace would continue onward to their house. It was an unfortunate coincidence that the most efficient path just happened to pass by Leelin. But it was nearly nine now, two hours past his 'appointment', so surely, there was no way he–

The door opened, and Ereta stopped in her tracks. Cold panic overcame her every sense, slowing time to a painful crawl. Her breath caught in her throat. Her heart pounded. She wasn't sure how she managed to gather enough air to put a tone behind her whisper, "*No.*" But no, what? No, this couldn't be happening? No, her and her friends couldn't be here, and they needed to turn around right now and run? No, please don't let this be what it looks like?

Because standing at Leelin's door, her hands covered in dripping red blood, was Hista.

Chapter 18

"Oh, *good*, little 'Reta's back. We've been looking for you all evening," Hista spat in her musical lilt across the short expanse of dusty ground that separated them. "Unfortunately, we had to get started without you. But no matter, you're here now. And you brought company?"

Run run run run run– Ereta's mind couldn't focus through the haze of her instincts, instincts that screamed at her to put as much distance between her and Hista as possible. But Leelin– and that *blood–*

"Where is he?" She shouted, or whispered, or something in between; it was hard to tell when her ears were filled with a loud roaring noise punctuated by the too-fast beats of her heart. *Thumpwhooshthumpwhooshthumpwhoosh*

"Who, your little friend? Oh, he's inside. We've had fun, him and I. He's a tough nut to crack, but I'm making progress." Her smile was a stomach-wrenching, beautiful, vile– an utterly perfect and utterly hateful thing. "But before I return to him, you and I have–"

"I'm sorry, but who the fuck are you?" Jace interrupted, her tone as regal and steady as ever, and as flatly unbothered as though she were asking the time. Ereta grasped her friend's arm in a silent plea, trying to somehow send her words through their contact, *No. Stop. Do not engage her. She'll hurt you, too.*

Jace shook her hand off. "And why are you covered in blood?"

Milo stepped up beside Ereta and grabbed her arm. He whispered into her roaring ears, "The Water."

And all she could do was reply, trying not to visibly move her lips, "Yes."

He nodded, but didn't retreat.

Hista did not deign to dignify Jace's question with a response, but instead continued addressing Ereta. "You can imagine my surprise when I received a letter demanding my return to this Lords-forsaken little town because apparently, I had *failed* in my Duty." Hista took a few confident steps toward Ereta. Her blood-coated hands were clasped in front of her with a chaste poise that contrasted grotesquely with the gore. Only a dozen feet or so separated them now. "But you and I both know that isn't true, don't we?"

Ereta said nothing. Jace stepped forward, partially shielding her. "Your failures are not Ereta's responsibility. Now, kindly fuck off so that we can return to what *had* been a relatively painless evening."

"As I'm sure you remember, Ereta, I left you dead in the dust. You had drunk all of your Water. You collapsed. You stopped breathing. The way I figure it, the only way you can be standing here in front of me now is if someone followed you on the Route and helped you cheat with extra Water. I intend to find out exactly who that person is before Tella's morning rise."

"Let him go," she said, unable to focus on anything else but the fact that Leelin was in danger and possibly even dead.

"No, I don't think I will let him go. What I *will* do is find out which of your little friends may have been involved." She spun on her heel and walked back to Leelin's front door, whipping it open and poking her head inside. "I need you. Outside. Now."

They waited in silence for a moment, and the door opened again, and out walked...

"*No,*" Ereta pleaded again.

"Which one of Ereta's friends should I speak with next, Mari? Do you recognize any of them?"

Ereta tried to swallow past a heavy knot in her throat. Almost everyone she cared about, except for Bellat, was here. Although she missed her warm, loving friend, and although Bellat's ability to calm angry nerves would have been useful in this situation, she found herself grateful that she wasn't with them. Bellat was home. She was *safe*.

Unfortunately, the rest of them were not.

Mari looked at the small group, her eyes calm despite the obvious danger of the situation. "That one," she pointed at Jace. "The redhead. I think they live together. And," she continued, looking over their faces again, "I've never seen her be too friendly with the tall one. Kilas, he's in her Cohort. Although it *is* possible that he assisted her. I don't recognize the others, and I don't think they'll have as much information as Leelin. He's her closest confidant."

"Mari," Ereta pleaded, her voice breaking. "What are you *doing*?" But in truth, she already knew. A feeling of betrayal swelled inside her, a feeling that was all too familiar, but no less potent than the first time she had encountered its ruthless, unpredictable sting.

Mari turned her head away and avoided eye contact.

I hope you make it, Mari had said to her at the Ration quarters. Had she meant it back then? Or was she on Hista's side all this time? And what about Leelin? Lords, was *Mari* the reason he was being tortured?

Hista nodded. "Yes, I agree he's the key. But if all else fails, they may be helpful in loosening her lips." The words bounced off her tongue in playful over-clarity. Hista smiled again, if she had ever stopped. "Guards?" She called, and five large men stepped forward after a long moment. They had been concealing themselves in the shadows, unseen until the moment of Hista's choosing.

Time slowed to a crawl as she ran through her options, which were distressingly few. They could turn around and run back the way they came, toward the social hall–but Milo and Jace weren't Runners, and the guards were likely trained to be swift. She didn't even know if *she* could outrun them anymore.

The guards crept forward, stepping in front of Hista, the combination of tight beige jumpsuits and odd, jet-black face masks making them appear headless.

Think think think–

To her right– between two houses, there was an alley that led back toward the Lek: not an option, as the Lek was crawling with guards of its own. Backward–the social hall, which had no means of egress excepting the main door. If they went inside, they would be trapped. They could potentially run around it and try to hide in the neighborhood beyond. Not a horrible option, though it was only a quick fix, and relied on everyone being able to run quickly enough to outpace their pursuers. She turned her head slightly to glance behind her, and her stomach dropped at the sight of a retinue of headless guards spanning the road, blocking the way they'd come. Caging them in from the back. *Fuck. Ok, other options.* Forward? Between them and the open desert beyond stood Hista and more guards. Surely, escaping into the open would be a poor decision regardless. Left–

Milo's house. Milo's house stood to their left, a mere fifteen or twenty feet away. But what, then? They could run in, and barricade themselves against the guards for a while, but the headless men would break through in mere minutes and they'd be in the same situation: moments away from capture. Was there a back door in Milo's house? She tried to think, tried to picture it. If only they could lose them in there somehow, but then Leelin would still be in Hista's clutches.

Suddenly and without any conscious effort, a stupid, ridiculous plan popped into the front of her mind, fully formed and ready. It wouldn't work, surely. But what else was there? She felt sick and tired and scared and she just wanted this to all be her first bad dream—

Focus. You can save them. You can save them all, if you play this right.

And so, going against every screaming instinct she had to devolve into a hopeless mess, she whispered to Milo.

"I can get us out of here, but you need to trust me, and we have no time to waste arguing. When I say, I need everyone to run into your house and barricade the door as best you can. I need all the time you can give me once we're in there. Can you do that?"

He was quiet for a moment, and then his broken voice was near her ear, "Leelin—"

"I can get him, too. We're out of time. Are you in?" She turned her face to look at him, and his brows were, for once, not furrowed. He seemed...broken. Which just looked *wrong* on him. He was the one who always knew what to do. But whatever he saw in her face with those red-flecked eyes, it must have given him some measure of hope, because his brow furrowed and he nodded, turning to tell the others while Ereta distracted Hista.

She looked at the woman whose face had long hid in the shadows of her mind, always telling her she wasn't good enough. Wasn't strong enough. Wasn't worth the people and things she had in her life. But staring at her now, the woman coated in blood and looking so Lords-damn bitter—as if she had been shaped by pain and nurtured by cruelty into a being of pure nightmares, Ereta felt no self-consciousness. It was with stunning clarity that she realized Hista's ire was born of something inside of *her*, and Ereta, rather than being the cause of that ire, was just an outlet for it. Maybe without that outlet, the hatred would build and build until it consumed the woman from the inside out. Maybe it already had. Either way, it wasn't Ereta's fault. It wasn't her responsibility. Just as Hista could choose to be hateful, Ereta could choose not to give a fuck.

With a sense of liberation at the realization, she let go of the fear she held of Hista's words. How could she be afraid of mere sentiment when her friend's blood was likely drenching Hista's clothes? Leelin was in danger. Leelin was *hurt*. And nothing Hista could say, no cruel-intentioned barb about her worthlessness, could shatter Ereta thoroughly enough that she wouldn't try to save him.

But *her* words, perhaps, could do some damage–especially if they were unexpected. Unprecedented.

"I've always hated you, and up until now, I thought it was because I was jealous, or because you spoke cruel truths that I didn't want to hear," Ereta told the woman, searching for words that would rile Hista's anger to the edge of distraction. "But *look at you*. You're rotten from the inside out. And I don't feel hate for you; I feel pity. I think it has been pity I felt all along. Pity that you live without compassion, without real love. You're a hateful bitch, and I feel sorry for you." And to Ereta's shock, that was true.

"How *dare*–"

"NOW!" she screamed, and they were running, a tight unit of bodies moving in unison to Milo's door. After what felt like the longest five seconds of her life, they were through, and Kilas slammed himself against the door, looking at her with fervent intensity.

"You'd better know what you're doing, because if *this* is the whole plan, all you did was buy us an extra two minutes of freedom. If that."

She nodded. "I need as much time as you can give me. *Please.*" Milo was flinging his important and useful things toward the door. The way he heaved massive stones over his shoulders made them seem like the weightless balls of crumpled paper strewn about the room. Jace stood nearby, impassive and not at all helpful, save for the shoulder she leant to supporting Chegg. He was still very, very out of it, and Ereta felt a twinge of relief that they hadn't attempted an escape that required more running. He wouldn't have made it.

She went to the far corner of the main room and knelt in front of the prisms. She wasn't sure if she could muster the calm she needed in order to summon the fissure, but surely, being in front of the objects that had made her tear with awe could only help–even if they now swayed black and colorless in the night.

She took a deep breath and closed her eyes, frantically searching for the slightest twinge of that encompassing warmth. But the panic had coated every inch of her body, inside and out, with a seemingly impermeable tension. Every muscle was taught, every sense over-sensitive, every dread preemptively activated.

You can't save them, her thoughts worried. *You can't even save yourself.*

She tried for a deep breath, but it caught in her throat as if her lungs were filled with dust. She silently loosed a wrenching sob, grateful that her face was away from her friends, who were noisily shoving things against the door as guards furiously beat against it. Glass shattered. Indiscernible yells of impatient demand echoed in her head. *I can't do this I can't I can't I can't–*

A hand touched her shoulder and she whipped her head up, eyes wide, to see Chegg's face looking down at her with a solemn smile.

"The small and pretty things are the most dangerous of all," he told her with a firm squeeze of her shoulder, his words still slurring a bit, "'cause no one ever sees 'em comin.'"

Tears welled in her eyes, and she nodded, letting her eyelids slide closed once again. The movement pushed a swell of tears past her lashes, and she felt the gentle, cool slide of it falling down her cheek. She breathed, and it came easier now–deeper. She thought about her dreams. She thought about the warmth in her soul when she crossed the fissure into the snow planet. She thought about Ima calling her

'Tiny', about skis and cold Water so abundant that the combustion of thousands of Leks wouldn't equal it. She thought about Leelin, and Jace, and Chegg, and Milo, and–

"What the fuck?!" Jace screamed, which was so completely unnatural to hear that Ereta had almost not recognized her friend's voice. But she held the connection, felt the tug against her eyes and willed it to strengthen and hold. She kept her eyes closed even as she felt the blow of cold, moist air against her skin. "Go," she told them, her voice loud but steady.

Milo's voice came from just beside her, "What is–"

"It's safe. Just *please*, go, I can't hold it much longer. Please."

She heard the shuffle of feet behind her, and then in front of her.

"What the fuck is that?" Kilas asked with frantic intensity.

"If you don't want to be captured, you need to trust me and go inside. It's safe, I promise. I've been there many times."

"*Many times?*" Jace questioned with scornful incredulity.

"You heard her. Let's go. They're almost through," Milo ordered, and indeed, she could hear the creak of the door beginning to open against the weight of the blockade.

Another shuffle of feet, and utterly terrified screams echoed out from her friends.

"What is it? Oh *Lords*, what is it?!" Jace cried out.

"This can't be real. This is a dream," Kilas whispered with more voice than he likely intended.

Milo and Chegg were quiet, but their breaths came so quickly that she could hear them both from several feet away. Then, Chegg spoke in his usual, casual tone, "You weren't exaggeratin', boss. I never saw *this* shit comin'."

O nce her friends were safely through the air fissure, Ereta stood and walked through, letting the tether go slack and the rip in worlds close behind her. Their breaths came heavy in the frigid air. Snows drifted from the sky, swirling in little white dots.

"Is it dangerous?" Jace asked, looking up and pointlessly attempting to dodge the individual snows as they fell toward her. Her feet shifted, crunching through a thick layer of powdery snow, and she loosed a yelp.

Ereta opened her mouth to answer–

"It's Water," Milo whispered. "It's fucking *Water.*" She supposed that she shouldn't be surprised that Milo had figured that out in just a few seconds, but still, it caught her off-guard to hear it confirmed by another person from her dry, desolate planet. *Yes, we who have toiled in grueling Duty all our lives to help create Water are now surrounded by more of it than we could drink in 100 lifetimes.*

"The Crown Lord's *shit* it's Water," scoffed Kilas.

"I ain't never seen Water look like this, boss–"

"He's right," Ereta interrupted with a confident authority of unknown origin. "It's cold Water. It's called *snow,* or so I've been told. And I know you have a lot of questions, and I promise that I will answer all that I can, but right now, we need to focus on saving Leelin."

Milo nodded, looking around with an awed fascination, his lips parted and his brow furrowed; and those deep brown eyes alight with burning embers that seemed frantic to process all of the implications of what they observed. "How are we going to do that?" he asked without pausing his observations.

"The same way we got here. I have to open another fissure." They all turned to look at her in blatant confusion. "An air fissure," she amended. "That's what I've been calling it."

"Cold burn me, Ereta, how long have you known about this?" Jace asked.

"*Later,*" Milo tutted at her. "The guards will be searching my house for a few minutes. We need to get to Leelin while they're distracted."

"Exactly. So..." she turned in a circle, attempting to orient herself.

"It would be ideal to open the...*air fissure* directly into Leelin's house," Milo mused, his familiar confident decision-making returning all at once. "Do you have any way of controlling where they open to on Veirbos?"

"We're not on Veirbos?" Jace squealed.

"*For the Lords' sake*, woman, get ahold of yourself," Kilas hissed at her. "What happened to the haughty bitch who couldn't be bothered to raise an eyebrow while I was beaten to a pulp?"

Ereta attempted to focus through the panic and fear and confusion that seemed to thicken the air around their group. "No, I don't think we're on Veirbos. And yes, I can control where they open. The direction and distance seems to be the same across both planets. So, if I walk five feet north here and open a new fissure, it will open—"

"Five feet North in Veirbos. That's fortunate. Really, *really* fortunate, and very unlikely in a way that raises a lot of questions. But for now, it's mostly just fortunate." Milo was nodding, encouraged by the news. "So we entered this way, facing South-East," he turned his body to face the direction in which they'd entered. "So we'll need to go about...I want to say 20 feet or so to the North-West to end up in the middle of Leelin's house." Ereta nodded and was thankful that he'd figured it out for her; thankful she wasn't alone in this anymore, and she wondered why she hadn't just told them from the start. Fear? But of what? *Rejection, denial, loneliness—*

She stopped her thoughts cold and began to follow behind Milo, who was already pacing North-West. He stopped firmly in the snow after a few moments, and seemed to be momentarily distracted by the crunch of his treads passing through it up to just below his knees.

He was muttering to himself, *"...significant compression, so it must be mostly air–"*

Ereta snapped in his face. "Focus, science boy. *Leelin.*"

Chegg snorted. "Science boy. I like that one, boss."

Milo's brow twitched before he shook his head and found focus. "Right here should be good," he said with confidence. "Right next to his bed. But we don't know what condition he'll be in, so we should really be prepared to find anything."

"He'll be ok," Ereta replied with a confidence that she didn't feel as she dropped to her knees and began focusing on Veirbos. Because he *had* to be ok. She couldn't consider any alternative.

"When you get it open, I'll go in and get him." He snapped at Kilas. "Come with me, he might need to be carried and it'll be quicker with the two of us. Chegg, how out of it are you?"

"Pretty out of it, boss."

"Are you sober enough to throw a decent punch?"

Chegg snorted again, but it gurgled, wet in his throat. "Punchin' ain't got nothin' to do with being sober. Well, maybe it does, I s'pose. The more fucked up ya get, the punchin' gets *easier.*" He cracked his thick knuckles and stumbled over to the group.

"Great. When we open it, you'll act as our guard while we get Leelin through. Punch anyone who tries to follow us. Knock them out, if possible. Once Leelin's secure, we'll come back through and fight them off with you until we can all escape. Do not, *under any circumstances*, allow them to cross the fissure. Keeping them out of this world will be far, far easier than getting them back out."

Milo kept giving directions and fastidiously planning for any complications in their plan as Ereta narrowed her focus on opening the fissure. It came fairly easily this time, and she knew it had worked when the smell of iron swam suddenly in her nose.

"Fuckin' Lords," Chegg whispered.

"Go! Go!" Milo's yell was cracking with emotion. She opened her eyes.

He's dead, she thought, the realization coming to her with clarity and *relief,* despite herself. Because to live with such injuries, that would be the *true* tragedy–

Then she heard Leelin's soft moan–saw his chest rise and fall once in a broken stutter–

"Holy Lords," she echoed in a whisper. She didn't remember crossing the fissure, but suddenly she was there, kneeling at Leelin's side, tears streaming down her face, her hands covered in a thick layer of his blood. "Leelin," she pleaded, her eyes clouding, "you're going to be ok."

"*E–Ereta,*" he murmured. "I'm so sorry."

"*Oh,* my heart, you have nothing to apologize for. *Nothing,*" she told him in a breaking, shaking voice as she soothingly stroked his blood-drenched hair.

"Ereta," Milo said from beside her. "We have to move him. Now." She nodded, tears dropping from her cheeks and landing in one of the cuts on Leelin's bare chest, but he didn't react. He was spread across the floor in a dark pool of blood. All over his body, strips of skin had been peeled away and tossed aside to lay beside him on the floor. Blood poured from the long, shallow wounds. There were so many she couldn't count. Twenty? Thirty? More? Hista must have just started on his face before they interrupted her, because there, running down his cheek, was one single strip of ripped flesh. The length of it was still attached to his skin, dangling grotesquely across his neck like a piece of thick, wet cloth. Her friend had been peeled apart, strip by agonizing strip, and it was the worst sight she had ever beheld.

There was a crash as the guards burst into the door. Leelin was in Kilas and Milo's arms, his mouth agape and eyes closed. He looked dead, just as she had thought he was when she first laid eyes on his mangled body. But his chest still rose and fell, however weakly. "Run," she encouraged, and whipped around to face the guards. There was one already towering over her, his arms out as if to grab her. But in a flash of white skin, the guard fell away, and Chegg stood there shaking his fist.

"Fuckers' heads are thicker than steel," he murmured. "Harder, too."

He turned again to punch out another guard, but his blow missed the man by inches and the force of it sent him stumbling to his hands and knees. In a flash, Kilas was beside her and Chegg, and then he was kicking and punching, which Ereta did her best to emulate as guards swarmed them. *So many guards.* They flowed in through the doorway in apparently endless supply beyond their original five pursuers. Milo joined them then, and leaned to mutter to her, "He doesn't have a lot of time. We need to get out of here. *Now.* All of us." He punched a short, stocky guard in the stomach and sent him sprawling into the puddle of blood. It splashed high into the air and fell back down to splatter over the man's crumpled body, giving the appearance that he had been the one bleeding. But no. *Leelin's blood. All of it.*

Ereta nodded, and began to back up toward the fissure, the other three men wordlessly taking her cue. The fissure was still open–she could still feel it. The effort to keep it there was as easy as breathing, and she wasn't sure why. *Maybe because your best friend is dying on the other side.*

Hista burst in with the newest cluster of guards, and blinked at the gaping fissure that they were retreating toward.

"They're trying to escape, you idiots! Go into their...hatch! Their escape hatch! Go into it!" The woman sounded utterly unhinged with fury and frustration and maybe even desperation. Apparently determined to do it herself because the guards were too slow, Hista's long, graceful legs bounded toward Ereta and consumed the distance between them in three effortless strides. Ereta didn't think; she pulled back her arm, looked at Hista's ire-laden, beautiful face–the face that had haunted her, held her captive at its mercy, stared at her and watched with delight as her heart had broken, the face that had beheld Leelin and probably fucking smiled as she peeled his fucking skin–

Her fist flew, and Hista was on the ground, her lip welling and a heavy drop of blood cresting–she blinked in confusion and maybe a little awe. *Did I do that?*

And then, Milo was pulling her backward, punching guards as they went, until she found herself shoved through in the fissure. Milo stood by its entrance with Chegg, both of them punching through it and wrestling guards out of the portal. "Close it, Ereta!" Milo bellowed. "You have to close it *now*!"

She blinked herself back into focus, and visualized the tug going slack–

Milo threw his outstretched arm against Chegg's chest–pushing them both backward as the portal slammed shut.

With all of the guards still on the other side.

Chapter 19

The snow reminded her of Ima.

Specifically, the snow reminded her of Ima's clothes, because it was the same color: a dark, thick–but somehow still bright–red.

Leelin's chest still rose and fell weakly, but at least he was alive. At least he was here. But was *here,* on another planet, lying outside in the snow completely naked, really the best place for him?

"Ereta!" Milo called to her, trying to get her attention while she stared numbly at the blood still oozing from Leelin's stripped skin. "We need to go back!" He was shaking her by the shoulders, but she couldn't tear her gaze away, because Leelin's skin was no longer the warm, dark brown she knew so well; it was gray and looked like Lords-damn *death* taken human form–

"Look at me," Milo whispered. He leaned forward until his forehead was against hers, and his face filled her vision completely, and his hands were gripping her shoulders and probably keeping her from floating away with the snows, and his eyes–

She took a deep breath and tried to focus on the tiny flecks of red that had always both scared and intrigued her. A different red than the blood. *Burning embers. Hot coals.*

"You're a survivor, Ereta," Milo told her with a smooth gentleness that wasn't quite a whisper, "and so is Leelin. But we have to act *now*, before it's too late to help him. Time is the most valuable resource we have. We can't afford to waste it."

She nodded against his forehead, focusing on the warmth of contact where his skin met hers. They were both sweating despite the cold, their hot skin slick against the cool air. "What do we need to do?" she asked him. She tried to fall into a space of calm obedience. Her part of the plan had worked, at least for now. But Milo was here, and he *always* knew what to do. She told herself that Leelin would live if she could just calm down enough to listen to Milo's instructions. Unsurprisingly, that thought didn't do much to calm her.

"We need to get back into my house," he told her. His breath was a warm reprieve from the assault of cold air. "I need supplies." She nodded and pulled away to numbly follow their tracks back to where she had opened the first fissure. Milo followed as she knelt in the snow. "Chegg! Kilas! Here, now," Milo ordered. "Jace, I need you to keep pressure on the wounds. Just keep holding that shirt over the cuts on his legs. They're the ones I'm most concerned about." Ereta chanced a glance back toward Leelin, and noticed that he was covered in bloodied shirts and coats. Her gaze returned to the three men, now awaiting her fissure, to find they had all stripped down to their underthings. If she had felt less terrified, the sight might have been a significant distraction. But she let her eyes close, and soon, the fissure was open again. The three men raced through, and a few long minutes later they were back, arms laden with bulks of clothing and fists gripping all manner of random objects. They all rushed back in again, and came out again with another armload of important and useful things.

Milo was the last one through. "No guards, thank the fucking Lords," he grumbled, and nodded at her. Even without words, she knew what the nod meant, and she let the fissure slide closed.

He hurried over to Leelin and began arranging things around himself as he spoke to his friend, "Hey, brother, you really outdid yourself with the dramatics this time," Milo shifted slightly and punched down snow in a wide circle around Leelin.

Leelin's eyes fluttered open, and his gaze locked with Milo's. His normally mischievous sage eyes were dull and tinged a sickly yellow. Her best friend smiled up at Milo, and ground out a breathy, stuttering response, "Y-you were r-right...my c-cock doesn't know w-what's g-good f-for it."

Milo spared a brief glance downward. "Well, your cock seems to be one of the only parts of your body she didn't skin like a bamboo stalk. You're a lucky fucker."

Leelin grinned a bit wider, but didn't find the energy to chirp out a full response. His voice faded and his eyes fluttered closed after a tense, weak, "Y-y-yeahhh."

Milo finished punching the snow down and began giving orders as he hastily pulled on a fresh set of clothes, the others following his example. "Chegg and Kilas, I need you to lift him while Ereta and I lay out a blanket. Jace, just keep putting pressure on his wounds as best you can." By the time he had finished speaking, Leelin's body had been hoisted into the air, and Ereta was smoothing out a wrinkled blanket to cover the circle. "Ok, put him back down," Milo instructed.

Kilas looked even paler than usual, but his face remained an unreadable mask of neutrality. Jace was kneeling in the snow, similarly pale, features twisted into disbelief, holding a mess of bloody cloth loosely in her hands, and silent with what might have been shock. "Pressure, Jace," Milo encouraged, but Jace stayed unmoving and maybe even unseeing. Ereta rushed over to her in a sudden burst of fervent desperation. She gently, but not too gently, clapped her hands onto Jace's shoulders. "Hey!" she yelled and shook her roughly. "Get it together. Listen to Milo. This is no time for you to lose your composure. You've never fucking lost it before. *Get it together*," she repeated. Jace blinked, shook her head slightly, and nodded in affirmation. "Pressure on the wounds," Ereta ordered, and hurried back to Milo's side, where he was hurriedly piling snow into a metal bucket. "What do you need?"

He reached to the side and grabbed a small flint and a container of what looked like oil. "Pile snow into this bucket and use this to melt it," he told her while extending the supplies. She took them, and Milo turned his attention to Leelin's wounds. He pulled out a needle, threaded it with a thin string, and started rushedly stitching one of the wounds on Leelin's leg while she finished gathering snow. She nearly lit the small jar of oil directly, but ultimately chose to rip her hood out of her pocket and soak it in the oil. She placed the bundle in the snow outside the circle and struck the flint. The fire took off quickly, but almost immediately reduced from a violent flare to a steady burn. She grabbed the bucket and held it over the fire. But that wasn't working, because her hand was *burning*–

She pulled the bucket back, hastily looked around until she found a long metal rod, and used that to suspend the bucket over the fire from a safe distance.

"Get it boiling–that's when you see bubbles rising from it. Let me know when," he told her over his shoulder, his hands stitching as fast as they could, Leelin's blood still pouring out of his wounds. "I won't be able to close them before he bleeds out," Milo said under his breath. Ereta kept holding the bucket aloft and tried not to process his words. "Chegg!"

"Boss?"

"Get every metal thing we have and heat the fuck out if it in Ereta's fire. While you're at it, gather anything that might burn–except for cloth–and bring it over to the fire so we can keep it going. Kilas, come help Jace put pressure on the wounds." Kilas had been tending the small fire by poking it with a rapidly singing bamboo rod, but he walked over at Milo's command, despite his usual resistance to obeying orders. If her best friend weren't dying, watching both Kilas and Jace be submissive might have been bizarre, if not entertaining. Maybe her and Milo could have watched and taken notes, like one of his experiments. *The effects of trauma on stubborn people's stubbornness,* they would call it. She shook her head. *Lords, I'm losing my mind.*

Kilas ripped fabric from discarded pieces of clothing and held the bundled cloth with firm hands over Leelin's pouring wounds. From the corner of her eye, Ereta saw his wince as he pressed on a particularly deep wound at Leelin's thigh.

Ereta yelped in surprise when the clang of metal tumbling into her fire rang out. "Sorry, 'Reta. Didn't mean to scare ya."

She nodded, watching the metal poles and hammers and bowls begin to shine with intense heat; the thinnest objects turned a bright, gleaming red almost instantly, and Ereta couldn't help a passing thought that it was the same red as Milo's eyes. *Not blood. Nothing like blood.*

"Anything that's glowing red, bring it to me. With something wrapped around it. Rubber! Wrap rubber around it," Milo ordered from his place at Leelin's side, where he was still frantically stitching.

Chegg strode off and returned a few moments later with a long strip of bamboo rubber. It took her an embarrassingly long moment to recognize it as an old, cut up Running tread. Chegg used the rubber to take firm grip of a slim iron pole, pulling it out of the fire and rushing over to Milo.

"Give it to me, carefully please," Milo ordered. It took another embarrassingly long moment for her to realize what he intended to do–

"*No!* You can't! You'll hurt him!" she cried, nearly dropping the bucket. His head whipped toward her.

"*Do not let that bucket spill,*" he ordered her through gritted teeth. "And yes, it will hurt him," his head turned back toward their friend. "But he won't die." Without hesitation, Milo pushed the iron rod steadily against Leelin's wound. Leelin's answering scream was as heartbreaking as it was earsplitting. "I'm sorry, brother," Milo choked. The scream split her head open and emptied it of everything but despair. It was a sound of such pain, such misery–she wanted nothing more in that moment than to trade places with him. To take it away. Smoke billowed up from Leelin's seared flesh in repugnant tendrils. The smell hit Ereta a moment later, and once it had, she was sure it would never leave her again: the scent of his burning flesh leaving its brand on her heart. On her *soul*.

Milo raised the bar and touched a different, still-red length of it to another wound. Leelin's scream rose anew between throaty sobs. It was pure, raw anguish. He passed out after a few moments, leaving a haunting silence in his wake. "Thank the Lords," Milo said to no one in a voice heavy with emotion.

Ereta couldn't tear her eyes away. "The Water, is it boiling?" Milo asked her in a slightly cracked voice as he set the rod aside and rose to fetch another. He grabbed a thicker pole out of the fire with the shredded scrap of rubber tread and peered over the bucket, nodding at the bubbles just barely dancing at its surface. The sight might have shocked Ereta, if she weren't already shocked in far more urgent ways. "Good enough. Bring it over. And find something...a tube. A thin tube. And a funnel."

"A what?"

"Never mind, actually, I'll find those supplies, I need very specific things. For now– Chegg!" Chegg hurried over instantly. "Take the bucket and put it in deep snow so that it cools. Ereta, you can do this part," he said confidently, holding out his hand to pass her the red-hot iron rod as Chegg took possession of the bucket from her trembling hands.

She balked. "I *can't*–" Lords, she sounded and felt pathetic. But there was absolutely *no way* she could–

"You can and you will. Time is everything. Do it now." He pushed his outstretched hand a smidge closer to her, and she raised a still-shaking arm to grasp an open stretch of rubber. He let his hand drop and nodded. "Good. Focus on the leg wounds first, then chest. Switch to a new implement when the red glow fades." He continued instructing her as he hurried about, gathering supplies. "Hold it so that it covers the open skin. Horizontal is best for the most coverage. Do multiple passes on a wound if necessary. Your goal is to stop the bleeding. Yes?"

"Yes," she affirmed in a breaking voice, but she was kneeling next to Leelin now, and the blood was sliding down his skin in a steady flow not unlike Water pouring from a tipped canteen. *Too fast.* She couldn't afford to delay; she focused on a particularly large cut along his upper thigh and, with a sharp intake of breath, pressed the rod against Leelin's skin.

The smoke rose once again, and the smell flooded her nostrils instantly. It smelled sweet and slightly rotted, like hot fucking *death*.

Mercifully, Leelin remained unconscious, although without his open eyes or piercing screams, it was harder to tell that he was alive at all. He could be slipping closer to his death, even now–

Focus. She raised the rod and pressed it into a different wound, inadvertently breathing in the smoke of his burning skin, while she watched for the subtle rise and fall of his chest. Again and again, she seared her friend's skin shut. She got up to retrieve a new implement, and when she returned with a large, hot bowl held by its rim, Milo was kneeling on Leelin's other side and fiddling with a thin rubber tube. He chanced a glance over the wounds Ereta had closed, but his hands never paused their machinations. "Looks good so far," he told her. "There are some bad wounds on his backside too, but let's finish up the big ones on his front and get the saline line going first."

"Saline line?" she mimicked.

"I'll explain in a moment. Where's the salt?" He looked around fervently and returned to Leelin's side a few moments later with a small jar of white crystals. He turned a large portion of the jar into the bucket–which he had, at some point, brought over from its place cooling in the snow. He seemed to think for a moment before muttering, *"Fuck,"* under his breath, rushing to his feet, grabbing another piece of rubber and then a skinny metal rod from the fire, returning, and plunging it into the Water. Smoke hissed and danced away from the liquid. He gently stirred, added more salt, stirred again, and repeated the process a few times before he nodded, apparently satisfied with what he saw within the bucket, and removed the rod. "Okay," he said to himself, or her? Or maybe no one. She had no idea what he was doing–

"Don't stop cauterizing," he instructed her.

"What?"

"The burning. Keep at it. I'm going to give him some saline." He began to fiddle with the thin rubber tube, which she noticed at a glance was now attached to a small, hollow iron needle. He seemed to ponder something for a moment before once again calling for Chegg, whom he had hold the bucket aloft while he fit a flared object–its mouth as wide as a hand on one end and its opposite tip tapered down to the size of a constricted pupil–under the bucket. The narrow end fit snugly within his rubber tube. He called for Kilas, who was ordered to hold the 'funnel' and tube in place while he gathered the needled end. He took a deep breath and began using the tips of his fingers to poke at each of Leelin's inner elbows, then his wrists, then finally his neck. On a long exhale, he pushed the needle under Leelin's skin, his other hand gently pinching the tube a few inches above.

"The Water, Chegg. Now," he ordered. With keen control, Chegg tilted the bucket over the funnel and let the Water pour down. Blood shot up the tube from Leelin's skin, stopping at the place where Milo pinched, and Ereta's breath stuttered, even as she continued cauterizing wounds.

"What are you *doing*?" She couldn't help but ask, but she supposed in hindsight that she probably *could* have helped the accusatory tone with which she asked it. The Water raced down the tube, flowing past Milo's fingers and briefly mixing with Leelin's blood before washing it back down into his body. The Water in the tube ran clear, and Chegg continued his slow, steady pour.

"So," he started, breathing easier now, "the heart pumps blood throughout the body. That's what keeps us alive. We aren't sure precisely what the blood does on the most fundamental level, but we know that if we deny any area–say, a toe–of blood for too long, it dies. So we need to keep blood flowing everywhere in the body. The problem with blood loss is primarily that there is not enough liquid for the heart to pump. That's why Leelin's heartbeat is so fast and unsteady: his heart is trying to make due with too little blood. Ideally, we would give him more blood, maybe from one of us, but such procedures are incredibly dangerous and have a high failure rate. For some reason, the blood of two individuals is not always compatible. When it is, it works really well. But I didn't think it was worth the risk to try. So we needed another way to give the heart more blood to pump, without actually giving it blood. So," he continued, shifting slightly and moving his hand to touch Leelin's pulse for a long moment, "we made something that will increase the volume of liquid in his system. It's a mix of sterile Water and salt, called *saline*, which is better for this purpose than plain Water because it's closer to the composition of our bodies. It will dilute the blood, which isn't ideal, but his heart will have more fluid to process and it will beat stronger. I'm hoping that's enough to pull him through until his blood can replenish itself."

"How in the Lords-damn *fuck* do you know all of this?" Kilas spat, ending his long tenure of silence.

Milo's eyes didn't leave Leelin, or the needle in his neck, as he shrugged. "I've gotten to help at a few infirmaries over the turns, particularly in the wake of Lek explosions, so I've seen some of these things done. I also read some interesting medical records at the Lords' City when I visited there a few turns back. This kind of science has been taking off recently. A lot of it is common sense; if you understand how the body works–or more helpfully, how it doesn't–you can make substitutions when needed to save someone's life. I'd only ever *heard* of the saline solution trick for blood loss, but I've experimented with making saline enough times that I was fairly confident I could get the proportions right, and the rest was made infinitely easier by the fact that I..." he cleared his throat, "*borrowed* some supplies from the infirmary last time I was there.'"

'The questions of science are above the laws of men,' he had told her in reference to the bamboo seeds.

"*Good Lords,* science boy, how many of your experiments are made possible by pilfered materials?" She hadn't meant to be so nonchalant in the face of their admittedly dire situation, but she was too tired—emotionally, physically, mentally—to filter her thoughts before they came flowing steadily out of her mouth. *Flowing like Leelin's blood.*

Milo thought for a long moment. His head tilted in concentration as his eyes darted back and forth over the horizon, tracking something invisible. "It would be easier to count the ones that aren't," he said matter-of-factly after a long silence, and despite herself, despite *everything,* Ereta laughed. Chegg joined in, his booming laughter a comfort to her ears. Jace was smiling, too, and even Kilas' sneer took on a more amenable quality. The corner of Milo's lip quirked up, and that familiar sight was a comfort, too, as their laughter peaked and then quieted to a steady silence.

Chapter 20

L eelin's shivering had started not too long after his wounds had all been cauterized. Luckily, the cuts on his backside hadn't been as severe or numerous as those on his front. The saline seemed to have helped, at least according to Milo, who checked the strength of Leelin's pulse almost obsessively.

But the shivering wasn't good. The dangers of hypothermia were perhaps the only medical phenomenon that Milo did *not* have to explain to their group.

Leelin was covered in clothing and blankets, but still, his body shook. He had been unconscious for over an hour now; Ereta didn't know if that was a good thing or not. Certainly, when he woke, his pain would be unimaginable. Even though she longed for his company, she found herself hoping that he would sleep through the most challenging part of his recovery.

"We need to block the wind better," she told the group as they sat huddled near Leelin, attempting and failing miserably to do just that; all of them were shivering, too. "Maybe use the snow? Build a barrier?"

"That's a really good idea," Milo answered. His usual sharpness was palpably dulled from what was likely a combination of exhaustion, shock, and worry. She was sure that each one of them shared those feelings in varying proportions, but Milo was especially ragged. He focused on little else other than watching Leelin, checking his pulse, inspecting his wounds, and repeating the process over and over and over. He would have had the idea to block the wind himself, she was sure, if he were in his right mind. "We could build up the walls and put something on top to trap the heat in."

"I'm sorry," Jace started in that familiar way that indicated she was certainly *not* sorry, and indeed, was about to point out something that she thought should be obvious to the others, "but are we planning to live out here indefinitely? Shouldn't we be–I don't know–trying to figure out how we're going to get home?"

"Have you been paying attention at all? We're not going home," Kilas spat, but his usual coldness was tempered by exhaustion.

Jace scoffed. "Of course we are. Don't be ridiculous."

Kilas shot to his feet and whipped his arms out to gesture at the expanse of snow that surrounded them. "Look around you, princess! We're treating fuck-face's wounds in the middle of nowhere! Don't you think we would have gone back to–*I don't know*–the infirmary, or one of our Lords-damn *houses*, if we could? We're here because we *can't* go home!" As quickly as he had stood, he then plopped back down into the tamped-down circle of snow. His legs pulled up toward his chest, arms resting across his knees in a defeated sort of way, and his unfocused gaze dropped to Leelin's shivering body.

Jace's lips became a thin line as she pressed them together. After a tense moment, she spoke, "So, what? We're going to just make 'new lives' out here in this stupid circle? What about nutrition allotments? What about all of our stuff? You can't seriously think we can survive out here–"

"I reckon it's not as bad as that," Chegg chimed in with unsettling levity. "Seems to me we lucked out. No more Duty, no more worryin' about Water. And we have science boy here," Chegg amiably cuffed Milo's shoulder, "with that brain of his, and 'Reta's pure grit, they'll turn this empty circle into a settlement bigger than home in a fuckin' quarter!"

Ereta's exhaustion had reduced her to an impassive eavesdropper in this conversation, but at the mention of a settlement, she perked up enough to interject. "There's a settlement here. From my house, it's about four miles. From yours, which is where we are–but on this planet, I mean–that would be three miles or so north and slightly east."

They all stared at her for a long, quiet stretch before Jace spoke, "Wait, are you saying there's a settlement *here?* On this...place?" Ereta nodded. "I'm sorry, but you're just telling us this *now?*" she asked with gritted teeth. "What the *fuck*, Ereta? We could have gone there to begin with!"

"*Hey.*" Milo's tone was tense. "Ease up. We couldn't have. You've walked through this shit, or tried, at least," he gestured to the snow around them. "It's up to our fucking knees. There's no way we could have walked there in time to save Leelin. We probably can't walk there now, at least not..." he trailed off, and his furrowed brows pinched further as he turned to look at Ereta. "You've been using Veirbos as a means to travel longer distances here, haven't you?"

She nodded. *Lords*, she could have saved so much time figuring all of this snow planet shit out if she had told Milo to begin with. In minutes, he had reached conclusions that had taken her hours of trial-and-error to parse out. "But that didn't seem like an option while we were being pursued like so many Duty-dodgers. We would have had to walk right through the middle of the settlement."

He nodded in turn. "No, that wouldn't have been an option. Honestly, it's not really an option now. We need to let the dust settle," he huffed a humorless laugh at his turn of phrase, "and focus on making this place hospitable until we can figure out a safe way to travel. We're cold, and exhausted. We need to warm up, rest, and regroup afterward." He clapped his hands together and stood. "Ok, so we're building walls out of snow. I'm thinking...shoulder height? My shoulder height," he specified, since taking the measure of any one of their group's shoulders would yield dramatically different results.

They toiled steadily despite their exhaustion. The tamping down of the snow, the shaping of the walls, all of it became more intuitive as they went. The snow behaved nothing at all like dust. It stuck to itself, and compacted into a useful rigidity with very slight pressure. They scooped snow up from the expanse around them and piled it higher and higher until they had what looked like walls. Everyone labored in heavy silence, shoring the walls and occasionally gathering armfuls of fresh snow to add to their height. Milo, for his part, had taken on one small section of wall and turned it into a small snow-tunnel so that they could enter and exit the structure without opening it up to the elements. Ereta had to stifle a giggle as she watched him finish up, because the way his body was shoved inside the small tunnel while he worked was a near-perfect reminiscence of how he had looked laying in that pipe yesterday.

She glanced around, noting the rest of their group distracted by their own tasks. Idly pondering if she was delirious with exhaustion, she quietly slipped inside the other end of the tunnel, crawling forward slightly until she was only a foot away from Milo's prone form.

"*Pssst,*" she whispered. "*Pssssssssssst, Milo?*"

He tilted his neck back and to the side until he could see her. The little crease in between his eyes was deep with confusion. "What are you doing?"

She cleared her throat and spoke in a full voice, "You tend to startle when caught unawares in pipes. I'm not confident this tunnel would survive the impact of your head." She turned onto her back and laid down in the packed snow, and stared wide-eyed and nearly delirious with exhaustion at the tunnel above her. The darkness made the snow appear gray, and despite the otherwise pitch dark, the white powder seemed to cast its own glow of light. She interlaced her hands over her stomach and sighed.

"*One time*, I hit my head. That's not a tendency." His hands resumed their machinations, patting at the snow above him with delicate precision.

She smiled just slightly to herself. "So, I want to fill you in on everything I know, and see if we can figure out a way to get Leelin what he needs without being captured by Hista."

"Hista," he repeated thoughtfully. "The Ration officer?"

She nodded, but realized he couldn't see her, and aloud, confirmed, "Yes."

He pressed some loose snow into a crack in the ceiling of the tunnel. "Some of the things you said to her seemed very...personal."

She briefly debated pretending that she was oblivious to the implied question in his statement and moving on, but she didn't think she could fool him, and wasn't totally sure that she wanted to.

She took another sigh. "There is a history between me and Hista. Maybe I'll tell you the whole miserable tale someday, but I would prefer that not be today." Her heart began to race as her thoughts brushed against the edges of unpleasant memories that she *really* didn't think she had the emotional energy to examine, despite having made rather massive strides that day with her attitude toward Hista's torment.

She paused and he was quiet, continuing to smooth little handfuls of snow into cracks and crevices. She took a deep breath and attempted to calm herself before speaking again, more quietly, "But I'll tell you this: if I had nightmares, she would be the object of them."

She heard him move against the snow, but couldn't tell if he was nodding his head or simply fidgeting around. "I *would* say something about the fact that people who use fear as a weapon are usually compensating for their own weaknesses, but you'd probably accuse me of pontificating, and I would prefer to not hear that today."

She snorted a laugh. "Noted."

They lay there, scalp-to-scalp, in comfortable silence as Ereta pitched in to help Milo shore up the tunnel with handfuls of snow.

"Will he be ok?" She broke the long silence with a whisper and was abruptly overcome with terrified anticipation of his answer, which she knew would be unflinchingly honest.

"I don't know," he answered after a moment. His voice was characteristically serious, but tinged with a deep sadness that they clearly shared at seeing their friend so gruesomely injured. "We did the best we could. But it's hard to tell if it will be enough. He lost so much blood. And even the smallest of wounds has the potential to turn fetid. If one of them does, it could poison his blood. He needs the infirmary. He needs the wounds cleaned, and I don't have the resources to do that here—"

"We're going to get him help, Milo," Ereta interrupted. She was surprised at her own confidence in that truth. Because it *was* the truth. They would get him help, no matter what. She tried not to think about the fact that *she* had been the uncertain one asking for reassurance just a moment before. Milo's fear had strengthened her, pushing her seamlessly into a role of calm authority. "He's going to be alright. He has to be."

Milo was silent for a stretch before his solemn whisper broke the silence again, "I did the best I could."

Her heart ached and tears welled behind her eyes. She stared at the ceiling of the snow tunnel. It felt like its own little world, separate from the grim reality of Leelin's battered body just outside. But certainly, without Milo, her friend would be dead. "I know you did. And you will keep doing your best, and he will be ok. You won't let him die."

He huffed. "You sound awfully sure."

She huffed back, and hers was almost a grim laugh. "Fire does not burn cold."

"**I** hate this," Jace lamented for what Ereta was positive was the billionth time. "I'm not made for the cold."

"It's no colder than Veirbos," Ereta assured her. *Again.*

"I don't like it there, either. And that can't possibly be true, besides."

"I think it just feels colder because of the wet."

"I'm not made for the wet either."

"Will you *shut up?*" Kilas hissed from several paces ahead. Apparently, his attempt to distance himself from Jace's complaining wasn't working as he'd hoped.

Jace stuck her tongue out at Kilas' back, but (predictably) continued complaining to Ereta, her voice raised so she could be heard over the crunching of the snow beneath their feet. "I just wish you had found a warm planet instead."

"Well, I didn't really get a choice."

Jace humphed as if to imply that she didn't necessarily believe that.

Step after step, they trudged endlessly through the knee-deep snow. It was exhausting, and nearly impossible to keep track of their distance as time slipped away and their pace remained agonizingly slow. The worst part, though, was the utter lack of landmarks. All around them, an endless expanse of white snow stretched to the distant horizon, from which the morning sun had almost fully emerged. She only had the indentations of their footsteps behind them to assure her they were making progress; it didn't do much to ease the persistent, nagging feeling that they weren't *really* going anywhere at all.

They had only been walking for thirty minutes, but her exhaustion was that of a far greater distance. But that could be in part due to the fact that she hadn't slept well, despite her attempts. They had taken two or three hours (honestly, she had lost count) to make their snow shelter before they settled down to sleep in the sparse time before dawn. She had curled her body around Leelin's unconscious form, clinging to him with her ear pressed to his too-fast heart. The others had slept close, too. It had been surprisingly warm. The walls of their snow-structure kept the frigid wind at bay, the sheets and blankets tossed over its walls formed a ceiling that trapped their sparse body heat inside as they huddled together under piles of more sheets and blankets and unused clothes.

No, her fitful sleep had not been due to cold, but due to the paranoia that every time she drifted off, she could hear Leelin's heartbeat fading. She had held him through the few hours that separated them from first light, with Jace at her back, Milo at Leelin's other side, Kilas next to him, and Chegg stretched stomach-down across Leelin's outstretched legs. The lot of them seemed to sleep through her many frantic awakenings; she would jolt into consciousness, terrified that Leelin was dead, and his heart would respond: *tha-thump tha-thump tha-thump,* and she would try to return to sleep.

She probably hadn't slept a full hour in total by the time the dawn's yellow-tinged sun had brightened their camp and she, Jace, and Kilas readied themselves to leave.

She thought of the soft kisses she had given Leelin: one on his lips, and one on his forehead. '*I'll be back for you, my heart,*' she had whispered before turning to leave him behind. At least Milo was with him, with Chegg there to offer his usual enthusiastic assistance. She trusted that Milo's inventive medical interventions and experiments were Leelin's best chance at staying alive while the rest of them sought assistance in Brafta. She hoped they would only be gone for the day, but in case it took longer, she was glad they had put in the effort to make a warm shelter for Leelin.

"It's probably been a mile, right?" Jace interrupted the silence and Ereta's wandering thoughts.

Kilas scoffed. "Not even close, princess."

It wasn't until nearly an hour later that she and Kilas were reasonably confident they had gone a mile. She knelt in the snow and thought of Veirbos. It took a bit longer to conjure the fissure, probably because most of the people she cared about were on the snow planet, and she didn't want to bring the one who *wasn't* into this mess until the danger was long passed. A minute later, she was relieved to open her eyes and find the portal looking upon the open desert. The group cautiously stepped through, and found the shadows cast by Tubat-So's Water tower a safe distance behind them. The orange sun of her home planet cast everything in a dim glow that felt strangely dreary after spending time under the snow planet's golden light. But at least Veirbos would offer a reprieve from Jace's complaints about the yellow sun being *"too Lords-damn bright."*

Ereta hurried them over to a nearby pipe on the Water network to better camouflage themselves in its shadow as they walked. She knew most of the way by heart already; the most pressing issue she currently faced was how she would fissure into Brafta unseen during the light of day. She considered the issue while Jace and Kilas alternated between arguing with each other and shamelessly gossiping, as they had done for the past forty minutes.

"...heard that he can't keep it in his pants. Though how he's managed to bag one mistress, let alone three, might be the biggest mystery on Veirbos. Lords, it's impressive he even found a wife in the first place with those *atrocious* teeth," drolled Jace with a dismissive eye roll.

"Not to mention," Kilas added, "I could weave myself a roomy overcoat just using the hair from his fucking eyebrows."

"We're here," Ereta interrupted them as she slowed to a stop. "This is as close as I want to get during the day, the settlement seems to get fairly crowded and we can't risk being seen going through the fissure."

"Why not?" Kilas asked as he lazily picked at his nails. "They wouldn't even know what they were seeing."

"That's...true..." Ereta responded, realizing for perhaps the first time that what they were doing wasn't *technically* against any laws on Veirbos, and presumably, on the snow planet (although they really had no way of knowing that for sure). Still, she couldn't help the feeling that opening a fissure was something the Lords wouldn't be too happy about. *How far under their boot am I if I'm ashamed of my behavior on their behalf, without them even knowing the behavior exists at all?* "But do we really want to attract attention to ourselves? At the very least, that would slow us down. And we need to get Leelin to an infirmary as quickly as possible."

Kilas sighed with performative force. "*Fine.* Lead on, then." He gestured with a dismissive hand flick as he turned away from her. Lords, she was beginning to understand why Leelin hated the man so fervently, not that she had ever particularly liked him.

The snow planet portal came easily, and she breathed a sigh of relief as a soothing comfort lightly danced against her skin. It felt so...right, to be there in that other place, and though she wondered if the others felt that too, she couldn't muster the will to ask. She led them through with a cautious eye at Brafta in the distance. Seeing it again stole her breath; it was even more massive than she remembered.

As they trudged toward the settlement, approaching the Western edge in a wide arc to avoid the road, bits of the town came into clearer view. She was closer now than she ever had been, able to see individual people and houses and the well-traveled, dirty snow of walkways. The closer they got, the harder her heart pounded with the sensation that all of this was, indeed, very very real. *Too* real–

"What are they *wearing*?" Jace inquired. "It looks like they're covered in blood."

"Yeah, I'm not sure why their clothes are like that. Initially, I thought maybe it was just the skiers, but I guess everyone has red clothes."

"That's bizarre. It looks gruesome."

Ereta shrugged, but with the thick blood that had poured freely from Leelin's injuries fresh in her mind, she couldn't really disagree.

"What's a skier?" Kilas asked. He had an irritating way of asking questions that made it clear he regarded his willing participation in the conversation as a favor to the other person.

"I think they're like runners on Veirbos, but I'm not entirely sure. They use those metal transportation strips and poles I told you about. I'll point it out to you if I see one."

As they walked closer, people began to take notice of them. They crossed the settlement's edge and proceeded up the leftmost massive stone slope that rose from the snow, and she couldn't help but notice the prolonged stares, and the murmur–

"They're whispering about us," Jace marked in full voice. Ereta elbowed her in the ribs. "*Ow!* You *cun–*"

"Try not to draw attention to us, yeah? At least fucking attempt to blend in." Even though Jace's whining was, truly, annoying–Ereta was grateful that she could be shamelessly direct with her friend.

Jace adjusted her shirt with haughty indignation. "I'm not capable of blending in."

"Neither am I," Kilas added in a bored, waspy drawl. She hadn't realized how similar the two of them were, if only in their unflinching arrogance.

She hissed at them under her breath, "*Yes, yes,* you're both positively stunning, now keep your heads down and *shut the fuck up.*"

The slope upward was dotted on both sides with small stone cottages that reminded her a lot of her own home on Veirbos, but somehow, these seemed entirely more...home-y. Thin smoke rose out of open pillars on the roof of each dwelling. Strikingly colorful fabric decorations, in brilliant reds and deep purples and bright whites, were slung over the entryways and windows of the homes, wafting delicately in the gentle breeze and giving the appearance that they were reaching out to brush against those who passed in friendly greeting.

People bustled around their houses and through the streets in a lively, disorganized dance. Even though the snow planet was, indeed, just as cold as Veirbos, the people here seemed much more content to be outdoors than they were on her home planet, where the streets were barren of all but those who *absolutely had to* be traveling them. The warmth that always coddled her on this side of the fissure swelled for an entirely different reason as she watched the townspeople smile and wave at each other as they flitted about. She couldn't help but wonder if somehow, someday, she might find that spark of belonging on this planet, too?

After a few long minutes, the cottages gave way to larger structures which seemed to be open to the public. People darted in and out of the buildings carrying bags and wooden boxes and swaths of colorful fabric. She wasn't sure what, exactly, the purposes of those buildings were. In Veirbos, there were only four types of buildings: homes, social halls, courts, and Duty buildings; places like the Lek refinery, the distribution center, the metal shop, and the Greenhouses. Those buildings were certainly not open to just anyone. They were locations where critical resources were fashioned and then distributed based on standard Issues and Duty-specific needs (like the specialized rubber treads given to Runners).

These buildings didn't look like any with which she was familiar; she wasn't at all confident that they would be permitted to enter, and trying might draw more attention than it was worth. Their non-red clothes were certainly already doing enough to prevent them from blending in. So she led their small group onward, hoping to find something like a social hall where she could more confidently enter to inquire about Ima.

But as they walked onward, the buildings shrank in size, and they were soon passing by small cottages once again. They neared the top of the stone slab, having marked nothing even remotely resembling a social hall.

"What exactly are we looking for?" Kilas asked, and she was surprised that neither of them had bothered to ask her that earlier. She supposed they were too caught up in observing the locals, as she was; and, if she knew them at all, attempting to find their bearings well enough that they could begin parsing out whatever lascivious affairs were scandalizing the townspeople.

"A woman. Ima. She should be..." she gestured vaguely to the entirety of the town. "Somewhere here."

Kilas picked at his nails. "How *help-ful*," he over pronounced with a pop of his thin lips.

She was starting to *truly*, actively dislike him. She felt a pang of sadness as her inclination to complain to Leelin about his enemy reminded her that her best friend was currently laying in tatters, fighting for his life.

"Look at this," Jace called from the edge of the cliff, and they made their way over to her.

Stretching from the edge of the stone all the way to the slab beyond it was a bridge. They had bridges across some fissures in Veirbos–though they were rare, short, and made of bamboo. This bridge was narrow, with over-wide planks of a strange yellowish wood. The structure swayed lightly in the breeze.

"It must be a half mile long," Kilas observed as he stepped toward it. Ereta followed, but as she did, her eyes fell downward–

"Dust fucking bury me!" she squealed in panic, throwing herself backward.

"Now who's drawing attention?" Jace drawled. But Ereta barely registered the red-clad passersby who had slowed to look at her as she panted heavily, heart racing. She realized she had ended up (somehow) kneeling on the stone with her fingers futilely attempting to dig into it as if it were the only thing keeping her from falling off the edge of the fucking world.

And maybe it was. Because she hadn't realized how Lords-damn high up this thing was. So high up. *Too high up.* She had little practice estimating *vertical* distance, but she knew it had to be at least three times the height of her recent fall into the fissure. Milo's words from when she had fallen into the fissure flitted across her consciousness: *"You're no more than 30 feet down. The impact of a fall longer than that would have shattered your bones."* Her breath came faster.

"Is she always this dramatic?" Kilas asked Jace as though Ereta were not there.

Jace scoffed and placed her hand in a long-suffering caress over her ample breasts. Or, Ereta supposed, over her heart, which was buried somewhere deep beneath them. "Oh, you have *no* idea."

Chapter 21

S *tuck in the Lords-damn fissure again. Dying in the dust on my Ration Route with a broken nose. Holding hands with Hista and fucking skipping.*

The list of places she would rather be swirled in Ereta's head over and over as she took trembling steps across the bridge. *Anywhere but here. Anything but this.*

"We should go back," she squeaked out. Again.

"We're over halfway. It will take less time to continue than it will to turn back," Jace's steps were sure and unbothered as she strode across the bridge in front of Ereta.

"But at least we know the places we've already walked are safe–"

Her words died on her lips at the sight of Kilas sneering at her from his place in front of Jace. "Cold fucking burn me, you are a helpless little coward."

Normally, Ereta valued brutal honesty. But Kilas' honesty had an intentional cruelty in it that Jace's never did. When Jace said something mean, it was because she didn't care to filter her thoughts. When Kilas shared *his* thoughts, he filtered them with the express intent of inflicting pain. And she really, *really* was starting to hate him.

"And *you're* an insufferable prick. We all have our weaknesses, but most sane people would prefer her company to yours," Jace's words filled Ereta with a small swell of gratitude–

She stopped short at the dizzying drop beneath her feet. Lost in her thoughts, she had accidentally glanced downward. Her heart pounded. *Not safe not safe not safe*–Jace looked back at her and rolled her eyes. "I told you not to look down, you helpless little coward."

Shaking, she resumed walking with slow trepidation and locked her gaze upward upon the back of Kilas' head to keep from peering into the fucking *gaping abyss* at her feet.

This is so Lords-damn stupid. She thought of how they had ended up *here:* willingly suspended on a narrow structure swaying breezily back and forth over the 100-foot drop to the ground below.

Evidently tired of putting in the barest effort to search on their own, Jace had meandered to a crowded area and loudly sighed, drawling, *"Oh, how I wish there was someone who could help me find where Ima might be."*

Predictably, this led to several handsome men crowding around with suggestions. *"I can help you search, miss!"* a chiseled older gentleman with tan skin and a rough black-and-gray beard had said as he took her hand and bent to kiss it. *"There isn't a man alive who knows Brafta better than myself."* The man, and in fact, all of the people in Brafta that they had encountered, shared Ima's accent.

"I know Ima personally," a beautiful, dark-skinned, almost frighteningly muscular man had boomed as he pushed his way to the front of the crowd. *"She lives on the third shard. I can take you there, my lady–"*

A tall man with shoulder-length blond hair–reminiscent of Kilas', but darker and a bit wavy–had scoffed and shouldered the muscular man out of the way. *"You must not know Ima at all if you think she'd be home after midday,"* he had chuckled piteously at the other man's ignorance. *"She's probably at the tavern. Over on the second shard. The bridge is the quickest way."*

And so, in spite of her many and loud protests, she had been unceremoniously herded toward the bridge and across its swaying planks, following all three men as they pushed past each other in ceaseless rounds, each seeking to reclaim the lead over their small group.

After what felt to Ereta like a small eternity, they mercifully set foot onto the solid stone of the second *shard*, which was apparently what the people of Brafta called the angled shards of stone. The bridge was anchored two-thirds of the way up the slope, and as they stepped off and Ereta tamped down the urge to fall to her knees and kiss the solid ground, she was immediately aware of how different this shard was from the first. It reminded her a bit of Tubat-So, if significantly busier. The buildings were all three to four times the size of the largest ones on the first shard. They were long and squat, and for all she knew, they might all be social halls of some kind. Like on the other shard, people flitted in and out of the buildings carrying various items–

"There!" Ereta barked at Jace and Kilas, pointing unsubtly at a flash of red as it came careening down the slope. It whooshed past the group with impressive speed and shot to the bottom of the shard in mere moments before turning sharply and disappearing around the edge.

"What in the all the *fucking Crown Lords' Water* was that?" Kilas' inquiry was quiet, but the sharp disbelief in his tone was not lost on Ereta. He was just surprised as she had been the first time.

"That was a skier!" she told him, smiling. She was glad that their guides had drifted ahead into a clump to argue with one another about *'who was leading the group,'* because she wasn't quite sure how she would have explained her companions' obvious ignorance of skis.

Kilas stared with his mouth slightly agape at the place where the skier had disappeared. His throat bobbed with a visible swallow. *"That's* how they travel? The method you mentioned? With the metal strips?"

She shrugged. "At least for longer distances. I haven't seen anyone *walking* through the deep snow outside the settlement." For the most part, it seemed that walking was the dominant form of transportation within Brafta, as it was on Veirbos. On top of the shards, most of the surface was clear of snow entirely to reveal bare, dry stone that was easy to tread upon–excepting a single three-foot-wide strip of packed snow that ran down the middle. She hadn't realized prior to that moment that the clearing and not-clearing of the snow had been done in intentional sections, presumably to enable skiers to move down the shards with greater ease.

"This way," the older Brafta native called. Jace strode after him as the other two guides mumbled to themselves with obvious irritation at their companion's leadership initiative. Ereta and Kilas took up the rear of the procession down the slope. Kilas made a point of walking just a few steps ahead of Ereta, making it clear that although they were walking in the same direction, they were most certainly not walking *together* and she shouldn't attempt to speak with him.

Ereta's thoughts drifted back to Leelin as she trailed behind the group. She watched Jace toss her hair casually over one shoulder before fondling the flexed bicep the muscled man had presented to her. Lords, if Leelin were here, everything about exploring this new world–meeting these new people–would be so much more...fun. Although she had spent her entire life in a beige, dust-covered wasteland, even the color and liveliness of Brafta felt *dull* without him beside her.

The de facto leader of their group strode to a stop in front of a yellow wood door. He pulled it open and stood, holding it ajar with evident pride to let the others file into the *tavern*. Ereta nodded at him in thanks as she passed, though he didn't seem to notice; his gaze was unsubtly devouring the sight of Jace's ass. *I suppose this place isn't too different from Veirbos, after all.*

Ereta stepped into the tavern and, for a moment, wasn't sure if it *had* been a door at all, and not a fissure into yet another strange planet.

Because she didn't understand the sight in front of her.

The massive room was dark–with only the faint, warm glow of sparse braziers to set its confusing contents into relief. Smoke filled the air in dense tendrils that cast the room's already dim affect into a deeper haze. The smoke carried a smell she had never encountered: deep and raw and stingingly rough and just a *tiny* bit sweet.

There were pots of green plants set about the space. Had she not encountered something similar at Milo's house, she mightn't have contained her excitement at the sight of the living, thriving greenery.

On one side of the room, a huge, high table made of the same odd yellow wood as the door stretched what looked like 20 or more feet from end to end. Behind it, a man flitted back and forth, pouring water from many different bottles into many different glasses in many different combinations. Ereta nearly jumped when he pulled a lever on the table and foamy water gushed out, splashing in equal measure into the glass he held beneath it and onto the floor below. She instinctively cringed at the waste before reminding herself that she was, in fact, on a planet literally *covered* in water.

On the table's opposite side, across from the bustling man, tall chairs were packed from end to end. People of all sorts sat in the chairs; most were larger than Ereta had ever seen in both form and stature. In fact, all of the people in the tavern were large. They were crammed shoulder-to-shoulder, sitting in small chairs and clustered around small tables throughout the space. The sight of too many people stuffed into a room was the only part of the tavern that was at all familiar to Ereta. *Like a social hall. Like a busy night at Intali.*

But the Intali cards and dice were nowhere to be seen. At these tables, the imposing figures dipped bits of rolled paper into and out of their mouths before puffing out clouds of massive smoke. She cringed again. Were they...*breathing* smoke? Looking around, it seemed that everyone in the Lords-damn tavern was participating in the bizarre practice. Similarly, they all greedily drank water from large, open glasses. But she felt a stab of pity when her eyes adjusted well enough to the dim light to discern–

"Ewwwww," Jace voiced with a grimace. "It's fucking *yellow*. Are they drinking fucking *piss*?"

Kilas grimaced and loosed a throaty noise of disgust. "That's absolutely foul. Even if it's not piss, it's the dirtiest Water I've ever seen. Piss might be cleaner."

Ereta had to agree. "It looks kind of like when the Lek had that pipe rupture a few turns back and the central Water line was clogged with dust. Our Issues were that same color for two days."

Jace nodded in agreement. "You'd think with all the clean snow they have around them, they'd be smart enough, or even have enough *self-respect,* to–"

"TINY!" A voice boomed from across the dim, smoky tavern. Ima stumbled over to Ereta, looking like she had taken enough Olchate to put several grown people to sleep and sloshing her disgusting water all over the floor. She made her way over with surprising speed, considering–and before Ereta could pull back, the snow planet woman pulled her into a crushing embrace. The water sloshed as the glass was pinned between their bodies, and the putrid liquid sloshed all over their clothes. The pungently acidic smell of it made Ereta want to gag. Ima pulled away slightly and roughly pinched Ereta's cheek with one sticky hand. "It's been an age! I was starting to think you weren't gonna take me up on my offer!"

Ereta's eyes met Ima's, and she took in the sight of the other-worlder. Her cheeks were flushed deeply with color. The lines on her face were of both age and experience; the woman looked thoroughly weathered, as though many turns of traveling at impressive speed through cold and snow had worn her skin down like dusty wind wears stone. But her otherwise toughened appearance was made soft by her wide smile and kind eyes. "I'm sorry it took me so long," Ereta said, returning Ima's smile. "These are my...friends." Close enough to the truth, even though she imagined Kilas, who was behind her and out of her sight, wincing at the descriptor.

Ima gently, but kindly, shoved Ereta sideways so she could navigate around her. She stumbled up to Jace and Kilas and looked them up and down with slow nods. "So Tiny brought tiny friends, eh?" she slurred. "Where are you all from, and what are they feeding ya? Or should I say, *not* feeding ya! *Ha!*" She looked over her shoulder toward the bustle of the tavern. "*Anyone order three sacks of skin and bone?*" She boomed at her fellow patrons. Sparse laughter and indecipherable chides floated back across the room in answer. Ima turned back to once again regard Ereta's companions, extending her hand in greeting. "Pleasure to meet ya! We'll get you straight–don't fret, loves. Stews all around!"

Jace and Kilas both looked deeply offended, by Ima's words or manner or both.

"Actually, Ima, this isn't a social visit," Ereta interrupted. "Is there somewhere we could talk? *Privately?*"

Ima ambled back in front of Ereta and looked her up and down, just as she had just done for Jace and Kilas. She frowned. "*Ackh,* Tiny, so sorry to say it, but you're not my type–pretty though you are–if a bit wanting in assets. Let's just say that, when *I* have private meetings, I tend to pick folk who can...*fill me up from end to end,* if you know what I mean."

"Ugh, *gross*," Jace lamented and Ereta fought the grimace that so desperately tried to take up residence on her face, since there was no way to *not* know what Ima's distressingly graphic words meant.

"Nothing gross about love, Tits, and judging by the look of ya, all tense and cranky? Yer prob'ly overdue a good impaling," Ima responded.

Kilas snorted so loud that several tavern patrons glanced toward the noise, Ereta included. His grin was positively decadent as he leaned toward Jace and repeated in a near-whisper, "*Tits.*"

"It's nothing sexual," Ereta clarified. *Perhaps I could have worded that more subtly,* she thought, but then again, Ima hadn't bothered to filter her words, either.

"Ah! Well, then, what's the need for privacy?"

"Um..." Ereta struggled to find the right words, realizing she hadn't considered how this conversation would unfold. It dawned on her that she had taken Ima's willingness to assist them, along with her overall acceptance and discretion regarding their situation, for granted. "Um..." she repeated to extend the silence. She needed to *think,* but with the stuffy smoke invading her nostrils and mixing unpleasantly with the putrid aroma of the dirty water on her clothes, she couldn't bring herself to focus on anything other than suppressing her insistent nausea.

Ima slapped Ereta on the back with dizzying force. "Out with it, eh? Ha! No worries, love–if it's such a secret, I'll bring you somewhere private. But don't be mistaking me, unless you're hiding an iron rod 'tween those skinny legs, nothing will cross these lips but words!" She shook her finger at Ereta in warning, but the kindness in her eyes remained.

"Understood," she replied with an awkward nod and an even more awkward attempt at a smile.

Ima turned, gesturing for them to follow behind. As she passed by the man behind the long table, she yelled at him, "Four ales, Chatre, and bring 'em to the back! Room two still under repairs?"

"Aye," the man chirped in response.

They made their way to the back of the tavern and parted a dark red curtain to pass through the narrow, high archway in the stone. Ereta had to gesture at their three guides to stay behind, which they did, if begrudgingly. Beyond the archway, doors lined either side of a long, barely-lit hallway. Ima swung open the first door on their left and ambled inside. They followed and Kilas pushed the door shut until it clicked behind them.

Ima fiddled with the room's brazier, and by its pale light, Ereta saw several leaning stacks of chairs. A window in the back of the space was covered up with a length of billowy red fabric just sheer enough to make out the shattered panes of glass behind it. But despite the broken window, the room felt warm, and mercifully clear of that hazy smoke.

Ereta turned back to look at Ima, who had pulled some chairs down from a stack and was arranging them in a circle. She took one of the seats and nodded in silent thanks at the woman, and Jace followed her example. Ima sat as well, leaving only Kilas, who stood to the side of the door with his arms folded and a look of indifferent superiority on his handsome face.

"I didn't know you were bringing all your friends, too," Ima pondered. "If I'da known *you* were on the table, Blondie, I might have been ok with this meeting being *private* from the start." She winked at Kilas, the look effortlessly seductive. Clearly, Ima had ample practice in attracting lovers.

Kilas grimaced and took to examining his nails. "Actually, I just so happen to share your inclination to be–how did you put it? *Filled from end to end.*"

It was Ereta's turn to snort, and Kilas' head whipped up to glare at her. "No! I'm not–I didn't mean–I don't care whether you prefer to be– it's just...that was unexpectedly...descriptive, that's all. I am happy for you," she paused and flushed with embarrassment. "Not *happy for you,* just...neutral. Totally neutral."

"Nice save," Jace encouraged. "If I tell you I love getting impaled by cock, will I earn your praise as well?"

Ereta gritted her teeth and looked at the floor, suddenly wishing she could disappear beneath it.

Ima's laugh boomed through the space. "What a strange lot you are," she noted, shaking her head and pulling a thin roll of paper from her pocket. She got to her feet and turned her back toward them, facing the brazier. When she turned back around, the paper was glowing red at the end, and smoke wafted from Ima's mouth.

Ereta winced. "What *is* that? It smells awful. Are you just breathing in smoke?"

Ima laughed again. "Alright, Tiny, no need for subtlety, now. I'll pass it 'round." She sucked at the stick, making the end glow brighter, before breathing out a thick puff of smoke and extending the object out to Ereta in offering.

"Actually," Ereta started, looking at the strange object. *This is as good a segue as any, I suppose.* She cleared her throat, "Actually, I don't know what that is, because my friends and I are from another planet." *Ok, maybe that was too abrupt,* she realized in hindsight the moment the words left her lips–

Suddenly, several things happened at once. Ereta heard a creek, and a loud bang, and then a crash, and finally, a high-pitched whine. She lifted her gaze: first, to Ima, who was staring with obvious irritation at the doorway. Following her stare, Ereta saw the source of the noises.

"FOR ALL THE LOVE OF THE BASEST FUCKING DUST-BREATHING LORDS–" Kilas was unleashing a barrage of swears in a loud, constant whine dampened only slightly by the fact that he was covering his nose and mouth with both hands. Blood trickled through his fingers. Chatre stood in the entryway in stunned silence, holding a now-empty tray. The former contents of that tray, presumably, were the now-shattered glasses that littered the floor in shimmering wet shards. The wafting reek of the putrid water moments later confirmed her suspicions. Clearly, Chatre had swung the door open too quickly, whereupon it had collided with Kilas' nose and rebounded into the tray, which spilled the water and knocked the glasses to the floor. She was glad of the occurrence–even despite the waste and Kilas' bleeding nose–because it spared her from having to actually *drink* the foul water.

"Give us a moment, will ya, Chatre?" Ima asked in an unfamiliar reserved tone. Her eyes turned to stare at Ereta with a still-furrowed brow. *I'd give good Water to see Ima and Milo compete in a staring contest.* She swallowed as Ima's penetrating gaze held her captive. "And Chatre?" the snow planet woman added, "Don't bring more ales just yet."

The door clicked shut behind Chatre, leaving the four of them alone once again. It was silent for a moment, and Ima's hard gaze never left Ereta's face. Then, suddenly–"*By the fucking forge*, I *knew* it!" she bellowed, slapping her knees. "After that time out in the snow, I knew something was off about you, Tiny, no offense. Another planet, eh? I wasn't far off the mark, then. I thought you might be some kinda spy, sent by the Main City Lords. Although, if you're asking me true, I'd say at least twenty of the fuckers out there," she gestured toward the tavern, "are spies already, and hide it far better than you lot. But another planet, I shoulda guessed."

Ereta chuckled nervously. Ima had accepted her declaration almost *too* easily. "Yeah, well, we are definitely not spies." She looked around the room for help, only finding Jace's look of aloof judgment and Kilas' freely bleeding nose. *No help there.* She turned back to Ima, who was smiling and looking positively gleeful. She cleared her throat again and looked at the stick in Ima's hands. "So what is that thing?"

Ima scoffed, "I don't know what kind of shit hole you crawled out of that you've never seen a roll." She carefully handed Ereta the paper, now half-burned, and took another one out of her pocket, taking it over to the brazier to light it. "Hold it up, that's it. Good. Now, close your lips around it, and you're gonna wanna breathe in deep, get it all up in your chest," Ima slapped her chest a few times in demonstration, "hold it, and then *breathe it out.*"

On a deep inhale, the smoke tingled in Ereta's throat, pouring down into her lungs and seizing them–

She coughed. And coughed. It was suddenly hard to get air, she was coughing *too much*–

Ima patted her on the back with enough force that it verged on uncomfortable. "You really are from another planet. There isn't a person on Scheal–excepting those in Lords-damn diapers–who can't take a roll hit better than that." *Scheal.* Was that the name of the snow planet? She wished she could catch her breath well enough to ask.

Ereta's eyes were watering heavily by the time the coughing finally abated a few minutes later. She thrusted the paper stick back toward Ima, who gestured at her to, instead, pass it on to Jace.

"Because you made it look so enjoyable," Jace said flatly, her eyebrows raised. Kilas' pre-emptive glare from behind his bloodied hands warned her to not even attempt offering it to him. So, she just...held it.

"Thank you for that, Ima," she said and hoped it sounded genuine, even though it really wasn't. The stale taste of the smoke lingered in her suddenly dry mouth. "So I opened a fissure–" No, wait–that wasn't right, she needed to explain...better. Better than that, right? Wait–better than what?

She blinked rapidly, trying to clear her suddenly murky thoughts. The door was wiggling. "Is he trying to get back in?" she asked, but no one answered. *I didn't say that out loud, did I?* "What is happening?" The door wiggled more. Everything wiggled. It was quiet. So quiet, why was it so Lords-damn *quiet?* And how long had it been since she'd started speaking? How long had it been since she'd stopped? *And stopped what?* Whatever she had stopped, it felt like hours ago. Everything was hours ago. The silence was loud in her ears. *How can silence be loud?* She turned to look at Ima, and the woman felt miles away. And she was wiggling. Was this real? Was *she* real? *Oh Lords, I might actually be dying–*

The distinct sting of another hard slap on her back pulled her attention from her panicking thoughts, if only barely. "First time's a doozy, but you'll get used to it," Ima's wiggling form chuckled.

"What's wrong with her?" someone asked. *Was it me? Did I ask?*

"Heh! No, that wasn't you, Tiny. Tits over there–"

"Jace."

"Got it. *Jace.* It's just the roll; first time can throw you for a loop. Takes a bit to get used to it. And Tiny's, well, *tiny,* and she took a hefty pull. Could have made a mess of a man four times her size. Her head'll be right in an hour or so."

"An *hour?!*" Ereta squeaked, because they were talking about her, weren't they? *An hour?* Until what, exactly?

"–will be alright, Tits. And next time, it won't be as strong. Someday, she'll barely feel it."

Her heart pounded. Oh Lords, what was happening to her? *Is this permanent?* And she knew with agonizing certainty that it was.

Her vision blurred and cleared in waves. What are those? *My hands.* So strange. She clenched and unclenched her fingers. "Am I doing that?" Were her hands hers? Was she her hands? Was she dying? *Yes, I'm dying. I have to die. This is my purpose. This is everyone's purpose. We are born to die, and that's all.* Leelin's bleeding form flashed through her thoughts. *This is everyone's purpose.* Her body went cold in abject panic at that sudden weight of hers and everyone else's mortality, and her vision blurred again–but this time, it did not clear, even as she faintly registered Jace's familiar touch on her shoulder. The darkness closed in, plunging her into blackness and mercifully taking her consciousness with it. Her last thoughts before plummeting into sweet oblivion were that, if this was death, she was glad for it; because her thoughts were finally quiet, and quiet was peace.

Chapter 22

There were no dreams lingering as Ereta emerged from sleep, but she hardly took notice; the aching in her temples occupied every frayed scrap of her attention. She groaned and reached up to futilely rub at them.

"*Finally*," she heard Jace's voice from somewhere nearby. "Her grace awakens. Are we set to leave as soon as she's up?"

"Should be," someone replied. Someone–*Ima*.

Everything rushed back to her in one dizzying barrage of memories. The snow planet. Leelin. The tavern. The smoke. *Oh Lords, the smoke.* She groaned again. "What *happened*?"

"Your eyes were bigger than your lungs. Bigger than your nerves too, Tiny, if I'm speaking true." Ima chuckled. "I've never seen someone pass out from one puff. Must've been quite a mess going on in that brain of yours."

"You could say that," she muttered. Certainly, she didn't claim to be emotionally stable at the best of times, let alone in the midst of a still-unfolding crisis, and certainly not when given a substance that altered her perception of reality itself. Ereta grudgingly sat up, realizing that she was sprawled on the floor. They were still in the room at the back of the tavern. She glanced around, marking Jace's bright red hair and Ima's imposing form. She didn't see Kilas, though.

"I thought I was dying," she said aloud by way of explanation for her freak-out, but if she was being honest, the words were just as much for her as for them. She struggled to wrap her head around the intense emotions she had felt before losing consciousness. It was a deep fear; a resignation to a miserable, dreary fate that had inspired panic in her, surpassing even that of her Ration Route, when she actually *had* been dying. She shivered at the memory and noticed her heart racing. *Oh Lords, is it happening again?* Suddenly fearing that the worst was not behind her, her breaths came in pants, and the room felt cold and dreary and everything was on the precipice of being fucking *terrifying* again–

"Calm down, you're alright, Ereta," Jace said with her usual flatness, yanking Ereta partially out of her spiral. "You just got a bit *high*, is all. That's what they call it. It's been a few hours."

"What was it?"

"Some kind of plant that makes people all loopy when you smoke it. Kind of like Olchate is at home, I guess, but based on your reaction, I'm guessing it's stronger–"

"That was *nothing like* Olchate," she interrupted between gritted teeth. Olchate felt like warmth and relaxation. The smoke had felt like undiluted torture. Like *insanity*.

"Well, they don't seem to have Olchate here, so I guess we'll take your word for it, since I'm certainly not trying a roll."

"Won't be so bad next time," Ima chimed in. "You have to build a tolerance. Might take a few tries, but you'll get there, Tiny."

Ereta wobbled up to her feet and took deep breaths in an attempt to settle herself. "No, Ima. I am *never* doing that again. *Never.*"

Ima chuckled and slapped Ereta on the back yet again, and in her weary state, it was almost enough to knock her over. "We'll see. You won't fit in too well 'round here if that holds true. And you'll have to fit in, since according to Tits, there's no going back to *Wareboos.*"

"*Veir-bos*," Jace corrected with a haughty pronunciation that seemed to imply she had taken offense.

Ereta came up short at the realization that Ima had attempted (however poorly) to speak the name of their home planet. "Y-you know–?"

Jace rolled her eyes. "Of course she knows. I told you: *it's. Been. Hours.*" She pointed at the ceiling as if Ereta could see the moons' position directly through it, which she (of course) could not. "Anyway, after your little stunt, I took over and told the old bag about everything."

Ereta turned to glance at Ima, who nodded in confirmation. "And as I told Tits, and Blondie–Lords favor that handsome mug–I'd be happy to help however I can. By the forge, we sure could use some new blood around here, if only for rutting! Brafta doesn't come by new folk often, but not for want of trying. You'll find us the most welcoming bunch on Scheal by a wide margin, that's for damn sure!"

Ereta barely processed Ima's words, but she nodded in acknowledgment all the same. *Lords,* her head hurt. But even through the pain and the lingering fog of passing out, she was acutely aware of the time passing all too quickly while Leelin waited back at their camp. *Dying.*

"Where is Kilas?" she asked, rubbing at her temples uselessly.

"Blondie? Getting fit for skis out back, last I left him."

Jace groaned. "Why do you refuse to even *try* using our names?"

Ima laughed and gave Jace, for a change, one of her too-hearty back slaps. "If there's one thing I've learned living out there on the snow, it's that you've gotta know yourself damn well, even if no one else does. Maybe especially then, for true. No sense hammering a dead nail, far as I'm concerned, eh? You're lucky I remember *something* to call you, full stop! Ha! Now we should be going, Tiny, soon as you're right in the head."

As she tried and failed to parse meaning out of Ima's words, she couldn't be sure that she *was* right in the head. *Dust bury me, this woman makes no fucking sense,* Ereta thought with more aggressive rubs of her aching skull. Maybe it was the lingering effect of the smoke still twisting the world around her, but she didn't think so. Regardless, she flashed Ima a weak smile and a nod in placid agreement, and gestured for her to lead the way out of room two.

"—To go sit somewhere and watch the moons turn. At least then, you will be of some use for once in your miserable life when I find myself needing to know the *fucking time.*"

"At least Kilas is still himself," Ereta noted to Jace as they approached their companion, who was berating a terrified-looking young man of no more than 16 or 17 turns.

The thin sheet of snow that had fallen that afternoon made soft crunching noises beneath their feet as they walked down the alley beside the tavern. Jace huffed a humorless laugh. "Yes, I suppose no matter what planet we might find ourselves stranded on, Kilas being an irredeemable prick can be our guiding fucking moon."

And by the dust, he certainly looked the part. Kilas stood just beyond the tavern's creeping shadows; the late afternoon's yellow sun set his already beautiful visage into otherworldly elegance, which (she supposed) was *technically* fitting. His nearly-white hair gleamed in the bright light, and the dust of newly-fallen white snow that surrounded his slender frame made it appear that he was *glowing*.

But despite his beauty, Ereta found that it was easy to break her stare from the man. Their short excursion together had fortified her already rising dislike. At some point in the past 12 hours, the idea of punching him in the face had become less an outrageous joke and more a distinct and unavoidable eventuality.

The young man who had been the unfortunate target of Kilas' ire squeezed past Jace and Ereta through the small alley, his head bowed and his arms clenched around a large bundle of fabric.

"I see your beauty rest did you no favors," Kilas spat at Ereta with a loathsome smirk.

The blow didn't have time to register before Jace spoke for her, "If you're going to bully someone, Kilas, perhaps you should find another star-eyed youth; Ereta has already been thoroughly disillusioned."

Ereta scrunched her face and looked up at Jace. "I'm not disil–" Jace raised an eyebrow at her, and she relented with a grimace and a murmur. She didn't have the energy to argue her case that her general attitude about life had been steadily improving in the few pentads since her near-death experience. And, she had to admit, her disinterest in arguing that point was in and of itself proof of lingering disillusionment. "Fair enough."

It was only when she looked toward the ground in resignation that she noticed–

"You're wearing skis!"

Kilas stood straighter, and the skis shifted forward an inch beneath him in response to the motion. He wobbled back and forth, arms waving to find balance, before eventually finding his composure and reclaiming his arrogant, straight-backed posture. "Yes."

"Can you use them?" She asked and walked around him in a wide circle, then knelt in the snow to examine the objects up close. "So strange," she murmured, reaching out her hand to touch the tread, which seemed to be fused to the metal itself–

"*Stop it!* Don't touch them. They're *fragile,*" he hissed at her.

"Fragile?!" Ima bellowed from down the alley, following her outburst with a deep chuckle that echoed ominously off the alley walls. She strode toward them with additional pairs of skis clutched clumsily in her arms. They shifted against each other with clangs and scrapes at each jostle of Ima's movement. Reaching them, she loosed her arms and let the skis fall into a messy, loud pile of iron against the stone. "They're solid metal. The only thing fragile here is you, Blondie." She winked at him, and Ereta smiled. She liked Ima more and more, and found herself wishing that she could swap out Kilas with her in their little group. Surely, there could be no better *get well* gift for Leelin than banishing Kilas somewhere in the open desert of Veirbos.

Ereta looked at the pile of skis before her and hastily counted. "That's only enough for two people. Didn't Jace tell you there are others?"

"Of course I told her. She probably forgot. Memories get faulty in old age."

"Calm your tits, Tits." Ima hiked a thick rope over her shoulder, and a large, shallow, oval bowl slid up closer behind her. "The sled'll hold the rest. And on the way back, it'll hold the infirm."

"Leelin," she corrected. "His name is Leelin."

"Not if she can help it," Jace murmured.

"Well? Those things aren't just for decoration, Blondie, though you do make them look awful pretty. Let's see how you're coming along."

Kilas tried to straighten further, but as he was already at his full height, the gesture was more of a self-important waggle of his shoulders. He huffed a breath and slowly lifted his left leg into the air, moved it forward, and confidently planted it down a foot or so ahead of his other foot. All at once, his outstretched foot slid forward, and his legs split apart until his groin nearly touched the snow. He tried to yank his legs backward, but the motion only served to knock him off-balance, and he fell hard onto his side.

"By the forge, it's been an hour, Blondie—what have you been doing out here? Staring at your reflection in the metal? Your skiing looks just as shit as when I left ya." She walked over and pulled him to his feet by the shoulders as if he weighed no more than a newborn babe. "Firstly, you can't go anywhere less your poles, I told you as much, unless you're going downhill, but even then, you should be holding them." She snatched his poles from where they laid against the wall and shoved them into his hands. He slid backward a tad from the impact. "Second, don't be lifting your lords-damn feet. There's no reason under Scheal's skies why those skis should leave the snow. The *poles* will be your legs." She gestured repeatedly in the air, balling her hands into fists to grab invisible poles and pull down and back, up and forward, over and over. She didn't pause her mimicry when she prodded, "Well? You waiting for the open plains to whisper your name? Ha! There's no invitation, Blondie, you just gotta do it, and leave your fear to feed the forge."

"*I don't know what that means,*" Kilas gritted through a tightly clenched jaw. Ima gave no signs that she intended to pause her gesturing. He took a shallow, irritated breath, stood straight (again), and slowly mimicked her movements. His poles' sharpened points made a faint *tang* as they passed easily through a layer of snow and struck the stone below. He did not move. "It didn't work."

Ima huffed. "Of course it didn't work. You've gotta *push*, Blondie. This part–" she emphatically pulled her fists back into her sides, "–needs to have some power behind it. I know you're not much for muscle, but you're not much for fat, neither, so it shouldn't take much of a push to get you moving. Go on. You can put some of that pretty anger of yours into it, if that helps. That's what I do. Just picture the face of some fucker you wanna throw off a shard, and imagine you're driving that point right down, deep into his fucking eye. I've crossed many miles by the power of my hate for the–"

"THERE you are!" a voice echoed off the alley walls. The looming shapes of multiple people drifted toward them, barely visible through the thick shadows. "Why'd you run off, beautiful? I know you found Ima, but I'd be happy to keep my post as your guide. For whatever you'd like to...*explore*." By the time the beautiful, heavily muscled man finished speaking, his face was sufficiently lit that Ereta could see the suggestive wink and eyebrow flutter he leveled upon Jace. She could also see the other two men behind him, blocked into the alley by the span of his form and futilely attempting to find a way around.

"I'm free as well," the older man called. "Let's not forget who *actually found* Ima."

"I know all the best places to eat on the second shard, my lady. It would be my pleasure to dine with you this evening," the third man–the blond one– added as he attempted to meet Jace's eyes by standing on his toes and peering over the muscled man's shoulders.

"OUT! The lot of you. I have no time today to wait for all three of you to make your best play at wetting your cocks."

"But–" some combination of the three started in unison before being abruptly cut off.

"But *nothing*. Back to the tavern with ya, or wherever you please, as long as it's far from here, else I cut off the sources of your lingering and chain all three of them 'round my neck."

And just like that, with hurried platitudes of departure, the three men scuttled back down the alley and out of sight.

"Right in the eye," Ima murmured, almost dreamily. A wistful smile crept onto her face as she stared after them into the shadows.

Something about Ima's speech–likely, the bit about her willingness to sever cocks and wear them as jewels around her neck–caused a shift in Kilas' attitude. Suddenly, he was perfectly content to follow her skiing advice. Ereta and Jace had hastily pulled on the treads attached to their ski blades and joined in the lesson.

In just under an hour, by her estimation, they were skiing across the small strip of flat ground that ran parallel to the shard's slope. Satisfied enough with their progress, Ima bid them take off their gear to walk down the shard on foot. *"I think I'll be well in the forge's fires before you're skilled enough to take the shard run,"* she had insisted. And as they walked down the steep slope toward the flat ground of the snow plains, a skier whipped past them in a blur of speed she could barely comprehend, and Ereta was grateful for her teacher's lack of confidence in their abilities. *We don't need to have anyone else in the infirmary today besides Leelin.*

Ereta had considered whether taking this time for them to learn skiing even made sense. But as soon as they were off onto the plains, pushing their poles into the snow and going a bit too fast for Ereta's comfort, she was sure that even despite the delay, this method of travel would save them hours (and any risk of getting captured if they fissured into Veirbos with Ima). "Why are we going so fast?" she yelled at Ima, who was trying her best not to pull ahead too far and lose the group in the increasingly heavy fall of snow.

"Most of the main runs are sloped," Ima called back over her shoulder. "They build up the snow at an angle so you're always moving slightly down, so you go faster, eh? They're sloped the opposite way on the run back."

By the time they had been skiing an hour, her muscles were thoroughly exhausted from the effort. Muscles she didn't even know she had burned with unrelenting intensity, but she didn't stop. Nor did she allow anyone else to stop for anything other than canteen refills; not that Jace didn't try. At the redhead's fifth insistence that she *"most definitely wasn't made for skiing,"* Ima had abruptly turned and skied up to her, cutting off Jace's path. The redhead nearly fell as she tried to stop before colliding with the large, intimidating woman. Before she could finish turning her skis inward to slow herself, the sound of a slap pierced the dense quiet of the snow. Ima grabbed Jace by the shoulders and shook her around a bit.

"The blood of that poor lad'll be on your hands if you keep us slowed, Tits. You're a weakness out here, and those pretty lips and feeding breasts won't skew me from knowing what link of the chain needs cutting free."

Jace's cheeks, a roughened pink in the assault of snow and wind, paled to white at Ima's words. Her lips thinned with tension, but she nodded, and Ima grunted, turning back and sliding her way to the front of the group. Ereta hadn't truly noticed before that Ima...had a temper. She had seen glimpses of it, but to Ereta, Ima had always been warm and kind. It was unmistakable now, though, after seeing her with Jace. The woman had an air of absolute authority about her that made even her self-assured friend shrink a bit; though part of what made Jace a queen in her own right was her ability to know when she was better off following than leading. Here, on this strange planet of snow and smoke, Jace deferred to Ima.

After a mere half hour, their path left the man-made slope and ventured into deep, open, flat snow. Their progress slowed considerably as they trekked through the powder. But still, their little camp came into view surprisingly quickly, with barely another half hour passing before she was close enough to yell, *"Milo!"*

And moments later, her heart racing, terrified of what she might find, she clumsily pulled up her skis beside the shelter's tunnel. Milo's messy brown hair popped out of the tunnel for just a moment before he shot straight up to his feet. His red-flecked eyes met hers; they shone bright against the waning light of early evening.

In her peripheral vision, she registered the small (but unmistakably genuine) smile that curled his lips upward. She didn't have the words to ask, but she didn't need to. He nodded once, and she knew: *Alive. Leelin's alive.*

For now.

"I'll not be waiting for ya. He's not looking great, and I'd sooner have him back at the infirmary than with his friends, eh? Especially since he's not awake to know the difference."

"That's fine, Ima. Thank you." Ereta fiddled with the strap around Leelin's chest, making sure it was tight enough. Her friend was bundled in blankets like a newborn babe. He had been several inches taller than the sled was long, so his legs were bent at the knees, but he otherwise looked reasonably comfortable.

Ima finished tying the sled's rope around her middle. "The infirmary's on the first shard, near the base. Ask 'round if you get lost. Most folks are friendly in Brafta. I'll have someone waiting for you at the main gate. Muscles, maybe, since you already know 'im."

Despite how insulting Ima's nicknames often were, they were nothing if not effective; Ereta knew *exactly* who muscles was. She smiled, her eyes still fixed on Leelin's unconscious form. She leaned down and kissed his forehead. She wasn't sure if he could hear her, but she leaned down to whisper to him all the same, *"You're doing so well, my heart. It's just a little further and you'll be safe. I have so much to tell you when you wake up—"*

"He can't hear you, and I'm low on patience," Kilas spat at her.

She grimaced at Kilas' words, which he had the fucking *audacity* to speak with an air of sourceless authority, and gave Leelin one last kiss on his cheek. *"Especially about how much I really, truly hate Kilas."*

Ima nodded back at her with a sad, knowing smile before pushing off her ski poles and gliding away. "I'll take care of him, Tiny," she called back over her shoulder. Leelin's sled pulled after her, but despite his considerable weight, Ima managed to build up decent speed in just a few pushes. By the time she disappeared into the curtain of falling snow, Ereta was sure the woman was moving significantly faster in the deep powder and despite the extra weight than their group had on the entire journey to camp.

"Some woman, ain't she?" Chegg broke the silence with a cheery clap of Ereta's shoulder. Between him and Ima, she was sure she would have a bruise tomorrow that spanned her entire moons-cursed back. They hadn't had much time to socialize; as soon as they arrived, Ima had unburdened her sled of skis and set to helping Milo and Chegg move Leelin. It had taken just a few minutes in total.

"She's something, alright," Jace agreed. "A bit bossy, if you ask me."

Kilas rolled his eyes. "Oh, spare me, *princess*. You just can't stand when someone else is in charge for once."

Jace rolled her eyes in turn. "Don't be ridiculous. Milo bossed me around for hours yesterday, and this morning."

"*That* didn't bother you because you don't see him as a threat. He's too...*you know*..." Kilas drifted off. His hand flourished in overlapping circles, as if he could unravel the air itself and find a suitable word within it.

"*Brilliant!*" Milo exclaimed from a distance away. "Absolutely fucking *brilliant!*"

Kilas scoffed. "I wouldn't say—"

"Did you all see this?" Milo rushed over to them with a single ski held aloft, gesturing frantically with its end, seemingly oblivious to Kilas' ongoing attempt to assault his character. He placed the ski gingerly on the snow as if he were placing paper-thin glass onto rough stone. Carefully, he pushed the lone blade back and forth with his fingers, then looked up at the group expectantly. His eyes were bright with amazement, and seemed to ask them if they, too, were seeing this.

"That," Kilas gestured dismissively toward Milo's place on the ground, "is exactly what I mean. Not a threat."

The features surrounding Milo's steadily pinched brow changed their affect almost instantly in response; morphing his visage from a look of anticipatory fervor to one of confusion. "A threat?"

"Never mind. Kilas is just," Ereta pinned the blond man with a sneer that she could only hope portrayed the depths of her dislike, "*being Kilas.*"

"Alright, children, let's get on with it," Jace mercifully interrupted them with a clap of her hands before Kilas could open his mouth to speak. "Lords know we could putter away the hours picking each other's self-esteem to empty husks. But I'm assuming there are beds and nutrition allotments back in Brafta, and you are all delusional if you think I would willingly spend another night in that piece of shit thing." She gestured toward their snow shelter. She clapped again. "I desperately need my personal space back. So let's go. Now."

Milo and Chegg pulled on their skis and stood unsteadily. Both men struggled with them more than the rest of the group had; Chegg seemed to think he could leverage his body weight in order to beat the snow under him into submission, while Milo couldn't seem to force his muscles to follow his brain's commands. Whenever any of them attempted to give him advice, he would shoot them a look and dismiss it. *"I'm aware,"* he would say to their suggestions that he adjust his stance, or shift his weight. He was clearly as uncomfortable with being unsteady physically as he had been when knocked off-balance mentally–like that day when she had seen him in the alley beside his house, looking for all the world like a lost child.

As the two men practiced, Ereta, Jace, and Kilas distributed their belongings (or, more accurately, Milo's belongings, since most of what they had had come from his home) into their packs. They had to leave behind some of the bulkier objects: the large bucket, a few bigger rocks, three metal poles, and several glass bowls and domes of unknown utility. They brought the rest for no other reason than they had nothing else to bring, and in the off chance any of it might prove useful back in Brafta, it was worth the slight extra effort.

By the time the two men were confident enough in their skiing ability to begin the journey back to Brafta, the night's moons were high and shining, Siga's crescent making its nightly trek east. Little puffs that looked like raw bits of puffy fiber sat low in the dark sky, occasionally obscuring the moons' soft light.

"What are those?" Ereta asked, her gaze fixed on the puffs. "I've never noticed them before."

"Ah," Milo attempted to push his poles harder and gain enough speed to ski to her side, but the sudden push instead made his skis cross together in the front, and he stumbled–his frantically waving arms attempting to restore his dubious balance. After a small struggle, he stood straight again with parallel skis and resumed his prior pace. He raised his voice to speak, acknowledging the reality that he couldn't and wouldn't catch up to Ereta's side. She slowed her own pace enough that the gap between them shrank slowly and steadily. "I believe it has something to do with the moisture in the air. They seem to be directly related to when the snow falls. They are thicker just before and during, and often disappear after. But what, exactly, they are? I'm not sure." He paused, staring upward in thought with his head cocked slightly to the side. "They seem to move on the wind, sort of like steam or smoke. Or breath when it's cold. Maybe that's what they are: moisture, or at least a form of it."

Ereta nodded and loosed a large exhale. Her breath became visible in the frigid night air before rising up and toward the sky. "They're beautiful, whatever they are." In her childhood, she had imagined what Veirbos might have looked like before the New Sun. She had imagined strange, tall plants bursting with shades of color. The white snow plains were barren of that colorful life, but that did not mean they weren't beautiful. She never could have dreamed up the bright yellow light of the sun on Scheal, nor the abundant water that took a shimmering, powdery form. The wonders of this world, and even her own, were things she could scarcely have imagined if not for having seen them with her own eyes. What other worlds–what other moons and suns–might be out there, and what wonders did they hold? Her heart swelled with the thought, and despite persistent, nagging thoughts that warned her against letting hope flourish freely, she let it.

Both Milo and Chegg were relieved when they crossed the threshold onto the smoother, tapered snow of the main run back to Brafta, which ran beside the Route they had taken into the plains. The rest of the journey passed quickly. Milo was as proficient with his skis as the rest of them by the time they could glimpse Brafta in the distance. Chegg, however, looked no more adept at skiing than he had when he had first strapped the blades on. He slowed the group's pace considerably, but apologized so genuinely and often that Ereta couldn't muster resentment. "Y'all make these fuckin' things look easy," he grunted from the back of the group.

"*We* are not suffering from a massive Olchate hangover," Milo reassured him.

Kilas scoffed–a sound that grated on her absolute last nerve–and muttered under his breath, "*Nor are we brutishly muscled simpletons lacking both grace and dexterity.*"

And at that, something in Ereta just...*snapped*. She couldn't take it anymore. She was tired, and scared for Leelin, and unsure about what the future held in every possible way. And she understood being rude to Jace, or even herself, but Chegg? *Really?* The man radiated kindness and positivity. Why break his spirit, but to be cruel? They were all frighteningly alone on this new planet, with only each other and Ima to rely on. Besides, hadn't they been through enough in the past two days without having to worry about infighting?

She pulled her skis around to face Kilas, staring up at him with seething rage. Her sudden turn and aggressive stop caused the snow beneath her to cut up from the ground in a splash of powder. He raised his eyebrows at her. "Will you *shut up?!* Lords, you are such *a miserable fucking prick!* We're not happy about this situation either," she gestured around to the rest of the group, "but you seem intent on making us all even more miserable as if it will help anything. I'll save you some time: It. Fucking. Won't! All your being cruel accomplishes is making us hate you. That's it! Is it worth it? Is it worth the effort you fucking expend coming up with the most cutting possible thing to say? You've done it! Congratulations! We hate you! I *hate you.* I am this close," she meant to leave space between her thumb and pointer finger as she gestured a visual aid for her patience, but her fingers were smashed together entirely. Which, she supposed, was actually a fitting metaphor. "*This fucking close* to opening a portal to Veirbos and shoving you through it and right into Hista's fucking lap. You're both miserable assholes who feed on other people's misery; maybe you'd be happy together." She couldn't help but huff a humorless laugh at the mental image of Kilas and Hista sitting across from each other, hurling barely-veiled insults back and forth without end. Maybe it would be better that way, if their cycles of inflicting misery were self-contained instead of poisoning the world around them. "If there is a single positive quality inside that pretty head of yours, I've yet to glimpse it. And if I die by my own hand before this ordeal is through, know that it's not because of the hurt your words inflicted, but because I decided it was no longer worth living if I had to tolerate your arrogant, self-centered, miserable, fucking *irredeemable* presence for another moment!"

She spat in the snow by his feet (a great insult on their home planet, where every drop of Water was scarce, though the effect was lessened as her expulsion fell to the snow) and pushed off her poles, turning around in a wide arc to resume the last of their journey to Brafta's looming gate. She was breathing hard. Her vision was hazy with anger and exhaustion as she attempted to focus on her destination: so close, and yet it felt farther than ever.

Chegg loosed a long, low whistle.

"Wow," Jace commented from behind her. "That was...really something."

She didn't turn back to see Kilas' reaction, if he even had one.

Neither did she turn when she heard skis sliding closer to her, nor when she heard Milo's voice coming from her side. "Anger issues?"

She huffed. "Sometimes." Well, more than sometimes. She felt angry a lot, but most of the time, it was directed inward, at herself. In her experience, when something went wrong or when someone treated her poorly, it was more than likely her fault. The bitter self-flagellation that followed most of the valid criticisms she received was always accompanied by a repeating chorus of the internal monologue: *you deserved it.*

So when there was a true injustice, directed toward her or not, it was a struggle to contain her ire; it was such a relief to feel justified fury at someone besides herself that she wasn't at all sure how to modulate it once it started spilling out.

She let her eyes drift sideways just enough to catch him nodding in her peripheral vision. "Yeah, me too. Sometimes." They traveled in silence for a moment. "It didn't help, did it?"

She considered, and was surprised to find that he was right; her tirade had given her no relief from the anger and frustration that had caused it in the first place. In fact, if anything, those feelings had dug themselves in deeper. Now they formed a hateful knot of slumbering wrath that sat like caustic bile in her throat. If she let it out again, what would happen? Would it simply hijack her tongue temporarily, using it as a mechanism to spit out angry words? Or would it sit there, choking her, *suffocating* her, until nothing but malcontent remained? That would be no way to live. While she no longer knew what her future held, she knew what kind of person she *didn't* want to be. She loosed a long, heavy sigh, and with it, some of the anger eased.

"No," she confirmed. "No, it really didn't."

They moved forward in silence, and with the slight reprieve of her ire came a swell of other emotions that threatened to overcome her entirely. Leelin was here, and she would be with him soon. But what then? What *next*? And would he ever be ok–ever be the same? What manner of life could they make for themselves, if any, on this strange planet?

Her heart beat a song of aching terror and tension as they slid beneath the shadows of Brafta's massive stone-and-iron gate.

Chapter 23

Muscles, whose actual name was Hinet, had been waiting for them just past the gate. He stood with his feet wide, hands clasped behind his back and chin slightly raised. He nodded curtly at Ereta, but his stern face broke into an easy, handsome smile when he caught sight of Jace trailing behind. While they removed their skis, Hinet introduced himself to Jace with an indulgently lingering kiss of her hand.

The snow around the gate was not the brilliant white of the plains; it had been trampled into a dense, slippery pack of grayish-brown slush. Ereta grimaced at the feel of grimy water soaking her cloth treads. She regarded Kilas' rubber-bottomed Running treads with longing as her sparse toes quickly surrendered into numbness.

Hinet seemed to know everyone he passed as they traversed Brafta's busy streets. The walk to the first shard had them winding around stone buildings that reminded her of the Duty buildings of Tubat-So: industrial-looking stone brick structures with no identifying markers or features. On her home planet, if you had to ask what the building was, you almost certainly weren't allowed in. She wondered if that was the case for the majority of buildings at the base of the shards; none seemed to be residential or public as those on the great slabs of stone had. She craned her head back to glance at the wide chimneys that rose from the rooftops of the settlement, spitting tendrils of thick gray smoke into the open sky.

It was while looking up at that wending smoke, walking along the side of the first shard, that Ereta took notice of the long rope-and-wood ladders that hung down at varying intervals from the slope's top. Her head nearly spun when she realized that the shapes on those ladders were actually people–Lords-damn *people*– dangling at least 60 or 70 feet off the ground and seemingly trusting in the surety of their own steps alone to keep them from plummeting to the ground below. Her breath hitched in her throat as she watched them move up and down the ladders.

Jace caught up and made to knock her shoulder into Ereta's side, but due to their height difference, the result was more of an elbow nudge. "You seeing those?" Jace nodded towards the nearest ladder, where a man in Brafta's customary deep red clothing was stepping off and onto the solid ground. Ereta tried to swallow down the lump in her throat.

Milo rushed up to her other side. He pointed at the ladder. "See, *that thing* would have been ideal when you were in the fissure."

"I recently discovered that I am not particularly fond of heights," she murmured weakly in response. As she watched the overlong contraption sway gently in the breeze, she could think of nothing else to say.

"Well, if you're going to insist we stay here, you're going to have to get over it," Jace stated without emotion. "Because I plan to find us a house at the top of one of these things."

Her heart warmed at the subtle confirmation that Jace wanted to continue being her housemate in Brafta. That conversation felt extremely premature, considering that they knew nothing about Duty or how they might obtain housing vouchers; it was a nice thought all the same. But that warmth cooled as Jace's sentiment sunk in. "At the fucking *top*?" she squeaked. Unbidden, an image formed in her head of a small stone bed teetering precariously on the top of the middle–the *tallest*–spire. She imagined herself laying on it, deeply asleep, and simply...rolling over and off the edge. She fought a shudder.

Jace shrugged. "Yeah. I don't like the idea of people looming above me."

Milo leaned forward so that he could see across Ereta to Jace on her opposite side. "Because you'd rather loom above *them*?"

Jace gave him a small, rare smile. "I thought Ereta was exaggerating when she went on and on *and on* about how smart you were. *'Milo's a genius, Milo's going to change the world,'* blah blah blah." Ereta felt her face heat with self-consciousness. Why did Jace have to be so Lords-damn *honest* all the fucking time? And why did her friend's impression of her sound like the voice of an elderly man with a raw throat? But she couldn't help but remember how Chegg had, similarly, told Ereta everything Milo had ever said about her, and she felt a little less awkward. *I guess we're even now.* Jace cocked her head at Milo, entirely oblivious to Ereta's embarrassment. "But you do live up to your reputation, *science boy*."

Milo straightened and furrowed his brow. "Funny how, in the end, *she's* the one who ended up changing the world for me."

And even though–in the most technical, literal sense, which was almost *certainly* the sense that he had intended–he was right, she once again found that she couldn't think of a single thing to say.

Brafta's infirmary could not have been more different from the one on Tubat-So, but it still managed to smell the same: a faint odor of iron (almost definitely blood) mixed with the over-clean scent of cleaning powder and–when one turned their head *just right*–a slight whiff of stale piss.

Upon arriving, she alone had been ushered through a dimly lit hallway that never seemed to fucking end. The others waited in the front room where Ima had greeted their group, but only one person was permitted to be with Leelin at a time, and she would be damned if that person wasn't her. As she walked down the hall, she felt like she had out on the snow plains. That no matter how far she walked, she wasn't really going anywhere at all, and her destination might remain forever out of reach. Equal feelings of anticipation and dread warred within her.

But despite her fear, the nurse eventually stopped in front of one of the closed yellow wood doors. And her fear of never arriving would have been a balm compared to the new fear that bloomed–the fear of what she would find on the other side of that door. The implications of how her life might be hinged entirely on Leelin. If he recovered, they could start to think about the bigger picture of their group's life on Brafta. If he didn't–if he...died?

She wasn't certain life would go on without him. Wasn't certain that her life *could* go on–

The Nurse pushed the door open, and her heart leaped into her throat.

Leelin was reclined on a strange-looking bed–it had a frame of metal that held a thin, soft-looking cushion aloft. His head was resting on a puffy pillow. His beautiful sage green eyes were closed; but not in that cold, rigid cast of imminent death. Now, his skin was closer to the pallor she knew, though not quite fully revived to that rich, deep brown. His clothes had been removed, and a red blanket covered his skin from the waist down. His chest rose and fell in deep, solid breaths rather than inconsistent spurts. Even despite the gruesome wounds, he looked for all the world like he was sleeping. When she heard a familiar soft snore growl out of his throat, she nearly sobbed in relief.

She approached the bed, heedless of the Nurse's presence, and stared down at her friend. At the man who kept part of her soul cradled in the balance of his survival. The man whose laugh and smile and voice calling her *little flame* had raised her from the walking death of grief that had all but consumed her when she had first arrived in Tubat-So.

She leaned down to him, barely noticing the tears that splashed against his warming skin. She pressed her forehead to his, closed her eyes, and breathed deeply: taking in his scent, taking in the gentle brush of his breath against her face, savoring the fact that he was alive, and that they were together.

"We made it, my heart," she whispered to him. "You *made it. Everything's going to be ok."*

She stayed there, savoring the reality of his survival, for several endless, beautiful minutes of peace. Her breath slowed to match the pace of his. She idly ran her fingers through the close crop of his now-clean hair.

It was only when a loud *"A-hem"* broke the silence that she remembered the nurse was there at all. Taking one more deep breath, she gently kissed his forehead and pulled herself away. She turned to the nurse.

"You his wife?"

"No," she responded.

"Well, who are you?"

"He's my best friend."

The nurse raised her eyebrows and glanced between her and Leelin. "And would he call you his?"

She blinked at the woman in confusion. "What?"

The nurse gave a loud, weary sigh. "Would he be comfortable with you knowing his personal health information?"

"Oh. Oh, yes, of course! Yes, please. Anything you can tell me."

The nurse nodded and sighed. "Well, those wounds are some of the worst I've seen, full stop. That he's still breathing at all is...well, it's *something*. But he's got a long way to go yet. Seems to have lost a lot of blood, and those burns are covering a bit less than half his body.

I don't anticipate that he'll wake anytime soon, not that we should want him to. The pain would be..." the woman trailed off and stared, frowning, at Leelin's sleeping form.

"...*something*?" Ereta offered.

"Yeah. Something," she shook her head, "but for now, the plan is simple: we clean and dress the wounds. We keep giving him fluids. We watch closely for signs of rot; that's really the biggest worry right now."

"And will he..." the question felt too important to ask all at once. Too imposing. Too broad.

"...*be ok*?" the nurse (helpfully) finished for her.

She tried again to swallow that persistent lump in her throat. "Yeah."

"There's no way to tell just now. He's lost a lot of blood, for true. And the wounds are significant. Luckily, if there's one thing Scheal's infirmaries know, it's burns–we've seen forge-made burns that wouldn't heal over at all because they're too large: there's no skin to grow together. *His* burns are all over, but the edges are pretty close, and the surrounding skin is still intact. So I'd say that's a good thing. There's cause for hope, but until his body replaces most of that blood, I doubt he'll wake, and of course there's a chance he might never wake at all. We just don't know."

The uncertainty was instantly frustrating, even though Leelin's chances were as good as she'd dared hope, and he was in the best place possible to care for him. She didn't know what the *forge* was, but it sounded like this settlement treated a lot of burns, and that was a boon.

"Is he in pain?" Like every question she had asked the nurse, she was more than a little afraid to hear the answer. She ran her thumb soothingly back and forth across Leelin's arm, though in truth, it probably soothed her more than him. She relished the feeling of his warm skin beneath her touch–the slight tickle of the soft hair dusting his arm. Those were comforting, familiar sensations that she had been unsure she would ever have again.

"No, I don't think so. He's out of it." The nurse walked over to the other side of Leelin's bed and brusquely snapped her fingers in front of his face. Ereta wanted to be irritated at her rudeness, but Leelin didn't so much as stir. "Mhm. Out of it," she declared with a nod.

Ereta stayed steadfastly by Leelin's side for the next hour: sitting on the iron chair by his bed, holding his hand, and observing the Nurses who came in near-constant shifts to tend his wounds. They used small containers of a pungent liquid to clean his burns before applying a thick layer of some thick, sticky substance and covering them in bits of clean cloth.

She leaned her cheek against his bare chest and breathed deeply. His heart beat softly against her cold-raw skin. As she stared at the bag of clear liquid that *drip drip drip*-ed into her friend through a needle-and-tube system (one that bore a *striking* resemblance to the one Milo had devised), she barely noticed that her eyes were slowly drifting closed. *Drip...drip...drip...drip...*

drip...

"T*iny.*"

She woke in a daze to the sound of Ima's voice and the weight of the woman's hand on her back, reminding her in no uncertain terms that the past two days had, for better or worse, not been a dream.

"Ima?" She tried to blink the sleep out of her eyes, but the room was dark, and truth be told, she wasn't ready to wake just yet. She was so Lords-damn *tired.* But for Ima to wake her–

She shot up and frantically felt for Leelin's pulse. *Tha-thump tha-thump tha-thump–* his heartbeat was weak but steady beneath her hand. "What is it? What's wrong?" She ran her hands over his forehead and along the un-bandaged stretches of his skin, desperate to tend any new ill that had befallen him while she had slept.

Ima squeezed Ereta's shoulder. "Nothing's wrong, Tiny. But it's late, and according to Brains out there, you've been awake for nearing two days straight."

Again, Ima's nicknames proved themselves startlingly effective, because Ereta didn't have to pause and ask who *Brains* was. But, now that she thought of it, she wouldn't have had to ask if Ima had simply called him Milo, either.

"I won't leave him," she said, and laid her head on his bare shoulder, as if she were claiming her place by his side. "You'll have to drag me out of here."

Ima chuckled. "I may yet. But here's hoping you'll listen to reason."

The silence sat for long enough that Ereta's eyes slipped closed again of their own accord. Ima's voice jerked them back open.

"Nothing's gonna change in a few hours, tiny, and you need to rest prop–"

"I'm. Not. Leaving. Him." She bit the words out. Her exhaustion was too thick to bother with niceties.

Ima sighed. "You're a stubborn little thing, eh? Not all sweet and fragile after all, I s'pose. Well I loathe to tell ya, but the nurses have been coming less often since you've been sleeping."

Ereta's eyes shot open. "What?" She sat up slightly. "What do you mean?"

"I have a feeling they don't want to disturb ya, with turning the lights on and moving him about and such. They wouldn't say so, not to my face, but I've been sitting just outside and they've barely checked on him in the past hour, where before it was every 20 minutes."

Ereta climbed to her feet and started toward the door. Her head spun with exhaustion and the room was full dark, but she kept moving.

"Where are you off to, then? Seeing reason?"

"Telling the nurses to come check him."

Ima sighed again, and a solid hand grasped Ereta's shoulder from behind, spinning her around.

Though Ereta still couldn't see Ima in the darkness, the woman's voice came from only a breath above; so close, soft and almost piteous. "They'll tend him better if there's no worry of disturbing ya. Come back in the morning, after a few hours of sleep and a good meal."

After a long, ultimately pointless argument, Ereta deferred to Ima and followed her out of the infirmary and into the brisk cold of night. Their walk to Ima's home passed in a daze of exhaustion, colored by streaks of dulled panic that accompanied crossing the two bridges that separated the infirmary from the third shard. *It's too dark to see the drop, anyway, Tiny,* Ima had tried to soothe her; not realizing that the resultant effect made that drop seem not smaller, but fucking *endless.*

But mostly, the journey was a blur, and Ereta was not conscious enough to form the memories of entering Ima's home and being tucked into bed.

When she woke out of her dream, the lingering colors and feeling of warmth felt more potent than usual. *"We will find each other,"* the words echoed in a comforting chant that soothed her otherwise aching bones. She smiled to herself, the soul-deep warmth a needed reminder that no matter how far she traveled, as long as she could dream, her true home was never out of reach. The feeling ebbed, as always, but didn't dissipate entirely. Instead, it faded to the low hum of comfort that colored her every moment on Scheal–for a reason she felt no closer to understanding now than when the sensation had brushed against her with the first air fissure on Tubat-So.

She shifted slightly, finding that the surface beneath her shifted with her weight. Just like Leelin's infirmary bed, it was some sort of soft cushion instead of a stone bowl like those in which she was used to sleeping. It felt odd; sort of like she was falling bit by bit as moved and the surface sank beneath her.

She opened her eyes to find that the yellow light of Brafta's sun was relentlessly glaring through the edges of thick, red curtains. Shafts of bright sunlight illuminated deep blue stone walls. She wrinkled her brow. What an odd thing, to put color on *walls.*

She sat up and took in the rest of the small room. It was, truly, lovely–the bed's sheets were the same deep red as the curtains. The floors were covered in polished planks of that odd yellow wood, which also made up a small table and something that looked like a dresser. Several tall, leafy plants grew out of colorful pots: two on the floor framing either side of the window, one on the sill, and two small ones on top of the dresser. Other than the plants, she was alone, and there was no trace of the others. She hoped they were with Leelin, keeping him company in her stead. Although he was likely still unconscious, if there was any flicker of awareness in him, she wanted him to know he wasn't alone.

The room smelled strangely sweet. Not sweet in the way that nutrition allotments were sweet, but sweet in a soft, warm way that was grounded in a base of smoky richness. She put her feet to the floor and stretched. Lords, her muscles ached. *Everything* fucking ached. She had no idea how long she had slept, but her body struggled to adjust to motion as if it had been held stationary for an extended period and her joints had all partially fused in place.

She grimaced at the musty smell that tickled her nose, but when she moved her head to avoid it, she realized... *fuck*. That smell was her. She needed to powder off, and find a spare set of clothes, and *eat*. She didn't dare hope that the nutrition allotments on Brafta were better than on Veirbos. Certainly, if the smell of their gross, yellow water was any indication, they had...*different* tastes on Scheal. Already, her standard for nutrition allotments had been unreasonably skewed by the delectable gel that Milo had made.

But she was hungry. Certainly too hungry to have high standards.

She would have pulled back the curtains and attempted to assess the time, but the bright light was already straining her eyes, mostly covered as it was. Whatever time it was, she needed to get back to Leelin as soon as possible, and she felt plenty rested regardless of how long she'd actually slept.

She glanced around the room. Her treads were nowhere to be seen. So, feet bare, she padded to the door, moving a bit unsteadily across the smooth wood as she tried to force her body past a creaky haze of rest and into wakefulness. She brushed her hands reverently over the leaves of a small plant she passed by, and she could swear that she felt its liveliness thrum a responding beat against her fingers.

She carefully pushed the door open. It groaned a little in protest as it swung open to reveal–

She felt that same, strange feeling of other-worldliness in the hall as she had when entering the tavern. Was this another Lords-damn planet entirely? What was she *seeing*?

The walls around the massive, square space were colored a bright purple. There were doors scattered along each of its long sides, each of which must have spanned 30 or 40 feet. A hallway ran along each side, connecting all the doors, but at the center? Nothing. Empty space. A strong iron gate covered three sides of the inner hallway, and the fourth side was partially open to gleaming wooden stairs with iron handrails winding downward in large circles. Strange, spindly green plants wrapped around the railings without pattern, conveying a sense of barely restrained wildness that made her heart swell. She inched toward the closest gate and peered down.

Her heart fluttered–the wood-and-iron staircase swirled downward a further two stories–the vines wending along with them–before ending on the edge of a massive, wide-open room. She chanced a glance upward to find that the staircase continued for an additional two levels above her. That knot in her throat returned in full, obnoxious force as she edged alongside the wall toward the stairs. As she stood at their entrance, her heart kicked into a full, nervous beat. Brafta had not only created her newfound fear of heights–the settlement seemed to relish any opportunity to fucking trigger it.

She took a deep breath and started gingerly down the steps; she gripped the handrails so tightly that her knuckles whitened. Despite her nerves, she looked up from the descending stairs to glance around each level as she wound downward. They looked the same as the one she had departed from–with lines of closed doors–though their walls differed in color. One was a blue slightly lighter than that in her bedroom, and one was a red so dark it was almost black. Step by careful step, the solid floor below grew closer.

She stepped off the bottom step and onto the polished wood expanse of the main level. "Tiny! Was starting to wonder if you'd sleep the rest of the turn, eh?" Ereta stared at Ima, who was lounging on a massive cushioned bench on the far side of the room, bare feet lit aglow by the massive, roaring *fire*–

"What the fuck?!" Ereta jumped back and pointed. "*Fire*–there's fire!"

Ima stood and lazily stretched her arms above her head. She spoke through a yawn. "Yeah, yeah. *Fire.* Your friends had the same reaction. Not to worry, Tiny, it's perfectly safe. The chimney pulls the smoke out–they said you had chimneys for some of your machines on *Weer-boos*, eh? Same thing here, but the fire stays put."

Ereta cautiously nodded. "Where's Milo?" She had a sudden, almost overwhelming need for him to be here to explain exactly why she *didn't* need to be afraid of this open, blazing fire, because Ima's explanation did little to calm her nerves.

Ima blinked at her blankly and clearly had no idea who she was talking about–

Dust bury me. "Brains?"

"Ah, Brains! He's over with your other friend. The infirm–"

"*Leelin,*" Ereta corrected through gritted teeth, hoping that Ima would replace her apparent nickname for Leelin with something more fitting for him once he woke, maybe *Flirt* or *Charming* or even *Horny.*

"Aye, well, he's been over there for a few hours now. Real pain in the arse, that one, eh? Won't stop asking Lords-damn questions. Always saying things." Ima waved her hand through the air dismissively.

"Yes, he does like to say things." Ereta smiled slightly. "And the others?"

"Blondie's been shut in his room since we arrived, and Tits has spent the past few hours in the *bath*–don't know what she's doing in there, for true. And Cheery's keeping sentry at the Infirmary. Loathe to leave Brains' side, I think." *So Chegg's nickname is Cheery.* That was fitting, and surprisingly close to his real name. She wondered if Ima would be willing to change her nickname to something a bit closer to *Ereta*, but all she could come up with off the cuff was *Error,* and she couldn't help but think that it was perfectly fitting. *Error. A mistake from birth to dust.* She shook her head in an attempt at dispersing that thought; for all she had been improving her attitude and self-esteem since her fall, it seemed that the instinct to be self-flagellating was dug in deep and would continue to insist upon itself whenever she let down her guard.

She again attempted to scatter her thoughts with a clear of her throat, glancing down at her filthy jumpsuit. "So, do you happen to have a cleanroom–?"

"By the forge's raging fires," Ima groaned with a roll of her eyes. "Would that you were here when I went through explaining to the others, eh? We don't have *cleanrooms* here."

Ereta blinked in surprise and chanced a doubtful glance around the rest of the room–

She had been so distracted by the massive fucking fire that she hadn't noticed anything else. But this place was absolutely *massive:* larger than the floors above by at least half.

Light pink walls and gleaming wood floors laid a canvas for a space that could only be described as...*alive*. The same spindly green plants that decorated the staircase continued their journey by wending up and down and across the walls, leaving no significant stretch of pink stone unadorned. Just like in her bedroom, there were potted plants littered across the space. But here they were *massively* tall and reached their leafy tendrils toward the ceiling as if they intended to someday burst through the sky itself.

On one side of the room, a massive wood table stood proudly, surrounded by at least ten chairs, all of which were decorated with soft-looking, colorful cushions. Those colorful cushions were everywhere in this room, in fact. Multiple lounges boasting intricate iron frames were scattered about the room in arcs and circles. Some were so small they might only fit one person, where others looked as if they could comfortably seat five or more. Massive windows spanned all sides of the room, with most stretching from the floor to the high ceiling above. They were ornamented with thin, flowing, light red curtains that didn't do much to stop the sun's light—instead, they filtered its tone to cast a warm, rosy hue. There were ornate iron braziers mounted on the walls, lit and flickering despite the abundant, bright light of the day's sun.

In the corner opposite the table and chairs, there were tall stone counters set into a crescent shape. They reminded her of the basin of their Waterroom in Tubat-So, but they were larger, with other strange structures surrounding them. There was another, smaller, mercifully unlit fire hole in the middle of the span of counters. And, notably, there were no Water Issues. Their absence should have been predictable, but the lack of them was nevertheless disconcerting to Ereta after a lifetime of planning her days around the need to be near her source of Water; after a lifetime of feeling an invisible tether pulling her back toward that which she needed to survive. The lack of that pull should have felt freeing, but instead, it felt like she had been cut loose to blow uncontrollably in an unforgiving wind, cast out to the whims and dubious mercies of the air around her.

She was distracted from her visual perusal by the firm and familiar clap of Ima's hand against her back. "There's a bathroom on your floor, but Tits has been occupying it for Lords-damn hours now. Heh. You can use any other you like, there's one on every floor 'cepting this one. Just a water closet down here."

Ereta nodded, but really didn't know what Ima was talking about. She followed the woman up the winding stairs, trying and mostly succeeding to ignore the drop that stretched beneath them as they climbed. They exited onto the purple-walled level where her bedroom was, and Ima led her around to a door on the opposite side. She knocked loudly.

Ereta heard a familiar, long-suffering, flat voice filter through the door. "Come in, I suppose," Jace called out.

For the third fucking time, Ereta thought she had stepped onto yet another planet. The air felt thick and hot with hazy moisture and carried a delicate, lilting scent. "What in all the Lords' spit..." her voice trailed off, her eyes widening as the haze cleared and bared the sight before her.

It was a small room, dominated by a massive, deep iron bowl in the center: oblong, with intricate lines in rich reds and purples winding around its sides, seeming to serve no purpose but decoration. A pipe extended from the floor into the bottom, and another curved around the top edge. At its base, elaborate curving legs held it slightly aloft from the polished stone floor. The top lip was rolled into itself to form a smooth, thick edge. And inside the bowl...

Ima loosed a long, low whistle. "By the forge, Tits, you'll have a woman questioning her tastes! Ha!"

And truly, the already hot air felt a bit more suffocating as Ereta took in the sight of Jace–

Completely and utterly *naked*, lying in the bowl, seemingly covered in...*No, that can't be.*

"It is," Jace told her, apparently reading Ereta's mind as a small, indulgent smirk flitted into the corners of her moisture-swollen lips. "It's *water.*"

Chapter 24

Jace's heat-flushed, swollen breasts seemed to bob gently in the clear liquid. Only her delicate pink nipples–framed by long, sodden tendrils of soft auburn hair–remained above the water's surface. Ereta felt the urge to avert her gaze, but couldn't quite force herself to do so. She had seen Jace naked many times, and *vastly* preferred men to women in the lustful sense–but she couldn't help but feel a twinge of heat in her core as her gaze rolled over the glistening curves of Jace's undeniably sensual form.

"Enjoying the view?" Jace's voice was a bored drawl, though she almost certainly relished the attention and made no move to cover herself.

"I reckon you'd need to be dead to appreciate *that*, eh, Tiny?" Ima nudged Ereta with her elbow.

"Yes," Ereta answered truthfully without breaking her shameless stare. "And perhaps even then."

Jace huffed and pulled her lips tight: the expression as close as her friend typically got to a smile.

"Well, enough of your lurking. You're letting out the heat." Jace shimmied her shoulders and sank back down into the water. She leaned her head back to rest against the edge of the basin, and her eyes slid closed. She lifted a hand out of the water and gestured a lazy shooing motion in their direction. "Run along now."

"What in the all the fucking Lords...what *is* this?"

Jace shimmied her shoulders again. "A bath," she answered in a tone that suggested it should have been obvious.

Ereta finally managed to break her gaze from Jace and glance around the room. Something that looked a lot like a cleanroom chair sat on one side. A mirror took up most of the wall on the other. The stone tiles around the iron bowl were mottled and dark with errant splashes of moisture that had swelled over the edge of the bath.

"And the point of a *bath* is..."

Jace scoffed. "To get clean, obviously."

"So instead of cleaning powder–"

"You soak in water. Correct."

Ima huffed. "*Weerboos* sounded right miserable enough before you told me you bathe in dirt."

Jace opened her mouth, presumably to correct Ima's butchered pronunciation, but Ereta cut in before she could.

"Seems like a waste."

"You're thinking about it like we're still on *Veirbos*," Jace cut a pointed glance at Ima as she drew out the word. "Water isn't exactly scarce here, in case you haven't noticed."

"I know, but..." But what? *But treating Water–or* water, *I suppose–so flippantly makes my entire life on Veirbos seem pointless.* "But how can the water make you clean if it's filled with the filth it removed from your skin? You're actually just making the clean water dirty, and then sitting in it, right?"

Jace's eyes snapped open and her top lip pulled back just a fraction. "You just *had* to ruin this for me." She stood in a swift motion, baring her full glory to the room. Ereta purposefully evaded her eyes before she could get sucked into another bout of shameless staring. "Ima, care to do anything about the fact that I'm soaking wet?"

"Careful with your words, Tits, 'specially when you're standing there with your twat bared to the wind." Ereta snorted loudly before she could stop herself.

"Oh, shut up. Are you both Lords-damn twelve turns old? Fine–I'll just drip all over the floor, then. Makes no difference to me." Jace stepped out of the bath, and a puddle began to swell at her feet as water streaked down her body. As she gathered her hair and wrung it out, Ima strode to a door against the far wall, opened it, and pulled out a stack of thick red cloths.

She handed one to Jace, who wrapped it around herself. "If you soak my floor again, it better not be with water." Jace ignored her and walked past them into the hall, purposefully bumping against Ima's shoulder as she did. The woman called after her, "*Or piss!* Not water or piss, so I'm being clear."

"Oh, you're being *very* clear." Jace's deep, almost inaudible tone carried something with it that wasn't quite frustration or annoyance–but exactly what it *was?* Ereta couldn't say.

As Jace opened the door next to Ereta's and shut it behind her with a loud *click,* Ereta nudged Ima with her elbow. "I think you and Leelin are going to get along really, *really* well."

Ereta stared at the pipes that poured hot, steaming water into the basin. A *bath-tub,* Ima had called it. She swallowed thickly. She wasn't sure she could sit in this basin of water only to drain it all away. The sense that the action was diminutive to her former life's values gnawed at her. *I could open a fissure to Veirbos right now and give this water to some Dutied who would likely weep at the sight.*

But really, she couldn't. She couldn't freely cross between the two worlds, at least not while she and her friends were being pursued by Hista and her guards. And, by this point, almost definitely the

Lords' guards as well, since the past two days of missed shifts had surely broken everyone's Duty oaths. They were fugitives now, and she didn't think that returning to Veirbos would ever be safe. As she stared at the expanse of hot, abundant water so deep she could cover her body in it, she tried to convince herself that was a good thing. But there was a slight, lingering fear that something about this whole situation wasn't right–that leaving the rest of her planet–and especially Bellat, the thought of whom made her heart ache–to toil indefinitely while she enjoyed the luxuries of Scheal couldn't be the end of her story. That she could do better for them, and for her.

Not that she had the first clue as to *how*.

She shook her head and sighed deeply, finally turning the tap on the pipe and stopping the flow of water. Resigning that she was not currently comfortable with the idea of a bath, she grabbed one of the red cloths and perched herself on the tub's rolled iron edge. She dipped the fabric into the water and ran the wet cloth over her filthy, naked skin.

It took a long time to clean herself this way, and she was ever-conscious of all the minutes that passed while she was not with Leelin. But removing the grime was important, especially because it was crucial that Leelin's wounds stay clean. Ima had explained that to her at length when Ereta had insisted that a simple change of clothes would do, and that she wanted to see Leelin right away. Predictably, she had relented at Ima's appeal to her friend's health and safety.

She rubbed the strange, foamy *soap* that Ima had given her onto her skin and then off again, working her way across her entire body. Slowly, the acrid smell of her filth gave way to that sweet, warm smell she had glimpsed earlier when interrupting Jace's bath. She cupped handfuls of water over her long, black tangles of hair, rubbed soap over their length, and cleaned away the foam with another few handfuls, letting the bit of excess water drip onto the floor. Luckily, the mess from Jace's bath was still there, and she doubted her extra mess would be noticeable when Jace returned to clean the floor, as Ima had said she would insist her friend do. *Let's call it payback for the hours of whining yesterday,* Ereta justified. She used her fingers to unknot her now-clean hair. It felt so strange, for her hair to be wet: it hung heavier, and her scalp chilled slightly with every brush of air that passed it.

Despite her hesitance, wiping herself with warm water felt luxurious. When she finished, she was sure she had never been cleaner. The bath stood in the center of the room, loosing tendrils of heady steam, ready for someone else to submerge themselves in its depths. She was proud of herself for not wasting that water, even though Jace and Ima didn't seem to care. And besides, she still wasn't convinced that soaking in a tub of dirty water made any sense as a method of cleaning oneself.

Back in her room, Ereta ran the dry cloth over her body thoroughly until most of the water on her body was soaked away. A neat pile of dark red clothes sat on her bed. Skin pimpling in the sudden chill of being slightly wet and entirely naked, she hastily pulled them on: overlarge undershorts, a pair of loose, long pants made of something thick and soft, a similarly soft chest wrap, and a thin, long sleeve shirt with a scooped neck that left her clavicles exposed. The clothes felt like everything in Brafta had: decadent. Indulgent and excessively enjoyable to experience. And while she tried to appreciate the sensation of comfort and safety, she couldn't help the nagging thoughts that pricked at her: *you don't deserve this. This isn't right. You aren't done.*

After carefully descending the spiral stairs to the main floor, she found Ima sitting with Jace at the massive wood table.

"Tiny! Come eat," Ima implored.

"She's gonna lose her shit," Jace muttered to Ima.

"What? You have nutrition allotments?" Ereta hurried forward. The nagging hunger in her stomach swelled at the barest thought of eating. But she didn't see any nutrition allotments when she approached the table.

"What is this?"

"Foods," Jace answered as she lifted a metal rod with a solid-looking, round, red thing stabbed onto the end and closed her mouth around it–

"What the fuck?!" Ereta yelped and involuntarily hopped backward a step. "What is *that?*"

"Tohld yoh," Jace said to Ima out of the corner of her mouth before turning back to address Ereta through a mouthful of that odd *thing.* "Wae're ohn ahnother thucking *plahnet*, Ereta. Wahy ahre yoh thill tho thocked thaht thahngs hahre ahre differahnt?"

Ima huffed. "It's a tomato, Tiny. S'pose your food is different on that planet of yours too, or so they tell me. That you only eat some paste or such. Tragic, if you ask me." The woman raised a glass of yellow water to her lips, closed her eyes, and drank deeply before setting it back onto the wood with a satisfied exhale and a hearty *thud.* Jace's glass of yellow water sat untouched in front of her. "We have real food here, for true. You'll have to learn how to chew it, though; don't be swallowing that shit whole like Brains and Blondie, or your stomach will be a right mess. It might be something of a mess for a bit anyway, until you get used to eating solid."

Jace worked her jaw in awkward, wide, circular passes. She stuck out her tongue at Ima, baring a mess of masticated red flesh. "Ith thith gud?" she asked through her open mouth.

Ima leaned forward a smidge and seemed to study the chunks on Jace's tongue. "Good enough, Tits. You don't have to keep showing me, though please yourself if you feel the need."

Jace closed her mouth and dipped her head slightly, and Ereta saw her throat flex in a swallow. "Come sit, Ereta. You need to eat."

"I..." Jace was right. She kept getting caught off guard by how different life was on Scheal...but maybe she needed to find a way to accept the shocks as quickly as they came. She was, after all, on a different Lords-damned planet.

She steeled herself and pulled out a chair. Ima grabbed a glass disc from a pile in the center of the table and heaped it with 'foods'; Several of the round, red things, a long, hard green thing that uncannily resembled a man's erect member, multiple thin strips of dark green sheets, and a pile of small round things the color of Veirbosian dust.

She tried *everything*, and the sensation of crushing the foods between her teeth did not get less strange as she repeated the motion. *Endlessly.* It was a lot of effort to chew. She was so hungry, but with every bite that came into her mouth, she had at least 30 seconds of chewing separating her from the satisfaction of swallowing it down into her aching belly.

But the taste? The taste was incredible. Strange, and maybe not delicious, but *interesting*. The red balls (*tomatoes,* Ima had informed her) were sharp and tangy with a hint of sweetness. The green sheets (*spinach*) were a little stringy and hard to chew, but they had a fascinating depth to their flavor that was entirely new to her.

She ate and chewed and swallowed over and over, until she was full to bursting with *tomatoes* and *cucumbers* and *spinach* and *soybeans* and–her personal favorite–*bread*.

As they finished their meal, Jace looked at Ereta with a hint of a smirk and raised her brows. Her cheeks were stuffed full and round as she spoke through the foods, "Nohw *thith,* I wath made fur!"

"Swallow your food, eh, Tits?" Ima slapped the auburn-haired woman on her back–the sudden expulsion of air forced the foods in Jace's mouth to spew outward and across the table.

Ima grimaced at the chewed bits. *"By the fucking forge,* Tits! You're one for making a mess, eh? You'll be cleaning that, in addition to the bathroom, for fucking true!"

Jace rolled her eyes and stabbed her *fork* at another fresh piece of foods. "We'll see."

"You live with her, eh? Is she always this Lords-damn *filthy*?" Ima asked Ereta, still leveling that grimace in Jace's direction.

But before she could answer, Jace loosed a low, wicked chuckle through her new mouthful of foods. She shook her fork at Ima. "Oh, yew hove *noh* idhea."

E reta wasn't sure if it was the bridge's swaying or the solid foods sitting in her stomach like a moons-cursed *brick* that made her want to puke. But step after trepidatious step, she continued forward toward the infirmary. *Toward Leelin.*

Although her morning had been strange and just a tad overwhelming, only an hour or so had passed since her waking when she, Jace, and Ima finally left the house—if a huge building that seemed capable of housing dozens could be called a 'house'.

As the door had closed behind them, Ereta had looked up at the massive stone brick structure, whose top stretched so high above them she could barely see it. *"What is this place? Some sort of fancy barracks for travelers? We had barracks in Tubat-So, but smaller, and with many more beds. And fewer floors."*

"Heh! It's my *house, Tiny.*" Ima had slapped Ereta on her back.

"Seems like a lot for one person," Jace observed, and Ereta nodded in agreement.

"It's not for one person. I just had to send everyone away when you lot came by. Not quite sure how to handle ya, for true. S'pose I'll let 'em come back once you stop gawking at the water like it's a Lords-damn treasure. Ha!"

And that was how they had learned two things: one, that Ima must be the best Lords-damn skier in Brafta to have gotten a housing voucher for *that* place (regardless of how many she shared it with); and two, that the woman was keeping her new wards somewhat of a secret from those closest to her.

Ereta finally, *mercifully* stepped off of the bridge and onto the solid stone of the first shard. Her stomach didn't settle with the steadiness of the ground, though. Lords, if she felt this nauseous and crampy despite chewing her food, she couldn't imagine the distress Kilas and Milo must have been in after swallowing their foods whole. Kilas hadn't responded with so much of a grunt of recognition when Ereta had knocked on his door before leaving. And truthfully, she couldn't bring herself to be even slightly regretful at the man's absence, even though it was due to his being in crippling intestinal distress and (she supposed) she should probably feel bad for him. She didn't.

When they reached the infirmary lobby, they were greeted by Chegg's loud, open-mouthed snoring. The sturdy man looked absurd stretched across the floor with all of his limbs extended at odd angles. One leg was perched up high on a tall chair, the other was blocking the front door and shifted slightly when they pushed it open. But Chegg didn't wake, and Ereta didn't push him. He was dressed in the red clothes of the snow planet settlement. He, Milo, and Kilas had all apparently chosen to bathe and eat before going to bed, though how they had stayed awake that long, she wasn't sure. Jace, like Ereta, had fallen asleep almost immediately when returning to Ima's home and had only awoken a few hours before Ereta. The others had slept for only a few hours before Milo and Chegg had woken and returned to the infirmary to be with Leelin.

And when Ereta had wended through the endless hallways of the infirmary and opened the door to Leelin's room, she was predictably greeted by *two* unconscious men.

Milo sat in a chair beside Leelin's bed—his head leaning forward against the cushion of his friend's bed.

Leelin looked the same as when she had left him, and at the sight of his chest rising and falling, Ereta loosed a breath she hadn't realized she'd been holding since she had first awoken that morning.

She walked over to Milo and gently shook his shoulder. He stirred slightly, but didn't wake. "Hey, *science boy*, I'll take over from here," she spoke in nearly a whisper while giving him another gentle shake. Finally, his head shot up, his brows already pinched into their enduring furrow.

"Ereta," he said when his glazed eyes cleared and pinned her. She sucked in a breath, the embers catching her in their keen grip. "How are you?"

"Me? I'm fine. How are you? And how is he?" She flicked her eyes over to Leelin.

"We're both fine. He seems better. Heartbeat's stronger." Milo turned and gently flicked the tube that continued to drip liquid into Leelin's arm. "Wounds were clean, last the bandages were switched. We just have to wait," it seemed he couldn't help the yawn that overtook his last words.

"Go back to Ima's, Milo. Get some sleep."

"Are you sure? We can wait in the lobby–"

Ereta laughed. "I think the infirmary staff would rather get Chegg *out* of the lobby."

Milo stood and made toward the door with a nod. "Alright–I'll bring him back to the house and we'll get some sleep. We can meet up later? All of us? We have a lot to talk about. Fuck, I have a lot to *think* about." He seemed to say the last to himself, not Ereta, as his eyes stared unseeingly at the floor and he ran a weary hand through his messy brown locks.

"Yeah, sounds good. Are you feeling...?"

"Better. *Much* better. For a few hours, I was grateful to be in an infirmary, since it felt like I might be dying. But much better, now."

"Good to hear. Kilas might be a different story. I guess we'll see, if he ever deigns to grace us with his presence. I couldn't get him to so much as grunt through the door before we left. He might actually be dead."

He nodded. "I'll check on him. So...later?"

She nodded and smiled at him. "Later." *Later, we'll get our questions answered. Later, we'll find out if Leelin is ever going to wake from this sleep. Later, we will figure out how to make a Lords-damn life here.*

A nurse bustled in, hurrying up to Leelin's side and ignoring them entirely. "Sorry, I know there's only supposed to be two of us. He's leaving now," she nodded in Milo's direction.

"Heh. Don't think I can call you out on it, lest the Lords themselves cut me down. Perks of being connected, I suppose."

It was Ereta's turn to furrow her brow. A quick glance at Milo showed her he shared the sentiment. "Sorry, what do you mean?"

The woman huffed, her hands preoccupied as she swiftly changed Leelin's bandages with the smooth confidence of a thoroughly practiced hand. "I mean that I'm not to be the one getting chewed out for daring to say something critical to the Lords' favored infirmary guests."

Ereta and Milo shared another confused look, and the woman finished up cleaning another bandage, gathering the soiled ones in her hand.

"Sorry," Ereta started again, and the nurse huffed as she started toward the door. But she paused after a beat, and turned slowly back to Ereta.

"What, you don't know?"

"Know what?" Ereta's heart began to pound at the realization that was dangling in front of her.

The nurse looked at both of them, and smiled slightly, as if relishing their torment. "That Ima's the Crown Lord of Brafta."

Ereta couldn't muster words.

The Lords-damn Crown fucking Lord? It seemed impossible; the implications were...vast, and although she didn't think Ima intended them harm, she certainly wouldn't have approached the woman at all if she had known she held the highest of all Duties. That she was, essentially, a queen.

"Guessing you didn't know, then." The nurse laughed again, shook her head, and left with a slight spring in her step.

"Well then," Milo started. She met his gaze and swallowed.

"Later?" *Later, we will come to terms with the fact that our guardian is the most powerful woman on the planet.*

He huffed, and the corner of his lips twitched up. "Later sounds good."

Milo turned to leave, but stopped in the doorway. "You saved us, Ereta. I know there's a lot we have to figure out—especially *now*—but without you, I think we'd all be dead, or something close to it. So thank you."

"Thank *you*, Milo. You saved Leelin's life. I'm sorry you got dragged into this mess."

He started out the door once again, and over his shoulder he shot her a tired but genuine grin. "Well, that makes one of us."

She smiled to herself and settled into the chair beside Leelin, gently stroking his hair. "I'm here, my heart. And I have *so* much to tell you."

And, as the hours passed by and Scheal's sun cast its yellow light across his beautiful face, she did; and she knew in her heart—in her Lords-damn *bones*—that her friend heard every word.

The sun had long set and the moons had long risen when Ereta finally finished her story and drifted into a peaceful sleep at

Leelin's side. As she slipped into dreams, she felt the tug–that had never quite gone away–surge anew. The sensation was almost painfully insistent, just like it had been that day she had first been blinded by the snow and yellow sunlight. The day she had fallen into the fissure. The day that everything had changed.

The tug pulled again, and she furrowed her brows against it, fighting the sensation off. In her drowsy, thoughtless state, she couldn't entertain anything other than her overwhelming desire to fall back into sleep. *Tug. Tug TUG*–against her wishes, her eyes flitted open at the insistent pull. She sighed peacefully at the realization that she already *was* asleep, caught in the haze of strange, wistful dreams. As her eyes drifted closed again, she smiled at the strange sight her mind had conjured–a strange tear in the air. It reminded her of the bath. An indulgent expanse of water, but instead of being confined to a tub, this expanse was like that of the snow planet's plains–stretching as far as she could see to every horizon. The dark water lapped a soothing beat. The phantom sensation of a warm, wet breeze tingled against her skin. As her consciousness sank into oblivion, she dreamed that a spray of warm water splashed against her cheek. She dreamed that a single, heavy bead of moisture sluiced down her skin, dripped off of her chin, and gently fell onto Leelin's arm. And she dreamed that Leelin, for the first time in days, stirred at the sensation. She felt his warm body shift just slightly beside her. Heard the slight moan that came from his lips before he stilled once again.

Definitely a dream, she thought to herself reassuringly through the thick haze of looming sleep. *A good dream.*

But it was not a dream at all.

Chapter 25

I 'm going to vomit all over the moons-cursed table.

Ereta's stomach must have overheard her thoughts; it grumbled in a loud echo of agreement.

But the Crown Lord of Brafta sat on the opposite side of the table, displaying a countenance that was both stern and resolute, and Ereta didn't hold out much hope that the woman would suddenly develop the capacity for sympathy.

"Please," Ereta begged nonetheless. Tears welled slightly in her eyes with the strain of speaking over her nausea without spilling her guts. But that wasn't saying much–tears came easily these days. Somehow, in the mere four days since she had come to the snow planet of Scheal, Ereta's body had grown accustomed to the abundance of water. Now that she didn't have to worry about dehydration, she found herself crying with very little provocation. Perhaps her emotions had been stifled for so long that they were aching for release, or perhaps she just hadn't previously allowed herself to cry enough to know how cathartic it felt.

Or maybe she was trying to drown the tug that had continued to pull her vision relentlessly over the past few days.

She forced her thoughts away from the sensation; nothing good could come of dwelling on it. Returning to Tubat-So–to Veirbos–was not an option, and that was where it was pulling her, right? *Back.* And she couldn't go back. Didn't want to.

"*Please* just let me go, Ima." A plump tear slid down her cheek with the choked words.

Ima rolled her eyes. "By the forge, I told you once or a thousand times, Tiny. *Finish* it, or stay here all night. You'll not be finding my pity, for true." Ima leaned across the massive wood table and pushed Ereta's half-filled plate closer.

Ereta clutched her bloated stomach. The smell of baked mushrooms wafted, unwelcomed, into her nose, its normally mouthwatering scent (that had tempted her only thirty minutes earlier into filling her plate to brimming) now utterly nauseating to her overstuffed stomach. "If I eat another bite, I *promise* you I'll vomit."

"Good folk burn in the forge to make the heat that grows your food. You'll be pissing on their ash if you let your meal spew."

Ereta grimaced, but couldn't fairly argue the point. It was her own fault. She couldn't seem to get the portions right when serving herself. At lunch yesterday, she had hungrily filled her plate and had to sit at the table for a Lords-damn *hour* before she managed to finish it all. When dinner came, she had taken a much smaller helping, and found that she was left with a distractingly empty stomach as she tried to fall asleep. And so, this morning, she had reverted to the previous extreme, letting her gnawing hunger vastly overestimate her stomach's capacity. Part of the problem was that no two kinds of food seemed to be similarly filling, so she really had no way to gauge her portions.

And Ima, for her part, seemed to have no limit of patience in waiting for Ereta to empty her plate, refusing to allow her to offload the extra onto someone else or–Lords forbid–put it in the waste bin.

She resolved that, in the future, she would take smaller helpings and go back for seconds or thirds if needed. It was just hard, so fucking hard to control herself when presented with an abundance of decadent smells, flavors, and textures. But this experience of sitting, forcing herself to eat past where her belly would stretch, was a waste of time—time she could otherwise be spending by Leelin's side at the infirmary.

"I didn't force all that on your plate, Tiny. By the forge, it's not even much! Lords favor him, Cheery eats thrice your plate and asks for more, and you can't even finish one! Were it to me, you'd eat twice that and be happy for it. You lot were nearly *starved*. If you don't eat, you'll never put any fat on, and be sure you'll die out there in the snow, eh? The wet makes—"

"—the cold ten times colder, I *know*. But I'm not out in the snow, am I?" she gestured around her—to the sheltered luxury of Ima's lavishly appointed home, which the woman seemed to forget about whenever she warned Ereta of the fact that cold snow was deadly. "And I won't need fat to keep me warm when I'm Dutied in the forge."

Ima slapped her hand on the table and chuckled deeply. "Think you're ready to face the forge, eh? I'd like to see those skinny arms of yours take a try at shoveling char for ten hours! *Ha!* If you need a layer of fat to be a skier, be sure you need thrice that in muscle to be a forger."

Ereta knew this, and she truly did plan to start building her muscles in the coming few pentads before Ima finished the tedious process of counterfeiting their Duty paperwork. And although neither her previous Ration reassignment nor her missing toes would prevent her from becoming a skier on Scheal, she didn't have any desire to return to her former life of long, isolated days spent traveling along a delivery network. Back on Veirbos, she had really started to enjoy her job in Combustion, which was much less isolated and far, far warmer.

But that job didn't exist on Scheal; the closest thing to it was Dutying at the forge.

Similar to how Veirbosians' lives revolved around Water, Schealians' lives revolved around Heat. There had been no such thing as a forge on Veirbos, since the waste heat generated through combustion was sufficient to warm their buildings and prevent their Water from freezing over. But on Scheal, they needed to produce fuel in such quantities as to Heat massive agricultural Greenhouses that fed all of the planet's settlements with a wide variety of colorful, delicious foods.

"If you don't like it, Tiny, you're free to go back to your dust planet and your man-paste."

"It's not–"

"Dust bury me, this argument again?" Jace strolled the last two steps down the wood-and-iron staircase and made her way toward the table. "We weren't eating *people*, Ima."

"You can't know that! Seems the clearest answer I can guess, for true, if you didn't have Greenhouses. And why the lot of you are skin and bones, if all you were eating was other scrawny folk, eh?"

But they *did* have Greenhouses on Veirbos (as they had all told Ima many times). They were simply much, much smaller than the ones on Scheal. With Water as scarce as it was, growing such a variety and quantity of plants had not been an option. Mostly, low-Water materials needed for textiles–such as bamboo and flax–were all that was deemed vital. The nutritional allotments that fed the people of Veirbos had been Lords-provided and of unknown composition. Milo theorized that they were made from some kind of dense, low-Water plant also grown in the Greenhouses. It was that theory that had tempted him to pilfer seeds from a Greenhouse in the Lords' City. Milo had nurtured the seeds into several types of seemingly edible plants, which he had then mashed into a flavorful paste.

Little had he known that he could have saved himself the time by simply consuming the plants whole.

Milo chimed in as he, too, stepped off of the circular staircase. "There weren't enough people on Veirbos to support a nutritional economy relying entirely on human fles–" His right foot flew out from underneath him, and his arms whipped out in frantic search of the handrail. He found it and just managed to regain his balance without finishing his fall to the hardwood floor.

"Lords *damn it,* Jace! How many times!" he bellowed as he stood, and Ereta knew without looking his way that his brow was scrunched in anger, eyes narrowed with ferocious intensity. She smiled to herself, despite her nausea. At least there would be some entertainment to distract her from her overfull stomach and the half-eaten plate of food that mocked it.

"What?" Jace asked with a flick of her thoroughly wet hair, splattering water all over the table–and, unfortunately, onto Ereta's still-unfinished plate of food. She grimaced; a quick glance at Ima's still-stern visage left no question that her food's slight sogginess would not exempt her from having to finish it.

Milo gestured to the puddle of water at the base of the stairs. His foot had dragged through it when he had slipped, leaving an evidentiary streak of water jutting across the floor. "There is a sign in the bathroom *clearly* outlining the dangers of–"

"If you have the right to post stupid signs in common spaces, I have an equal right to ignore them." Jace cocked her head and held out her hand to inspect her nails. Ereta's eyes shot to Milo in anticipation of his response. Jace's ambivalence toward common courtesy had inspired Milo to resume his habit of engraving little warning signs near potential hazards or areas of common use. The one in the bathroom, which he had made after slipping on one of Jace's bathroom puddles and cracking his forehead on the iron tub, read:

PLEASE DRY SELF AND FLOOR THOROUGHLY BEFORE EXITING

WATER IS SLIPPERY

Anger and retort were building in Milo's crimson-fleck eyes as he idly rubbed the mottled black-and-purple bruise that spanned half the width of his hairline, but it was Ima who spoke first.

"Who's saying they're *common* spaces, eh? Don't be forgetting that you're a guest in *my* house, Tits, and it's by my grace that you're allowed to bathe at all. I told you that first day to stop dripping all over my floorboards, and I'll not be warning you again, be certain."

Ever since learning that Ima was the Crown Lord of Brafta, Ereta wondered how she had not realized it sooner. The woman's air of brutal command underpinned her every interaction; despite her usual light-hearted affect, she did not waver an inch in her convictions. Everything about how Ima handled conflict made it clear that she was used to having complete, unilateral authority.

Unfortunately for Ima, so was Jace (despite having no title to justify it).

"Are you insinuating that you'd not let me bathe? I find that hard to believe. I suspect that *accidentally* walking in on me in the bath is the best part of your day, *your highness*." Jace grabbed a plate from the counter and walked to the stone-countered kitchen–where Ima prepared their meals–to fill it.

The Crown Lord of Brafta lit a smoke roll and leaned back in her chair. She took a deep drag–as if the smoke would disperse into her body and pour through every inch of her marrow in search of patience–held it for a long moment, and slowly released plumes of wending smoke through her nose and lips. "It's not the best part of my day, but the *better* part of my day that you spend in that bath. Four hours and some yesterday, eh? By the forge, there's no fault found in me walking in if you never leave."

Ereta was used to a lot of things about Scheal, but Ima's odd cadence and dialect often left her parsing meaning for long moments after the woman finished speaking. She was doing her best to adopt the foreign speech patterns; most importantly, the lot of them needed to unlearn their tendency to swear about dust and Water and start swearing about the forge. She was glad that the practice of swearing at all was something that the two planets held in common.

Jace had filled her plate with baked mushrooms, a slice of bread, a pile of leafy green foods, and a scoop of piping hot *rice*. Lastly, she smothered the lot in a scoop of thick, chunky brown sauce before plopping down next to Ereta and pulling the full, steaming plate of foods toward her.

Ima fought against the smile that crept onto her face while watching Jace dig into her meal. She seemed to delight in cooking and, for the first few days, the Crown Lord had even insisted on serving them herself, claiming that they needed assistance to unlearn their poor eating habits and get used to *'properly eating something besides mashed people, for true.'*

Jace leaned her elbow on the table, pointing with her fork as she spoke through a mouth full of foods: "Dat's uh good poin', dis ish your house, so you shud be well awaya da fack dat dere's a baffroom on ev'ry Lords-damn floa."

Ima took another long drag of her smoke and let the smoke billow out in a single huff of air.

"By the fucking forge, I told you a thousand times, Tits, *best be done eating your food* 'fore you go flapping your mouth. And best be getting them pointy elbows off my table, too, eh? They're bony enough to dent the wood."

Ereta pushed her chair backward in an attempt to withdraw from the smell of Ima's roll. She didn't think the smell alone could cause the symptoms she had felt when smoking the strange herb directly. However, she wasn't willing to risk it; she doubted whether her frayed nerves could withstand another episode. Her last smoke had left her deeply uncomfortable in her own skin long after it ended. She frequently recalled the feeling of not being entirely certain where or who she was, or if she was alive or dead, or if being alive or dead even really mattered at all. Combined with the lingering distress of watching Leelin nearly die, soaking the snow red with his blood–

She shook her head. It was nearly unbearable to let her mind wander into those memories.

Jace leaned back in her chair and swallowed loudly as she rolled her eyes. She had a habit of speaking through mouthfuls of foods, which seemed to anger Ima more than almost anything else Jace did–and that was saying something.

"Be sure I'm aware of the rooms in my own house, but your floor has the largest bath. That's why I let you stay there, to be host-like, eh? Keep on my nerves about it and I'll move you to the loft where there's not but a sink basin to wash up in."

Milo had filled a plate and now came to sit between Jace and Ereta. Ima got to her feet and ambled over to the kitchen. A small fire crackled in the small hearth that was used to warm their foods. Now that she was used to open fires blazing, Ereta found them strangely calming. It was a marvel that something as destructive as fire could be contained into submission as a charming, crackling ambiance of warmth.

Jace chewed another large bite of foods. "Yoo wown't moov mah room–"

"Lords have *fucking* mercy! Brains, I need you to make one of those dumb little signs you do, but about eating and talking." She grabbed a large iron utensil and used it to angrily poke at a tray of mushrooms.

Ima loved to make foods, and even without a point of reference, the blend of flavors in Ima's creations assured Ereta of the Crown Lord's cooking expertise. Ima's dark hair swished back and forth across her broad shoulders as she fussed with her food-cooking receptacles: stirring and prodding, flipping and tossing.

Milo finished chewing his own mouthful of foods and swallowed. His face was predictably stern as he replied, "The signs are important and useful reminders. They are *not* dumb. People tend to be more mindful of their actions when common errors are forewarn–"

Ima waved a careless hand in his direction. "Yeah, yeah. But make one all the same. And let it be a notice, Tits, that if I catch you breaking a rule again 'spite it being etched in metal, I'll take full license to toss your ass into the loft."

Jace smiled, displaying the partially chewed foods splotched over her teeth. "Weyul shee."

Ereta idly stroked the leaves of a plant. Her *favorite* plant, if she was being honest, although she hated to favor one on principle. They were all unique and beautiful in their own ways. Since her first full day in Brafta, she had made a point of touching every plant in Ima's home at least once. Whether it was another kind of dread-easing, obsessive ritual or simply a need to connect with the vibrant beats of living, thriving things was unclear and, she thought, probably unimportant.

This specific plant was special; its leaves were as large as her head, and their pointy stair-step edges swelled away from the branches in the shape of a teardrop. Its smooth, pliant flesh was thick and dark green with shocks of bright yellow running through. Ima called it a *sunlight fern*, and due to its fussiness, it was the only one of its kind in the house. The plant needed full, long stretches of yellow sunlight each day, and preferred daily watering and a consistently warm environment. That was the other reason she favored it; it lived in front of the window that was closest to the massive fireplace. That was where Ereta lived, too, when not sleeping or eating or visiting

Leelin—In a wide iron bench positioned so close to the fire that its heat sometimes singed her skin.

She didn't know much about the future that awaited her in Brafta, but she *did* know she never wanted to be cold again.

She closed her eyes and dipped her head backward. Her eyelids lightened in the rays of golden sun that streamed through the massive window at her back. But the light only served to cast a bright bath of attention onto the ever-present tug. Her awareness of it nearly overwhelmed her thoughts. *Don't acknowledge it,* she told herself. *If you ignore it, maybe it will go away.*

Her fingers traced the delicate vines of her favored plant, and though her movements were languid, she was feeling anything but patient. Anything but calm.

Milo had left not long after finishing his second helping of break-fast. Every morning and every evening, he took an hour to visit with Leelin and check his wounds. Ereta trusted the nurses at the infirmary, but getting Milo's opinion was her true guide pipe, if only because she had seen his expertise proven on multiple occasions.

His hour was nearly gone, and Ima was due to walk Ereta over to the infirmary. But the Crown Lord had never returned from escorting Milo, and she was starting to get frustrated. It wouldn't be out of character for Ima to have stopped at the alehouse on the way back from the infirmary. For Ima, drinking at the alehouse seemed to be the equivalent of holding fucking court. Indeed, she hadn't witnessed Ima doing anything else one might remotely call "Lordly Duty." Certainly, cooking elaborate meals for houseguests and berating naked women for dripping water onto the floor didn't count.

Eager to both ease her nerves and encourage her stomach's digestion, she got up from her seat and began pacing. *Should I just make my own way?* Oh, Ima would be furious. She had insisted after their first day that they go nowhere on Brafta unescorted. Ima was oddly wary of her own settlement and did not have a single person with whom she trusted the secret of the group's origins. A pentad and a half into their stay, Ima had still not allowed even one of her household staff to return for fear of them learning the Veirbosians' (and now her) secret. Instead, she took on the cooking and cleaning herself, after which she would become despondent and stomp off to the alehouse to drown her burdens in gallons of piss-rank ale, returning in the late hours of night muttering under her breath about 'people-eaters' and 'dripping wet tits'.

After her experience with smoking rolls, Ereta had declined to partake of ale, which was apparently another form of inebriating substance that had to be drunk like water.

The sound of a plate scraping against wood made Ereta's head snap upward.

Across the great room, Kilas pushed back his chair and stood.

"Finished already?" she asked him. He had only started eating a few minutes ago. It had taken her a full two hours to finish her massive break-fast.

He turned to look at her with a pre-formed sneer pulling up one corner of his thin, tense lips.

"Your stomach is feeling better, then, I take it?"

Kilas turned and started toward the stairs without acknowledging that she had spoken. Indeed, he hadn't spoken to her (or anyone, as best she could tell) since she had yelled at him just outside the front gates of Brafta. She had never thought Kilas to be sensitive, but he certainly seemed to be holding a grudge. She didn't want to apologize, but neither did she want to endure the aggressive, simmering tension that seized her awareness whenever Kilas entered a room. And besides, Kilas had said far more offensive things to her than she had said to him, hadn't he? He'd called her ugly on multiple occasions, and weak on far more.

So what did she want from him? Truly, she wanted him to apologize so they could move on. But it was becoming abundantly clear that he had no intention of speaking to her, and *that* just made her angrier. She had made a tacit peace offering, extending a suggestion of forgiveness to him by showing that she was willing to speak with him again. And *he* was the one who should be apologizing, so why not take her easy out and just... get over it? Let it go?

That he continued to ignore her despite her kindness–which she didn't even want to give to him in the first place–coaxed her simmering anger into a swell of indignant rage. *How dare he? How fucking dare he? I should be the one ignoring him.*

She rose and stalked toward him, savoring the bright, intoxicating taste of her own righteous fury. "You know, Kilas, you *really* have a lot of fucking–"

The door burst open, and Ima rushed in. *"Tiny!"* she bellowed, her hands framing her face to magnify her already booming voice.

"I'm right here," Ereta winced from directly beside Ima.

"Tiny!" Ima spun and grabbed Ereta by the shoulders. She shook her firmly. "Coat and treads! *Now!* No time to waste!"

Ereta yanked herself out of Ima's too-strong grip and rushed over to the door-side rack that held her coat. She glanced down to confirm that her treads were already on, and in her peripheral vision caught the movement of Kilas' feet retreating upstairs and out of view.

Later. She would confront him later.

"What's going on?" She pulled on her coat. "Is Leelin ok?"

Ima huffed. "Well, I s'pose that depends on how you define it. Hollering like a newborn babe left naked in the snow, but breathing and beating his heart, so I reckon that's good enough for now, eh?"

Ereta blinked, her eyes widening.

She still wasn't especially adept at understanding Ima, but she was fairly certain she was interpreting that last part right.

"Leelin's awake?" she blinked as Ima smiled in silent answer. "Leelin's awake," she echoed.

But this time, it was not a question.

Chapter 26

Lords, it would take hours for this feeling of fullness to recede to any measure of comfort. Her break-fast sat in her stomach like a stone brick. If she thought about it for too long, she would likely vomit it up. Likewise, if she kept up her current brisk walking pace, she would likely vomit it up.

There were actually very few courses of action which didn't end in her puking up her guts. She thought about just getting it over with and letting the retching happen, but knowing Ima, she would probably force Ereta to eat whatever she spewed, Lords literally forbid she *disgrace the ash of the elders*.

But she couldn't force herself to slow down. Leelin was awake. For how long? And in what state? She had not lingered to badger Ima with further questions, but now that she had time to think, she couldn't help but wish she had gotten at least a little more information from the Crown Lord.

Ereta glanced over her shoulder and pinned Ima's form far in the distance. She had hollered at Ereta for walking too fast, and Ereta was sure she would be yelled at for leaving her escort behind later. Ima didn't like them to wander Brafta alone. Ereta found herself pondering, not for the first time, the reason behind Ima's apparent lack of trust in her own people. As consumed in thought as she was, she barely noticed the dizzying drop that stretched beneath her as she took the final few steps across the second shard bridge. She ate up the yawning distance of the first shard in what felt like mere moments. At some point, her walk had become a run; a truth she only noticed when she felt the jarring impact of her joints as she slowed to a stop on the downward-pitched slope. She clamored into the infirmary and started down the hallway without pause. She was distantly aware of someone calling after her, likely telling her to *stop* or *wait* or something equally pointless. They would have to physically restrain her to keep her from going straight to Leelin's side, the one-visitor-at-at-time rule be damned. She paced back into a run, but where the trek down the first shard had happened in a blink, her frantic dash down the infirmary hall seemed to go on forever. The muted off-white of the walls blended into an endless void as she frantically sprinted through the winding halls. Though Ereta did not have experience with nightmares, she imagined that this was what they might feel like: an eternity spent desperately running toward a destination that would remain forever just out of reach.

But she knew it wasn't a nightmare when she rounded one last corner to behold a loud, familiar voice that echoed in her ears and heart.

"If you insist on groping my ass like that, at least have the tenderness to kiss me first," Leelin's voice whined in an overstrained, overloud pant.

Ereta wasn't aware of her body's movement. She blinked, and suddenly she was in the doorway staring wide-eyed at Leelin. *Awake.*

He was lying on his side, facing away from her, as Milo seemingly tended a wound on his rear. "If I did kiss you, would you finally stop whining?"

"Try it and find out."

"Leelin," the words fell through Ereta's lips on a choking sob.

Leelin shot up straight instantly at the sound of her voice. *"FUCKING SPITTING FUCKING DUST!"* he yelled nonsensically, clearly overcome with pain as his body crumpled back into itself. *"Owowowowowow—"*

"I told you not to move quickly," Milo scolded with a shake of his head.

Leelin shot his friend a searing look over his shoulder. "You might as well tell wind not to blow, or fire not to burn."

Milo, who was hunched over Leelin's wounds again, glanced at Ereta, the corner of his lip tipped up just slightly. Even in her state of hurried concern, his eyes pinned her, as they always did, seeing entirely too much. And there was a shadow of something else in his eyes, too; something complex that Ereta did not recognize or dare to parse. She swallowed.

"My dearest, loveliest, most sexually appealing, *gentlest* friend," Leelin implored her in a strained coo, "will *you* come tend my ass wounds and rescue me from this *brute's* indelicate prodding?"

A presence ambled up to her side, but she didn't have even a moment to register who, exactly, it was before a waspish drawl cut into the silence like a knife.

"Such pretty words. But will you tend *my* ass in return? When you are healed, of course."

Dust fucking bury me alive.

Leelin, who was still curled up and facing away from the doorway, visibly stiffened at the sound of Kilas' voice.

"Out," Leelin breathed, his voice barely cresting a whisper. "Get him *out*, Milo, or I swear to all the Crown Lords on Veirbos I will rip open my wounds just to drown him in my blood."

Kilas confidently strode across the room, his movements striking an effortless balance between delicate grace and plotting malice. "A toothless threat, seeing as the Crown Lords of Veirbos aren't here to hold you accountable." Milo stepped away from Leelin, subtly covering his friend's naked body with the pull of a sheet as he stood straight and angled himself between Kilas and the bed.

Milo was a few inches shorter than Kilas, but he met the man's gaze evenly and with the promise of physical force. The solid bulk of muscle on his chest and arms had already visibly swollen given a few days of proper nourishment, and they now strained the thin cotton of his shirt. That shirt (like most clothing on Brafta) was red, enhancing Milo's already vivid red-flecked eyes so that they glowed with arresting intensity. Height difference and all, Milo cut a starkly intimidating figure next to Kilas, who (by contrast) had become downright *gangly* since leaving Veirbos. Unperturbed, Kilas continued his lilting drawl. "Or were you not aware that your precious *flame* has stolen you away to another world?"

Her heart rose into her throat. With Leelin just barely emerging from his days-long sleep, she was sure that this was not the ideal way for him to learn about their (admittedly shocking) circumstances.

"I am aware of nothing but my sudden desire to return to unconsciousness," Leelin spat.

"Leave, Kilas," Ereta said with more confidence than she felt as she stepped up to his side. "He doesn't want you here, isn't that obvious?" Kilas' white-blonde hair, which was usually smoothed flawlessly into a shining curtain, was tied at his nape with a tattered red string. His thin strands stuck out at odd angles, giving the impression that he had pulled back his hair just before a long, restless sleep. She had seen him so sparingly and from afar over the past few days that she hadn't noticed how...*disheveled* he'd become. His sharp features had sharpened further, his cheeks were hollow and sunken, his normally keen eyes were glazed, and his under-eyes had taken on a hue of blotchy purple. *Has he been eating? Or sleeping?*

Kilas sneered at her through a sideways glance. "Why would I take advice about knowing when I'm not wanted from *you,* of all people?"

Ereta winced at the words, which threatened to drag her somewhere deep and cold and hateful–a pit of self-loathing out of which she had been attempting to climb for pentads. Her gaze fell and settled numbly at her feet–

At the periphery of her vision, the tumble of Kilas' long limbs sprawled across the floor. For a moment, she could only stare at his motionless form; at the blood that began to slowly drip out of his now-crooked nose.

She snapped her head up to find Milo grimacing at the man's form while rubbing the already lightly bruised knuckles of his right hand. "I'll get a nurse," he muttered, starting toward the door.

"Fuckfuckfuckfuck–" Leelin's strained whimpers rose to a tense pitch as he attempted to maneuver onto his back. At the sight of Kilas, who was clearly unconscious, a slow, wide grin crept onto his face. "Well, well, *well*," he muttered, knuckles white as he steadied his weight on the iron crossbar of the bed. "Look at *you*, Milo, defending my honor. If I had more blood in me, I might just blush."

Milo groaned, or maybe growled, as he stalked wordlessly out of the room.

Ereta swallowed thickly and said nothing.

Because *she*, evidently, had enough blood to blush. She knew–as did Leelin, despite his attempt to diffuse the tension with humor–that it hadn't been *his* honor that Milo had been so moved to defend.

Hours spent at Leelin's side blended into each other in a timeless blur of love and laughter. Kilas had begun to stir slightly by the time nurses–plus Ima, who had arrived shortly after Ereta to a scene of blood and chaos–came to haul him to another room, where she supposed they would treat his nose and any other injuries he'd sustained from Milo's punch.

Leelin had tried to insist that the nurses not clean the puddle of Kilas' blood drying on the floor. *"Let it be a warning for him,"* he had told them, *"and decoration for me. I enjoy looking at it. Something to brighten the mood in here."* Their refusal to obey him had made him particularly whiny in a way that would have been irritating if it weren't so endearing to hear his voice again. Not even his insistence that he was *"dying again"* (demonstrated with a dramatic flourish that brought the back of his hand to rest on his forehead) and that they were Duty-bound to *"obey his last wishes"* proved sufficient to convince the nurses.

She sat with her friend through his cycles of waking and napping. He could only maintain his characteristic vigor for short stretches before he exhausted himself and drifted into sleep. Mostly, their conversation was light-hearted and easy, as if they were both reluctant to delve into the more serious topics that weighed on their shoulders and hearts. But soon, the shadow of that which remained unsaid grew imposing, and Ereta knew she could delay the inevitable no longer when Leelin's eyes fluttered open from sleep for the third time that day, and his sage-green eyes met hers.

"Could you hear me? When you were asleep?" she asked him before she could lose her nerve or overthink where to start. "I spoke to you. I told you a story."

He smiled at her, not disguising the sadness beneath. "I remember your voice," he told her. His voice cracked a fraction, either with emotion or disuse. "I remember knowing you were here." He grabbed her hand in his and squeezed. "It made me feel..." he trailed off, eyes dropping to their joined hands. She just barely glanced the well of tears that swelled in his eyes before he cleared his throat and blinked in rapid succession. "Well, anyway, I heard you, but I don't remember what you said."

She attempted to gentle her tone and squeezed his hand in return. "And what, exactly, *do* you remember, my heart?"

He stiffly plopped his head against the pillow and closed his eyes. "I remember being at my house, waiting for Mari," he began, and though his eyes stayed closed, he smiled slightly. "I knew she would come, of course. And she did, but ultimately, not in all the ways I was anticipating she might."

Ereta couldn't help but snort at that, but he continued unfazed, "She arrived with a woman. Your Ration officer. The blonde. I admit, I was...disappointed. After all the fucking *effort* I put into seducing Mari, I had hoped to first enjoy her alone before involving others. And I never cared for the blonde, anyway–much too frigid."

Ereta smiled to herself, just slightly. The idea of Hista being turned down by one of *Ereta's* lovers filled her with some sort of perverse satisfaction that she didn't care to examine too closely.

Leelin continued, "I told her as much, but, you know, *nicely.* Told Mari that I had been expecting her, and her *alone.* But the blonde ignored me and walked right the fuck inside before I even realized it. So I followed her, and I got...dizzy? She must have done something–given me something, I dunno. I passed out and woke again sometime later bound up with rope. And then..."

She squeezed his hand. She knew what came next, and she wouldn't push him to share if he wasn't ready. How could anyone ever be *ready* to share something like that?

"She asked me about you. About the Ration Route. About your *'accomplices.'*" He huffed and rolled his eyes, which then halted and fixed unseeingly on the ceiling. "As *if* I would betray you to anyone, let alone some cunt wielding a rope and a knife in such a thoroughly non-consensual way."

Ereta smirked and chuckled again, despite herself. She wasn't sure if he was simply *unable* to take any conversation–no matter how grave–seriously, or if his interjections of levity were purposeful efforts for the benefit of his own sanity.

But the light in his eyes dimmed slightly as he continued, "She questioned me. I don't remember much, besides the pain and a vague memory of hurling some spectacular insults at her, none of which I can recall in any detail. It's a pity; they were quite creative. Some of my best. But I think," his throat bobbed, "I think she was fucking...*peeling* me?"

Ereta said nothing–just squeezed his hand again in silent reassurance. She wouldn't push–she knew all too well what it felt like to be pressured into sharing something before she was ready. But he continued without tears or complaint, just a brief, answering squeeze of her hand.

"At some point, she untied me, and I guess moved me around? It's all fuzzy. I remember blood, and I remember calling for Mari to help me. I remember..."

For the first time since his story had begun, Leelin's eyes locked with hers. "I remember knowing I was dying, and that my one regret was that I couldn't do anything to save you from the same fate. To so much as *warn* you, and Milo–"

The strain of his voice, the renewed swell of his tears, the truth of his words; it was all too much. She leaned forward and pressed her lips against his forehead as tears of her own began to flow freely. She felt them drop from her cheekbones, likely landing on his barely warm, still pale skin.

"Oh!" he added in a soft voice. He pushed her back slightly until they were eye-to-eye once again and used his thumb to brush away a tear. "And, *of course,* I remember Milo telling me that she hadn't wounded my cock. I suppose I could have died happy then...if only I had known for certain you were safe."

"I was," she whispered. "We all were. We are. But there are things I have to tell you. Things that might be a bit...difficult to accept."

He brushed a strand of her hair behind her ear and smiled at her before pulling her close and brushing his lips against hers. His next words came out as a whisper, his warm breath cooling the wet streaks left by her tears, "As long as my cock is still intact, little flame, there's *nothing* you can tell me that I can't manage."

Hours later, Ima beckoned for Ereta to approach her where she leaned against the Nursing station outside of Leelin's room. Her voice was a low, conspiratorial whisper, *"Well? How'd he take it, Tiny?"*

"As well as can be expected, I guess." Ereta rubbed her eyelids with her palms, applying enough pressure that it almost hurt. The tug faded into the background of her awareness, if only for a moment, and she was grateful for the bliss of its reprieve. It wasn't that the sensation itself was that uncomfortable; more so, it was a pain that she felt acutely in her heart when she thought of returning to her home planet, a deep pit of dread that yawned open in her mind, beckoning for her to plunge into its depths and bathe in a tangle of questions that held no answers.

As she released the pressure on from her eyes and blinked, little black and white dots danced across her vision. Ima came slowly into focus before her. What time was it? She had no idea, but she had a feeling that Ima would soon drag her back to the house for a meal. She couldn't say that the prospect was entirely unappealing. Ever since she'd been eating more, she'd found that her hunger had (paradoxically) only grown *more* potent at mealtimes. Her stomach felt just as uncomfortably empty now as it had felt uncomfortably full only hours earlier.

"Dust fucking bury me, I forgot to tell him about the fucking foods!" Though nothing she had told him had been sufficiently shocking as to cause his loss of consciousness, the difference in nutrition between Veirbos and Scheal was a glaring omission when detailing the bizarre nature of their circumstances. Luckily, the matter of him eating wasn't necessarily urgent. While he had been unconscious, the nurses had periodically inserted a hollow tube into

Leelin's nose and down his throat, through which they had poured an unsettlingly familiar nutritional gel.

Ereta loosed a deep, weary sigh. It must have been late, perhaps after midnight–or maybe telling Leelin about Brafta had drained her energy faster than the mere passing of hours could. Either way, he was exhausted, too. She had left him in a deep sleep.

"You!" Ima presumptively snapped at a passing nurse. "Yes, *you*, Thin-Lips! Bring three meals to Leelin's room. Big ones, eh? *Full* plates. And make his bland food. Bread, maybe, and some potatoes. And for this one," Ima slapped Ereta's back with her usual bruising force, "bring the lot, eh? For me, too."

The nurse nodded obediently and walked away, but as she did, Ereta noticed that her lips were indeed pulled into a tight, slight line. *Thin-Lips.* She supposed she couldn't truly complain about her nickname–or any of their group's names: *Blondie, Tits, Tiny*–

Ereta blinked through the throb left by Ima's slap. "Wait. You called Leelin...*Leelin*?"

Ima turned to look at Ereta and scoffed. "'Course I did. You've been moaning his name like a spurned lover for over a pentad, for true. Be sure I meet a lot of people, but I would have to be pretty damned thick to miss that one, eh?" Ima rapped her knuckles against her skull.

"I just thought...the nicknames?"

"Right, for when I can't remember the true name. Not the case with him, not with all your babbling. If only you'd used your own name as much, maybe I'd know it by now, eh? Ha!"

Ereta couldn't help but smile at Ima. "Actually, you calling me 'Tiny' doesn't bother me as much as it used to. You say it so often that it's practically lost all mean–"

CLANG-Dong CLANG-Dong CLANG-Dong

The piercing sound of a massive bell ringing somewhere nearby would have drowned out Ereta's words if it hadn't already shocked her into silence–because that sound...Lords help her, she knew that sound. They had the same one on Veirbos. She had heard it ring out in the Lords' City just a few times before.

And when it had, news of a Lek explosion had followed not long after.

"Not again," Ima murmured with uncharacteristic fear in her voice. She cursed and ran down the hall without explanation. Ereta was barely aware of the Crown Lords' bellowed commands as she passed nurses in the hall, "It's the forge! Best be getting all the beds ready! *Every single one!* I'm talking to you, eh, Brown-eyes? NOW!"

By the time she stumbled out the Infirmary door and into the chill, snowy air of Brafta to stand at Ima's side, she could already smell it. It smelled like...well, her first thought was that it smelled like Milo. *Wood smoke.*

But then she took another breath, and her heart began to pound with a familiar sense of dread.

Because underneath that not-unpleasant smell of wood smoke, there lingered just the barest hint of another scent she had only recently come to be familiar with.

The smell of burning flesh.

Chapter 27

Leelin

A loud sound startled Leelin out of sleep. What the sound was, he had been too far-gone in unconsciousness to commit to memory. But he drifted awake nonetheless.

As it had been so many times since he'd regained consciousness, Leelin woke from his too-short nap disoriented by his unfamiliar surroundings. But unlike the other times he had awoken, he was presently alone.

He *hated* it. Being alone was its own form of torture for Leelin. He needed to be around people, feeding off of their energy, engaging with them—feeling the pulse of life that can only come from trading words and emotions with other people.

Lords only knew why, despite knowing that about himself, he had still chosen to Duty as a Runner, thereby relegating himself to endless hours of tedious solitude. But he had made up for it, at least partially, by spending every free hour of his turns as a Runner on Veirbos in the company of a lively array of friends and lovers. Often, those two designations were one and the same.

But that was not the case for the friend who, only seconds later, strode through the doorway of his infirmary room.

It wasn't for lack of trying that Milo had never been his lover. When they had first met a few turns ago, Leelin had been instantly attracted to the man. But Milo didn't share Leelin's proclivity for lovers of any/all genders, preferring (with the few dalliances in which Leelin knew Milo had engaged) to bed women alone.

Even now, and despite the fact that Leelin thought of him as more of a brother than anything else, Milo was undeniably striking. He stalked into the room donning his usual, neutral expression of deep concentration. Leelin had often teased that, with how often Milo employed them, the muscles that pulled down his eyebrows might be strong enough to lift a moons-cursed Water tower.

"Thank the Lords you're here, Milo. I'm terribly *lonely.*" *Too real. Keep it light.* "Also, I haven't jerked my cock in *days*, what with my terrible injuries and unconsciousness. With your *vast* experience in the matter of self-pleasuring, perhaps you might–"

"I think something's happening," Milo murmured as he pointedly ignored Leelin and walked over to the small window on the far wall, peering behind its thin red curtain. "Did you hear the bell?"

"No. At least, I don't remember hearing it, but *something* woke me up."

Milo tilted his head to one side. "I think that's smoke. And with the bell…"

Leelin swallowed. Milo didn't need to finish that thought. Everyone on Veirbos had known what a bell meant. And with the smoke, it seemed that it meant something similar here.

"How far are their Leks?" Leelin asked, suddenly a little nervous. "Are we in any danger? And where's Ereta?"

Milo closed the curtain and walked to Leelin's bed. He dropped into the chair beside it with deceptive casualness, but his concern was evident in the deeper, more stern furrow of his brow and the way he ran his hand through his mess of tousled brown hair. "They don't have Leks here. How much did Ereta tell you?"

"Ah," Leelin swallowed again. "The *snow.* I suppose I should have guessed. No need to make Water when the planet does it for you?"

Milo nodded. "But they have something called a *forge*, which I understand to be some type of heat generation facility that uses large fires. It might be that."

Leelin stretched, wincing at the pain that shot across his skin, and tried again to lighten the mood. "You must be relieved that you don't need to drink your piss anymore. But then again, I always suspected it was more a matter of want than need, in which case there's no reason for you to stop now."

Milo huffed, which was–for him–essentially a belly laugh.

"Just wait till you see *ale*–it's what they drink for fun around here. My *perfectly clean*, filtered Water is a boon in compariso–"

The yellow-wood door, which had been cracked open only a fraction, swung full open and hit the wall with a loud *bang*.

"In here!" Ima bellowed, beckoning someone toward the door.

A nurse backed into the doorway, pulling something in–

"ABSOLUTELY *NOT*!" Leelin bellowed with all of his strength, which wasn't much at all. "Over my FUCKING DEAD BODY–"

Ima was across the room in a flash of red canvas and dark hair. She grabbed Leelin by his shoulders and he hissed as she impressed the firm pressure of her grip on his wounds. She didn't seem to care. She shook him slightly, and he swallowed a yelp of pain. Ima spoke to him through clenched teeth, her nearly-whispered words both a threat and a promise. "The fucking forge is burning. People are *dying*. It'll be over your dead body, for true, that I'll have folk pass from this life unneeded because of your little lover's quarrel with Blondie. We need the rooms. More, we need the people not *dripping flesh from their forge-fired bones* to be kept away from the others, out of the Lords-damn way. You'd be damn *grateful* to be in the state you're now in if you saw what I've seen coming out the forge's fires, eh? There may yet be a dozen of your enemies sharing your damned bed for all I give a fiery fuck about your comfort."

She spat the diatribe in what felt like an instant and an eternity. Fuck, she was...*terrifying.*

He kind of liked it, if he was honest. He had half a mind to say, *"Yes, mother,"* and kiss her cheek in response, but he truly wasn't ready to have his flesh peeled from his bones yet again.

Also, it probably wouldn't be appropriate given the disaster that was unfolding just outside.

Kilas was pushed into the room on a slick metal oval...thing that slid his bed across the stone floor with seeming ease.

The nurse settled Kilas–who was awake and looking so fucking *smug*–on the far side of the room. Facing Leelin.

Leelin glared at him and turned away to look toward the window.

Milo was tense. His eyes darted between Leelin, Kilas, and Ima, who was now almost out the door. "Brother..." Milo started, pity in his eyes. "I have to..."

Leelin nodded at Milo. "Go save the world, science boy. I'll be *fine.*" He spat the last word as a warning to Kilas, hoping his silent meaning was conveyed. *Do not rile me. Do not bait me. I am in no mood, now or ever.*

Milo bared the edges of a smirk at hearing the nickname, which Ereta had given him while Leelin had been...well, in pieces. His friend nodded and hurried out the door after Ima. Knowing him, he'd probably *accidentally* discovered that his snot doubled as an effective burn salve. Leelin grimaced at the idea, suddenly too aware of the unidentified goop covering the raw bits of his flesh.

"Well, *roomie*," Kilas started, his awful, stupid voice poisoning the air into something dark and thick and putrid. "Looks like we finally have some time alone."

And dust bury him, Leelin found himself tempted to walk out of the infirmary and throw himself into the blazing fire of the forge.

"Because that ended so fucking well last time it happened," Leelin grit out under his breath, and the memory clawed at him as if it were a living thing fighting desperately to be recalled.

But he swallowed and forced it back down deep.

Where it belonged.

Chapter 28

Milo

Milo rubbed futility at the incessant pressure that had taken up unwelcome residence in his head. He could see at least three more Dutied being carried down the hall. If the fire had been as massive as the smoke and the burning smell (that now permeated even the deep indoors of the infirmary) seemed to indicate, they would be far from the last.

Milo jogged over to meet the first in this new batch of Forge-Dutied patients. He was sprawled out on a stretcher between two serious-looking women who didn't seem to so much as mark Milo's presence. The patient squirmed in evident agony, loosing small moans beneath his breath. Milo rapidly assessed the man's burns. "Level two," he designated the case aloud to no one in particular. "Bring him to room seven."

The women nodded mutely and walked around him and down the leftward hallway, not bothering to ask what right he had to be giving orders, or what Level Two meant. He barely had to glance at the next patient before designating her a level three. There were a few burns on her cheek and arms, but her shirt and pants weren't so much as singed. Not to mention, the woman was alert, sitting up and glancing frantically about the infirmary, looking more frightened than injured. He grasped her by the shoulder and squeezed gently, attempting to still her frantic gaze and failing. "Did you breathe in any smoke?" She took a moment to process his question before shaking her head. *Good.* He hadn't thought so; he could usually smell the patients who had been exposed to the acrid smoke from around the fucking corner. "You'll be alright, then. The worst is over."

Her rapid breathing didn't slow, but Milo nodded at the two rescue workers carrying her to continue on to room fourteen all the same. He thought she might be at risk of psychological trauma, otherwise she might have been a level four: the least urgent designation he had created to categorize the injured now being brought in from the forge fire.

How could they have survived this long without a formal system of triage? Well, he supposed that many of them hadn't, in the end. How *stupid*–how infuriatingly *inefficient*–

He stopped himself before he could get carried away on a familiar tide of righteous indignation.

...But *really.* They had the resources to staff a cross-Duty team of rescue personnel, but they didn't know to set up triage closer to the disaster site? Instead, they just wasted time, energy, and space dragging every fucking Dutied that came out of the fire straight into the infirmary, whether they came bearing a single blister or an expanse of mostly-melted flesh.

He needed to get to the Forge as soon as possible. Any minute now, Ima would (hopefully) halt the unnecessary flow of non-critical patients to the infirmary, which was currently overwhelming the staff and resources that the gravely injured needed. He had told her to do as much, requesting that only stabilized level one and two patients be brought to the infirmary until they could get a hold of the situation.

He had since quickly trained two other nurses, along with Chegg (who already knew some of the basics from his Lek safety training) to assess trauma levels and sent them off after Ima with supplies. Which (even considering that this was a different planet) should have been the *very bare minimum* of competence expected of an Infirmary in such an emergency. The failure was made even more egregious by the fact that (according to Ima) such fires occurred with disturbing regularity. It had taken every spare fiber of concentration he could spare to keep his temper in check when she had informed him that the last such incident had occurred only five pentads prior. *Five fucking pentads.* And he only knew now–after cataloging the infirmary's rooms to determine available resources and existing patients' stability–that there were no less than four people *still* in the infirmary for wounds suffered in that fire. But he hadn't had the time to make that point to Ima, who had been on her way to the Forge just seconds after he'd ordered her.

He had given a *Crown fucking Lord* orders. *Him.* A nobody. An other-worlder. And cold burn him, Ima had obeyed and departed for the Forge without protest or question. He filed the knowledge away to examine later. It said something about good leadership, clearly, though until he had sufficient time to reflect on the full circumstances and compare them with what he already knew about successful leadership, he didn't want to draw any firm conclusions as to what.

...But can it really be called successful leadership if she allowed such incompetence to fester in the first place? Does it matter that she's listening to good sense now, instead of appropriately allocating her resources to determine that there was a problem to be solved in the first place, let alone how–

"Level four," he declared aloud, his thoughts about Ima still a whir that faded to the background as he performed the more crucial tasks in front of him. "How calm are you? On a scale of one to ten, one being panicked," he asked the woman who was lying on the stretcher before him.

The woman twisted a lock of her hair around her finger again and again, which might be a marker of either arousal or anxiety. He strongly suspected the latter. "I don't know," she answered, meeting his gaze. "I guess...a seven? Or a six. Wait–are halves allowed? Maybe a six-point-fiv–"

He nodded and looked up at the rescue team that held her aloft. "Room fourteen." They started to walk, and with a quick glance back to ensure there were no other patients currently tearing down the hall, he followed along at the woman's side.

"There's a woman in room fourteen. She's fine–about as injured as you are, but she seems worked up. I'm hoping you can help keep her calm. Or, at least, calmer."

The woman scoffed. "*Me*? But I don't know the first thing–"

"You already know everything you need to know," he interrupted. "Just be there with her. Listen to her. Tell her everything is going to be ok and *believe* it. If she doesn't calm, or if her anxiety starts to make you feel unsettled yourself, call for a nurse. There's one doing rounds of the level threes every five minutes, give or take."

The woman's throat bobbed, but she locked her gaze with his and nodded, resolute. "Great. Thank you–"

"–Pashne," she interrupted with what he assumed was her name, even though he honestly hadn't intended to ask, and by the time she said it had already fully turned his back on her to head back down the hall. He looked at her over his shoulder as she was carried away.

"Milo," he called back, though he didn't know why, except that it was the polite thing to do.

"See ya later, Milo," the woman called, her voice reaching his ears after its bounce through the long hall. And that courtesy, he couldn't return, because *later* was too far in the future for him to consider fully, let alone predetermine his whereabouts *later* or calculate with any degree of certainty the likelihood of seeing the woman again. She would probably be discharged long before *later* came to pass.

Right *now*, the hallways were empty, which meant that Chegg and Ima and the nurses had started setting up the triage site at the forge.

And *that* was where he needed to be.

Chapter 29

Ereta

Ereta somewhat reluctantly walked out of the lovely, only *very* mildly stifling heat of the infirmary and into the chilled air and soft amber glow of Scheal's midnight moons. It looked a little like Veirbos–except for the snow, of course–with a thick haze hanging stiffly in the air like dust.

But this wasn't dust. It was smoke from the fire that was only a few hours past blazing out of control.

Ereta sat on the stone staircase at the rear entrance of the infirmary, letting her legs dangle off the side. The fire was Brafta's second in five pentads. Milo had, predictably, taken charge of the disaster with confident ease: enlisting Chegg as his second-in-command and assigning the Infirmary Dutied to various tasks as systematically as if he were dealing out a round of Intali cards. Each Dutied filled a role, and the roles together formed a larger system that practically managed itself.

He had been at the Forge site for most of the day, sorting patients into categories based on the severity of their injuries before bringing the most severely injured back to the infirmary. He hadn't stopped once (at least, not that she had seen) in the nearly 24 hours since the bells had first rung. She had chipped in where she could to help the injured, but mostly, she stayed out of his, Chegg's, and the nurses' way.

"You taking a break, too?" Her eyes pulled upward to meet a soft red glow above her as if her thoughts had summoned him. Milo should be intimidating, towering above where she sat. But all she felt was...relief. He had a way of framing situations so analytically that she could be sure the truth was laid bare in his words. Honesty was the trait that endeared her to her closest friends, and at some point over the past few days or pentads, Milo had tiptoed into that category.

"Of sorts," she replied with a huff. "Escaping a fire of my own." He smoothly lowered himself down to sit beside her, and when she met his eyes again, he somehow looked no less imposing than he had while standing. He nodded.

"Leelin and Kilas?"

"Leelin and Kilas," she confirmed with another huff. She rubbed her chilled hands together and stuffed them into each other's sleeves, attempting to forestall their freezing. "They've been at each other's throats all day."

Milo grabbed her arm with sudden urgency and pulled it toward himself, furrowing his brow as he cupped her hand in his and inspected it closely. "What—what are you doing?" she asked him, only very slightly concerned. Truthfully, it felt...nice. In a few seconds, his hands had warmed away the worst of the chill in her fingers.

"Checking for burns," he muttered, and the ember glow of his eyes peered up at her through messy brown bangs; that one corner of his lips kicked up slightly.

A joke. He's joking. It was a rare enough occurrence and she was so fucking *tired* that it took her a moment too long to understand. He pulled his hand back from hers. *Shit.*

"You can't blame me for being nervous," she spat out frantically before he could think that his joking was unwelcome, which it certainly wasn't. Being joked with was one of her favorite things.

How else could she have stood so much of Leelin's company? "Last time you were left alone with my cold digits, I recall waking up missing a fair number of them."

His head was tilted back, gaze fixed on the moons. The quirk in his lip returned. "That's not what happened and you know it."

Of course, she knew it. Milo hadn't cut off her toes; he had only stopped by a while after the nurses had to redo the messy stitches they'd given her. The new stitches were, presently, almost completely healed.

But that response wouldn't be any fun, and she needed some fun, especially after *hours* of keeping Leelin and Kilas from tearing each other to pieces. She'd only been willing to leave them when they'd both fallen asleep.

"Do I? I'd bet my day's Water—or...uh, fire, I guess—that you have a finger-cutting knife in one of your pockets right now."

Milo lazily waved a hand. "That knife could be for anything. That it's sharp enough to cut through fingers just means that I take good care of my tools, but isn't predictive of its use."

"So you're saying that you *do* have a finger-cutting knife?"

He reached into an overcoat pocket and indeed retrieved a small knife, setting its sheathed blade and smooth wood hilt on the stone between them in answer.

"I have a knife that is, *I suppose*, sharp enough to *possibly* cut off fingers if circumstance absolutely necessita—"

"Just say 'yes,'" she performatively shook her head before tilting it up to the moons as if he were the bane of her existence and not a salve to her burned nerves. "Like a fucking scholar of old."

He laughed. Actually fucking *laughed,* low and rumbling. Quick, too—she marked only a few white puffs of haze leaving his nose in bursts of warm air before he stilled and resumed staring at the moons with her.

It would be generously called a chuckle from anyone else, but from *Milo*? For whom a barest smirk was equivalent to a hearty giggle?

"I know I'm supposed to say something about fire," he said in eventual reply, and she could still hear the smile in his voice. "But I don't care to remember what."

Ereta laughed now, too, but her laugh was less impressively won than his. Catching her breath, she leaned over and knocked her shoulder against his. "Fire has a certain temperature," she answered with a smile. "Maybe hot, or possibly cold, depending on what planet you're stranded on–but either way, it probably burns all the same."

She caught him nodding out of the corner of her eye. "Probably," he mused, voice sounding far away, and as they sat there in comfortable silence, Ereta was surprised to find that she wasn't cold at all.

A minutes-long stretch of quiet later–during which Ereta *may* have *possibly* started to nod off into sleep–she heard Milo's voice cut through the silence of the falling snow.

"The moons are the same," he murmured aloud. "That doesn't make any sense."

She didn't think he was talking to her; he seemed to be thinking out loud.

She looked up at the three tiny circles of faintly glowing light and did the same. "It really doesn't, does it?" They hadn't had time to talk through all of the many confusing implications of the fact that they were on another planet. Life, she found, had fought to settle into normality against every instinct that told her to stop and revel in how *ridiculous* this entire situation had become. They had left a desert planet, on which they had toiled all their lives in service of

Water, just to stroll through a rip in the world and onto a different planet that was *covered* in cold water, but still had the same moons as their home planet? And–even more confusingly–had a different sun?

"If we were somewhere near Veirbos, you'd think they would at least be in different positions. You know, like from another angle?" she added. "But they're...*exactly* the same, down to the minutes."

The moon cycles were so complex that Ereta doubted they would be coincidentally found in exact replica on some distant world. All Veirbosians were raised to learn the sequences of the interplaying objects that marked their days down to their minutes–sometimes even seconds. Cold burn her, she sometimes still found herself reciting the sometimes-nonsensical rhymes that had been relentlessly drilled into their brains at the childhouse:

> *Siga at its Zenith and we know it's come ten/ We mourn our sweet Tella; Pri is mid, a thin bend.*

> *In the hour of three Pri shows its full circ' / But when Siga is clipped to the right of its smirk / Then Tella will sit either steadfast or sure / Telling right it's three-one and left it's three four.*

> *"Eighteen hours gone," Tella droned from full dark, "Pri's mark stops at two and Sig' to eight 'ere her arc."*

There were *so many* fucking rhymes. Some even tracked the days.

Surely, the fact that those rhymes matched the moons she gazed upon from Scheal...

"The world isn't just a series of random occurrences, Ereta," she found herself mocking aloud in yet another terrible imitation of Milo's deep rumble. *"Everything happens due to action and reaction."*

He huffed. "Close enough, and I agree it bears repeating. This *means* something. It has to."

"I guess there never was a simple explanation for all of...*this*," she gestured vaguely at the planet around her. "We just got caught up in it, and at some point just started ignoring how strange it was that we're here at all. It's just that...I don't know, it's just another place, isn't it? There are things to do. People to help. People to hate. It's easy to forget that we should be Lords-damn terrified."

"We should," he agreed without hesitation. "But you're right. We got lost in it. But I've actually been thinking–"

"I'm shocked."

"*Funny.* I've been thinking that we should go back to Veirbos."

Her body's temperature seemed to plunge rapidly at that, until she felt like it met the chill of the air itself.

"Hista," she choked out by way of explanation and denial and fucking *refusal*–

"Not forever. Just a...visit. A short one. In the Lords' City, there's an archive. I was allowed inside it by the Crown Lord so that I could dig through old medical records–you know, look for some way to treat people injured in Lek explosions–and what I found was actually really fascinating. Did you know that a man once lived for several minutes after being cut in half? A plate of iron impaled him, but it was so hot that it seared to his skin and kept his blood and innards from pouring out. So he was just *there,* for multiple minutes, totally conscious and aware of everything. That led me to a fascinating theory about blood pressure–"

"Milo," she interrupted gently, *softly,* so as to get him back on track without dimming his enthusiasm. "The archive?"

"Oh. Sorry–yes, the archive. So when I was down there, I wandered around and saw a section that was gated off. Lots of stuff in there, it alone was half the size of the rest of the archive. I tried to break in, but I didn't have the right tools, though if I went there now, with notice? I'd bring fire, and a metal rod. Melt the lock–"

"Or, we could walk there in Brafta..." Ereta hopped in to finish the eventual line of this particular thought before it diverted too egregiously.

"Right," he finished, looking at her with a slight grin. "And open a fissure into that locked section from there."

"And no one would ever know we had been there, at least not until long after we'd left with a sizable chunk of their most treasured secrets, which might even include information about the moons–"

"And we could take it all back to Brafta and spend our time going through it, compile the data, and reassess–"

"And we could get Bellat!" Ereta finished at nearly a shout, giddy and utterly swept up in the plan. Milo cocked his head at her in silent question. She lowered her voice, "I...I've been thinking about Bellat–or, trying not to, I guess–it just seems...*wrong* that we left her there. She's my friend. *Our* friend."

Milo studied her for a moment, brows drawn together.

"I know it's a risk to go back, but if we're going anyway, maybe–"

"I wish we could bring them all," he said with a note of what sounded like dejection, or maybe anger. "I don't want to leave a single fucking person behind on that miserable desert. I just don't know how we even attempt to arrange that, especially without knowing more about where we truly are." He gestured idly in the direction of the moons. "But I agree. We get Bellat this time..."

She was nodding so enthusiastically that she thought her head might snap from her body and tumble into the snow. "...And then later, somehow, maybe using whatever we find from the locked archives, we bring the rest?"

He looked at her, pinning her in place with the warm brown of his eyes that seemed to glow now in and of itself, dimming the red flecks to a soft accent. He gave a quirk of his lip and a single nod. "We bring the rest."

She smiled: a wide, genuine thing that almost ached. They were going back to Veirbos, yes–but to get *answers*. And more importantly, to get Bellat. And *most* importantly, to start trying to find a way to rescue everyone who toiled in a miserable existence on Veirbos. "We can do it. We can find a way, whatever it takes," she stated firmly, and she was surprised at how much she believed it.

He smiled now, a little wider than normal, and tilted his head back to look up at the familiar moons of an unfamiliar planet's sky.

She tilted hers back as well, caught in a swell of hope so potent she couldn't–didn't dare–try to temper it.

She almost missed the words he spoke a moment later. They were soft, but carried a smile, and she knew his hope was just as brimming and bright as hers, "After all, no matter where we go, fire probably burns in some way or another."

Epilogue | Another Realm

Embrase

We are closer to each other now; I can feel it.

If I usually see Ariame–feel them–through a fog of layers, then it is now as if one of those layers has been peeled away. Something has happened in the physical realm, and I have a feeling that the tether we recently began fastening between us is responsible.

The tether holds taut as I fade away.

"I love you," I tell them through the bond, "We will find each other."

Being parted from them is always painful, but ever since that one layer lifted, parting has felt less like a loss and more like a promise. We are closer than we have ever been.

And surely, if the tether can break through one layer, why not all of them?

I will find Ariame. I know it as keenly as I know the agony of their absence.

Again and again, I chant my vow to my soul's mate; also a warning to the darkness that dares to take them from me:

"We will find each other."

.

.

.

END OF BOOK ONE

FORGOTTEN HEIRS
1. **By Dust & Duty** March 3, 2024
2. **By Frost & Forge** *Summer 2024*
3. (to be announced) *Fall 2024*
4. (to be announced) *winter 2024*

Pronunciation Guide

Characters

Ereta—————-Uh-retta
Jace—————Jace
Leelin————Lee-lin
Kilas—————-Kai-less
Mari—————Marr-ee
Bellat————Bell-aht
Milo—————Mai-low
Hista————Hist-uh
Chegg———Chegg
Ima————Eem-uh
Hinet————-Hin-nett
Chatre————-Shut-ray

Places, things

Tubat-So————-Too-baht Sew
Veirbos————-Vair-bose
Lek————Lehk
Intali————In-tah-lee
Olchate———Ole-caht-eh
Brafta———Brahft-uh
Scheal————-Sheel

Glossary

Term	Definition
Allotment^	A general term for everything the Lords provide to the Dutied (housing vouchers, nutrition, Water, basic items for everyday life).
Betting Glass	A glass of a certain size that represents a common measure of a Water bet.
Betting Stones	Stones used to represent Water bets during Intali.
Childhouse	Where non-heirs are communally raised. There is usually one Childhouse per settlement.
Cleaning Powder	An oil- and processed dust-composed powder used for cleaning skin and hair. Powder is applied, adheres to dirt and grime, and is brushed away using a roughened rag. Soiled powder falls through the cleanroom grate*.
Cleanroom	A room used for personal hygiene needs, including powdering off*, using the cleanroom chair*, primping in the mirror.
Cleanroom chair	An iron bowl that is sat on and used for personal hygiene. Waste collects in the bowl, and pulling an attached lever releases a rush of high-powered air that sweeps the waste into the cleanroom pipe*.
Cleanroom grate	A metal grate placed over a hole in a cleanroom* floor. Soiled cleaning powder collects there. Periodically, the drain needs to be manually emptied.
Cleanroom pipe	An iron pipe that moves biological waste from individual homes/buildings to a central processing facility.
Cohort^	A common group of Dutied* who share Shift* schedules.
Combustion^	1. A Duty assignment at the Lek Refinery. 2. The Duty process of burning hydrogen and oxygen gases to create Water* vapor.
Court^	Where the Lords make laws for each settlement and city
Crown Lord^	The single Lord who rules over all of the others from their Court in the Lords' City.
Cycle of Three^	The moons' primary cycle at midband* that happens every 400 days. Marks one turn*. Celebrated as a holiday.
Distribution Center^	Where Expediters gather deliveries, supplies, and dispatch Runners.

Dutiless^	Those who have chosen to not perform Duty and do not receive nutrition, housing, supply, or Water allotments.
Duty^	The labor for which each citizen is responsible in return for nutrition, housing, supply, and Water allotments.
Expediter^	Those who coordinate the Delivery Network on Veirbos
Fabricator^	One who shapes raw metal into various objects.
Fissure	A crack in the ground. These run throughout Veirbos and new fissures crack open often due to weak points in the rock of the planet's surface.
Greenhouse^	Where the plants used to make textiles and nutritional gel are grown. Hortisans are Dutied at Greenhouses. Greenhouses are not open to the general public (high security).
Heat	The waste product of Combustion that is used to warm buildings and keep Water in the network from freezing.
Heir^	The chosen children of the Lords and other Courtly aristocrats. These nobility often have many children in search of an heir, but what makes heirs unique is unknown to the people of Veirbos. All children not chosen are raised communally in the Childhouse*. NOTE: Only aristocrats are permitted to reproduce. All other citizens are provided with a contraceptive in their nutrition and Water.
Hortisan^	A Dutied who tends to the plants grown in Greenhouses. Those plants are used to create nutritional gel and textiles, and the Greenhouses are heater by waste heat from Combustion*.
Infirmary^	A building where Dutied nurses care for the injured.
Intali	A betting game where players wager portions of their Water Issues.
Issue^	The spherical glass container into which daily Water allotments are deposited (every 24 hours) via Water Network pipes.
Lek	
Refinery^	The building where Water is created through Combustion.
Masons	Dutied who carve stone. Stone is commonly formed into stone brick: a simple rectangular cub shape used to build buildings.
Midband	The theoretical line that separates the Northern and Southern hemispheres

of Veirbos.

Term	Definition
Molters	Dutied who create glass from pulverized rock.
Moons	Refers to the three moons which, together, are used to mark time in Veirbos.
New Sun^	The orange Sun that has shone on Veirbos since replacing the Old Sun a millennium ago, per established Veirbosian history.
Nutritional Allotment^	A gel that is provided to all Dutied to meet their body's needs. Runners' allotments contain a stimulant. All citizens besides Lords and Heirs receive a contraceptive in their nutritional gel.
Olchate	A drug that causes a feeling of contentment and relaxation. Traditionally taken by all players at the beginning of a round of Intali.
Old Sun^	The sun under which Veirbos thrived a millennium ago, before being replaced by the New Sun.
Pentad	A count of five days.
Pri^	Smallest moon, warm golden color. 7.5-day orbit. Irregular shape, quick movement. Marks shorter time intervals.
Quarter	A span of 100 days. Every turn is split into four equal quarters.
Ration Officer^	The individual—usually an accomplished Dutied in their field—who oversees the Ration punishment.
Ration Quarters^	The sealed outbuilding where the Rationed muster sequester prior to their punishment. Need of the Ration Quarters varies based on Duty punishments.
Ration Route^	The Ration punishment for Runners, in which a Route must be Run on severely diminished allotments.
Ration^	A punitive measure taken when a Dutied does not perform their tasks as written by their Duty Oath (Ration punishments vary for each Duty)
Route^	Specific to the Duty of Running: a segment of the Runner Network* assigned to an individual Runner on Shift. Routes are out-and-back in most circumstances. Some Routes may be extended and require overnight travel.
Runner	The grid-like system of Running Routes that ensures supplies and

Network^ correspondence can travel between any two places on the planet.

Runner^ A Dutied who travels via Routes across Veirbos to transport correspondence and supplies.

Shift^ A designated time block within which a Cohort is scheduled to perform their Duty.

Siga^ Largest moon with a silver-white glow. 30-day orbit. Prominent craters, full every 15 days.

Social Hall A place where Dutied socialize and play Intali*.

Tella^ Smaller moon with a subtle blue hue. 15-day orbit, synchronized with Siga*. Phases from crescent to full.

The Lords' City^ The Capital of Veirbos, from which the Crown Lord rules.

Tubat-So^ One of the Lek settlements on Veirbos, located in the North-East corner of the Western hemisphere.

Turn A measure of 400 days, and the length between instances of the Cycle of Three*.

Veirbos^ A cold desert planet under the New Sun* and three moons.

Water Network^ The system of iron pipes that distributes Water from the central Water tower of a Lek* to individual Water Issues. Also used for desert wayfinding.

Water pipe A pipe in the Water Network* that delivers Water to Issues every 24 hours.

Water^ Liquid that sustains life and whose creation drives all Duty on Veirbos

Waterroom The central room of most homes, where Water Issues* are installed for each resident.

Acknowledgements

Thank you to Dave: for always giving me strength, acceptance, belief, and encouragement when I can't give them to myself.
Thank you to Patty, who has changed my life in innumerable ways. In the darkness of my own kind of fissure, you threw me a rope, anchored it, and told me I had the strength to climb out. I will be forever grateful.
Thank you to Regina for pushing me to go for it, and for being the first person to fall in love with this bizarre creation of my brain. I couldn't and wouldn't have done this without you.
Thank you to my alpha and beta readers.
Thank you to my computer, whose backspace key was tragically cracked in half during the writing of this book.
And most of all, thank you to *you:* the person reading this right now!
When I first wrote this book, I never intended for it to see the light of day. To have one person (let alone multiple people) spend time reading these words of my heart is an honor and a privilege. Thank you, thank you, thank you!

.

.

Follow me on Substack for series updates and exclusive (always free) content: kcphillipsbooks.substack.com
Instagram/Threads: @kcphillipsbooks

.

.

ABOUT THE AUTHOR

K.C. Phillips is a reclusive, mysterious, and eccentric writer who deeply resents society and fears the opinions of the general public. (She's definitely not a regular person with a corporate job, a husband, and a house filled with cuddly pets...because that wouldn't be nearly intriguing enough).

Don't miss out!

Visit the website below and you can sign up to receive emails whenever K.C. Phillips publishes a new book. There's no charge and no obligation.

https://books2read.com/r/B-A-ERXCB-JPCUC

BOOKS 2 READ

Connecting independent readers to independent writers.

Milton Keynes UK
Ingram Content Group UK Ltd.
UKHW041908120324
439302UK00005B/387

9 798224 900237